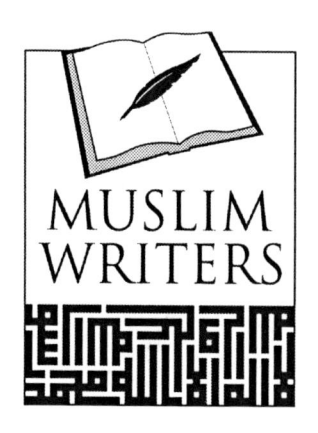

MUSLIM WRITERS

Also by Jamilah Kolocotronis

**Echoes Series: Echoes (Book 1)
Innocent People
Islamic Jihad**

Rebounding

Book Two of the *Echoes* Series

by

Jamilah Kolocotronis

Muslim Writers Publishing

Tempe, Arizona

Rebounding

All Rights Reserved © 2005 by Jamilah Kolocotronis
No part of this book may be reproduced or transmitted in any form or by any means, graphic, electronic or mechanical, including photocopying, recording, typing, or by any information storage retrieval system, without the permission of the publisher.

This work is a work of fiction. Names, characters, places, and incidents are the product of the author's imagination or are used fictitiously and are not to be construed as real. Any resemblance to actual events, organizations, locales, or persons, living or dead, is entirely coincidental.

Published by Muslim Writers Publishing
P.O. Box 27362
Tempe, Arizona. 85285
USA
www.MuslimWritersPublishing.com

Library of Congress Catalog Control Number: 2005935796

ISBN 978-0-9767861-3-9
ISBN 0-9767861-3-3

Illustrations by Shirley Gavin
Book cover designed by Zoltan Rac-Sabo
Interior design by A.P. Fuchs

Printed in the United States of America

Author's Note

Because I wanted to show significant developments in the lives of my characters, I have set this story in the future. The first chapter begins in the year 2015.

I cannot pretend to be a prognosticator. I have made some general predictions about technological and political events of the future. These may turn out to be true, or I may be way off base. Time will tell. Please don't let my fortune-telling shortcomings distract you from the story.

Acknowledgements

Alhamdulillah, this book has reached the completion through the help of many.

First of all, I must recognize the mercy of Allah, Who created me and has given me the ability to write.

And, though long overdue, I have to say that I have always appreciated the love and support of my parents, my father Thomas (who died in 1989) and my mother Shirley. Everything I've been able to do for the last thirty years comes from the strong base they provided for me as a child.

My husband, Abdul-Mun'im Jitmoud, and our children have patiently tolerated my long hours in front of the computer even when they had to take over the cooking and household chores. Along with their general encouragement and support, they have served as springboards for bouncing off ideas and storylines.

Two women have been instrumental in helping me refine a very rough draft. Huda Malzone read Rebounding in its very early stages and provided valuable feedback. Pamela K. Taylor, the editor for Muslim Writers Publishing, read a later version and provided invaluable advice for fine-tuning the story and unifying the diverse storylines.

I would like to thank my publisher, Linda D. Delgado, who has been consistently supportive and demanding, which is a great combination. Her tremendous help made it possible for this book to be published.

Finally, I have to mention Najiyah Helwani, my Kansas City writing buddy. We met weekly while I was writing Echoes, and she gave me some great advice for that book. When she finished reading Echoes, she asked me what comes next. Najiyah's question prompted me to sit down and write Rebounding, the second book in the Echoes Series.

Rebounding

Table of Contents

Prologue 1

Evie: A Blast from the Past 3

Joshua: Keeping the Faith 23

Evie: A Journey 315

Epilogue 351

Prologue

On the day Evelyn Adams learned she had breast cancer, she did three things.

First, she cried.
Then, she prayed. For the first time since her mother had died of breast cancer, twenty-seven years earlier.
And she decided to start enjoying life.

A year later, when Evelyn Adams knew she had beaten the cancer, she did three things.

First, she stopped praying.
Then, she retired from the insurance company.
And she opened her own catering business. She called it "Evie's."

Evie: A Blast From the Past

"I like the dreams of the future better than the history of the past."
- Thomas Jefferson

He calls on a Monday evening.

I should have known something would go wrong. Everything has been so right.

I have been cancer-free for five years now. My business is thriving. Brad and Beth keep busy raising their two boys, Kyle and Matt. Chris and Melinda moved to a nice new house last year to make room for their five. Joshua and Aisha are living their dream of happily ever after with their three boys, and another one on the way. And all of my grandchildren are the sweetest things on earth. Except Jennifer. She can be a little difficult at times; but, after all the years I spent worrying about Joshua, now it's his turn to worry about his daughter. I have had enough worry to last me a lifetime.

When the phone rings, I'm reading a novel and enjoying one of the late days of summer out on my deck. For the first twenty years after I moved here, I barely remembered that I had a deck in back. I was always too stressed. In the last several years, since my cancer diagnosis, I have spent as much time as possible out here, soaking up the sunshine and enjoying the fresh breezes. Before the cancer, I worked hard to maintain my place in the rat race. Now I take the time to enjoy the serenity of my backyard. The wind blows softly. There's a slight chill in the air. Soon I will need to call one of my grandchildren to help me rake the leaves under my elm tree.

Some robins built their nest in the branch above my deck. I watched all spring and summer as they raised their family. The little ones are ready to take off on their own and leave their parents with an empty nest. I wonder if they'll think about their children after they're gone. As much as I think about mine. I had brought my phone outside with me because I don't like to miss their calls. I don't know why I didn't just check the caller ID. It would have saved us all a lot of trouble.

"Hello Evie. How are you?"

The voice tickles my brain. A blast from my past. When I finally identify it, my stomach turns.

"Hello, Sam."

"I would like to see you."

5

I cannot even remember how many years I foolishly waited for him to call me like this. He missed me. He wanted to come back to me. Now I know I don't need him. He is many years too late.

"You shouldn't be lonely. You have Cynthia."

"Not anymore. She died almost a year ago. Breast cancer."

I feel like giggling—I finally beat Cynthia at something—but I force the corners of my mouth to turn down and say, in the most solemn voice possible, "Oh, that's too bad." Later I'll giggle. I'm terrible. How could I hate her that much?

"Yes, I've been very lonely this past year."

"What about your children?" *Not the ones you had with me. Those brats you chose over our sons.*

"Celia helps me some, but she has her own life. And Sean doesn't talk to me much. He likes his independence." *So even Cynthia's brats know what a bum you are.*

"Your other children are doing very well, by the way. I am very proud of them." *Not that you would care.*

"That's why I'm calling, actually. During this past year I have had a lot of time to think. I'm an old man now. I know that I've made many mistakes in my life. And possibly my worst mistake was the way I've treated our boys."

Possibly "your worst mistake?" What else have you done? Blown up the Hindenberg? Led the attack on Pearl Harbor? Sabotaged negotiations for peace in the Middle East? Helped the Grinch steal Christmas? I don't know what to say. I don't know what to say because you are such an idiotic old man.

"I said I want to come see you, Evie, but what I really want is to see my sons again."

"I doubt that they'll agree to see you."

"Could you talk to them for me? Tell them how much their father wants to see them again before he dies."

"You're dying?"

"No, but I am old and I'm not in the best of health. We never know."

Rats. "Why should I be your advocate? Have you forgotten all the yelling and cursing? And the cheating. Not to mention that little note you left on the kitchen table."

"No, I haven't forgotten. It was Cynthia. She's the one who made me leave you. She's the one who wouldn't let me see the boys. It's her fault, not mine. Now that she's gone, I'm free to rebuild my relationship with them."

Blame the dead lady. In a few more minutes, he'll have me feeling sorry for her. I am starting to wonder how she put up with him all those years. "Sure, Sam, it was Cynthia. Do you really think I'm going to believe that?"

"You can believe what you want, but it's the truth."

This is getting very deep. How could I ever have been attracted to that man? I must have been insane. "Whatever you say. Listen, I'm a busy woman. I don't have time for your nonsense." I want to say something else, but I do need to preserve my dignity.

"All right, then. I'll let you go. Just promise that you'll talk to the boys for me."

"I don't have to promise you anything."

"No, you don't; but do this for me."

"Why?"

"Because you loved me once." *Oh, please.* "Because we shared the wonderful experience of creating three children together." *No wonder he always made salesman of the year. He should have been a politician.*

"I can't listen to any more of this garbage. Why don't you call your sons yourself? That would be different."

"Just talk to them for me, Evie. Ask them if they want to meet with their father. I'll respect their wishes."

"All right, I'll ask them, but I don't think you'll like their answers."

"Just ask them. That's all. I'll call you back at the end of the week."

"Thanks for the warning. I'll be sure to wear my boots."

"Goodbye Evie."

"Goodbye, Sam." *And good riddance.*

So he wants to see his boys again. Thirty-seven years after he walked away from them. He is right about one thing. It was Cynthia. Not that it was Cynthia who made him leave or Cynthia who made him stay away. It was Cynthia who fulfilled his needs. Now that she's gone, now he finally has time for his sons.

I will go ahead and talk to them about it. It will be good for a laugh.

I wonder if any of them actually would like to see him. Brad is the only one who halfway knew him. I wonder how much he remembers. I know Chris just remembers the presence of a man for the first few years of his life. Joshua barely knew him at all, but he has carried the hatred and the bitterness, just as I did. Joshua had to look to men like Abdul-Qadir and Dr. Evans to fill the gap his father left. Fortunately, the men he found were a hundred times better than his real father.

∞

I stop by Brad's house on Tuesday evening. First to be born, first in everything.

I'm lucky to have caught him at home. Now that his boys are older, he is always running somewhere with them.

When I pull up, he's in the garage working on that car of his. That old yellow Toyota is practically an antique. His Lexus is still brand new. I don't know why he keeps tinkering with that old yellow car. He should have it towed to a junkyard.

I park at the end of the driveway and walk toward him. I chuckle when I see a beer can sitting next to him. Only one of my sons knows how to relax with an occasional drink.

He looks up from under the hood of the car. "Hi Mom. What brings you out this way?"

"Oh, I just happened to be in the neighborhood and I thought I'd stop by."

"You just happened to be in Evanston?"

"Not exactly, but I did want to visit my oldest son."

"Come on in." He wipes his hands on a greasy rag, and we walk through the garage into the kitchen. "So what's up? We have

Rebounding

the house to ourselves. Beth went to exercise class, Kyle's still at football practice, and Matt has tae kwon do. Can I get you something?"

"Do you have orange juice?"

"Sure. Let's sit at the breakfast bar, and I'll get you the juice. So why are you here? I know you have a reason for coming."

"Yes, I do. Maybe you'd better sit down first."

"What's wrong? Is it your health?" He washes his hands at the kitchen sink, pours us each a glass of juice, and sits on the stool next to mine.

"No, nothing that serious. It's a family matter."

"What did my brothers do this time?"

"It's not your brothers. It's your father."

"Sam?"

"The one and only."

"What happened? Did he die?"

"Not yet, unfortunately, but Cynthia did."

"Ding, dong, the witch is dead. Let me guess. He wants you to take him back."

"No, not even Sam is that delusional. He wants to see you boys."

Brad's expression changes. I see it in his eyes. "He does? Really." He stops and looks down. "It's about time, I guess. After he missed our ball games, graduations, weddings, children's births. . ."

"What do you think?"

"Honestly, I don't know." He stares at his glass. When he speaks again, his voice is soft, as if I'm not here. "I was almost eight when he left. He was my dad. He was far from perfect, but..." He stops, and swallows hard.

"But what?"

"But when you're seven, it's hard to understand. One day I had a dad, and the next day I didn't." He stops again and looks at me. "Did you know I cried every night for a week after he left? I waited until I thought you were asleep."

"Yes, I knew. I should have come in to comfort you, but I was too hurt and confused myself. I couldn't do much for any of you boys for a long, long time."

"But you were there. And that mattered." He stops again. I didn't know it would be this difficult for him to talk about Sam. After all these years.

"I don't know about seeing him again. I've hated him most of my life, but part of me wants to see him, to know who he really is. And I want to know if he loves me now." I know he won't cry in front of me. He closes his eyes, and I turn away as he surreptitiously wipes away a tear.

I touch his hand and say softly, "So what do you think?"

He looks at me. He's fully in control again. "Why don't you ask my brothers? If both of them want to see him, I will too."

"I'll do that. And I'm sorry I didn't give you a better father."

"You did the best you could, I guess. And half of who I am comes from him, whether I like it or not."

"Yes, you're right. In spite of everything, he is your father."

∽

I stop by Chris and Melinda's house the following evening. All of their children are busily engaged, from Ruthie typing at the computer to Martha babbling in her playpen. They all know how to entertain themselves. Chris will not allow a television or video game system into their home.

He must be preparing a sermon. Books are scattered across the table, and he's written several pages of notes.

"Come on in, Mom. Sorry for the mess. Here, let me clear a space for you. So what's going on? Is everything okay?"

We sit at the table. Melinda brings over a tall glass of root beer. And I tell Chris about the phone call from Sam.

"He said that Cynthia has died, and he wants to get to know his boys again."

"That's interesting. What did you tell him?"

"I said I would ask each of you what you want."

"What did Brad say?"

Rebounding

"No, you need to tell me what you think first. I don't want you to call Joshua after I leave, either."

"I won't." He stops, and plays idly with his pen. "I barely remember him. He was tall, but I was only four, so everyone was tall to me. He had a deep voice. When he carried me on his shoulders, I thought I was king of the world. I thought he loved me, but one day I woke up, and he was gone. He didn't say goodbye. He just never came home again."

"You sat by the front door for hours at a time, waiting for him. I remember now."

"And when we went to the store, I searched for him. I thought maybe he had died. Just like old Mr. Robbins, who used to give me candy every time we passed his apartment. One day Mr. Robbins wasn't there, and you told me he had died. I thought my daddy must have died, too.

"Then, when he came back with some Christmas presents, I was really confused. Especially because he left again without playing with me. Later, I understood what he had done." He looks down. "I thought he loved me."

"Yes, well, I thought he loved me, too."

"I think about him sometimes, in those quiet moments with my own children. I love them too much to ever think of leaving them. And I can never understand why he didn't love us enough to stay."

"I don't know, Chris, except to say that he didn't leave you boys. He left me."

"No, he left us too. Otherwise he would have done whatever he could to be with us. The way Joshua did for his children."

"You're right. I wish I could erase the pain."

"I think it might be a good idea to see him again—at least we can have closure instead of always wondering why, and thinking about what should have been—but only if both of my brothers want to see him."

"That's what Brad said."

I stop by Joshua's house the following evening.

"It's quiet in here. Where are the children?"

"Aisha and Sharon took all of the boys over to Umar's house. They wanted some time to play with their cousins before school starts. Would you like some tea?"

"Yes, tea would be nice."

He puts the water on to boil and we sit at the kitchen table.

"Joshua, someone called me a few days ago. Someone I never expected to hear from again. Your father."

"Sam?"

"He told me that Cynthia died last year. He claims she kept him from seeing his sons."

"You don't believe that, do you?"

"You should know me better than that. The point is, now he says he wants to establish a relationship with you boys. He wants to meet with the three of you."

"What did you tell him?"

"He persisted, so I finally told him I would ask you boys if you want to see him."

"What did my brothers say?"

"First, tell me what you think."

"I don't know. My first instinct is to say no—it took me so many years to get over my anger, and I don't want to go through that again—but I don't remember what he looks like. I don't really remember anything about him, except that he didn't come to see me when he said he would. And he yelled and cursed at you every time he did come."

"You heard that?"

"I couldn't help but hear him. I hated him for hurting you."

"I didn't know. You wanted to protect me?"

"Yes, but I was too young. And I kept hoping he would change. But then he disappeared completely from our lives. And I have never forgiven him for that."

"But you just said that you're not sure if you want to see him."

Rebounding

"I guess it's mostly curiosity. I want to know what he looks like. And I want to know if he's changed. He's older now, so maybe he really does want to be a father to us."

"You really don't know what he looks like?"

"No. I can't remember."

"Look in the mirror. You'll see your father. Except for the beard, of course, and the dimple in your chin. Your dimple comes from my side of the family."

"So that's why you projected your hurt on to me."

"I suppose it is. I still regret those years. Of course, I'm sure his hair is gray now, and he has wrinkles; but if you meet him, you might see a future version of yourself."

"If both of my brothers want to see him, I will, too."

"That's what your brothers said."

"Then I'm glad we're together on this."

~

We all agree to meet at my house on Monday evening. Sam has never seen my new place, even though I've lived here for nearly thirty years now. That shows how completely he has been out of our lives.

I don't know how it will go this evening. My boys are all ambivalent about seeing him again. They still want his love, after all this time, but they are unforgiving of the hurt he has caused.

Sam arrives first. I had hoped one of the boys would be here when he came. I don't want to be alone with him. If he tries anything and, knowing Sam, he just might, they could find their father dead in the foyer.

He's old. He's actually only one year older than I am, but he looks much older. His hair is completely white, and he looks thin and frail.

"Hello, Evie. How are you? You look good."

"I know. I wish I could say the same for you. You're a little early."

"I want to talk to you first, before the boys come. Can I come in?"

"Come on in." *Don't try anything, old man. I've taken classes in self-defense.*

He walks slightly bent over, but that could be an act to gain my sympathy. He looks around as I lead him toward the patio room.

"You've got a nice place here. I see you finally got the hardwood floors you always wanted. And the art work is impressive. Cynthia couldn't tell a Monet from a Rembrandt, but you always did have good taste. Yes, very nice. I am impressed."

"I did very well after you left me. I'm sure you know that I've opened my own catering business."

"How could I miss it? Your name is all over Chicago. You always were a good cook, I'll say that for you. Nothing like Cynthia. I had to teach her how to boil water. Our kids thought that home cooking meant ordering in."

"That's enough, Sam. You made your choice. Whatever problems you had with Cynthia, I don't want to know about them. Apparently you loved her enough to stay away from your children."

"That wasn't my fault. Cynthia wouldn't let me see them."

"Don't lie to me. I had hoped we were past that. Let me tell you about one of your sons. Joshua, the one who was just a baby when you walked out. The one you never wanted. The one who looks just like you. When he was twenty-three, he walked out on his wife and children. It took him a year or two to clean up his act, but once he got himself straightened out, he did everything he could to see those children again. For the past several years, he has worked very hard to be the best father possible to his children. That's the difference between Joshua and you. You never even tried."

"Twenty-three? That was pretty young to have a family."

Give me a break, Sam. You were twenty-one when Brad was born. Or have you forgotten? "Your son went through hell during his teenage years. And do you know why? Because he didn't have a loving father to guide him and support him and show him right from wrong. All of your children have suffered, but Joshua has suffered the most. You might want to remember that when you

Rebounding

meet him." I think of Brad. He has suffered in a different way, but I don't want to talk with Sam about Brad. On some level, I am still afraid.

"You're right, Evie. I've been a terrible father. Even Cynthia's children hardly want to be around me. But I'm just an old man now. I hope my boys can forgive me and let me try to be their father again."

"We'll see. Whether they do or not will be entirely up to them."

The doorbell rings. I wonder which one will arrive first. I go to open the door, and smile. All three of my sons stand there on the porch, shoulder to shoulder. I guess I have done something right.

I walk with them into the patio room. Sam stands up when he sees them.

"There you are." He smiles. "My boys." He keeps looking from Brad to Chris to Joshua with a puzzled expression on his face. "I can't tell which one of you is which anymore. You're all about the same size now."

Brad steps forward and extends his hand. "Hello, Dad. I'm Brad, your oldest son. I cried after you left."

Sam smiles, and nods. "Did you? Well, hello, Brad. Now I recognize you. You've grown into a nice looking young man."

"I'm Chris. I used to call you Daddy, but now I don't know what to call you. I waited for you to come home. I thought you had died."

"Yes, Chris, now I remember. You were just a little bit of a thing, always playing with your toys."

"Hello, Sam. I'm Joshua. You have never been Dad or Daddy to me. Only Sam."

"Joshua. You're all grown up now, aren't you? I guess you do look a little like me. Except for that beard. Have you just come back from a camping trip?"

"No, Sam."

"Well, here we are. My boys." Sam shakes his head. "You're a tough crowd, but you're right. I've been a terrible father. I can't even tell one son from the other. Why don't we sit down and try to get to know one another again? What kind of work do you boys do? Brad. You go first."

"I'm in engineering. I work for a large Chicago-based firm. Over the last several years I've supervised some important projects here in the city."

"Good. I always knew you were a smart boy. Got straight A's on your report card, didn't you? And when you were little, you were always trying to make something."

"You remember that?"

"Sure I do. I've forgotten a lot of things, but I still remember playing with my oldest son and his erector set."

"Actually, it was Legos, Dad."

Sam frowns. "Yes, boy, it was. Now I remember. What about you, Chris? What is it you do?"

"I'm an instructor at Redemption Bible College. I train young men and women to do God's work, both in this country and overseas."

"That's interesting. I have to confess that I have never been very religious. Your mother's the one who always wanted to go to church." All of my boys look at me and grin. They think they know me. Sam doesn't notice. "She made sure that every one of you was baptized before the devil could get your soul. That's good, Chris. Sounds like you're doing some good. Okay, now Joshua. What about you?"

"My brother-in-law and I run a nonprofit agency on the south side. It's called The Caring Center. We established the center to meet the needs of the underprivileged. And I've been a Muslim for the last thirteen years."

"I was wondering. That would explain the beard, then, and the strange clothes. It sounds like you and your brother-in-law are doing good work, though. Just as long as you don't blow up any buildings. Guess your center doesn't do any of that, does it?"

"No, Sam, it doesn't." Joshua remains calm. I almost wish he would get upset. Sam deserves it.

"I get it. Brad makes the buildings, Joshua blows them up, and then Chris comes to pray for everyone. Don't you see? Isn't that funny?" He laughs loudly. My boys just sit there, stone-faced.

Rebounding

"Okay, maybe that wasn't a good joke. So what about your families? I must have some grandchildren running around out there. Brad, did you ever have any children?"

"Yes, I have two sons. We decided to bring pictures of our children. Here's my oldest, Kyle, and this is Matt."

"Look at them. Those are two handsome boys you have there. That little one looks kind of skinny, though. You had better try to put some meat on him."

Brad looks down. "Yes, sir, I will."

"That's a nice family, Brad. And what about you, Chris? I imagine you have a large family, being as religious as you are."

"My wife and I have five children. Three boys and two girls. Here is their picture."

"Oh, yes, they're nice-looking kids, but the two oldest are wearing glasses already. I hope you don't make them read that Bible all the time. They're kids. You've got to let them have some fun, too."

"Yes, they do."

"And Joshua, I guess you have a whole herd of kids. I've heard how you Moslems like to pop those babies out, one right after the other." Sam laughs. "Do you have a whole harem of wives, too?"

Joshua takes a deep breath and answers calmly. "I have been married twice, but only one wife at a time. I have six children—three with my first wife and three with my second wife. We are expecting our fourth in a few months. These are my children."

Joshua hands Sam the picture. Sam stares at it. I should have remembered. I had forgotten the way he is. It has been so long, but I should have remembered.

"Now Joshua," he says slowly, "these three older children are fine looking, very fine indeed, but the younger ones are a little dark, aren't they? Don't tell me you went and got yourself married to a nigger."

There is stunned silence. Then Joshua gets up and stands over Sam. His face is very red. I'm frozen to my seat. It's like watching an accident and not knowing what to do to stop it.

17

His hands are clenched. His voice is tense, but he doesn't shout. "You are my father. One little drop of liquid that made me who I am, that made me look like you. That little drop made you my father. Because you're my father, I won't smash your face in. A Muslim is not allowed to hit his father, even if his father is a damned idiot.

"I'm going to show you another picture." He pulls a photo from his wallet and holds it in front of Sam. His face is red, he's breathing hard, his left hand is clenched, but he's still not shouting. "This picture was taken on our wedding day. This beautiful woman here is my wife. And this man here; he is my Dad. He's the one who taught me. He's the one who loved me like a son. He's the one who didn't want to leave me. He's been dead for eleven years now and he's still a hundred—no, a million—times more of a man than you are. You aren't good enough to kiss his feet."

Joshua takes a deep breath. He looks like he is going to hit Sam, but after a few seconds he lowers his fist, and spits in his father's face. "Go to hell, Sam."

He turns around and walks out, slamming the door behind him. This is the first time I've ever been glad to hear Joshua slam a door.

We're quiet for a moment, but then Sam starts up. Just like old times. He stands and shakes his fists at the door.

"Don't you walk away from me, boy," he yells. "And don't you dare curse at your father." His face turns red, too, as he shouts curses at the door.

I remember that look on his face. I remember when he looked at me that way. I reach over and touch Brad's arm. I know he remembers, too.

Finally Sam can't go on. He sits down and tries to catch his breath. I wish he would go ahead and have a heart attack, and let the rest of us live in peace, but after a few minutes his breathing becomes normal. He stares at the door for a moment longer. Then he turns back to Brad and Chris, and smiles. I remember that smile, too. That's the first thing that attracted me to him, even more than his dark curly hair and his deep gaze. I always forgave him, every time he flashed me that boyish grin. His hair is white and thinning now, but his smile hasn't changed. It took me a long time to realize how dangerous his smile could be.

"That Joshua always was a troublemaker, since the day he was born. Couldn't get a decent night's sleep with all that crying. That's okay. I still have two sons I can get to know."

"Count me out." Chris gets up and walks away.

"Brad. You always were my favorite son. I know you'll stand by me."

"Don't give me that shit. I remember what kind of father you were. And yet, all these years I have wanted to see you again. I hoped we could have a real relationship now, but you'll never change. You are a pathetic old man." Brad follows his brothers out the door.

I'm seething too. Not cringing, like I used to. I feel emboldened. Probably because he looks so frail.

I try to control my temper. If Joshua can do it, so can I.

"Are you satisfied, Sam? Is that how you show your love? Or do you still not know how to love?"

"I was just expressing my opinion. It is still a free country, isn't it?"

"I want you out of my house. And don't you ever come around here or try to call me again."

"Evie, don't be that way. It's not my fault you raised three boys who don't know how to respect their father."

Joshua said, the other day, he remembers Sam cursing at me. I remember that, too. I might have yelled back a little, but mostly I just took it. And I don't curse. I've never cursed. There are times, though, when polite language simply won't do. I let go with all the frustration, all the hurt, and all the anger. And I don't choose my words carefully this time.

The old man gets up, his back straighter now, walks quickly out of my house, and hops into his car. I'm still screaming at him as he drives away. I'll probably hear about it from the Meyers tomorrow, but I'm getting tired of worrying about what they think.

When the old man is gone, I go to look for my boys. I find them in the back yard, huddled together.

"Can I join you?"

We all huddle together and breathe deeply, letting go of the anger and the pain. When everyone is calm again, Joshua remarks, "I have just come to realize that the day Sam left was the luckiest day of my life."

We all go out for a late dinner to celebrate. Now we are truly free of Sam.

During dessert Brad asks, "Mom, what did you ever see in him?"

I know his question has many layers, but I just smile and say, "I don't know. I hate to admit it, but maybe I was a little like that, too. And he was a good-looking man, though you wouldn't know it to see him now. He was a smooth talker, too. He promised me the world, and I believed him. I guess I would have to plead temporary insanity."

Chris asks, "You were the religious one?"

"Compared to Sam, I was. I took you boys to church almost every week. And I made certain you were all baptized."

"So," he grins, "maybe there's hope for you yet."

Before he gets into his car, Joshua asks me, "Is that really how I'm going to look when I get old?"

"No, Joshua. You have a beautiful spirit, and that's what will shine through."

As I drive home through quiet streets, I think about my boys, and how much they have been hurt.

And I think about Sam.

Our families went to the same church. He was smooth and good-looking. I first noticed him when I was fifteen, but he always had a blonde bombshell on his arm. Cynthia. Then one day, I saw him without her. A few weeks later, he came up after the service and started talking to me. Every girl I knew wanted to go out with him. I felt proud when he chose me.

At first he was the perfect gentleman. He opened doors for me and took me to nice restaurants. I fell in love with him one evening when we were walking out of the movie theater. The night air was a little cool, and I had forgotten to bring my sweater. He gently placed his jacket around my shoulders.

We became engaged on Christmas Day. He came to my house and got down on one knee, right there in front of my family. It was so romantic.

Two months before the wedding, we had our first fight. We were strolling down the sidewalk when he turned to look at another girl. I gently scolded him. When we reached the front porch of my house, he began screaming at me. He accused me of not trusting him, and even suggested that I might be cheating on him. He threatened to end the engagement. I cried and begged him to forgive me. He walked away. I sat on the porch and sobbed, but he came back ten minutes later and took me in his arms. We walked quietly into the house. Mom was in the kitchen. She didn't hear us come in. We sneaked upstairs to my room. He was the lover I had always dreamed of.

Two weeks later, my younger brother, Rob, told me he didn't trust Sam. Rob said he'd seen Sam driving down the street with another girl only two days earlier. I called Rob a liar. Sam had told me he had to work late that night so he could take me some place nice for our honeymoon.

A month before the wedding, my parents asked me if I was sure about marrying Sam. They had heard he had a temper, and Dad said, "There is just something about that boy I don't like." The next day I told Sam what they had said. He was angry. He said they didn't like him because his family wasn't as successful as ours. I held him and whispered I would always love him, no matter what anyone said.

Two days before the wedding, one of my friends told me Sam had made a pass at her. I accused her of being jealous because I was marrying the best-looking boy in Chicago and she didn't even have a boyfriend.

They all tried to warn me, but I married Sam anyway. And soon regretted it.

We had a wonderful honeymoon. He took me to Niagara Falls. Five blissful days of love.

When we came back to Chicago, I dedicated myself to being the perfect wife. We were happy, until I told him I was pregnant. He smiled and kissed me; then he started coming home late.

The first time he hit me, I was six months pregnant with Brad. He had just come home, and I demanded to know why he was late again. He slapped me in the face, and then he pushed me and shouted obscenities. He only hit me once, that first time, but I was terrified. He stormed out of the apartment, and I huddled in a corner, sobbing. An hour later he came back in, carrying flowers, and begged me to forgive him. Every day for the next week he brought me flowers. And I forgave him. Every time he hit me, I forgave him.

I knew he loved me. And I was sure he would change. That became my mission in life—to help Sam change.

We went to church together every week. He didn't want to go. That's the only thing I could force him to do. Probably because he wanted to keep up appearances. He always cared deeply about what other people thought of him. So we got all dressed up once a week and pretended to be the perfect family. And while he sat in the pew, looking handsome and clever, I bowed my head and prayed that our marriage would work.

But, of course, it didn't.

After he left, I forgot the cruelty. I remembered only the love, the sweetness. His deep brown eyes, and the grin that melted my heart. I hate to think of all those months and years I wasted, hoping he would come back to me. I chose to remember the good times, and forgot the bad.

Brad and I have never talked about it, all these years—the hours we both spent in fear of him—but I can tell he has never forgotten.

At least I stood up to him today. I have wanted to tell him off for the last forty-five years. I finally did it.

But I should have given my boys a better father.

Joshua: Keeping The Faith

*"What lies behind us and what lies before us
are small matters compared to what lies within us."*
- Ralph Waldo Emerson

Part One

I am finally free of Sam. No more wondering who he is. No more wishing he had stayed. I finally confronted Sam.

As soon as I walk into our house, I hug Aisha and hold her close to me. (As close as possible, considering that she's six months pregnant.) Sam will never know what a beautiful woman I married.

She asks me how it went. I tell her that Sam is an idiot and leave it at that.

The next evening, while I'm sitting at the computer working on the budget for The Caring Center, she comes up from behind and hugs me.

"Thanks for standing up for your woman," she whispers into my ear. She must have talked with my mother.

The best thing to come out of that meeting is that I conquered Sam. The second best thing is that my brothers stood by me. I think it was hardest for Brad. He has never talked about how painful it was for him, as a seven-year-old, to see his father walk away. He has never talked about Sam at all, but I'm sure he really hoped to have Sam back in his life. Still, he stood with me. We've come a long way.

Umar and I opened The Caring Center seven years ago. At first, after I finished my degree at Lake Forest College, I kept working with Fawad at the restaurant and considering my options. I couldn't see myself being tied down to someone else's company or organization. I usually like to make my own rules. Umar and I started talking about opening up our own agency, and finally we sat down one week and drew up a proposal. We managed to get the initial funding and licensing, and pass through all the other bureaucratic obstacles.

And we're still a good team. He uses his background in social work and counseling skills to develop programs and work with our clients. I use my business experience and communication skills to perform the administrative functions and convince community leaders to support our mission. So far we have a food bank, a wellness clinic, a youth program, and a small thrift store. We offer classes in basic life skills, and help for those who want to start their own small businesses. We're careful to make our services available to all, regardless of background or belief. Our clientele is a rainbow of nations and ethnicities. Over the last few years, we've hired a few staff members to help us. We also rely heavily on volunteers. And we are a good team.

Because our responsibilities at the center are very different, it would be possible for Umar and me to go for days without talking to one another, except when we meet briefly at midday to pray. We've taken care of that by making it a point to eat lunch together.

A couple of days after the meeting with Sam, Umar says, "I heard you told your father to go to hell."

"It sounds pretty bad when you put it like that."

"He is your father."

"But he insulted my family."

"Yes, I heard about that, too. Don't you think I haven't run into his type before? I still get called that from time to time. Sometimes I get stares when I drive down the street. Some people think that a black man isn't supposed to own a nice car. If he is driving one, he must have stolen it. I just got pulled over again last Saturday for driving while black."

"But he was talking about my family. And what makes it worse is that he is my father. Aisha is his daughter-in-law, the mother of his grandchildren."

"But he didn't care enough to stick around and raise you. Why should he care about them?"

"My point exactly. That's why I don't feel bad about what I said."

"I don't know. You need to be more careful next time before you just fly off the handle."

"And, if you had been there, what would you have done? Smiled and said, 'Yes sir, Mr. Adams. Whatever you say, Mr. Adams.'? Maybe you could have shuffled in with a mint julep and really made his day."

"You think you're being funny, but Dad used to tell me that a little 'yes sir' and 'no sir' would get me a long way. How do you think he got as far as he did? Not by being angry."

"But he was talking about my wife and children."

"I understand that, Isa. I also understand that you still don't have much experience with prejudice. You've rarely had to deal with it on a personal level."

"I guess you're right, but I'm not going to bow down to racists like Sam."

"That's not what I'm suggesting, but it wouldn't have hurt you to be a little more tactful. Anyway, you have to watch out for his kind. They don't take lightly to being put in their place."

"Like Brad says, he's just a pathetic old man. He can't do anything to me."

∽

After a few days, the whole incident with Sam has been forgotten. Things are good. My family is happy and healthy, and excited about the new baby. My relationship with my mother and brothers has never been better.

And another grant came through last week. We can go ahead with our plans to build the Jim Evans Memorial Youth Center on a vacant lot next to our building. The Jim Evans Youth Center will include a fully equipped gym, meeting rooms, a coffee shop, and a library and media center. It's the biggest project we've taken on so far. This morning, I wrote up the press release with some background information on who Jim Evans was—the educator who really cared about kids, my father-in-law, who really cared about me. We've scheduled the groundbreaking for early next March.

Umar walks into my office on Tuesday morning while I'm working on a new grant application. He forgot to bring his lunch. I glance at the clock. He's too early.

"What are you doing here?" I say between key strokes. "I wasn't expecting you for another hour or so."

"I need to talk. I just received a disturbing phone call." His hands are shaking.

I stop typing. "What's wrong? Is anyone hurt?"

"No, not exactly. Can I sit down?"

"Sure. What is it?" I'm closing in on the deadline for this grant, but it sounds like this is more important.

"It's a family matter."

"Is it Safa or the kids? Is Aisha okay?"

"Don't worry. They're fine."

"Don't tell me that Aunt Arlene had another stroke."

"No, nothing like that. I want you to just listen. We used to talk all the time about your past. Have you ever thought I might have some secrets in my past, too?"

I laugh. "You always have secrets, Umar. It took me a good six years to be able to figure out what you were thinking, and sometimes you still surprise me."

"That's not what I'm talking about."

"Okay. I know that you had a temper. You told me about that. What else could there be? I don't think you're a secret agent, though that would explain a lot. I don't know. Does it have to do with a woman?"

"Yes, it does."

"I always knew you had it in you. So what's the problem? She called and said she wants to see you again?"

"When I went away to college, I met a girl. Michelle. This is a long story. Are you sure you have time?"

I need to finish this application, but I'm not going to pass up on an interesting story. And Umar's hands are still shaking. I think he could use a friend.

"Go ahead."

He looks down at the floor, speaking so softly I can barely hear him. "I met her during freshman orientation. She was smart and funny. And she thought I was smart and funny, too. We could talk about anything, from Freud to the Flintstones. We had a class together, so we became study partners. Then we started dating. We went to the movies and out for pizza. When we walked across campus, I held her hand. When I dropped her off at her dorm, I kissed her. I wasn't a Muslim yet so it was no big deal. It was all very innocent, at first.

"The fall semester passed quickly, and we went our separate ways for winter break. I thought about her every day. We didn't call or write, but I missed her every day.

"I never told anyone about her—I wanted to keep our relationship my own special secret—but I think Dad knew. The day before I went back to school, he asked me to sit down with him at the kitchen table. We sat at that table, and he started out by saying he was proud of me. He emphasized the importance of taking my school work seriously. He reminded me how hard he had to work to put himself through school, and how much easier my life was. He warned me not to get distracted from my studies, and not to let my grades slip to the point where I would lose my scholarship. I needed to be serious for the next few years, he said, and after I received my degree I could relax and think about other things. We never talked about girls or sex, but I think he knew what was on my mind."

"You had those things on your mind, too? So you weren't always so serious."

"No, not always. I drove back to Chicago with his lecture still ringing in my ears, but she called me five minutes after I walked into my dorm room. My roommate wasn't due back for another day, so I told her to come on over. When I opened my door a few minutes later, and saw her standing there, I forgot all about Dad and his lecture." He stops, and shakes his head. "Our relationship changed that night. She's the only woman I've ever been intimate with. Besides Safa, of course."

"You are full of surprises. I never would have guessed."

He looks up at me. "I am a man, not a robot! Anyway, for the next few months my entire life revolved around Michelle. I went to my classes, and did the minimum amount of work required, but I rushed through everything so I could be with her. We were in love.

"By March we were talking about marriage. We spent quiet hours sharing our dreams for our life together. We would find an old house somewhere in the city and refurbish it. We would both earn our doctorates, and open up a joint counseling practice. We would name our first daughter Lisa. And our first son would be Derek.

"I lived in a dream world with Michelle until the middle of April. Then, one day after class, one of my professors called me aside. I was in danger of flunking his course. I knew that if I didn't perform well on his final, I would lose my scholarship.

"That conversation woke me up. I realized that I was in danger in all of my classes, not just his. Michelle and I talked about it, and we agreed to study more, but I couldn't study. I couldn't stop thinking about her.

"It was the last Wednesday in April when our lives changed. When we met that day, she was very quiet. I thought she was worried about finals. I told some jokes, trying to make her laugh, but she wouldn't even smile. We went to my room. I started to kiss her, but she stopped me. She told me she was pregnant. She said our baby would be born that December."

It's a good thing we're not eating lunch, because I would have choked. "You got a girl pregnant when you were eighteen, too? Why didn't you say anything? It would have been nice to know I wasn't alone."

"No one has ever known. I was too ashamed."

"Ashamed because of the pregnancy?"

"Not only that. Let me finish. We spent all that afternoon and evening trying to come up with a solution. We could get married, but how could I support a family? She could have the baby and give it up for adoption, but what about her studies? Or she could have an abortion. When she left my room that night, we still hadn't decided what to do. Looking back, I think she really expected me to marry her.

"I spent the next two days thinking about it. Finals were coming, and I couldn't study. I asked her not to see me. I needed time to think things through on my own. And at the end of the two days, the only solution which made any sense to me was abortion."

"Abortion? You wanted to kill your own child?"

"I didn't know what else to do." He stands up and starts pacing. "I couldn't go to Dad. Can you imagine how angry he would have been? Didn't you consider abortion when Heather first told you?"

"No, not really. Brad suggested it, but I couldn't ask her to do that. As hard as it all was, part of me wanted to be a father."

"Not me. Not then. I wasn't ready. I had to finish my studies. I borrowed money from three of my friends. They didn't ask me why I needed it. I knew I would have to get a summer job so I could pay them back in the fall."

He stops pacing and leans on my desk. "I told her on a Saturday. She cried. We fought. I screamed at her, and forced her to take the money." He stops again. It takes him a moment before he can continue, in a softer voice. "I screamed at her. And she turned around and walked away from me."

He starts pacing again. "I pushed myself to concentrate on my finals. I passed my exams and kept my scholarship, but she was gone. Her roommate wouldn't tell me where she was. I assumed she was recovering from the procedure. I would see her again in the fall and try to make up with her. We could still keep seeing each other. We just needed to be more careful. And maybe, after I had my degree, we would still get married."

He stops, and looks out the window. "But she didn't come back to school in the fall. Her roommate told me she had transferred to a community college near her home. I never saw her again."

"So it was Michelle who called just now?"

"No, not Michelle. It was Beth, Brad's wife."

"What does my sister-in-law have to do with all of this?"

"She said that a case had just come across her desk. There is a boy, a young man really, who is a patient at the hospital where she works. He has leukemia and needs a bone marrow transplant." He looks at me. "His name is Derek. His mother's name is Michelle. She and her children have all tested negative as possible donors. Michelle asked the hospital to help her locate the biological father so he could be tested. When Beth saw the name, Anthony Steven Evans, and the birth date of the father, she said she thought it was probably me. She was right."

I stare at him for a moment before I say quietly, "So you've had a son all these years, and you never even knew?"

"No. I thought she had the abortion. And it's been tearing me up inside." He starts pacing again. "At first I rationalized it to myself. I kept my scholarship, and my father was still proud of me. Wasn't that more important than risking my future?

"But that December, I thought about her. I thought about the baby which should have been born. I struggled with depression. And I came close to losing my scholarship again."

He stops pacing and looks down. "It was even harder to live with after I became a Muslim. The first time I read the Qur'an, I was shocked when I came to the passage describing the creation of a human being inside the womb. That was the first time I cried about it, because I knew I had told her to kill our child. I felt like a murderer."

"That's why I never could have talked with Heather about having an abortion. Because, somehow, I knew that he was a real person. Even before I ever held Michael in my arms."

"I wish I had known that. Instead I've had to live with the guilt. I kept trying to convince myself I had done the right thing. If I had married Michelle, I might not have become a Muslim. I might have lost my scholarship and had to drop out of school. I might have disappointed Dad."

"But I became a Muslim, and finished school, and was loved and accepted by Dad. And Michael has had the chance to live his life."

"I know. Believe me, since you married Aisha, there have been many times when I've thought about how much I admire you. I've never told you that." He looks at me. His face is expressionless, but his eyes show the pain.

I know he's suffering, but I'm irritated. "When I first met Aisha, you made me feel like scum for what I had done. Why did you act like that, knowing you had done the same?"

"I don't know." He looks down again. "I guess because I was so bitter about my own experience. The only way I could live with myself was to become cloaked in self-righteousness. I became a different person. I stopped telling jokes and I stopped laughing. I stayed away from women. I became old. Until Safa came into my life.

"And I still have felt haunted all these years. When Dad died, I thought of the grandchild he should have seen. When Aisha gave birth to Jamal, I thought of the child I had killed. And when I held my Sakeena, on the day she was born, I thought about my other first child. The one I would never hold. The one who would never cry.

"I was so hard on you, I guess, because I knew how selfish a man could be. I didn't want anyone to do to Aisha what I had done to Michelle."

"You know, don't you, that Dad would have been much angrier with you for telling her to abort your child than for losing your scholarship. Children were everything to him."

"I know that now, but I didn't know that when I was eighteen."

I walk over and hug him. He cries softly for a few minutes, until he manages to regain control. We both step back. "So how soon can you be tested?"

"I'll go to the hospital this afternoon, insha Allah."

"You will have to tell Safa, you know."

"I know. And she won't like it. She was married to Raheema's father. I don't think she'll understand."

"If she kicks you out, you can always spend the night at our place, but you're going to have to tell Sharon, too."

"And how do I tell her that I wanted to get rid of her grandchild?"

∽

Umar leaves, and I try to get back to my work. I think I'll just work through lunch. I'm not very hungry now.

Heather and I never talked about abortion. I never thought about God back then, but I still knew that there was something special about our baby. Besides, neither one of us got along very well with our families in those days, and we both needed someone to love. I only married her because I was afraid of her father, but I never could have asked her to get rid of Michael.

And Michael is such a great kid. He's just started his senior year of high school. He's been on the honor roll every year. He wants to go to college in Boston and live with Marcus, who works in a research lab out there. I've told him he's going to have to get a scholarship. I earn enough to support a family but not enough to send a kid to college. And Heather's husband, Peter, is an artist. Besides, they have a kid of their own, a little girl, and he doesn't have to worry about taking care of my kid.

Neither Michael nor Marcus is a Muslim yet. They're both really great kids, and they listen to Umar and me when we tell them about Islam, but they're not ready to make that commitment.

Jeremy is a Muslim. He's been praying and fasting since he was ten or eleven. He got his driver's license a couple of months ago, and he has a weekend job. He's trying to save enough money to buy a car.

Jennifer is the one I'm worried about. She's so rebellious. She used to be such a sweet little girl. Then, a week or so after she turned twelve, she changed. It seemed to happen overnight. The worst part is her mouth. I've wanted to slap her a few times because of that mouth. I worry about her and the boys, too. I sure don't want her turning up pregnant. I've tried to talk to her, but she won't listen. Maybe I should ask Heather to talk to her. She can tell Jennifer about what a jerk I used to be, and how she needs to stay away from guys like that. Jennifer doesn't remember the fighting, and the divorce, and the custody battle. She doesn't know how hard Heather and I had to struggle to get past all that.

And Umar got a girl pregnant and told her to get an abortion. Now that I think about it, it actually explains a lot. That's why he is always uptight. I used to wonder about that. Sharon and The Doc were always so upbeat; I wondered what made Umar so stern and sour. Now I get it. That's a lot of guilt to live with all these years.

Rebounding

I'm thinking too much. I need to get back to this grant. I'll have to stay late tonight and overnight it. I'd better call Aisha and let her know I'll be late. She won't like it, but it's her brother's fault.

When she answers, I can hear Luqman shouting happily in the background. He never stops. He was like that even in the womb, Aisha tells me.

Jamal and Muhammad are still at school. They go to an Islamic school not too far from our home. The principal keeps asking Aisha to come teach there, but she wants to stay home with the kids as long as we have little ones. With another baby coming, that could be a while. She does volunteer at the school, and sometimes they call her in to substitute.

"Assalaamu alaikum, Hon. I wanted to let you know that I'll be late tonight. I have to get these papers in the mail. You can go ahead and eat without me. I should be home by eight at the latest, insha Allah."

"But, Isa, we're going to Umar and Safa's house tonight. Don't you remember? Ismail and Mahmoud will be there, too. You've been looking forward to seeing them."

I sure did forget. Umar's little secret blew it right out of my mind. I'm sure Umar has forgotten, too. "That's right. There's been so much going on at work that I completely forgot. How about if I meet you there?"

"Okay, then. Love you."

"I love you too."

Before getting back to work, I run by Umar's office to remind him about tonight. He's in the corner, on his prayer rug, bowing down to Allah. He stays that way—with his head touching the floor—for a long time. I don't know if he's praying out of thankfulness that she didn't have the abortion, or out of regret for the mistakes he has made. Probably both. I write a short note and leave it on his desk.

I finally get the proposal typed up and in the mail. By the time I'm ready to leave the office, it's just starting to get dark. I pull out my prayer rug and say my evening prayer before heading over to Umar's house. I'm the last to arrive.

Sabeera answers the door. "Assalaamu alaikum, Uncle Isa."

"Assalaamu alaikum, Sabeera. How's my favorite second grader?" I playfully tap her nose.

She giggles. "I'm happy." She takes my hand. "Come on. They're in here."

She leads me to the family room. Mahmoud and Ismail are sitting on the couch, having a lively conversation in Urdu about the political situation in Pakistan. Twenty-three people died in Karachi this morning. Another bombing. I don't know where Umar is.

"Assalaamu alaikum, guys. How you doing?"

They stand to greet me. I haven't seen them in a long time. It's not like the old days when we lived together at the house. Now we all have jobs and families. No more staying up late with pizza and video games.

Mahmoud and Halima have four girls now. They're all very well behaved. I know Aisha would like Jamal to marry their second daughter, Naila. He is getting to be a big boy, but they have a lot of years before we have to start thinking about that. Naila is very sweet, and Aisha thinks she would be the perfect daughter-in-law. I'm not ready to go through all that with my kids yet.

Michael probably will be ready for marriage and kids in a few years, but I'm not ready. It's hard to imagine that I was just a few months older than Michael is now when Heather got pregnant. Fortunately, Michael is too smart to get himself into that kind of a mess. He's too busy with soccer and keeping his grades up to worry much about girls, but, now that I think of it, it could be on his mind. Maybe I should have a talk with him.

Ismail finally got married about six years ago. After all the matchmaking he did for everyone else, it was Aisha and I who matched him up with Amal. She and Aisha went to college together. Amal, who was born and raised in Chicago, made

Rebounding

Shahadah about a year after Aisha did. I had fun turning the tables on Ismail.

They have one son, and little Zaid is enough of a kid for any parents. That's how Ismail must have been when he was little.

I've been lost in my thoughts again. Ismail is talking to me. I come out of my daze.

"Hey, man. What are you now, a workaholic? I remember when we couldn't even get you out of that bed."

"You should talk, dude. I saw that new car out there. What happened to your little red clunker? You must be working pretty hard to afford that nice machine."

"Man, I got rid of the red clunker a couple of years ago. You ain't even been paying attention."

"Dude, you better pay attention to Zaid before he knocks over your tea." Ismail scoops Zaid up and starts roughhousing with him. No wonder Zaid is so hyper.

"So how have you been, Mahmoud?"

"I'm good. We're all good. Halima still teaches Qur'an at the school, so we're busy these days, but she enjoys it, and the girls like having their mother at school with them. I think she teaches Muhammad too, doesn't she?"

"Yes, she does. And Muhammad loves the way she teaches. Because of her, he loves reading the Qur'an. And his recitation is really coming along. We're glad she's his teacher."

"That's good to hear. Usually the only parents she hears from are the ones who complain."

"I'll have Aisha write her a nice note."

"That would be great. I know it will make her day."

"So where is Umar? He left the office early to go run some errands, and I thought he'd be here by now." *He went to the hospital to see if he can save the life of the son he didn't know he had when he woke up this morning.*

"Man, he's been acting weird all evening." Ismail puts his son down and Zaid runs off to play with the other kids. "When we came over, he was real quiet. I know Umar's not too talkative, but he was something else tonight. Is he having any problems at work?"

37

"Not that I know of." *Not at work.*

"Anyway, he went to go see Safa in the kitchen and he's been gone for a long time. I don't think he's helping her with the food. I hope not. I've tasted Umar's cooking."

No, Umar, don't tell her. Not now. Not with all of us here. At least wait until we're gone.

Umar and Safa come out of the kitchen a couple of minutes later.

"Where were you, man?" says Ismail.

"I just needed to help Safa with something in the kitchen."

"You didn't do anything to the food, did you?"

Safa smiles. "No, I needed him to fix one of the shelves in my cabinet. Don't worry. I won't let him near the food." I guess she's tasted his cooking, too. He does barbecue. And I guess his other cooking isn't that bad, but he'll never be able to compete with his wife.

I make eye contact with Umar. He shakes his head. He hasn't told her yet. I should have known. She is still smiling.

∽

A couple of days later, during lunch, he tells me that the first blood tests show he could be a match. He'll be going back for more tests next week.

"I haven't told Safa yet. I thought I'd wait for the initial test results. Could Aisha and you watch the kids tonight? I'll take her out to dinner first. It might help."

"I doubt it, but it's worth a try. Sure, we'll keep the kids."

"The strangest thing is, these last couple of days, I keep thinking about Michelle. I remember spring break, when Michelle and I made excuses to our parents so we could spend that time with each other. We were together every second. I start to wonder if that's when Derek was conceived. I remember her soft skin, and the way she looked at me. And I remember that her favorite flowers were violets. I bought some on my way back to campus that fall, hoping that we would make up and pick up from where we left off, but she wasn't there. I put them on the

Rebounding

windowsill in my dorm room until they died. Then I threw them in the trash. I keep remembering."

"Be careful, brother."

He doesn't seem to hear me. "I stopped at the store to buy milk yesterday, and I heard our song. 'My Destiny' by Lionel Richie. We thought we would be together forever. Sometimes I wish I could go back to that Saturday morning. If I could go back, I wouldn't scream at her. I wouldn't let her get away from me." He stares at his coffee mug.

I've never seen him like this before. I take him by the shoulders and look at him straight in the eye. He is in a very dangerous mood. "Listen to me, Umar. Remembering is what got me into trouble with Heather."

He comes out of his daze. "Yes, I guess you're right. I understand that now. When a relationship is left unresolved, and the memories are so strong, it is hard to just ignore it, isn't it?"

"It sure is. I don't think you should see Michelle. You have a good thing going with Safa and the kids. You don't want to do anything to mess that up."

He sighs, and shakes his head. "You're right. I love Safa, of course. She's my wife. Anyway, I asked about Michelle when I went over to the hospital. She refuses to see me. I'm sure she hates me. And she's married. Derek must have been pretty little when she got married because he has her husband's last name. He probably thinks that guy is his father. Michelle won't have anything to do with me. She just wants my bone marrow to save our son's life."

"It's better that way. And I'll make sure we have a spare blanket handy, in case you need to sleep on our couch tonight."

∾

By the time I get home, Umar's kids are already here. There are kids everywhere. Our three boys make enough noise on their own, without any help. Especially little Luqman, who thinks jumping and screaming are a way of life. When you add Umar's kids to the mix, the noise level is deafening. Of course, Raheema is a young lady now. She's helping Aisha get the dinner together. And Sakeena tries hard to be like her big sister, but his three youngest are something else. Even the girls. And I wouldn't trade their noise for all the loneliness in the world. I love it.

Along with our three boys, and Umar's three youngest, we have a few animals to add to the chaos. Aisha's cat, Frisky, lived a good long life in this house, but she passed away from old age a year ago last spring. A week later, a boy in Jamal's class announced that his cat had just had a large litter. A month after that, there were handmade signs on the school bulletin boards advertising free kittens. Aisha talked with the boy's mother, who desperately wanted to get rid of the fluffy little creatures. We ended up taking two, one for Jamal and one for Muhammad. I convinced the boys to name them Mario and Luigi. I used to spend hours playing that game.

When we first brought them home they looked so innocent. Just two little bundles of fur. Mario is an even mixture of black and white, and Luigi is mostly black with white around his eyes and paws and on the tip of his tail. We were happy to have cats in the house again, but they were kittens. We spent the next two months trying to tame them. At the same time, Luqman was going through his terrible twos. Those were trying times.

They're a little calmer now, but when the kids get going, they like to join in. Right now they're leaping around the family room, trying to keep up with Sabeera, Tasneema, Ahmad, Muhammad, and Luqman as they jump from the couch to the chairs.

We have a couple of other animals, too. We inherited the fourth grade class guinea pig at the end of the last school year. And I bought a white cockatoo for Aisha last Eid because she has always wanted one. The guinea pig doesn't make much of a fuss, but the cockatoo squawks and yaks all day, and needs a lot of attention. Jamal would like an iguana too, but Aisha draws the line at reptiles. I think they're kind of cool, but she has the last say on pets because she's the one who usually ends up taking care of them.

I join in on the kids' game, grabbing Luqman and tickling Ahmad. Muhammad jumps away from my grasp and nearly

Rebounding

knocks over the lamp. Sabeera and Tasneema giggle. I raise myself up and tower over them. Then I chase all the kids around the house, roaring. They scream and run away. As we run through the kitchen, Aisha scolds me. "Isa, sometimes you're as bad as the kids."

"I know." I grab her and give her a quick kiss before chasing the kids back into the family room.

They jump on to the couch. "You can't get us here, Uncle Isa," says Tasneema.

"That's what you think." I grab Tasneema, Luqman, and Ahmad and tickle them. Sabeera tries to rescue them while Muhammad jumps on my back. Then he jumps off and barely misses the lamp again. Fortunately, that's the only breakable thing in this room.

I want to keep the game going, but I'm starting to get tired. I'm not as young as I used to be. I plop down on the couch. The kids climb on me. "We got you now," yells Muhammad.

I let them crawl on me. I'm too distracted to go after them. I keep thinking about Umar's son. I won't tell Aisha about her secret nephew yet. She'll be irritated when she finds out that I knew and didn't say anything, but Umar needs to tell Sharon himself. No matter who tells Sharon, she's going to be angry.

Umar and Safa got their own place soon after Sakeena was born. Aisha and I still live in the Lincolnwood house, the one we all moved into after Dad died. We're buying the house, on a rent-to-own basis, so I guess we'll be here for a long time yet. I can't imagine living anywhere else.

Sharon still lives with us here. She never did go back to working in a hospital, but she has been a visiting nurse for several years now, since Aisha quit teaching to have Muhammad. She can still do the work she loves, and she has the flexibility to travel back to Moline or just take some time off.

She's been in Moline these last few weeks, trying to figure out what to do with Grandma.

Sharon's father died three years ago. I'm glad I got to know Grandpa before he died. He was a good man. And he even got used to the idea of Aisha being married to "a white boy." He

41

loved playing with Jamal and Muhammad. Jamal cried when Grandpa died. That was the only grandfather he'll ever have. Luqman was only two months old when Grandpa died, but at least he did get to hold him.

Grandma has been on her own for the last three years. After Grandpa died, she insisted on staying in her house. Things had been going well until last month, when she fell and broke her hip. Sharon rushed there to be with her. Now that Grandma is getting better, they're all worried about letting her live alone again. They've called a family conference. All of Grandma's children will be there. Aunt Laura flew in from California, and Uncle Frank drove up from St. Louis to see how Grandma is doing and decide what should be done. Aunt Debra, Aunt Vivien, and Uncle Paul still live in Moline. And Sharon stays in the house where Aisha grew up, the house where Dad lived.

So she already has a lot to deal with. And when she comes back she's going to hear about her long lost grandson. She will not be pleased.

The kids are running around the family room now. "Over here, Uncle Isa. Come get us," Tasneema screams. I forget about everything else and go back to chasing them.

I'm about ready to collapse when Aisha comes in and says loudly, "Time to break it up. Dinner is ready." I call a time-out and herd all of the kids toward the bathroom to wash up.

When we get to the table, I count heads. Someone's missing.

"Where is Jamal?"

"He went to do his homework as soon as he came home. I'm glad he's being so responsible," says Aisha.

I'm impressed. I go up to his room and knock on the door. "Jamal, dinner time."

"Just a minute, Dad."

I hear some noise in there, but it's not the sound of books. It sounds a lot more like a video game. He is a normal boy after all. I'll talk to him about it later.

Dinner tonight means macaroni and cheese with fish sticks. It's a lot easier to just eat kid food sometimes, especially when we have so many kids to feed. And Aisha doesn't really like to cook, even when she does have the time and energy to do it. Once in a while she'll be inspired and turn out a really delicious meal, but usually Sharon does the cooking around here, when she's in town. And sometimes, especially on the weekends, I still like to get into the kitchen.

We finally get everyone to sit down and eat. Aisha is at one end of the table, I'm at the other end, and all of the kids are in the middle. She shouts across to me, "How was your day?"

"What?" I'm sitting next to Umar's son, Ahmad, who bangs the tray on the highchair and babbles loudly.

"I said, how was your day?"

Ahmad throws his cup on the floor, and Sakeena jumps up to get it. He likes that, so he does it again. And again. When she's not fast enough, he throws some of his macaroni down, too.

"No, Ahmad, no," Sakeena says firmly. He giggles and reaches for her with his dirty hands. "No, Ahmad. Here, drink your juice." She gives him the cup. He throws it down again.

I've been watching the drama of Ahmad and Sakeena and have completely forgotten about Aisha.

She tries again. "Isa, can you hear me?"

That's right. I was trying to have a conversation with my wife. "What did you say again?"

She shakes her head. "Never mind."

Ahmad laughs as he smashes a fish stick with his fist. Umar's son is something else. Umar's son. He waited a long time to have a son. His first three children were girls. He didn't know he had a son all along.

After dinner we leave Raheema, Sakeena, and Jamal to straighten up the kitchen and clean Ahmad's mess around the highchair. Aisha gets Ahmad cleaned up and puts him in the playpen. I put on a movie for the other kids in the rec room, or "wreck" room as Aisha calls it. The cats stretch out and watch the movie with the kids, and the bird stops her chatter for now. We finally have a little peace and quiet. My wife and I go into the family room and relax together on the couch.

"How was your day?"

"It was okay. Nothing unusual." *Nothing I can tell you about, anyway.* "Did little Maryam give you a lot of action today?" According to the sonogram, it's a girl this time.

"She sure did. I think she's even more active than Luqman was, if that's possible."

"Well, she will have three big brothers to deal with. I guess she'll have to be tough." I put my hand on Aisha's growing abdomen, waiting for the next kick. It doesn't take long. She's strong. "I think we have another soccer star here."

Aisha stretches out on the couch while I massage her legs and feet. "That feels so good." She closes her eyes. She's asleep by the time Umar knocks at the front door.

"Assalaamu alaikum, Isa. It's much quieter than usual in here."

"We cheated. We gave the kids ice cream and put in a movie. Come on in. So how did it go?"

He looks around. "Where's Aisha?"

"Sleeping on the couch. Why?"

"I don't want her to know yet. I still have to deal with Safa."

"I guess she didn't take it too well."

"She listened politely, and all during my confession I could see those little signs of anger popping up, one after the other. First she pressed her lips together. Then she clenched her hands in front of her. She smiled tightly. And when her voice got higher, I knew I was in serious trouble. Then I made things worse. I told her that I'm hoping to get to know the boy, and she told me she doesn't want another woman's son in her house. I replied that I have been raising another man's daughter. That's when she asked me to take her home. And it was a very cold ride."

"Oh, Umar, you're usually smoother than that. That really was not a smart thing to say."

"No, it wasn't. Her circumstances were totally different. I don't even feel that way about Raheema. Most of the time I think of her as one of mine, and I've always tried to treat her that way. It just came out."

"Do you need me to wake Aisha up so you can sleep on the couch?"

"No. Let her sleep. I think I can face my own wife. When I get home she will probably be in the kitchen."

"Aisha and I just yell it out. I wish she would cook instead."

"No, you don't. I lie in bed and listen to the clatter of pots and pans. All night long. And every little clang reminds me of what I did wrong."

"At least you eat really well."

"Yes." He doesn't look too happy about it. "She makes the special desserts we usually have for Eid. And we eat a special curry every night. The children love it, except for Raheema. She knows. Every time her mother starts cooking all night, Raheema keeps looking at me, trying to figure out what I did wrong. Sakeena is probably old enough to figure it out now, too. It's wonderful food, but I don't eat much. I feel too guilty."

"She really cooks all night?"

"Yes, until she decides to forgive me. Then she comes into the bedroom and acts as if nothing ever happened, but that's not going to happen tonight. I don't think either of us will get much sleep for the next couple of nights. I don't know, it could take a week or so this time."

"Remember. There's always the couch."

"No, I've already hurt Safa. She's upset, and she needs me to be there. Besides," he smiles a little, "I can't deprive her of the opportunity to make me feel guilty. In fact, I'd better get home now so she can get me started on my guilt trip." He walks down the hallway and shouts in his deepest voice, "Where are my girls?"

"Baba!" Tasneema comes running toward him, a doll cradled in her arm. Sabeera is close behind.

He picks them up and swings them in the air. They shriek with laughter.

Umar is a good dad. It's too bad Derek doesn't know that. I doubt that he ever will. Even if Safa does learn to live with it, I don't think Michelle will ever let him back in her life.

Sharon comes back into town a week later. Umar has already gone through a second round of tests. He's still waiting for the results.

He says that Safa is still cooking all night. He has bags under his eyes. "But I bring her flowers every day and help around the house more. I think she's starting to soften up."

He comes over on Saturday to talk with Sharon. He gives her a potted tulip. It's her favorite. He asks her to sit down at the kitchen table. And he asks me to stay. For moral support, I guess.

"How are you, Mom? How's Grandma?"

"She's recovering well. She refuses to live anywhere but her own home. We finally decided to hire someone to stay with her and help her out. But she's eighty-nine years old. She won't be able to live on her own too much longer. I think that eventually she'll go to live with your Aunt Debra, or I might move back to Moline to take care of her."

"That's good. Um, there's something I need to tell you. It's important."

"You're not even listening to me, are you?"

"No, I guess I'm not. I need to tell you something. It's important."

"You just said that. What is it?"

"Well, you know when I was in college? I didn't tell anyone, but I had a girlfriend back then, during my freshman year. We were very serious about one another. We had even started talking about marriage. And we, um, I, um. . ."

"You are not going to tell me that you have a child with her, are you?"

"Yes Mom, I do."

"Oh, Tony, I thought I raised you better than that. Why didn't you say anything all these years?"

"I didn't know. That is, I knew she was pregnant, but when she told me, I panicked. It was right before finals. I didn't want to get distracted and lose my scholarship and disappoint Dad and

Rebounding

you. So I gave her some money and told her to get an abortion. She walked away from me, and I never saw her again."

"An abortion? You told this girl to get rid of your child because it was an inconvenience to you and your plans? I know I didn't raise you like that."

"I know. You didn't, but I panicked. I didn't know what else to do."

"You had two parents, didn't you? Why didn't you come to us?"

"I didn't want to disappoint Dad and you."

"Disappoint us? Tony, I have never been disappointed with you until this minute. Your studies were important, of course, but didn't we teach you about the importance of family? Family has always been more important. I thought you knew that. And of course your father would have been angry—what father wouldn't be?—but we would have stood by you and the girl. We would have helped you every step of the way."

"I know that now. So, anyway, she didn't have the abortion. My son was born that December, but I didn't know it."

"Thank God she had more sense than you did. Where is he now?"

"He's in the hospital, the one where Beth works. He has leukemia. I found out about him because his mother was looking for me. He needs a bone marrow transplant."

Her voice becomes softer. "How long have you known?"

"About two weeks now. They've been running some tests. I might be a match."

She shakes her head. "I hope you can help him, but I don't know what else to say. This is too big for one little plant. You should have filled the house with tulips, the way your father did when I was upset with him. And your father never did anything anywhere near this big." She's quiet for a moment, then she starts to cry. "This is the first time I have ever been glad that your father isn't here with us now. Having relations with the girl when you should have been concentrating on your studies, having an illegitimate child, that would have been enough to make him

47

upset, but turning your back on the mother of your child. . . That's the worst of it."

"What would Dad have said if he knew he had an illegitimate grandchild?"

"He would have been angry. Very angry. Growing up fatherless in East St. Louis, working as a teacher and a principal, he saw too many children without fathers. It bothered him greatly. And he never would have wanted that for his own grandchild. Besides, we both expected great things of you. There was a time when we thought you would earn your doctorate, like your father. Don't you know how hard he worked to get out of the ghetto and make something of himself? He didn't waste his time chasing after girls. We thought you were serious about your studies, like he was."

"That's why I never said anything."

"I just told you he would have been angry, but after he got over being angry he would have helped you and the girl. It's not the boy's fault that you weren't married to his mother. He was still our grandchild. And don't you know how much your father wanted to be a granddad? After Angela got married that was all he ever talked about. All the things he was going to do with his grandkids. Didn't you see how he was after Angela told him she was pregnant? I think that's what made him strong those last few days. He didn't live to see Jamal, but he had another grandson all those years. It breaks my heart just to think of it."

"I'm sorry, Mom. I was young. I didn't know what to do. I wish I could make it up to Dad and you."

"I never thought I'd given birth to a fool, but that's what you are, Tony, that's what you are."

She gets up and goes upstairs. Aisha walks in from the family room. "What's going on? Is Mom upset? I thought I heard her crying."

"Sit down, Aisha. There's something I need to tell you." He takes a deep breath and blurts it out. He tells her about the call from the hospital, and a shorter version of his affair with Michelle. "So, I have a grown son who needs me."

"No, Umar, I don't believe it. There must be some mistake."

Rebounding

"It's true, and the only mistakes are the ones I committed."

"No, Umar, not you." She looks at me. "Did you know about this?"

"Yes. Umar told me the day he got the call."

"Why didn't you tell me?"

"I wanted to, but Umar had to tell Safa first, and then Sharon. That's why Sharon is crying. And that's why Safa has been sending food over every day for the last week or so."

"You told her to get an abortion?" She starts to cry. "And Dad had a grandson and he never knew it." She cries harder. Of course, when she's pregnant she cries easily, but I almost feel like crying, too. Thinking about Dad.

"I'm sorry. I was afraid. How could I tell him that I got a girl pregnant? He would have gone through the roof. I know, now, that I was wrong. I hurt a lot of people with my foolishness. Hopefully I'll be a match, so I can do a little, at least, to make up for my mistakes."

"I'm going upstairs to be with Mom. I don't believe you, Umar. I never believed you could do something like that."

Umar and I sit at the table for a long time. Finally he says, "At least Safa is close to forgiving me, I think. Hopefully Mom and Aisha will be able to get past this, too."

"You just told your pregnant sister that you planned to get rid of your unborn child. And you just told your widowed mother that she and your father had a grandson all those years when he wanted a grandchild so badly. They will probably get past it, eventually—people do—but don't hold your breath."

"But it was over twenty years ago."

"But there are always the echoes, rebounding again and again. Did you forget?"

"No, I didn't forget, but I didn't know they would be this loud."

∾

A few days later, Umar finds out that he is a match. He comes to my office right after getting the call.

"I can do it, Isa. I can help Derek." He's so happy that he laughs out loud. The only other times I've ever heard him laugh were when he was playing with his children.

He still has to go through a series of examinations to make sure that he's fit to be a donor. Then they'll perform the procedure. And it will take at least another three months after Derek receives the marrow to know if he is cured. But, from what Umar tells me, this is the only option. Derek has been listed on the national registry, but it's especially hard to find anonymous donors for African-American patients. Umar's marrow is, most likely, Derek's last chance.

Safa has stopped cooking all night. Umar tells me that she's still not happy about it, but she has learned to accept the fact that he had a life before he became a Muslim. She's still not ready to accept Derek, though.

Aisha also has a hard time accepting it. We talked about it the day after she found out.

"I can't believe it. Not Umar."

"Why not?"

"Because he's my big brother. I've always respected him. And I always thought he was nearly perfect. He found Islam first. He's the one who taught me. He's taught me so much, since we were young. Now I don't know what to think. I don't know who he really is anymore."

"He's still your big brother, the one who taught you, but he's not perfect."

"No, I guess he's not, but weren't you shocked when he first told you?"

"Sure I was. He's my big brother, too. I've always depended on him to know what's right. But the whole thing happened a long time ago, before he took Shahadah. I know how it is to have a past."

"I still can't see it. I remember when he went away to college. I didn't see anything then."

"But you know that he's always been good at keeping secrets."

Rebounding

"Yes, but I never imagined he had such a big secret of his own."

"Are you still angry with him?"

"Not angry. Just disappointed. And I knew Umar then. I can't picture him being that kind of person."

She's trying to get past it. I know she had a long talk with him yesterday. After their talk, things seemed to be back to normal between them, but I know she is still disappointed in him.

Sharon hasn't said anything about Umar's child. I think she would like to pretend it never happened. He's trying to make it up to her. He and Safa are coming over more often, and each time they visit they bring her something. One time it was a box of chocolate eclairs. The next time, they brought a bag of red apples. Another time, he gave her a book she's been wanting to read. Not tulips, though. I'm sure he'll never bring tulips again.

He asks her how her day went, and she tells him what she did, but it's not the same. I think back to those days after Dad died, when Sharon relied on Umar to get her through the grief. Now a barrier remains between them.

Part Two

I'm trying to be supportive of Umar, but I need to concentrate on Aisha. Her ankles are swollen and she's always tired. And there are still the three boys to take care of. Her doctor says that everything is progressing normally. Sharon and I help out as much as we can, but I worry about her, anyway.

I'm worried about Jennifer, too, and her attitude. When I picked her and Jeremy up from Heather's last night, she wouldn't say two words to me.

When she does talk, she has a foul mouth. This morning, when I asked her to wash the breakfast dishes, she cursed at me and walked away. I wanted to slap her across the face, but I've never hit my kids, and I still remember being a teenager. I knew that hitting her would only make things worse. Much worse. I just took a deep breath and let her sulk.

I'm working at the computer when a boy comes to our house to pick her up in his car. She tries to sneak out, but his car needs a new muffler and he has the music turned up full blast. I follow her out and stop her on the front porch.

"Where are you going?"

"Out."

"Who's the boy?"

"A friend of mine."

"What's his name?"

"Why do you need to know?"

The image of Heather's father flashes suddenly in my mind. I am becoming Heather's father. Now I understand him. And I will do everything I can to keep that boy from treating my daughter the way I treated Heather.

"Jennifer, you are not getting into that car with that boy unless I know his name, his address, his cell phone number, and the names of his parents. And he needs to get out of that car and come into the house to talk to me himself."

"You can't tell me what to do."

Rebounding

"Think again." I grab her arm.

"Let go of me."

"No. Not until I find out what I need to know."

The boy watches from his car. He has long hair and an attitude I can feel from all the way over here. There is no way Jennifer is getting into that car with that boy.

I'm holding on to her and I will not let go. Her lips are in a pout and she will not tell me anything. Finally, after honking a few times, the boy gets tired of waiting. He gives me the finger, shouts out a curse, and drives away.

"I don't believe you. Do you enjoy ruining my life?"

"Go inside, Jennifer."

She curses at me and runs into the house. I stand out on the porch and take a few minutes to calm myself. That boy thinks he's going to take advantage of my daughter. Then he has the nerve to flip me off. He'll be sorry if he ever dares to show up around here again.

And Jennifer. She should know better. She wasn't brought up in the streets. Hasn't she learned anything all these years?

I take several deep breaths. I can't hit her. I can't scream. I just have to keep her safe. I just have to let her know how much I love her.

When I do finally go into the house, I can't find her anywhere. My heart beats faster.

What is going on with this girl? This morning was bad enough, but the way she was just now. And that boy. I know what he had on his mind. It hasn't been that many years since I was his age.

I don't know where she is. She's not in her bedroom, or in any other room of the house. I start to panic. I keep running up and down the stairs, looking in each room a second time. She could have sneaked out the back while I was still on the porch. She had better not be with that boy.

I haven't checked the basement. It's the only place she could be. If she's still here. I turn the knob and walk quickly down the steps.

53

She's here, sitting in a corner, her face turned toward the wall. At least she's here.

She glances back at the sound of my footsteps, then quickly turns to the wall again. She's crying.

I want to scream at her. I want to take her by the shoulders and shake some sense into her, but I remember myself in my mother's garage. I take a few more seconds to calm myself. Then I walk over and touch her softly on the shoulder.

"Jenny, I think we need to talk."

She keeps staring at the wall. I stand behind her for a few minutes, waiting, but she won't look at me.

I go upstairs, but I come back down every hour or so to check on her. Every time she sees me, she turns away, but she knows that I'm here, that I care.

In the evening, I call Heather. Peter answers.

"Hi Peter. This is Joshua. I need to speak with Heather, please."

"Is it important?"

"It's about our daughter."

"You two need to do a better job of controlling that girl."

"I know. That's why I need to talk to Heather."

I'm not that crazy about Peter, but he's a whole lot better than the guy she used to see. He treats my kids well. And Heather is happy.

"Hi Joshua. What is it?"

"It's Jennifer. She tried to go out with a boy today. He drove up in a car with a lousy muffler. He had long hair. And she wouldn't even tell me his name."

"Oh, that sounds like Brandon."

"You know about him?"

"He's come to our place a few times. She's gone out with him before."

"And you're okay with that?"

"No, not really, but she has to make her own choices. If we try to tell her what to do, she'll just rebel. I'm working to keep the lines of communication open with her. You didn't lecture her, did you?"

"No, but I stopped her from going out with Brandon, or whatever his name is. She's sulking in the basement right now."

"Listen, Joshua, you need to learn how to deal with her. She's not a little girl anymore. You have to give her some space to live her own life."

"Heather, she's only fourteen years old."

"I was fifteen when a boy with long hair and a bad car came to pick me up. My dad tried to stop me. That only made me more determined to see you. That's why I got pregnant when I was seventeen."

"You don't understand. That boy with the long hair and the bad car would have gone after you whether or not you were angry with your father. Your father just made it more of a challenge for me. Besides, don't you want to protect Jennifer from guys like that?"

"Of course I do. That's why I'm thinking about putting her on birth control. I don't want her to have to struggle the way I did."

"So she won't get pregnant, she'll just be free to sleep around? Is that your idea of a solution?"

"I don't want to do this right now. Peter and I are trying to have a quiet evening at home."

"Listen, if you don't work with me on this, I will take you to court. I don't want my daughter going out with boys who look like that, I don't want my daughter on birth control, and I don't want you making excuses for her."

"So what do you suggest?"

"I think we need to sit down, the four of us, and come up with a plan to help our daughter. And I want her to have to follow the same rules in both households."

"I'm sure not going to make her wear a scarf, if that's what you want."

"No, she doesn't have to wear a scarf, but I don't want her getting pregnant. And I want to keep her away from boys like the one who got you pregnant. I understand guys like that. I understand them better than they understand themselves."

"What's wrong, sweetie? Is he giving you a hassle?" I hear Peter in the background.

"No," Heather whispers, "it's okay."

"Do you and Peter want to come here, or should we go to your place?"

"I think it's better if you come over here. Your boys are too noisy. I can hardly hear myself think."

"Okay, why don't we do it tomorrow at six. I'll bring Jeremy and Jennifer back and then we can talk."

"Why don't we ask her to be a part of it? Maybe it will help her self-esteem."

"No, we need to have a discussion among the four of us first. I want to make sure that we are all on the same page. After we do that, then we can bring her in to talk with us."

"Okay. We'll see you then."

After I hang up, I put two scoops of chocolate ice cream into a bowl, pour on some hot fudge, and smother it all with whipped cream. The Jennifer I've always known loves chocolate and whipped cream. She turns away when she sees me, but I leave the bowl next to her. When I go back down, an hour later, Jennifer is asleep and the bowl is empty. I bring her a pillow and a blanket and kiss her lightly on the head before I go to bed.

I am not going to lose my little girl.

☙

After the morning prayer, I go downstairs to check on Jennifer. She's still asleep. She looks so sweet. Could she be the same girl who cursed at me yesterday?

I run up to the kitchen and fix up a batch of chocolate chip pancakes. I put a plate of them next to her just as she opens her eyes.

"Hi honey. Are you okay?"

"I guess so."

"I hope I didn't hurt you when I grabbed your arm."

"No, it's okay."

"I brought you some pancakes. You must be hungry."

Rebounding

"Yeah, I guess so."

"You're a good kid. Do you know that?"

"I don't know. I guess."

"I love you, Jenny." I brush her blonde hair out of her eyes. "I want you to always remember that." I give her a kiss on the cheek and head upstairs.

A couple of hours later, I find her sitting in the family room, reading a book to Muhammad and Luqman. I just have to remember to treat her the way I wanted, really wanted, my mother to treat me when I was her age.

I've barely seen Jeremy all weekend. He works at a fast food place, and he likes to spend most of his spare time with his friends. I don't mind, just as long as I know where he is and who he's with, and he keeps up with his prayers.

At least I see Jeremy more often than I see Michael. My high school senior keeps so busy with his job and extracurricular activities that I don't expect to see him on any kind of regular basis. He does stop by about once a week . Usually around dinner time. We eat and talk, and he plays with his little brothers before he leaves. He is so grown up. I'm glad that I was able to spend some time with him when he was small, when he still needed me.

Jeremy looks surprised when both Aisha and I come out to the car to take them back. "Why are both of you coming?"

"We need to meet with your mom and Peter. We have some issues to discuss."

"They both have to come because they want to talk about me," says Jennifer. She smiled a little today, but now she slouches. "They think I'm some kind of freak and I'm gonna ruin my life."

That sounds so familiar. "Aisha, why don't you sit in the front seat with Jeremy? I'd like to sit in back with Jennifer."

"Sure. It's easier to get in and out of the front seat anyway."

Jeremy is a smart boy. He takes his place in the driver's seat, turns on the radio, and pretends to listen to the game while I talk with his sister.

"There's something I have to tell you, Jennifer. Maybe I should have told you sooner, but it's not easy to talk about."

"I know. I'm running with the wrong crowd. I have a bad attitude. I'm a mess."

"No, I'm not going to talk about you. I'm going to talk about me. Do you remember that time, several months ago, when you asked me if I smoked weed when I was young?"

"Yeah, I remember. You turned red and changed the subject."

"I wasn't ready to talk about it then, but I'll answer your question now. When I saw that boy who tried to pick you up yesterday—"

"Brandon. His name is Brandon."

"Okay, when I saw Brandon yesterday, the thing that bothered me the most was that he reminded me of me. When I was a teenager, until about the time Michael was born, I was a total mess. I did smoke weed. I also drank heavily. I had long hair and a bad attitude. I fought with your grandmother all the time, and a few times I even pushed her against a wall. Everybody thought I was some kind of freak. And I hated myself. Sometimes I just wanted to die."

"Yeah, I know how that is, but what does all that have to do with Brandon and me?"

"I also chased after women. I think you've had some sex education classes in school. When I was a teenager, that was all I wanted from a girl. I didn't want her companionship and I couldn't care less about her personality. All I cared about was what she could give me. I treated your mother that way, too. That's why our marriage wouldn't work. I was with her because of the way she looked and the way she made me feel. It was all about me. I didn't care about what she needed, and I didn't even know who she was on the inside. The only thing I cared about was that she was hot."

"Mom was hot?"

"Sure she was. Take a look at some of the old pictures if you don't believe me. I asked her out because she was hot, I used her to fill my own needs and, when you were still too little to really know me, I walked out on her. By the time you were three, I had changed completely, but when you and your brothers were very,

Rebounding

very small I was still very bad. I'm not proud of that, and I've worked hard to change, but I thought that now, since you're getting older, maybe it's time for you to know."

"I already knew some of that junk, mostly from Kyle, but what does that have to do with me? Brandon's not like that."

I have to ask. "Jennifer, have you had sex with Brandon?"

"I don't have to answer that."

"Jennifer."

"No, not yet." Her voice becomes smaller. "But he wants to."

I relax a little. "That's what I thought. Because you're a pretty girl. Brandon would probably call you hot. And a boy like Brandon is only after one thing. I should know."

"It's not like that, Dad. Things are different now. Brandon says he loves me."

I have to keep myself from laughing, because she is so serious. "Do you know how many times I used that line? It worked almost every time, but I didn't mean it. I didn't know what love was. Not until I met Aisha."

"Did you lie to Mom, too?"

"My worst lies were the ones I told your mom. I treated her very badly. Fortunately, we've been able to get past that now. Remember that if a guy really cares for you he won't try to put the move on you. If he really cares for you, he'll put your needs and concerns first, over his."

"You didn't do that with Mom, did you?"

"No, not with your mom. Only with Aisha. She's the first woman I ever respected, and the first woman who ever respected me. And you don't have anything in a relationship if you don't have respect. Love is nice, very nice, but you have to have respect too. And later I think you need to have a good long talk with your mom about boys and sex and all that. Just don't be shocked when she tells you what a jerk I used to be."

"But you changed. Maybe Brandon will change too."

"I'm sorry," says Aisha, "but I have to butt in. Jennifer, when I married your father he was still a little rough around the edges, but he was trying very hard to change. I just helped him finish the process. Don't get involved with any man unless he's already

59

trying to change, on his own. Your dad got a good job on his own, he went to college on his own, and he became a Muslim on his own. If he had quit his job, or not gone to college, or not practiced Islam, he would have been history. He knew it, too. You need to let a man know that you have high expectations. And one more thing, do you know why your dad changed?"

"I don't know. I guess he just got tired of all that junk."

"That's part of it, but the main reason he changed was because he wanted to be a good father to you kids."

"I didn't know that," Jennifer says softly.

"Neither did I," says Jeremy. "Thanks Dad."

"Yeah, thanks."

Thanks, Aisha.

～

Heather and Peter live in a downtown condo. Their place looks like something from a magazine, with Peter's brightly-colored paintings on the wall, white carpet, white furniture, glass tables, and fragile, artistic knick-knacks everywhere. Their daughter, Brianna, is four. A quiet child. I can't imagine bringing our boys to this place.

Peter greets us with his usual charm. "Come on in. How are you, Joshua? It's been a while. And look at you, Aisha. Any day now."

"I have about a month left."

"I don't know how you two manage. Our little Brianna is a handful. I don't think I could handle a whole houseful of little ones."

Aisha smiles. "We get by."

While we exchange pleasantries, Jeremy and Jennifer walk past us and head for their rooms. They like Peter well enough, they've told me, but sometimes his banter can be annoying.

By the time we're comfortably seated, Heather is walking in from the kitchen, carrying a tray. "Hello Joshua, Aisha. How are you? Aisha, you look like you're due any day now."

"No, not for another month yet."

"That's good," says Peter. "I don't think I'm up to delivering a baby today."

I hate lame jokes. And if he thinks he's going to get anywhere near my wife. . .

The three of them chat for a few minutes longer. It's mostly Peter, but Aisha plays along. Sharon did teach her to be polite. I try to be patient, until I just can't take it anymore.

"Okay, why don't we go ahead and talk about Jennifer. That is why we came."

"If you insist. I just thought it would be better if we're not so serious all the time," says Peter.

"I understand, but my mother-in-law is watching the kids, and I really don't want to take advantage of her, so I think we'd better get to the point."

"Okay. You're the guest."

"I don't mean to be rude, but I've been concerned about this for several months now. Jennifer is not a little girl anymore. She's a very spirited, and very pretty, young lady. And I want to make sure that we all work together to keep her on the right path."

"I agree," says Peter. "She needs to be reminded of the proper way to behave."

"I don't know," says Heather. "I think she's just acting out. It's pretty normal for kids that age. Give her a couple more years and she'll outgrow it."

"But what is she going to do while we're waiting for her to 'outgrow it'?" says Aisha. "Think of all the trouble she can get into."

"Just because you were Little Miss Perfect doesn't mean you can tell everyone else how to live their lives," says Heather.

"What? Where did that come from? This isn't about you or me. We're talking about Jennifer."

"What's wrong, sweetie?" says Peter. "There's no need to get personal."

"Joshua made it personal. Yesterday he said he didn't want Jennifer to get pregnant, like I did. Who do you think made me pregnant? And now he thinks he can tell everyone else what to do."

"Heather, on the way over here I told Jennifer about what a jerk I used to be. We've been through all this before. You were a good-looking girl who trusted the wrong guy. The thing is, I don't want Jennifer to be another good-looking girl who gets taken advantage of by another guy like me. I've already told you I'm sorry. And your life is good now, but now I understand why your father tried to keep you away from me."

"I should have listened to him."

"Yes, you should have. And I'm going to do my best to make sure Jennifer listens to me. I was afraid of your father, but any guy who tries to mess with my little girl is going to be terrified of me."

"I see what you're saying." She pauses a moment, then nods. "I guess Jennifer is lucky that you're her dad."

"That's the nicest thing you've said to me in over fifteen years. Okay, so now we have to decide what to do. I won't ask Jennifer to wear a scarf, not unless she wants to, but I do have other conditions. First, I don't want her dating at all. At least not for a few more years. Then we can renegotiate, if necessary. All of us need to know the names and phone numbers of her girlfriends, as well as their parents' names. We need to know where she is and who she's with when she goes out. Finally, I want to restrict her media access. No R-rated movies. Limited time on the internet. And we have the right to know what kind of music she listens to."

"Man," says Peter, "I'm glad you weren't my dad. Do you think all of that is really necessary?"

"Yes, I do, but I don't want to just take things away from her. We need to encourage her to get involved in extracurricular activities, help her with her school work, and involve her in more family activities. You and I, Heather, also need to spend more one-on-one time with her. When I was her age, and wild, what I needed the most was my mother's love and attention. I think, I hope, that a lot of love will get her through this. Whatever we do, she needs to know that we care, but sometimes caring means being strict and holding the line. Are you with me?"

Rebounding

"That sounds way too strict. What's she going to do for fun? And no boys at all? Don't you think that's unnatural? How is she going to feel when all of her friends are dating, and she's the only one without a boyfriend?"

"I don't know how she would feel, but I would tell her to get new friends. We can't raise our daughter under the banner of 'everybody's doing it.' Besides, she needs to get involved in other activities. We can show her that there's more to life than music, movies, and boys. Hopefully, she'll become so busy that she won't miss those things. And that's what will raise her self-esteem, especially when she knows she doesn't need the attention of a male to make her feel good about herself."

"Have you been watching Oprah?" Peter teases.

"No, I've just been thinking a lot about my own youth. It took me a long time to realize that I didn't need to pursue and control women in order to feel good about myself. Now I need the love of just one woman to keep me going." I squeeze Aisha's hand.

"I know what you mean. I didn't have the struggles you did, but I know that I felt a special comfort when Heather came into my life." He puts his arm around her shoulders, and she smiles. "I think what you're saying is that someone doesn't need to experiment with members of the opposite sex in order to find the one who is right."

"Exactly. I'm glad we agree."

"It still sounds restrictive, but I see where you're coming from. And I want what's best for Jennifer. Okay, I can accept your conditions. What about you, Heather?"

"It still sounds strange to me—especially the part about no dating—but, now that you mention it, I did want my parents' love. Especially my dad. All he did was yell at me. And my mom was distant. We've made amends, but we're still not close. That's why I thought I needed a husband and a baby when I was seventeen, to replace what was missing in my life. So I guess, if we give Jennifer that love, she won't need to go looking for it somewhere else."

"What about you, Aisha?"

"I agree. I'll do whatever it takes to bring our sweet little girl back."

"Heather, why don't you ask Jennifer to come in here?"

And the four of us talk with her. She doesn't like it, but she doesn't argue too much. It's hard for a fourteen-year-old to take on four parents who present a united front. Now we have to make sure we follow through.

❧

Jeremy borrowed my car last Friday night so he could go out with a couple of other guys. I let him take it, with the conditions that he told me where he was going and who he would be with, he called once in a while, and he remembered to make his prayers. They went to see an adventure movie and then out to eat. He didn't get home until nearly midnight. I waited up. He was full of excitement over his new freedom. I was nervous. He hasn't had his license that long, but I guess I can't hold on to my little boy forever.

Umar will be going into the hospital for the bone marrow extraction next week. Derek will start the process soon to get his body ready for the new marrow. We talk about it every day during lunch.

"I keep turning it over in my mind. Michelle didn't have the abortion. I have a grown son named Derek. He's sick. He needs me. And the guilt. You can't imagine the guilt I've carried all these years. I'll finally be able to do something to redeem myself."

"Is Safa able to deal with it now?"

"It's difficult for her because she was raised as a Muslim. She still has trouble understanding how I could have been such a different kind of person than I am now. I told her yesterday that the difference between me then and me now is as wide as the ocean, but she's still trying to accept that I had a life before Islam. Before this happened, I don't think she really thought about it. And I never wanted to talk about it. She does support me in trying to help Derek. That part she understands. Helping

Rebounding

someone. Helping family. And speaking of family, how is my sister these days?"

"You know how it is. The baby moves all the time, and sometimes gets into very uncomfortable positions. Her ankles are swollen. She's always tired. She can't wait for it all to be over. Everything is ready now. Baby clothes, crib, everything. We're excited, even though this is our fourth. Now we just have to wait."

"Things are looking good, Isa. In another month, insha Allah, you'll have another daughter, and I'll have helped Derek back to health. The center is receiving more grants and helping more people. The Jim Evans Youth Center is on its way. Things are looking very good."

After Umar leaves, I think about the new baby. I can't wait to hold her in my arms. I could never have imagined that I would have seven children, and I never knew that I would be able to love them all.

Jeremy and Jennifer come over on Friday, as usual. After dinner, I sit with Jennifer on the couch. She says that Heather had a talk with her.

"Mom told me about how it was when I was little, and before I was born. I didn't know how hard it was for her. Why did you leave us?"

"I was bad to your mother, and we fought all the time. I hated myself. I felt like I couldn't hold on anymore. For the first couple of months after I left, I didn't do anything except hang. Mahmoud and Ismail let me stay with them, and they helped me get my life together."

"Did you leave because you hated me?" she says softly.

I reach over and touch her cheek. "No, Jennifer, I have never hated you, but in those days I was so messed up that I wasn't quite sure how to love you. I love you now. You know that, don't you?"

"Yes Dad, I know." She scoots over and puts her head on my shoulder.

"What about you? Do you hate me, now that you know how bad I was?"

"No, I could never hate you. You're my dad."

We have a good weekend together. On Saturday, she tells Aisha to sit down and rest while she takes care of the kids. I take her out for lunch on Sunday. We talk some more, and I think she understands now why she has to be careful. I don't know if this is a permanent change, or just the calm before another storm, but it's a good weekend.

Part Three

I wake up on Monday morning thinking about Sam. That hasn't happened for years, probably not since Dad died. I feel uneasy. Of course, I always feel uneasy when I think of Sam. Umar told me that I need to watch out, but Sam is just an old man. Unless he has friends who like to dress up in white sheets, which wouldn't be a complete surprise, I don't know what he can do to me. Still, I'm uneasy.

I get some good news when I walk into the office. The grant came through, the one I was working on when Umar told me about his son. We can expand our services to include ESL and citizenship classes. We already have a waiting list. It's good to know that we can help.

Umar is going into the hospital tomorrow. He plans to stay late tonight to finish up his work. They need to keep him overnight tomorrow for observation, to be sure there are no complications after the procedure. Those are rare, but the doctor recommended that he stay one night, and take at least one more day off from work to rest. I'll miss eating lunch with him these next couple of days.

"So how are you feeling?" I ask Umar over our last lunch for the time being.

"It's good knowing that I can finally do something for Derek. I'm nervous, too, but not about the procedure. We'll be so close. I wish I could see him. Though from what I understand, he's in isolation now, preparing his immune system for the transplant. I also keep wondering if I'll see Michelle."

"Remember what I told you. I've been there, brother. Forget about Michelle. Remember what you have with Safa."

"I know. You're right. Safa plans to go with me to the hospital tomorrow. The closer we get to the extraction, the more supportive she's become. It sounds strange, but in some ways this situation is bringing us closer together."

"That's great. What about the kids? Who's going to take care of them tomorrow?"

"Mom said she'll watch Tasneema and Ahmad for us. I think we'll bring them over to your place tonight. We can drop the other girls off at school, but you might need to pick them up. Safa will call and let you know. I wish we didn't have to do this right now, with Aisha so tired and just a couple of weeks away from delivering, but we have to go according to Derek's timetable. And I'm afraid he's running out of time." He looks down. "I need to see him."

"Have you tried?"

"Derek doesn't know I'm his father. I had to register as an anonymous donor."

"Which means?"

"Which means, according to hospital rules, I won't be able to see him until a year after the transplant. And even then, I don't know if Michelle will allow it." He shakes his head. "I'm worried, Isa. He might not make it."

I know he doesn't like to cry, but a couple of tears roll down his cheeks. I grip his arm. "Just keep praying."

He nods, and a few more tears escape.

∽

Umar brings Tasneema and Ahmad over in the evening. They like staying at our house sometimes. They play with Luqman and Muhammad. I give them ice cream. And their Grandma rocks them and tells them a story before putting them to bed.

I'm in the middle of peaceful dreams when I feel my arm being tugged. Then I hear my name. "Isa, Isa, wake up. My water broke."

It's Aisha. Her water broke. We have to go. Now.

"Okay, Hon, I'm awake. Go on out to the car. I'll tell Sharon we're leaving."

I throw on my nearest clothes and pound on her bedroom door. "Sharon, wake up. Aisha's water broke."

Rebounding

She's up and opening the door in seconds. "You go on ahead. I'll take care of things here. Just get her to the hospital on time."

Aisha is downstairs, still struggling to get her shoes on. It's been hard for her these last few weeks. I help her into her shoes and coat, hold her arm, and guide her out. Halfway to the car, she stops and doubles over.

"Hold on, Hon. We'll be there soon, insha Allah."

It seemed to take forever for Jamal to be born, but each of our other children has come faster. We got to the hospital only an hour before Luqman screamed for the first time. Her doctor warned us that this time Aisha needs to leave home immediately.

It started snowing during the night, but I don't have time to warm up the car and clear off the windshield. I just clear off enough to be able to see, and we're off. The roads are slick, so I have to drive slowly. But not too slowly. We have to get there on time.

I'm on the highway. It's a little before dawn and the traffic is light. I'm making good time, even with the road conditions. I can tell the contractions are getting harder. She leans over, gripping the door handle. I give her my right hand and she squeezes tightly. She moans softly. Then she lets out a short scream. There's not much time left. A few more miles. A light coating of snow covers the highway. I can't drive too fast, but I'm making good time.

Then she screams out, "I need to push."

We're not going to make it. I pull off, onto the North Avenue exit. I plan to drive to a parking lot, or pull into a side street, but she screams again. I stop on the ramp and pull over as far as I can. I grab my cell phone and call 911. While waiting for them to answer, I get out of the car and help Aisha into the back seat. She can barely walk.

All these months, I've been thinking about what I would do if it came to this. I was afraid I would have to deliver Luqman. This time I've rehearsed it in my mind. I think I know what to do, but I wish I had put a pillow and blanket back here, just in case.

It seems like it's taking forever for the operator to answer.

"911. What are you reporting?"

Finally.

"My wife is having a baby. She has to push."

"Is this her first child?"

"No, it's her fourth, and the last one was quick."

"Where are you?"

"North Avenue exit, off the Kennedy Expressway. Should I let her push?"

"Get her into a comfortable position. I'll connect you with a paramedic."

It takes just a second before we're connected. The contractions are hard and almost constant. She holds on to me, gripping my hand so hard it hurts. She shivers. The engine is still running. I reach over and turn up the heat. I hear a friendly voice.

"Sir, I understand that your wife is in labor."

"Yes, and she needs to push. Can she go ahead and push?"

The paramedic talks to me calmly, walking me through the birth of our child. Aisha pushes once, and I can see the top of the baby's head.

"That's good, Hon. We're almost there."

She rests until the next contraction. Then another push.

And our little girl is born. She whimpers.

"She's here. She's here."

"How does she look? Is she breathing?"

"Yes, she's breathing. Can you hear her crying?"

"Yes. Good. Now find something to tie off the umbilical cord. Do you have a shoe lace?"

I take the lace from one of my athletic shoes and tie off her cord. "Do I need to cut the cord or anything?"

"No, she'll be fine just like that. Hold on. The ambulance will be there soon."

The baby cries softly. I put her on Aisha's chest. Aisha is laughing. It's cold, she's shivering, and she's laughing. I take off my coat and wrap it around my wife and daughter. The three of us huddle in the back seat until we hear the sirens and see the flashing red lights. I wrap them up tightly and go to greet the paramedics.

Rebounding

Aisha is still shivering. They wrap her up in blankets. Then they wheel Aisha and the baby to the ambulance. I watch as the door closes on my wife and daughter, and the ambulance takes off, the siren going.

Aisha is shivering. And the baby sounded weak. I get into my car and drive as fast as I can behind the ambulance.

When I get to the hospital, they give me some papers to sign and ask me to wait in the emergency room. I want to see my wife and daughter, but they tell me to wait. I pace for a while, until I happen to glance outside and notice that it's almost sunrise. I wash up, then kneel down and pray, remaining prostrate for a long time. Please, Allah, please let them be okay.

A few minutes later, Aisha's doctor comes over to me. She delivered all three of our boys.

"Assalaamu alaikum, Isa. How are you? I hear that you had a very memorable trip to the hospital this morning."

"I didn't expect to take over your job. How are they?"

"They're both stabilized." I breathe again. "Aisha was stressed from the birth, and she was also suffering from mild hypothermia because she left the house without changing into warm, dry clothes. I can tell you both took seriously my admonition to get here quickly. She's fine, though. She's resting now. Her body temperature is back to normal, and she's feeling stronger. She's already been admitted and taken up to maternity. They'll bring her some breakfast soon. With a little rest and some nourishment she'll be as strong as ever."

"What about my daughter?"

"She's not as strong as your others were. And she's a little smaller, of course, but not too small. Her initial Apgars were low, but she has shown subsequent progress. She has already been washed up and checked out. They will take her to your wife soon so she can begin nursing. Don't worry. It was a very eventful birth, but they will both be fine."

"Can I go to see them now?"

"Yes, certainly, though we do have a little more paperwork for you to complete first. I think you probably remember where maternity is located."

"The fourth floor, last time we were here."

"That's it. Congratulations on the birth of your daughter. You did a good job, by the way."

"Thanks. I guess if we have any more, we'll have to camp out at the hospital."

She laughs as she walks away. "I doubt that Aisha will be thinking about having another one any time soon."

I rush through the paperwork and head for the elevators. On my way up, I say another silent prayer of thanks. They're okay. We made it.

I walk into her room. She's nursing the baby. I stand near the door, looking at my wife and child. We made it. They're safe. Everything will be okay.

When Maryam finishes nursing, Aisha hands her to me. I didn't have a chance to look closely at my daughter in the car. She has my round face. She has a full head of curly black hair. And I just thought I saw her smile. I won't tell anyone about that, though. They'll say it was gas.

I hold her close to me and perform the ritual that every Muslim father performs for his newborn. In her right ear, I softly recite the words of the adhan, the call to prayer. In her left ear, I recite the words of the iqamah, indicating that the prayer is about to start. Then I just hold her, studying her. She is a little smaller than her brothers were, but she came two weeks early. She has all of her fingers and all of her toes. She fusses a little. I hold her close and rub her back until she burps. As she goes to sleep, she curls up into a little ball and clings to my chest.

She is the most precious thing I have ever seen. I think of Jennifer. If I had held Jennifer when she was born, if I had known how to love her then, I probably wouldn't have left. I still have a long way to go to make it up to her.

I gently place our sleeping baby back into the bassinet. Aisha has finished eating her breakfast. She looks tired. I kiss her.

"You did a good job, Mom."

"You weren't too bad yourself, Dad."

"She's beautiful."

"Yes, she is."

"You're beautiful too." I kiss her again. "Get some rest. I'll call the family."

I go into the waiting room to make my calls. I need to call Sharon, Umar, and Mom. That's right. I can't call Umar. He's having the extraction done. At the hospital. This hospital. Right now, I think. I hope it goes well for him. I hope it goes well for Derek.

"Hello?" Sharon sounds tired. I doubt that she was able to go back to sleep.

"You have a new granddaughter. She's beautiful."

"How is Angela? Did you make it to the hospital on time?"

"No, not quite." I tell her about our highway birth. "It was scary, but they're both okay."

"You did a good job. Thank you, Joshua, for taking care of them."

"What else could I do? How are the other kids?"

"They're a handful. I managed to get Jamal and Muhammad to school on time. Muhammad was full of questions, of course. It's the little ones I'm having trouble with. Ahmad and Luqman together are too much."

"Do you need me to come home?"

"No, you should stay there with Angela. I'll manage. Hopefully Safa won't be too much longer." She pauses. "Did you know, Joshua? Did you know about Tony's child?"

"He told me when he found out, a couple of months ago now. Before that I didn't know anything about it. One time, many years ago, he mentioned that there was a girl he once thought about marrying, but he didn't say anything else about her at the time."

"I'm still having a very hard time with this. Part of it is because of his relations with the girl, though I suppose I shouldn't be too surprised about that. And part of it is because of the secret. I think the secret is what bothers me the most. He should have come to us."

"He was scared."

"But he told her to get an abortion. Tony grew up in the church. He knew how we felt about that. What about you,

Joshua? When you were eighteen, and you learned that you had a child, did you ask her to get an abortion?"

"No. I needed my child. Before he was born, I felt like I had nobody who really loved me—not even my mother, in those days—but Tony was trying to get through school and avoid disappointing Dad. In his own eighteen-year-old way, he thought he was doing the right thing. Do you remember when he used to laugh and joke?"

"Yes. He was usually a happy little boy. Until he went to college. Then he changed."

"I think the guilt is what made him change. I never knew Tony to be really happy. There was always something there, holding him back from enjoying his life. Now I understand what it was."

"I see what you're saying. I guess he has suffered, hasn't he? Maybe he needs the support of his mother."

"I think he does."

"I'll call Safa in a couple of hours to see if she can watch the children. I need to come to the hospital to see my children. And my new granddaughter."

"I'll see you soon."

I'm glad we had that talk. Now I have to call my mother.

"Evie's. May I help you?"

"Hi, Mom. Do you think you could send some food over to the hospital?"

"The hospital? What's wrong?"

"Aisha had the baby. Early this morning, before sunrise. You have another granddaughter."

"Already? Isn't it too early?"

"Two weeks early. She's a little smaller than the others were, but she's healthy. And, Mom, I had to deliver the baby."

"You did? Really! I knew Aisha delivered quickly, but I couldn't imagine it would be that fast. So the baby was born at home?"

"No, on the Kennedy Expressway." I tell her my story. I don't tell her how afraid I was. I'm still afraid that I did

Rebounding

something wrong, that somehow I could have hurt the baby, but Aisha is okay. And Maryam is okay.

"Good for you, Joshua. That must have been quite an experience. Is Aisha ready for visitors?"

"I'm sure she'll be happy to see you."

"I'll come this evening then. I can't wait to see my little Maryam."

Mom and Sharon will make sure everyone else hears the news, but I do call the school and ask the secretary to tell Jamal and Muhammad that they have a new baby sister. I don't want them to worry. Then I go back into the room to be with Aisha and Maryam.

It isn't until lunchtime that I remember to call the center. Umar and I are both gone. I hope Dora has everything running smoothly.

Dora has been our administrative assistant for almost seven years. She's efficient and professional. And she's fluent in both English and Spanish, so she can communicate easily with most of our clients. She and I speak mostly in Spanish. I don't want to forget what I learned in college.

"Hello Dora. It's Joshua."

"Where have you been? Don't get me wrong, it's nice with both of my bosses out. No letters to proofread, no calls to the pizza place. Joshua, you've had a few phone calls."

"My wife had the baby early this morning. In all the excitement, I forgot to call you."

"Congratulations then. Is it a girl?"

"Yes, and she's beautiful."

"All right. The next time Mr. Richards calls, I'll tell him you have a good reason for not getting back to him."

"Mr. Richards. I forgot. I need to set up a meeting with him."

"Don't worry, Joshua. I'll take care of it. Tell Aisha I said congratulations. And take care of that little girl."

"I will. Thank you, Dora."

I know she'll take care of everything while we're out. She does have to retype some of my letters. Even the computer can't always help me with my grammar. She's willing to order lunch for us. And she gives Umar and me the time we need to work on our projects. I wonder how long it is until Secretary's Day. We need to order a special bouquet.

Sharon comes in the afternoon. Safa has all the little ones, and she'll pick the older ones up from school.

"She asked me to tell you congratulations. And the extraction went well. Tony will rest here in the hospital tonight, but they should let him go home tomorrow. I'll go visit him in a little while. I think we need to talk."

"I think he'll like that."

"You know, Joshua, it's odd. Since Jim died, I have always associated hospitals with death, but now two of my children are in the hospital, giving life to their own children. I keep forgetting that hospitals can be about life, too."

I decide to run home while Sharon is at the hospital. I need to change my clothes and, in all the excitement, we forgot Aisha's suitcase. When I walk outside, I remember that my coat went with Aisha and the baby in the ambulance. I don't know if I can get it back. At least I didn't leave anything in the pockets. I run by an outlet store to buy another coat. And I pick up some new shoelaces while I'm out.

The house is too quiet. I miss my kids. I wonder how Luqman will adjust to his new baby sister. I can't wait to bring them home.

On my way back to the hospital, I pick up a pint of mint chocolate chip ice cream. Aisha has been through so much. She smiles when I walk in and give it to her.

"Thank you, Isa. That's just what I need."

I cradle our daughter while Aisha eats. I keep examining the baby, looking for some sign, some indication that something is wrong. Something must be wrong—I don't know how to deliver a baby—but she's fine. And Aisha is fine. I have to stop worrying.

Rebounding

After she finishes the ice cream, Aisha says, "I wonder what the boys are doing. I miss them already. Especially Luqman. I've never been away from him this long before."

"I'm sure he misses you too."

"Could you go get them?"

"Are you up for a visit? I know you're still worn out."

"I am, but seeing my boys will make me feel better. Please, Isa."

"Okay, if you think you can handle it. Call Safa and tell her I'm on my way."

Safa has them ready and waiting when I get there. Muhammad hugs me. "Daddy, I missed you."

"I missed you too, Big Guy. Are you ready to go see your baby sister?"

"Yeah!"

"Hold me, Daddy."

"Okay, Luqman." I pick him up, and he clings to me. He loves Aunt Safa and his cousins, but he's still little and he still needs us.

"Thanks, Safa. I'll bring them back in a little while. Can you keep them here tonight?"

"Yes, of course. Please give Aisha my salaam, and tell her to get some rest."

"I will. Let's go see Mom, guys."

"Mama!" Luqman yells.

Jamal is quiet. I talk with him in the car. "So what do you think about having a sister this time?"

"It's okay, I guess. Does she cry much?"

"No, not too much."

"That's good."

We walk in, after I remind the boys for the third time that we have to be quiet in the hospital, and take the elevator up to the fourth floor. I hold Luqman. He's afraid of elevators.

Aisha smiles when she sees us. Luqman cries out, "Mama." I lift him up on the bed and Aisha holds him. I don't think he even notices the baby. He just needs his mother.

Jamal has been through all this before. He walks in, hugs his mother, and smiles at the baby, but he's not too excited. He knows that babies cry, and have stinky diapers, and need a lot of attention.

Muhammad walks over to the bassinet and stares at the baby. He was only three when Luqman was born, and he didn't pay too much attention to his baby brother then. He studies Maryam's hands and feet, and traces her face with his finger. We remind him to watch out for her soft spot, but he's gentle with her.

"She's so little. Did I used to be that little too, Mama?"

"Yes, Muhammad, you did."

Aisha is very happy to see them, but after about fifteen minutes she starts to look tired. Then the baby starts crying.

"Okay, guys, I think we need to go now. Mom has to stay here tonight, but I'll bring her and your baby sister home tomorrow, insha Allah. You're going to stay at Aunt Safa's house tonight."

Jamal says, "Okay," and kisses his mom. Muhammad starts to ask questions, but I have to stop him because once he starts, he'll never stop. I pick Luqman up from Aisha's bed. He cries and reaches for her.

"It's okay, Big Guy. Mama will be home tomorrow." He keeps crying. Aisha looks like she's going to cry too. "Don't worry, Hon, he'll be okay."

I lead the boys out of the room and down toward the parking garage. Luqman starts to scream. I rush him through the quiet halls of the hospital as quickly as possible. When we get to the parking garage, his screams echo, rebounding off the walls. Muhammad laughs and shouts, trying to produce echoes of his own.

Finally I get them to the car. I buckle Luqman, still screaming, into his car seat and head back to Umar and Safa's house. Gradually his screams die down and he falls asleep.

Jamal is still quiet. Just before we get to the house he says, "She's nice. Maybe I'll like having a little sister."

"I'm glad you approve."

Rebounding

Raheema comes outside and carries Luqman, still sleeping, into the house. Safa comes to the door.

"Will they be coming home tomorrow?"

"Yes, probably in the afternoon."

"I can't wait to see my new little niece."

"She's beautiful. Thanks for taking care of the kids for me. I know you have your hands full."

"It's no problem at all, Isa. They're nice boys."

I give Jamal and Muhammad each a hug. "I'll see you guys tomorrow, insha Allah."

"Okay, Dad."

"Bye Daddy."

They give me their hugs and kisses, and I head back to the hospital.

※

Before heading back to Aisha's room, I go to see Umar. I'm sure Sharon has already been by.

On my way there, I pass a tall, thin black man coming down the hall from the opposite direction. I don't think too much about it until I get to the room. That's the door he just came out of.

"Assalaamu alaikum, Umar. How are you feeling?"

"Walaikum assalaam. I'm fine. It wasn't too bad. I'm a little sore, that's all. I keep thinking about Derek. I wonder when they'll start the transplant."

"I just saw a man in the hallway. Was that—?"

"Yes, that was John Williams. Michelle's husband. The man Derek thinks is his father. He said he was probably breaking some rules by coming to see me, but he had to meet me. He told me that Derek looks just like me. He asked how I could have been so stupid as to let such a wonderful woman as Michelle get away from me. And he thanked me for giving his son a second chance. I asked him if he would let me know how Derek does, and gave him my email address. He said he couldn't make any promises. And I told him I would like to meet Derek one day. He said he understood. I think he's a good man. I'm glad Michelle found someone like him."

"So you're finished with all the remembering?"

"Yes. That was so long ago. I was a different man then."

"Did Sharon come?"

"Yes. Oh, congratulations. I heard about my niece. I heard about the delivery, too. That must have been quite an experience."

"Don't tell Aisha, but I was terrified. I'm still worried that I did something wrong, that something's going to be wrong with the baby, but she's beautiful."

"I can't wait to see her. And thanks for talking with Mom. We cleared the air now."

"Does this mean I'm going to see some of that joking, laughing Tony you used to be instead of the somber brother-in-law I've been stuck with all these years?"

"You never know."

"Well, I need to get back to Aisha. Have a good rest. I'll see you tomorrow, brother." We hug.

"I'll see you, insha Allah."

※

Mom is in the room with Aisha. She brought a huge balloon bouquet, all in pink, proclaiming, "It's a girl!" She gets up and gives me a warm hug.

"Aisha told me what you did, there on the side of the highway. I'm proud of you, Joshua."

"Aisha had to do all the work. I'm just relieved that they're both okay."

"So I finally have another granddaughter. It's about time. And she is so precious."

"She's so small."

"You were even smaller than that when you were born. A full month early. I worried about you at first, but you have always been a fighter. You wouldn't let a little thing like size keep you down. I think this little girl is going to be a fighter, too."

I glance over at Aisha, who has been quiet. Her eyes are only halfway open. "I think she will be, too, but we probably should let her mother get some rest."

"Oh, I'm sorry. Of course, Aisha, after all you have been through. I'll see you tomorrow. Oh, and Joshua, I brought some food over. You probably haven't eaten all day."

"No, I guess I haven't."

"That's what I thought. You'll find some spaghetti in the bag over there. I put in some slices of my apple pie, too."

"Thanks Mom." I give her a hug. "We'll see you tomorrow."

After Mom leaves, I sit on the bed and hold Aisha's hand until it's time for me to go. We both need to rest. Tomorrow will be a busy day.

∽

I sleep very well, exhausted by Maryam's dramatic arrival. Mom's spaghetti and apple pie help, too. When I wake up, I'm full of energy. And excited about bringing my little girl home.

First, I rush around the house, picking up things here and there. I don't want Aisha to come home to a mess. I vacuum and throw a load of clothes in the washer. I make sure the baby's things are all in place. And I'm ready to go.

Sharon is in the kitchen, chopping vegetables. I stop to talk to her on my way to the door. "I'm heading to the hospital now. Do you need anything while I'm out?"

"Just to have my daughter and granddaughter safely at home. I'll see you in a little while, Joshua."

"Is that your special beef stew on the stove?"

"Yes, it is."

"I can't wait to eat some of that. I'll see you soon."

While climbing into my car, I remember that I haven't told my older kids about their new sister. I hope they haven't left for school yet. I call on my cell.

Peter answers again. "It's Joshua. Are my kids still there?"

"They're heading out the door."

"Could you get one of them for me? It's important."

"Which one do you want?"

"Let me talk to Jennifer." I want to tell my little girl about her sister and reassure her that she will always be special to me.

"Hey Dad, what's up?"

"Aisha had the baby yesterday. It is a girl."

"Great. So how is she?"

"They're both doing fine. I'll bring them home later today."

"Maybe I can come over to see her soon."

"I know she'd like that. Jennifer, I want you to know that you'll always be my little girl."

"I know, Dad."

I hear Michael shouting in the background. "Let's go. We're going to be late."

"Hold on, will you? Aisha had her baby. We have another sister."

"Great. Tell Dad congratulations, but we have to go."

"Okay. I have to go, Dad. I'll talk to you later."

"Okay. Bye."

She sounds so different than the girl who cursed me when I asked her to do the dishes. Now she's happy and sweet and full of life, as if she were a little girl again, but I know something about mood swings. I wonder how long this will last.

∽

I decide to stop by the office before going to the hospital. I need to check on that meeting with Mr. Richards and let Dora know we haven't forgotten about her. I'll have to get back to work tomorrow, but I hope I won't have to stay too long today.

"Hello Dora," I say as I walk in. "Did you schedule that meeting with Mr. Richards? I think he'll be able to get us some extra funding. Any other important messages? Any response yet on my latest proposal?"

Dora doesn't say anything. I look up. She's frowning, and Dora never frowns. She speaks to me slowly and softly, in English. "You have some visitors, Mr. Adams. They're in your office."

Rebounding

Mr. Adams? What kind of visitors? What's going on?

Two men are in my office. Both wearing black suits. One sits at my computer. The other is looking through my file cabinet.

"Excuse me. This is my office. Can I help you?"

"Joshua Adams?"

"That's me. Who are you?"

They flash some badges. The one by the file cabinet does the talking. "We're with Homeland Security. We need to ask you some questions."

"About what?"

"You will have to come with us."

"I'm not going anywhere."

"We have the authority to take you into custody."

"What authority?"

"You need to come with us. Where is your partner?"

"My partner?"

"Tony Evans. Where is he?"

"He's in the hospital."

"Would you care to tell us which one?"

"No, I would not care to tell you."

"Never mind, we'll find out. Let's go."

"Go where?"

"You're coming with us."

I could fight them. And get into worse trouble. I don't know what this is about. I need to stay calm. I can feel my face turning red, but it's better if I just stay calm. I breathe deeply, close my eyes, and say a short silent prayer.

I'm still making du'a when the guy who was at my computer comes over, pulls my arms behind my back, and puts me in handcuffs. He leads me out of the office.

The cold metal presses against my wrists. My heart pounds.

"Take it easy. You don't need those. You said you had some questions. You didn't say anything about arresting me. I didn't do anything wrong. Don't you at least have to read me my rights?"

"Not anymore. Not for terrorists."

Dora watches, her eyes wide, as they walk me out. I yell out over my shoulder, "Dora, call my mother."

83

I don't know what this is all about, but my mother will help me. My mother will know what to do.

Evie's Interlude: Terror

I was with a customer when Dora called, telling me that Joshua had been arrested. I asked Charlene to take over, grabbed my purse, and ran out the door.

While I drive to the hospital to get Aisha and the baby, I make a few calls of my own. First I contact Walt Thompson. I know he can help us. I tell him that Joshua was taken away. He promises to get right on it.

Then I call Sharon. We agree not to tell Aisha yet. I know she's strong, but she has just had a baby. We don't want to subject her to that kind of stress.

Next I call Brad. He just got off the phone with Beth. They've already come for Umar. Brad says he'll call Chris.

I was afraid this would happen one day. I wonder if Sam had anything to do with it.

Joshua

Part Four

They push me into the back seat of an unmarked car and drive away. I didn't get a good look at those badges. Are they really with Homeland Security? Why would anyone else want me? Why would Homeland Security want me?

What should I do? Cooperate? Resist? Demand my rights? I have to get to Aisha and bring the baby and her home. If I cooperate, they'll have to let me go.

I'm still in the car when my cell phone rings. It's in my pocket. I can't get to it with these handcuffs on.

"I need to answer that. It's probably my wife." I twist around and try to get into position, but it's no use. The phone stops ringing, but I left the speaker on. I hear Aisha's voice.

"Assalaamu alaikum, Isa. They're releasing us early. We're waiting for you. I can't wait to bring Maryam home and have our whole family together again. I love you, Hon. See you soon." Then there's silence, and she's gone.

"Hey, I need to talk to my wife."

They act like they don't even hear me.

They pull up to a nondescript building, drag me out of the car, and lead me inside. One of them reaches into my pocket and takes my cell. They take me to a simple office and tell me to sit down. It doesn't look like an interrogation room, just a simple office. Why would they want to interrogate me, anyway?

I know what it is. They're looking for another Joshua Adams. I must have a doppelganger somewhere who counterfeited money or transported a dead body across state lines. I need to tell them. It's all a mistake.

"Look, you have the wrong guy. There must be lots of guys named Joshua Adams. You just picked the wrong one. If you'd take the handcuffs off now, I really need to get to my family."

"Okay, Adams, if you think you don't belong here, then you won't mind answering some questions. What was the purpose of your trips to Pakistan? Why have you been sending money to

Karachi? How well do you know Ahmed Ali, also known as Abu Hamza?"

Ahmed. Abdul-Qadir's oldest son. What does all of this have to do with him? The last time I saw him was a few years ago, when I took Aisha, Jamal, and Muhammad to meet Abdul-Qadir. Ahmed was married and had a son. He and his wife sold sweets in the market. Why do they want to know about him?

They know a lot more about me than I thought they did. I don't know why they brought me in, but I need to be careful. I don't want to open my mouth and get myself into more trouble.

"I think I need to speak to a lawyer."

"Tell us about Abu Hamza. We know you have some connections with him."

I want to tell them that I've known "Abu Hamza" since he was sixteen. He likes to play soccer with his brothers and their friends. He prays regularly. He's good to his parents. He dotes on his young son, Hamza.

But they probably won't listen.

"I need to speak with a lawyer."

"We need answers, Adams. It will be better for you if you cooperate. We have men over at your office right now, gathering evidence. There's nothing you can hide. Tell us what we need to know."

"Will you let me go to my family?"

"Maybe, if you tell us what we need to know."

"What do you need to know?"

"Tell us about your connections with Al-Jahidia."

"Who is Al-Jahidia?"

"We know that members of Al-Jahidia have been responsible for at least three fatal bombings in the last month. What is your connection with them?"

"I need to speak with a lawyer."

This is unreal. I'm supposed to be on my way to the hospital right now to pick up Aisha and the baby. She'll wonder where I am. I hope Dora called my mother. My mother will know where to find a good lawyer.

Al-Jahidia? I've never heard of them. What is this about?

Rebounding

The office. He said that they have men over at the office. What will they take? What will they leave? What will I go back to? When will I be able to go back? How long will they hold me?

"We'll leave you for now so you can think about your situation. Sooner or later, you're going to have to cooperate."

I'm led to a smaller room. The handcuffs are removed. They leave, and the door locks behind them. And the irony of it all is breathtaking. All those years, when I was shoplifting and using drugs and driving around drunk, all those years they left me alone. Now, when I'm settled down and taking care of my family, now they bring me in.

I wish I could call Aisha now. She's waiting for me.

I wonder what time it is. I forgot to wear my watch this morning. I was so anxious to get to the hospital that I didn't take the time to put it on. Now I have all the time in the world, but I don't know what time it is.

I quietly recite Qur'an for a long time. Then I touch my head to the floor and pray. It must be time for the early afternoon prayer. I don't know how clean this floor is—I hate to think of how dirty it could be—but I have no choice. They took my new coat when they brought me into this room. I can't take my shirt off. I try not to think about it. I try to figure out the direction, and I say my prayer on the dirty floor. I pray as if my life depends on it. When I'm finished, I recite Qur'an again.

I try to concentrate on the verses I'm reciting, but my mind wanders. I wonder if they have Umar. He must still be feeling weak. I hope they leave him alone. He's not the one who went to Pakistan, but he has gone to Bangladesh a couple of times to visit Safa's family. Is that enough to bring him in? Just for going to visit his mother-in-law?

I wonder what Aisha is doing now. By now Dora has probably called my mother. By now my mother has probably told Aisha why I haven't come. By now they probably have my computer and all my files. By now they are probably calling me a terrorist.

Why? What did Ahmed do? Did he fight in Kashmir? Did he join the resistance in Afghanistan? I doubt that he went all the way to Syria to join in the fighting there. Was he behind any of the bombings in Karachi? Or was he just minding his own business when, somehow, he said the wrong thing at the wrong time to the wrong person?

Could they be talking about another Ahmed Ali who lives in Karachi and has a young son named Hamza?

And what is all this business about Al-Jahidia? I guess it's an organization. I've never heard of it before in my life. It sounds almost like they pulled the name out of thin air, but they act like I have some connections with this mysterious group. This whole thing is crazy. I feel like I've been thrown into the middle of a bad spy novel.

I sit in one of the hard plastic chairs and put my head on the table, overwhelmed by it all. I fall into a light sleep, but I don't sleep well. Someone screams at me, threatening me with torture. He slaps me, hard, in the face. He laughs when my face starts to bleed. He says that I will never see my wife or my children again. I cry out. He comes closer, until we are nearly nose to nose. I look closely at the face of my torturer. It is Sam.

I wake up, gasping. I seek refuge in Allah from Satan. I seek refuge in Allah from Satan. I repeat it over and over again, a prayer in a time of adversity. I seek refuge in Allah from Sam.

I sit in a corner of the room, on the bare concrete floor, and recite the Qur'an. I have to recite until I forget that hideous face. Until my fears are overcome.

I'm still reciting when the door opens. A man walks in. I don't know him, but he looks like he's on my side. He's tall, and his hair is completely gray. He probably played football in his college days. He looks confident and distinguished in his gray three-piece suit. I stand up. He offers his hand.

"Hello, Joshua. My name is Walter Thompson. I'm a good friend of your mother's. She has asked me to represent you."

"Why do they want me? What am I charged with? Why am I here? What's going on?"

"Hold on. Be patient. We'll get to all of that. I need to ask you some questions first." He opens his briefcase and takes out a handheld computer. "I'm told that you refused to provide any information until you could speak with a lawyer."

"Yes, that's right."

"That was a smart move."

"Mr. Thompson, before we start, do you know anything about my family? I was on my way to pick my wife up from the hospital. Our baby girl was born yesterday."

"Your mother asked me to tell you that they are fine. She's brought them home from the hospital, and your mother and your in-laws are taking good care of them."

"And what about my brother-in-law, Tony Evans? The agents asked about him."

"They located him. The doctor insisted that he be allowed to remain at home tonight. He will be brought in tomorrow. If he agrees, I will represent Mr. Evans as well."

"How bad is it? What do they have against us?"

"First, tell me exactly why you traveled to Pakistan. I want you to begin with your first trip."

"Okay. That was so long ago, though." I rub my forehead and try to understand. What does this have to do with anything?

"I had just become a Muslim. I was having a hard time changing my lifestyle and giving up my old bad habits. My friend, Mahmoud, arranged for me to live with his uncle in Pakistan for six months so that I could get away from my old life and get used to practicing Islam."

"I need to speak with Mahmoud. What is his last name?"

"Is that necessary? He has a family now. I don't want him to be dragged into this."

"Perhaps he can clarify the situation."

"Okay, as long as you can promise me that he won't be brought in, too."

"Nobody is going to disturb your friend, but I need to ask him some questions."

"His name is Mahmoud Ali."

"So Mahmoud sent you to live with his uncle. Is his uncle named Abdul-Qadir Ali?"

"Yes, he is."

"And what happened once you arrived in Karachi?"

"Nothing much, really. Each day, I went with Abdul-Qadir and his two oldest sons to pray in the mosque. Every morning, I attended classes at the mosque. In the afternoons, I helped Abdul-Qadir at his store."

"These classes you attended. What exactly did you study?"

"I learned how to recite and memorize the Qur'an. And I started learning how to read, write, and speak Arabic."

"Did you, at any time, become involved with any political organization?"

I almost smile. This reminds me of the first time I met The Doc, but the stakes are different. "No. I went to school, helped Abdul-Qadir at his store, and went to the mosque. That's all."

"This school you attended. Was it a madrassah?"

"Yes, it was a religious school."

"I'm sure you are aware that the word 'madrassah' has taken on an added connotation, as a place where young men are trained as terrorists."

"Yes, I know. I have tried, over the last several years, to clear up that misconception, but it's getting harder."

"Our purpose right now is not to educate. Our purpose is to clear your name. At the madrassah, were you ever instructed in regard to jihad, whether in terms of philosophy, methods, or both?"

"Only in a general sense. There are several references to jihad in the Qur'an. Jihad means struggle, and the greatest jihad is the war we wage against our own desires. When Muslims do perform military jihad, we must never kill or injure civilians. And property must never be intentionally destroyed. I did learn about the ideas and the rules of jihad, but if you are asking me if someone tried to recruit me to attack American interests. . . no, that never happened."

"But you do have an understanding of the philosophical principles of jihad. Joshua, if someone approached you and asked you to give material support to a military effort coordinated by Muslims against a non-Islamic state, such as the U.S., would you agree to do so?"

"I'm sure it would help if I could say no, absolutely not, but, to be honest, I can't say that. I believe that Muslims have suffered many injustices in recent years. If I were asked to help those who are oppressed, I would do what I could."

"That's not the answer I was hoping for. The charges against you are very serious, and I want you to rethink your answer in light of that. You are accused of participating in a money laundering scheme to provide funds for terrorists operating out of Karachi. It is alleged that you, and your brother-in-law, established The Caring Center for this purpose. Is that a plausible scenario?"

That is ridiculous. I can't believe what I'm hearing. I feel like screaming, but I have to stay calm. I close my eyes and take another deep breath before answering.

"Are you asking me if The Caring Center is a front organization for funding terrorism? Absolutely not. If you're asking me if I would be willing to commit a crime in order to help terrorists, then no, I wouldn't. If you're asking me if I would ever contribute money to help oppressed Muslims, then yes, I would do that."

"I appreciate such a thorough answer. The next step, then, is to prove that the purpose and activities of The Caring Center were strictly legitimate. Agents have already seized materials from your office in an attempt to prove illegal activities. Will they find anything, either on your hard drive or in your hard copy files, to support their case?"

"No, not at all. I'm in charge of the books, and all of the financial information for the center is on my computer. I also have letters soliciting funds, and grant applications I've submitted. Nothing in my files points to the kinds of illegal activities you mentioned."

"Are there other kinds of illegal activities indicated in your files?"

"No, of course not."

"That's why you must be careful not to answer any questions unless I am present. You could have just implicated yourself without realizing it."

"I'm not a lawyer, Mr. Thompson. I'm just trying to take care of my family and make a difference."

"I understand that. I simply wanted to emphasize the importance of not trying to be your own lawyer. So far you've done the right thing. I don't want you to slip. Tell me about this group, Al-Jahidia. What is your relationship with them?"

"Not only have I never heard of Al-Jahidia before today, but the name sounds suspicious to me. I don't know anything about a group named Al-Jahidia, and I actually doubt that such a group exists."

"The government seems to be very certain that this group does exist and has perpetrated dozens of documented terrorist acts. Not only that, they claim to have some evidence linking you with the group."

"I can't imagine what they would possibly have."

"Very well. I'll look into that." He enters some notes into his handheld. "What about your correspondence? When was the last time you were in touch with Abdul-Qadir Ali?"

"I sent him a letter about a month ago, but neither of us has ever discussed political issues in our letters. We talk about our families, our work, daily life."

"What about phone calls?"

"I call him several times a year. I'm planning to call him again in a few days to tell him about the birth of our daughter. You have to understand that Abdul-Qadir is like a father to me. And he is a quiet and gentle man. Exactly the opposite of a terrorist."

"The government isn't interested in Abdul-Qadir himself. It's his son, Ahmed. I'm told they have information from overseas informants stating that Ahmed Ali is a member of Al-Jahidia and is personally responsible for numerous bombings in Karachi. In addition, Ahmed Ali, or Abu Hamza, is reported to have fought alongside the insurgents in Kashmir."

"Mr. Thompson, the title 'Abu' simply means 'father of.' I have three names. My mother calls me Joshua. My wife, brother-in-law, and Muslim friends call me Isa. And, sometimes, I'm also called 'Abu Jamal' because I am the father of Jamal. And Tony is also Umar or Abu Ahmad. The media has taken the word 'Abu' and made it sound sinister. It's really very simple."

"That is all fine and good, but I need to know about your relationship with Ahmed Ali."

"When I first met Ahmed, he was a shy teenager. Over the last several years, he has finished school, gotten married, had a son. That's really all I know about him, but I can't imagine him being involved in those kinds of activities. He is as gentle as his father."

"Did you meet with him when you went to Pakistan four years ago?"

"Of course. He and his wife invited us for dinner. And I went over once before we left. We had tea and sweets."

"Did he inform you of his political activities?"

"No. We did have a general discussion about the conditions in Kashmir, but he didn't say anything about being involved there."

"Did you give him any money?"

"Yes. He and his wife have a small business, but they have trouble making ends meet. In Islam it is highly encouraged to give in charity."

"I'll accept your intention as charity, but that's not how law enforcement views it. They also claim to have records tracing amounts of money transferred on a regular basis from you to Abdul-Qadir over the past several years. Are you going to tell me that was also charity?"

"Yes. You haven't seen how he and his family live. I make a decent salary. And I've told you that Abdul-Qadir is like a father to me. I want to help him."

"Joshua, what is the source of your salary?"

"The Caring Center, of course."

"The Caring Center is funded by grants and donations. So, in effect, law enforcement will attempt to prove that you are misdirecting the center's funds to support terrorist activities. Do you see how much trouble you're in?"

It hits me. This is real. "Yes, I do."

"You will be transferred to an interim holding facility where you will be booked—mug shots, fingerprints, the works. In a few days you will be arraigned before a judge. At that time you will enter a plea."

"I'm not guilty. You have to believe that."

"I do. I've known your mother for a long time, and she's told me quite a bit about you over the years, so, in a sense, I feel that I knew you even before we met. I believe that you did not willfully commit criminal acts. I know you thought you were doing the right thing, but you've made some decisions that leave you vulnerable to suspicion. At any rate, I've gained quite a bit from our talk just now. I will work hard on your case, and I think I can help you, but it will be rough these next few months. You need to be prepared."

"But I've tried to do everything right. I went to Pakistan to learn about Islam. I've helped Abdul-Qadir and Ahmed when they needed money. Umar and I opened The Caring Center so we could help people. How can that be wrong?"

"It's the way things are these days." He puts the computer back into his briefcase. "I need to go. Do not answer any questions unless I am present. Your honesty, oddly enough, could get you into even more trouble. Can you remember that?"

"Yes, I'll remember. What about my brother-in-law?"

"The charges against him are as an accessory. They intend to show he was aware of your illegal activities and assisted you in covering up the facts. Those charges will be more difficult to prove. However, I'm sure they plan to cite his trips to Bangladesh, as proof of his sympathies, to support their case."

"So it doesn't look good, does it? For either of us."

"That depends. There are many variables. The political climate is unstable, and a single event somewhere in the world, especially in Pakistan, could affect your case. You need to stay quiet unless I am present. And I need to see what they've come up with from their raid on your office. All of those things will enter into the balance."

"What about my family?"

"It will be hard on them, that's for certain. I will try to have you released on bail. Your mother is ready to provide whatever is necessary for your release. Unfortunately, your arrest has already been aired on radio and television. Something along the lines of 'Man delivers baby on expressway, now arrested for terrorism.' I'm sure you can expect something in the newspapers tomorrow."

"When can I see my wife?"

"Not until the arraignment, at least, but you need to prepare yourself for the possibility of a very long separation."

This can't be happening. Maybe I'm dreaming. I pinch myself, hard. That hurt. And I'm still sitting in this tiny room with this man who says he can help me. It's no dream.

"Can you get a message to her? Tell her I love her, and tell her not to worry about me."

"I'll give her the message. You need to stay strong and be patient. Your life has changed now. There is no going back." He stands up, ready to leave me alone again.

"I'm trying to understand that. I still don't know, though, how this could have happened." I pause, lost in my thoughts, until I remember Thompson standing there. "Thank you for taking my case. I'll cooperate with you however I can."

"Good. I should be back in about two days, earlier if they insist on questioning you."

Two days. "That's something I'm still trying to grasp. I'm not going home today, am I?"

"No, I'm sorry. The earliest you could possibly go home will be after the arraignment—which should be early next week—but only if the judge allows you to be released on bail. If he denies bail at that time, you could be held until the trial."

"How long will that be?"

"I don't know. I can tell you that justice moves very slowly these days, particularly when the charge is terrorism. It could take a year. Maybe longer."

A year! I've been in custody for a few hours now and already I feel trapped and restless. How could I possibly hold on for a year? And it's not just me. "What about my family?"

"Everyone will do whatever they can to help them."

"What if I hadn't stopped by my office this morning? Would they still have taken me in?"

"They found Tony, didn't they? Take care, Joshua. I'll do my best."

"Yes, I'm sure you will." *Please get me out of here.*

Mr. Thompson walks out, the door slamming behind him.

～

I need to pray. It must be time for the late afternoon prayer. I should have asked Thompson to bring me a watch. There is no water. I make a dry ablution, tayammum, by patting the floor and making the motions of ablution. It's the best I can do.

I'm reciting Qur'an when the men in the black suits return. They take me away and book me on charges of fraud, money laundering, providing material assistance to terrorists, and promoting terrorism. They take my clothes, shoes, wallet, and car keys. I'm strip searched and given an orange jumpsuit and rubber-soled slip-ons to wear. I'm led down a hallway and taken to a cell. The door slams behind me.

How did I get here? Going to Pakistan? Giving money to Ahmed and Abdul-Qadir? Since when is it criminal to travel and give in charity?

And they're saying that Umar and I used the center to funnel money to terrorists and provide Al-Jahidia with a legitimate outlet here in the United States. Will they look at the good we're doing? The classes, the clinic, the youth center. All the people we've helped. Or will they only see what they want to see, searching for the evidence to prove their charges?

I can't lose hope. I didn't do anything wrong.

I think it's time for the evening prayer. At least now I have water. I wash up, grateful for this small thing. I recite Qur'an until I think it's time for the last prayer of the day.

After the prayer, I lie down on the bed. And I think about my family. Aisha and the baby are home, but I'm not there. What is she doing right now? What is she thinking right now? This morning I was imagining how nice it would be, bringing her and the baby back home with me, but tonight she's alone. We're both alone.

I fall asleep. I don't sleep well. I toss and turn, with disjointed images, threatening images, flashing through my mind.

A dream comes into focus. I can see my house. Sam is there, in the kitchen. I tell him to leave, but he doesn't hear me. Jamal walks into the kitchen, looking for me. Sam sees him and starts cursing him. He slaps Jamal across the face. Jamal cries out. Sam stands over my son and keeps hitting him until Jamal is lying on the floor, sobbing. I reach for my son, but he is so far away. Aisha comes in to see what is wrong. Sam grabs her. Aisha tries to push him away. She calls for me, but I can't move. I can't get to her. Sam puts his hands on her. She screams.

I wake up. Thankfully, I wake up. I look at the walls and the bars. Nothing soft here, nothing to hold on to. I seek refuge in Allah from Satan. I seek refuge in Allah from Satan. I seek refuge in Allah from Sam. I go to the sink and make my ablutions. And I pray for a very long time.

I'm reciting Qur'an when I hear some noise in the corridor. They're bringing in another prisoner. I listen as the footsteps come closer. There's no other sound. Just the slow shuffle of tired feet.

It's Umar. He's probably still sore. When he passes he just looks at me, and nods. He looks sad and tired. I want to talk to him. We can help each other get through this, but he can't stop. I listen as they take him to another cell on my side of the cellblock. I can't see him. He's probably pretty close, but he might as well be a million miles away.

Time passes slowly. There is no time. No digital display. No hands moving around the dial. No large window, even, to show the track of the sun. I sit and think and pray and recite and hope. And time seems to have stopped.

I'm sitting on the bed, still trying to erase the nightmare from my mind, when I hear a welcome sound. It's Umar, softly making the call to prayer. I guess he has a watch. I guess he managed to keep it. I wash up, and, when Umar prays, I follow him. I don't know where he is, I can't see him, but we can still pray together. We are still connected.

After the prayer, I sit on the bed and think about the nightmares. What do they mean? I have never had dreams about Sam, except for that once before Dad died. What do they mean this time?

And how did Homeland Security get involved in all of this, anyway? I've always been careful. I don't go to political rallies. I've never signed a petition, sent a letter, written an article. I've gone to hear some speakers at the masjid, along with hundreds of other brothers. I went to Pakistan, but thousands of Americans have. I've sent money overseas, but so have many other people who have family and friends in other countries. How did they ever become interested in me?

There had to be an informant. Someone who wanted to bring me down. Someone who hated me so much that he wanted to take away everything that was important to me. And the only person who hates me is my father. Sam.

In the Qur'an, we are told to respect and honor our parents. They gave us life. They loved us and took care of us. We owe them everything.

Sam did help give me life, but that's all he ever gave me. And even that was unintentional. He wishes I had never been conceived, never been born. He never loved me. He never took care of me. What do I owe him? I probably shouldn't have told him to go to hell, but he insulted my wife and children. And what has he done for me? He helped me come into existence. That's all. Is that enough for me to owe him anything in return?

And now he's trying to destroy me. I'm sure of it. Even the fact of my existence is too much for him. He can't stand me. He will do his best to make my life hell. He is my father, but how can I owe anything to a father like him?

❦

There are other prisoners in the adjoining cells, and some of them complain when Umar makes the call for the late afternoon prayer. The guy across from me looks pretty irritated. I hear a few of the others cursing, but I need this connection.

Again I wash up and pray behind him. I don't know for sure the direction I should be praying in. I'm so confused, so disoriented by everything that's happened, I can't tell north, south, east, or west in here, but I do the best I can and bow down to Allah.

They bring meatloaf and mashed potatoes for dinner, on a tray. The meatloaf tastes like cardboard and the mashed potatoes taste like paste, but I'm hungry. I manage to eat it all.

When I'm finished eating, I call out, "Umar. Can you hear me?"

"Assalaamu alaikum. Yes, I hear you." His voice sounds tired, but strong.

"Walaikum assalaam. That's great. Do you know what's going on?"

No response. I wait a minute and call again. "Umar?"

"Walter Thompson told me to stay quiet. Don't worry, Isa. It will be okay. I think we'd better just make Isha and go to sleep."

"But I have to know what's going on. How are Aisha and Maryam? What are we doing here?"

"Not now." He makes the call to prayer.

I follow him in the final prayer of the day, then lie down again on the hard bed. I seek refuge in Allah from Satan. I seek refuge in Allah from Sam. I repeat this over and over again as I try to ward off the evil of my nightmares.

I sleep peacefully this time. No more Sam, but I do dream of Aisha and our children. I'm holding her, comforting her. I'm gazing at Maryam as she sleeps in my arms. I'm wrestling with my boys. When I wake up and look at the hard cell surrounding me, I feel a loneliness greater than anything I could ever have imagined. I ache for them.

It's early morning, and Umar's call is soft and low, but I've been waiting for it. Again I follow him, bowing down to Allah in submission and despair. He's my only connection outside of these walls and bars around me, outside of my own fears and yearnings within me.

They come to get me right after lunch. I haven't prayed yet. I don't want to miss my prayer, but I need to get out of here, if only for a moment.

They take me to another small room, just like the first. A metal table, four plastic chairs, and a bare concrete floor. I wait. Finally Thompson walks in.

"How are you, Joshua? Are they treating you well?"

"I have three meals a day, a place to sleep, a sink, and a toilet. It's not the Hilton, but it's not Abu Ghraib. The isolation, though. No one to talk to. Nothing to do. Not even a clock in the cell. That's what's killing me."

"They're hoping to break you down. You have to be strong."

"I got a glimpse of Tony yesterday when they brought him in. I can hear his voice, and we're able to pray together. When can I see him?"

"You've been talking with him?"

"I tried, but he refused. He makes the call to prayer, and leads me when I pray. That's all."

"Good. Don't initiate conversation with him, or anyone else for that matter. Whatever you say can and will be used against you. You must remember that."

"I'll remember, but when can we meet? And how is my family?"

"Tony and you will not be able to see one another. Not until after the arraignment, at least. Your family is fine. I stopped in to see them on the day of your arrest. Your wife was surrounded by family and friends. And I just called your mother on my way over here. She said to tell you that Aisha is doing well. She's strong, and she's praying for you. Your mother, brothers, friends, and in-laws are providing meals, and they are prepared to support Aisha and the children for as long as necessary. Your older daughter, Jennifer, has moved in with your wife to help her take care of the children and the household."

"That's great, but what about her school?"

Rebounding

"Apparently your ex-wife has made arrangements to get her back and forth to school from your house. Everyone is behind you. Your mother appeared on a local news station this morning. She expressed full confidence in your innocence."

And twelve or thirteen years ago she thought I was a terrorist and a rapist. She's the one who wanted me in jail then. Time changes everything.

"Now we just have to convince the guys who are keeping me here." I pause. I have to ask. "There was a local informant, wasn't there?"

"Yes, there was."

"It was my father. I know it was my father." *The infamous Sam.*

"Don't worry about that now. We have to concentrate on getting you out of here. They will be coming in soon to question you again. Don't answer anything unless I nod. I will touch your arm if I think you are offering too much information. If I touch your arm, just stop. I'll take it from there."

"What about Tony? Have they questioned him yet?"

"Yes, but he's an easy client because he doesn't readily give information. They offered him amnesty if he would agree to testify against you. He adamantly refused. You two are close, aren't you?"

I can't believe they did that, though I guess I shouldn't be too surprised. "Yes. I know he won't turn against me. Not even to save himself."

"I could tell."

"What about the center? What will happen to it?"

"The center has been shut down. Computers and files were confiscated and the accounts have been frozen. It's gone. I'm sorry."

"Shut down? They can't do that. What about all the people we were helping? What happens when they show up to get food from the food bank or help from the clinic? What about the classes? And the youth center? We have to build the youth center." My voice is getting louder. I pound the table as I speak.

"Settle down, Joshua." He puts his hand on my arm. "I understand how you feel, but they can do that, and they have. The building is off limits. There have already been numerous stories in the media. Some other agencies are stepping in to help. You had quite a large clientele, but they are receiving help from other places."

"That's good to know, at least." *But it's not enough.*

Two men wearing black suits walk in. The last people I want to see right now. I don't know if they are the same two men who came for me. I was too upset to look closely at their faces. They sit across from me. Thompson stays by my side.

"You've had some time to think about your situation, Mr. Adams. Your lawyer is here, as you requested. I want to remind you that if you cooperate, it will be easier for you. Do you understand?"

"Yes, I understand."

"Why did you travel to Pakistan the first time, in 2002? What was the purpose of that trip?"

Thompson nods. "I had just converted. My friend arranged for me to stay in Pakistan with his uncle so that I could learn Islam, get away from my old lifestyle, and study Arabic and Qur'an."

"What is your friend's name?"

I don't want to say. I don't want them coming for him, too, but Thompson nods. I'll have to trust him. "His name is Mahmoud Ali."

"You arrived in Pakistan and stayed with Abdul-Qadir Ali in his home. Is that correct?"

"Yes."

"Is that when you became acquainted with Ahmed Ali?"

"Yes. He's Abdul-Qadir's oldest son."

"What types of activities were you involved in during your first stay in Pakistan?"

Thompson touches my arm and whispers, "Keep it simple."

"I helped Abdul-Qadir at his store, I took classes in Qur'an and Arabic, and I went to the mosque to pray."

"Were you connected with a madrassah during that time?"

I look at Thompson. That could be a loaded question.

"My client attended a religious school for the purpose of studying Qur'an and Arabic. The name of the school is

Rebounding

Madrassah Al-Taqwa, but it is not a madrassah in the political sense. His studies were limited to Qur'an and Arabic."
"Is that correct, Mr. Adams?"
"Yes."
"While you were studying, did you learn verses of the Qur'an pertaining to jihad?"
Thompson nods. "Yes, I did."
"And what is your opinion regarding jihad?"
Thompson touches my arm. "My client's opinions are not relevant."
"Tell us about Al-Jahidia."
"I have never heard of Al-Jahidia."
"What would you say if we told you that we have recovered documents from your office linking you with terrorist activities carried out by Al-Jahidia?"
I jump up and shout, "I would say that you are lying!"
Thompson touches my arm. "Settle down, Joshua." He turns to the agents. "I was not informed of the existence of these alleged documents. I insist upon being able to examine them before my client is questioned any further in this regard."
"We also have bank records showing a regular transfer of funds to Abdul-Qadir Ali over a period of years. What was the purpose of these transactions?"
I sit down and take a deep breath before answering. I have to stay calm. I can't let them get to me. "Abdul-Qadir is not a rich man. I have helped him out whenever I could. He was very kind to me at a time in my life when I really needed his kindness."
"Did Abdul-Qadir ever ask you to send him money, for any reason?"
"Only once, about six years ago."
Thompson touches my arm and whispers, "You didn't tell me about this."
"It's okay. One of his daughters had an accident and needed special medical treatment. He called and asked me if I could help with the expenses. I sent five hundred dollars to help him out. You should have it in your records." I can't keep the sarcasm out of my voice.

Thompson touches my arm and shakes his head.

"And that was the only occasion?"

"Yes."

"We want to move now to your relationship with Ahmed Ali, also known as Abu Hamza. Did you meet Abu Hamza during your first trip to Pakistan?"

"Yes, but he wasn't known as Abu Hamza then. He took that nickname after his son was born."

Thompson reminds me again with a touch on my arm. I don't have to tell them too much.

"What was the nature of your relationship with Abu Hamza at that time?"

"We were friends. He was sixteen. I was twenty-four. We prayed together. Sometimes we'd play soccer, along with his brother and friends."

"Did you ever discuss politics with Abu Hamza during that visit?"

"No." I almost say that I couldn't have cared less about politics then, but I have to keep it simple.

"When was your next meeting with Abu Hamza?"

"When we visited Pakistan four years ago."

"With whom did you travel?"

"My wife and our two oldest sons."

"What was the purpose of that visit?"

"I wanted Abdul-Qadir to meet my family. He has been like a father to me."

"And you had a meeting with Abu Hamza during that visit?"

"I guess you could call it that. He and his wife invited us for dinner."

"Were you aware of his political activities?"

"No, I wasn't." *I'm still not convinced of his political activities, either.*

"Did you discuss politics during your meeting with him?"

Thompson touches my arm. "I don't think that my client's dinnertime conversation is relevant to your case."

"Are you aware that Abu Hamza has been killed in a firefight with Pakistani police during a raid on militant headquarters?"

Rebounding

I close my eyes. For a moment I can't say anything, but I won't let them see me cry. I open my eyes and take a deep breath. "No, I am not aware of that."

"He has left behind a pregnant wife and a child. Do you want to help your family, Mr. Adams?"

They're trying to get to me. I can't let them get to me, but I can't answer.

"What is it that you want from my client?"

"First, we want him to tell us the names of other operatives in Karachi. We're certain he has much more knowledge than he has admitted. We also need information regarding the past operations and future plans of militant leaders of Al-Jahidia, and the extent of his involvement with that organization."

"And how will this benefit him, assuming he does have that information?"

"Any cooperation your client gives us will reduce his time of incarceration and help him reunite with his family."

I wish I did have some information for them. At this point, I would tell them almost anything so I could get out of here. I consider making something up. They wouldn't know the information was false, and I could go home to Aisha. I could tell them names, dates, anything. It doesn't have to be true.

But it's not right. It might cause another innocent man to be taken away from his family.

"I don't have that information. I can't help you."

"Then we can't help you, either. You need to prepare yourself for a very long separation from your wife and children."

They leave. After the door slams, I turn to Thompson. "Is it true what they said about Ahmed? Is he dead?"

"I don't know. It could be true. Or it could be a trick to make you more ready to 'confess.' I need to talk with Abdul-Qadir. He might have some information to help your case."

"I don't want to bother him."

"If his son is dead, he is already bothered. At any rate, I'm certain he will want to help you."

"Okay." I give him Abdul-Qadir's phone number, which I've memorized over the years. "I hope it's not true."

111

"I hope it's not, either. In addition to the loss of your friend, it will make your case much more difficult to defend."

Thompson leaves and I'm taken back to my cell. I keep thinking about Ahmed. It can't be true. He should be with his family right now. I hope he's alive. I say my prayers, and include a special prayer for Ahmed and Abdul-Qadir.

I'm lying on the bed, still trying to digest everything that's happened in the last seventy-two hours, when a guard approaches. "You have a visitor."

A visitor? It can't be Aisha, though I wish it was. I've already talked with my lawyer today. I don't think he'd come back so soon. Who is it?

I must have been thinking out loud because the guard says, "It's your spiritual advisor."

Spiritual advisor? The imam?

He leads me into the room. There, sitting at the table, is Chris. I wait until the door is closed and the guard is gone before I laugh out loud.

"My spiritual advisor, huh? You wish."

"I am ordained, you know. All I had to do was flash my credentials and tell them I wanted to talk to you about matters of faith."

"Okay, Chris, I know I can't go anywhere, but don't try to take advantage of my situation. You are not going to convert this prisoner."

"I know. I just wanted to see you. How are you, Joshua?" He stands up and hugs me. He's only done that a few times in our lives, all in the past few years. It feels so good to be touched by another human being. I hug him back. I almost cry. I hold on to him. I have never needed Chris before.

We step back. I'm still feeling emotional. I've been so lonely. And Chris is here for me. For the first time. We've never been closer.

"So how are you doing?"

"I'm okay. It's hard to keep up with all the activities around here. It was basketball this morning, followed by rugby. I just got out of the pool. And I think I'm having dinner with the president."

"It gets lonely, doesn't it?"

"How are they, Chris? How are Aisha and the kids?"

"They're good. Aisha is strong. She smiles and pretends that everything is okay. Melinda is over there with her now. She needs someone to talk with, too."

"I need to see her. I need to see my baby. I need them all."

"I know. Little Maryam is the sweetest thing. She doesn't cry much, either. She's a good baby."

"What about the boys? Do they know anything about what's going on?"

"They saw it on the news. The TV was on, and your picture flashed across the screen. It caught us all by surprise. Jamal is quiet. Muhammad keeps asking questions. Luqman stays close to Aisha."

"My lawyer told me that Jennifer is helping out."

"She's been a very big help. It's getting harder for Sharon to keep up with the kids. Jennifer is there to make sure they finish their homework and get to bed on time. She comforts them, too. She hugs them, and tells them that everything will be okay, and you'll be coming home soon. You should be proud of her."

"I am. Very proud. What about Umar's family? How are they holding up?"

"Safa is strong, like Aisha. And they're both getting a great deal of support from your friends. I know that they've frozen your accounts, both business and personal. Brad and I will make sure your family is taken care of. And Mahmoud, Ismail, and Marcus have pledged to take care of Umar's family. Neither of you has to worry about that."

"This is the second time you've taken care of my family. That first time, I left them. I feel like I'm being punished for what I did then."

"This time, it's not your fault. You have to believe you'll be exonerated, and, in the meantime, you must be strong. Mom and Walter Thompson are working hard on your case. Thompson is working pro bono, by the way. And Mom has turned into an investigator. You should have seen her on the news. She was even interviewed by one of the major networks this morning. She won't rest until you're out."

"We've come a long way, haven't we? Did you know that there was an informant?"

"I suspected as much."

"I think it was Sam. He's the one who turned them on me."

"It's possible. I don't know what the old man is capable of. Mom has said that, too. If she ever finds out for sure it was him, he's a dead man."

"I didn't do it, Chris. I didn't do anything wrong. I was just trying to help people. How did it turn out like this?"

"I don't know. It's easy for things to get turned around these days, but I know you didn't do it. You weren't even a very good liar back in your wild days."

"I sure did try, though, didn't I? Umar says that our past deeds come back to us, like echoes. They just keep rebounding through our lives."

"That makes sense, but they're not accusing you of drunk driving. These charges are much more serious. Unless, this time, the echoes go all the way back to Sam."

"I just want him out of our lives, once and for all."

"You shouldn't have told him to go to hell, but I understand why you did it. And I might have done the same." Chris stands up. I don't want him to leave so soon.

"So aren't you going to advise me on matters of faith? Otherwise, you'll be lying."

He sits down again. "Sure, Joshua. Be patient. I'll keep on praying for you. You might as well go ahead and pray, too. I don't know if it will help, but I guess a little prayer never hurt anyone."

He still hasn't given up on wanting to convert me, but that's not why I feel agitated. "It's not right. I was supposed to pick Aisha and Maryam up from the hospital. They can't take me away from my family like this."

"There is one good thing in all of this. Maryam was born two weeks early. Think about how you would feel if she had been born while you were in prison. It's a small thing, at least, to be grateful for."

"I guess, but I hope I'll be out in two weeks."

"I don't know about that. It doesn't look good. I don't know what Walter Thompson is telling you, but I think you may be in much longer. You're accused of being a terrorist. That's the most serious thing they can call a man these days."

I stand up and pace around the room. "They have to let me out. I didn't do anything wrong. They have to know that."

"Settle down, Joshua. I know that, and almost everyone else knows that, too. I'm just trying to get you to face the reality of your situation."

"You're telling me about reality? Try getting strip searched. Is that real enough for you?"

"Take it easy. I can only imagine what you're going through. Remember, I'm on your side."

I've been trying to stay calm since I first saw those men in my office. The pressure has been building, but I don't want to take it out on Chris. We spent half our lives fighting, but for the last several years we've managed to keep a fragile peace between us. I don't want to ruin it.

I stop pacing and close my eyes. I take several deep breaths. Chris reaches over and grips my hand.

When I'm calm again, I open my eyes and sit down at the table. "In that case, at least I was there. But it's not enough. I need to be with her now."

"I know it's tough. I don't know how I would feel if they took me away from Melinda and our kids. I know it would hurt."

"Yeah, it hurts plenty. Well, give them my love. And tell them that I didn't do it."

"The only people who think you did it are the ones who are keeping you here. You wouldn't believe the response your case is getting. All those people you've helped over the years are coming forward. They can't do much, but they are speaking out."

"Let me know when they have the 'Free Joshua and Tony' rally."

"I'm serious. You've done a lot of good these last seven years. And those are the echoes that are rebounding outside of this place."

"I just hope that they're loud enough to be heard in the courtroom."

We talk a while longer, and I hug him before he leaves. I never thought I could feel this close to Chris.

"I'll be back in a week."

"I guess I'll still be here."

"Be strong, Joshua. Your family is taken care of. Everything will turn out right in the end."

I hug him one more time. Then he has to go. And I'm alone again.

∞

Umar passes twice in the next three days, but he can't stop. We can't talk. He just looks at me with tired eyes, and nods.

When Thompson comes back three days later, he looks grim. "I've spoken with Abdul-Qadir. It's true. His son was killed last week by Pakistani security forces."

I wasn't prepared for that. They're wrong about me, and I was hoping they were wrong about Ahmed, too. He gives me time to process it.

"How is he?" My mouth moves, but I can barely speak.

"He has just lost his son, but he's accepting. According to Abdul-Qadir, Ahmed and another man were visiting with a friend when some men burst in shooting. Everyone in the apartment was killed, including the friend's wife and child. He said there was no firefight. And Ahmed never went to Kashmir."

I still have trouble finding my voice. Thompson continues. "I was unable to ask Abdul-Qadir more complicated questions because of the language barrier. I will need a translator."

I hadn't thought about that. Abdul-Qadir and I always speak in Urdu.

"Is there someone you could recommend?"

I clear my throat. "I don't know any professional translators, but you could ask my friends. Either they can translate, or they can refer you to someone. You can ask Mahmoud. I've already given you his name. Or Fawad. Fawad Choudhury. He's the owner of Karachi Kitchen, where I used to work."

"I'll check on that."

"Did you tell Abdul-Qadir about me?"

"I had to. He needed to know why I was calling, and how I knew about Ahmed. He asked me to tell you congratulations on the birth of your daughter. And he said he will pray for you."

That's Abdul-Qadir. He has just lost his son, but he's still thinking of me.

"I also need someone to work with in Karachi. I want to check out the different accounts of the shooting, and I need more information on Ahmed's activities for the past several years. Can Mahmoud or Fawad help me with that?"

"They should be able to. Or you can ask Ismail. Ismail Mohamed. He's lived in this country for the last twenty years, since he was a teenager, but he always seems to know what's going on."

"You're becoming much more cooperative."

"I keep thinking about Ahmed. I believe Abdul-Qadir's account. This doesn't just concern me and my family anymore."

"We still have a lot of work to do, but the conflicting accounts do intrigue me. At any rate, I think I'll be having quite a few conversations with Abdul-Qadir."

"Please, tell him I said salaam."

"Salaam?"

"Yes. And tell him that I am very sorry to hear about Ahmed."

"I'll tell him. Don't forget. The arraignment is tomorrow."

"Will Tony be there?"

"You will be arraigned separately, but you may have the opportunity to see one another. Remember, do not discuss the case with him."

"I'll remember." I think about what Chris said, and I want to ask Thompson if he thinks they'll let me out, but I guess I'm afraid of what his answer will be.

When I go back to my cell, I think about Ahmed, and Abdul-Qadir. I need to talk to him. I need to remind him that we all belong to Allah. And I need to remember that myself. Life is short, and uncertain.

∞

They let me wear my own clothes to the arraignment. Something so simple as putting on my own clothes. . . I never imagined how good it would feel. I can still smell the fabric softener Aisha buys. It reminds me of home. I don't know whether to laugh or cry.

Umar and I are taken to the courthouse separately. I catch a glimpse of him as he leaves the building. Then I look around me. There are people, and cars on the road, and a blue sky. It's cold, and snow is piled up against the curb. I didn't know that it had snowed again. I have a small window in my cell, but I didn't notice. The walls and the bars have swallowed me up.

It takes a few minutes to get from the jail to the courthouse. I enjoy the ride. As if I had never seen Chicago before.

I walk into the courtroom and glance at the spectator section. They came. Our wives and our mothers are here. Mom and Aisha smile at me. They look so good. Sharon and Safa see me, too, but they're looking for Umar. He'll be arraigned after me.

I stare at Aisha. She gestures behind her. For the first time, I notice that the courtroom is full of people. I recognize many of our clients and volunteers. The mother who brings her three small children to the clinic. The man who just opened up his own bookstore. The seventeen-year old boy who helps organize basketball games. The woman who runs the thrift store. Mrs. Lewis, who teaches a class in CPR, waves at me. Mr. Lopez, who was laid off almost a year ago, gives me a thumbs up. I can't believe it. They're here.

Rebounding

Dora sits next to Aisha. She smiles sadly. My brothers are here too. Chris nods. Brad just looks at me, frowning. He rubs the back of his neck. He always does that when he's worried.

Thompson greets me and shows me where to sit. He reminds me of the procedure and tells me to relax. That's what Zakariya said before the custody hearing. I hope this court appearance turns out better than that one did.

When he's finished, I turn to look back at Aisha. I gaze into her eyes. She is strong. I wish she had the baby with her. I wonder who is watching all the kids.

Thompson touches my arm. I have to turn away from Aisha. The judge walks into the courtroom, and we all rise. I have never agreed with that practice, but it's wiser to go along and try to make the judge happy. I'm in enough trouble already.

The charges against me are read. Fraud, money laundering, providing material assistance to terrorists, and promoting terrorism.

"How do you plead?"

"Not guilty on all counts."

My plea is entered. Then Thompson begins his argument to have me released on bail. I have seven children, including a newborn, all of whom live in the Chicago area. My mother, brothers, and their families live here. Most of my wife's immediate family lives here. I would have no reason to try to flee.

But the charges against me are serious. And there is the fear that I would continue my alleged terrorist activities through electronic communications. Bail is denied.

Aisha gasps. It's not very loud, but I hear her. I look back. She's crying. Before I can say anything, I'm led away. And I hear the judge pounding his gavel as my supporters loudly protest his decision.

On the way out, I pass Umar coming in for his arraignment. We stop for a few seconds only. He says, "Trust in Allah, brother." I nod, and I am taken away.

I'm being transferred to the federal prison to wait for my trial.

Part Five

This time I don't enjoy the ride. I don't know how long I'll be there. How long it will be before I can see Aisha again.

The routine is similar. I'm given a prison uniform to wear and my own clothes are taken away. They humiliate me with a thorough strip search. Up against the wall. Exposed. They probe. No privacy. I hold my breath and pray. Orange jumpsuit. And I'm taken to a cell.

This time I have a cell mate. He could be twenty-five or he could be forty. His face looks unnaturally old. His hair is long and stringy. He has tattoos on both arms. He's thin and pale. He's lying on his bed, and he doesn't look up when I walk in.

It's time for the prayers. I wash up in the sink and spread out my prayer rug. Aisha managed to get me a prayer rug through Thompson, and they let me keep it. I raise my hands and silently begin to pray.

"What the hell are you doing?"

I ignore my cell mate. All through the prayer he yells and curses at me. When I'm finished he says, "Are you one of those damned sand niggers?"

My nerves were already on edge, and now I'm ready to hit someone, but I have to stay calm; I don't want to make things worse. I clench my fists and hold back.

"I am a Muslim," I say quietly.

He starts ranting against Muslims. He keeps going on and on, all about terrorists and ragheads and dirty, lying sand niggers. His rant must last for at least an hour. I can't stand it, but I have to control myself. I'm already in prison. I don't want to be charged with murder, too. I punch my pillow, lie down on the bed, close my eyes, and try to ignore him.

Every time I make my prayers, he curses and rants. Every time I start to get annoyed—annoyed enough to do something—I think of Aisha crying in the courtroom. I can't make things worse.

At first I can barely concentrate on my prayers, but after a few days I start to get used to him. Even a loud obnoxious cell mate is better than no cell mate at all. His noise drowns out the noise in my head.

He doesn't rant all the time. Sometimes he sleeps. He sleeps all night, then most of the next day. Sometimes he's so still that I glance over to make sure he's still breathing. Other times, he jerks around wildly in his sleep. He must be in for drugs.

I've been here for three days when Thompson comes to see me.

"Tony was released on bail. His role, according to the charges, was only as an accessory. As long as you're in prison, the thinking goes, he will not be a threat."

"I'm not surprised, but anyone who has ever been around us knows that Tony is usually in charge. There's only been one time when I was able to boss him around, and that was right after his father died. He had his guard down. I'm glad he's out, though. He can take care of his family, and I know he'll watch out for Aisha and the kids."

"I have been making some progress with my investigation in Karachi. Mahmoud put me in contact with a local translator, so I've been able to get a more detailed statement from Abdul-Qadir. By the way, he asked me to give you his 'salaam' also. What does that mean?"

"It's a greeting among Muslims. It means 'peace'."

"I see. Peace." He nods. "I also gave him your message regarding Ahmed. He regrets that you are in prison because of his son."

"No, that's not right. Ahmed didn't do anything to hurt me. It's just a difficult situation."

"He realizes that. And I've come to realize that the key to your case is in Karachi. We need to track Ahmed's life for the past eight years and try to contradict the statements made in the charges against you. If we can prove that Ahmed was not involved with the bombings in Karachi, and he did not go to fight in Kashmir, then the case against you will have no basis. You cannot be accused of supporting terrorism if the person you were supporting was not involved in terrorist activities."

"It sounds so simple. How difficult will it be?"

"The hardest part, of course, is getting reliable contacts in Karachi. I've already taken the first step. Your friends have given me some good leads. Especially Ismail. You're right. He does seem to know what's going on. So I have a good translator now, and I am making progress in Karachi. If I can get the evidence I need, I can prove that their entire case against you has no basis."

"What about their charges of my connections to Al-Jahidia, whatever that is?"

"I mentioned that to Abdul-Qadir. He has never heard of any organization by that name, and he also expressed his doubts that such an organization exists. Homeland Security has not yet provided me with the evidence they claim to have found in your office. I will try to learn more about this alleged organization through my Karachi contacts, once I have those firmly established."

"That sounds encouraging, but I'm afraid to get my hopes up."

"I understand. Be patient. I do have some good news for you. Aisha will be allowed to come visit you every other week. You can expect her this Sunday."

"That's the best news of all. Thank you, Mr. Thompson." I grasp his hand. I feel like hugging him.

"That's the first time I've seen you smile. Don't worry, Joshua. I'll get you out of here."

When I go back to my cell, my cell mate is awake and he's at it again. I don't even hear him. Three more days until I see Aisha.

In a quiet moment, before I go to sleep, I think about the connection between Ahmed and me. Am I in prison because of what Ahmed did, or may have done? Or was Ahmed killed because of me? Thompson said the shooting happened last week. Was that before or after I was brought in? Could Sam possibly be that powerful? Could he hate me that much?

Do Sam's friends wear white sheets, or black suits?

~

Islamic congregational prayers are held here every Friday, but I'm not allowed to attend. I'm a terrorist.

The Muslim chaplain visits with me on Friday afternoon. "Assalaamu alaikum. Joshua Adams. I heard about you on the news."

"Walaikum assalaam. Yes, I guess I got in my fifteen minutes of fame. Too bad I was in prison. I didn't get to enjoy it."

"Don't lose hope, Joshua. Keep up your prayers. And trust in Allah."

I remember Umar. "Yes, that's right. And I like to be called Isa."

"My name is Yahya. Let me know if I can do anything for you."

"There are two things, actually. I wonder if you could get my brother in here to see me. He's an ordained minister. He should know by now that he's not going to convert me, but it would be nice to see him again. His name is Chris Adams, and he teaches at Redemption Bible College. If you could."

"I'll see what I can do. What's the second thing?"

"Just talk to me. It gets lonely, and I haven't seen another Muslim since I got here."

"That's not a coincidence. The idea is to keep you as isolated as possible. You are a suspected terrorist. So what do you want to talk about?"

I should ask him about some deep religious matter, but what I crave right now is just basic everyday conversation.

"How is the Super Bowl shaping up this year? Do you think the Bears will make it to the playoffs?"

We talk for a while, half an hour maybe, about normal life on the outside. The little things I never paid much attention to before. Then he has to leave.

"I'll see you next week, Brother Isa. Assalaamu alaikum."

"Walaikum assalaam." I'm sorry to see him go.

I am a suspected terrorist. As a terror suspect, I don't have even the normal rights of most prisoners. Limited opportunity to interact with other prisoners. No Friday prayer. No computer access. No mail. No phone calls. And no conjugal visits. Like Thomspon said, they're trying to break me.

I am a suspected terrorist. I turn the words over in my mind. Over the last several years, I've seen the stories on the news when different guys have been arrested for terrorism. I always figured that they deserved it. I wonder, now, how many of them were just like me.

On Sunday morning, I try to look my best. I can't do anything about the clothes, but I do wash up and comb my hair. My beard is getting scraggly. I wonder what Aisha will say.

I'm taken to a large room. There are other prisoners in here meeting with their family members, but I don't notice anything around me. All I see is Aisha. She waits for me, on the other side of the glass. She looks so good.

She smiles. We reach out, trying to touch each other.

There are tears on her cheek. I wish I could hold her. I stare into her eyes. I don't want to ever lose sight of her again.

I pick up the phone and talk to her. "Assalaamu alaikum. How have you been?"

"Walaikum assalaam. We're okay. We miss you. Everything is different with you gone, but we're okay. Your brothers are paying our bills, and I haven't had to worry about cooking. Someone is always showing up with a curry or a casserole. Jennifer has been a great help. She takes care of the boys so I can concentrate on Maryam. I don't know what I would do without her."

"How is Maryam? How are the boys?"

"Jamal and Muhammad ask about you. Luqman is very clingy. It's been hard for him, with a new baby sister in the house and his daddy gone, but Jennifer spends a lot of time with him. He follows her everywhere. He even cries when she has to go to school. Maryam is beautiful. She's a good baby, which helps. Two days ago she smiled at me. I took a picture of her yesterday. Here she is."

I study the picture. She has changed so much in just a short time.

"I'm sorry I never made it to the hospital that day. There were some men in my office who had other ideas. I heard your message on my cell. They were bringing me in when you called. I was handcuffed, and they wouldn't let me talk to you. I wanted so badly just to talk to you, and tell you where I was, but before they removed the handcuffs they took away my cell."

"They put you in handcuffs?"

"Yeah. I guess I'm pretty dangerous."

"This whole thing is crazy. How could they accuse you of terrorism? Don't they know who you are?"

"They think they know." I look into her eyes. "It is so good to see you again. I was worried about you."

"I was worried because you hadn't come yet and you didn't answer your cell. Then your mother came. I kept asking her where you were, but she just said you couldn't come and you had asked her to come get us instead. When I got home, both Evie and Mom sat down with me and told me that you had been taken in for questioning. I didn't understand what they were talking about. Later, Walter Thompson came to our house and said he had talked with you, but you couldn't come home. He wouldn't say why. I didn't understand why you were being held, and why you needed a lawyer. It wasn't until I heard the news on TV that I knew you had been charged with terrorism. I felt like I couldn't breathe, but Mom and Evie were there, and Aunt Arlene and Amal and Halima and Melinda and Beth and. . . everybody. Even Dora. They helped me get through that night. The next day, Heather and Jennifer came over. Heather sat with me for a while, and we talked. She said some nice things about you, which surprised me. And then Jennifer said she wanted to stay with me and help out. Everybody's been so good, but I just want you home."

"Me too, Hon. I miss you so much." I don't know what else to say. I try to dry her tears through the glass.

She tries to smile. "I didn't want to cry. I don't want you to worry. We'll be okay. Walt is working hard on your case. And you should see your mom on TV. She knows how to handle those reporters."

"I bet she's something. How's Umar doing?"

"He's okay. He came over that night with Safa, but he was still weak. They should have left him alone. At least they didn't come to his house to get him. They let Walt drive him in the next morning. Now he feels guilty, being at home with you still in prison. I think he's starting to get a little depressed. He just stays around the house, not doing much of anything. I guess you know that they closed the center."

"Yes, Thompson told me."

"Marcus, Mahmoud, and Ismail are helping him financially, but he feels bad that he can't support his family. I don't think he'll be able to work at all before the trial, and it's getting to him. Oh, I have some good news, though. Marcus asked me to tell you salaam."

"Marcus said salaam?"

"Yes, isn't that great? Mom called to tell him about the baby, and about what's going on with you and Umar, and he told her he'd become a Muslim a couple of weeks earlier. I don't think she needed that kind of shock just then, but she is getting used to it now. He'll be coming into town in a few weeks for a visit. Maybe they'll let him come see you."

"Maybe. That would be great. That should help Umar's spirits, too."

"It should, but I'm worried about him. He thinks he should be here with you."

"Tell him not to worry. I have a really obnoxious cell mate, but the food is edible and no one's mistreating me. I'm glad he's out because I know he'll take care of you. Tell him I'm okay. I just miss my family. More than I can say."

"We miss you too, Isa. Every minute of the day."

There's nothing else that needs to be said. We gaze at each other and try to reach beyond the glass.

"I love you. Kiss the kids for me. Tell Michael and Jeremy I'm thinking of them. And give Jennifer a big hug from her dad. Tell her I owe her a great big banana split."

"I'll do that. Walt is a good lawyer. He'll get you off. I know he will. I love you, Isa."

One more look. Then the guard comes to take me back to my cell.

I haven't felt this good since the moment I saw those two men in my office. Thompson is working hard on my case. My family is taken care of. I saw Aisha. Things are getting better every day.

∽

When they first brought me in, I tried to keep track of every hour. Later, I began to count time by days. Now it is weeks. I've lost my freedom, the center is gone, and I can't go home with my wife, but I know everything will be okay. As long as I can see Aisha every two weeks.

My cell mate is starting to calm down. He still rants when I pray, but his rants don't last as long. Finally, one day, after about ten minutes of yelling, he asks me, "Why the hell do you pray all the goddamn time?"

I want to tell him he should try it—it might improve his language—but I don't mess with men who have tattoos. I just say, "I'm a Muslim. We pray five times every day to help us remember God."

A few days later, he stops yelling and we start talking. He is in for drug possession. That's why he's been in such a bad mood. He doesn't have the right connections in here. He can't get a hit.

A lot of his story sounds like mine. Broken family. Failed marriage. Kids he may never see again. After he's finished, I tell him a little about where I used to be. He's even thought about suicide before, but, like me, he didn't quite have the nerve.

His name is Troy. He's twenty-nine. This is his second bust for drugs. He can't quit. He's been doing meth for the last few years, and that stuff is hard to beat, but he wants to clean up his act so he can see his son and daughter again. He shows me their picture. They're cute kids.

"My wife, Courtney, took that picture two years ago. My ex-wife now. Then a few weeks later, she packed up the kids and left. She won't let me see my kids. She took out a restraining order against me. I never wanted to hurt her. It's the drugs. Sometimes I get a little crazy."

I hadn't noticed.

"My little girl is nine now. Her name is Danielle. She likes to sing. She can make up a song about almost anything. In the mornings, she would go around the house singing. Always happy. My little boy is six. Alex is a tough little guy. He started walking when he was only nine months old! Can you believe that? He was always so happy to see me. He probably wonders why I'm not around anymore.

"Courtney and I have been together since we were fifteen. We got married right out of high school. Things were good, but right after Danielle was born I got drafted and sent to Iraq. January 2007. You wouldn't believe the things I saw over there. The things I did over there." He turns away from me. "I still have nightmares."

A few minutes pass before he talks again. "When I got back to the States, I got into the meth. I guess I wanted to forget. I love my wife, I love my kids, but once I started, I couldn't stop. I tried to stop, a couple of times, but I always went back. My wife—my ex-wife—got tired of waiting. I guess I can't really blame her."

He fidgets while he talks. He must have come in right when I did, because he's still got some of the drug in his system. I knew a guy in high school who did meth, back before it was so popular. One night I tried it too. I came through it okay, but he ODed. I found his body on the couch the next morning. After that you couldn't get me near the stuff.

Troy starts to sit quietly and watch me while I pray. And when I finish, he asks me questions. Why did I become a Muslim? Was it hard? Was I really a terrorist?

"How did you get your life together?"

"I don't know how together it is. I'm in here, aren't I?"

"You know what I mean. You found a way to see your kids. You got remarried. You have a nice family now. And I know you don't belong here. I do. You don't."

"I would have, a few years ago."

"That's what I'm talking about, man. How did you do it?"

He keeps bugging me, so I tell him the whole story. By the time I'm finished, he knows every gory detail of my life. And he knows how Islam got me out of my mess.

"Man, I could do that."

"Yeah, I think you could."

"I'm gonna do it. I'm gonna clean up my act so I can see my kids again. Maybe Courtney will take me back. I still love her. Maybe she still loves me too."

~

Thompson drops by every few days to keep me updated. I'm not sure if most lawyers come to see their clients this often, but I am sure he has Mom pushing him to check up on me.

Yahya meets with me too. Every Friday afternoon. He says he can't get Chris in to see me, but he brings me news from the outside and keeps me company once a week.

~

A few days before Aisha's next visit, Thompson tells me he'll be going to Pakistan.

"I appreciate all of this. You've already gone out of your way for me. Chris told me you're even working pro bono."

"I believe in your innocence, Joshua. I have to do what I can to get you out of here."

"What about your practice? I'm sure you have other clients."

"A few, but, to tell you the truth, I've cut back on my case load. I've been talking about retirement for the last few years now. Your case can be my last hurrah."

"You don't look that old."

"I'm pushing seventy."

I wouldn't have guessed that. He looks good for his age. "I guess your wife is looking forward to having more time with you."

"My wife and I divorced after our youngest daughter left for college. It's just me. At any rate, I believe I'll be able to get the answers I need in Pakistan. Abdul-Qadir has started tracking down people I need to talk to. Once I prove that Ahmed had no ties to terrorism, their case against you falls apart."

"I can't tell you how grateful I am."

"It's an adventure. I have never been to that part of the world before, but I wish that when you wanted to learn about Islam, you had gone to Tahiti instead."

"I hear that they have nice beaches, but I don't know if many Muslims live there."

"It's been a rough winter so far this year. I'd settle for the nice beaches."

"So I guess I won't be seeing you for a couple of weeks. Have a safe trip. Be careful. And give Abdul-Qadir my salaam."

"I'll do that."

∽

When Aisha comes, she brings another picture of Maryam with her. She is so much bigger than I remember.

"She looks so sweet. How are the boys?"

"The same. Jamal and Muhammad keep asking me when you're coming home. It's hard to explain where you are and what's going on, but I had to tell them. I think everyone in their school knows. Umar told them a little about his experience in the prison, and how he made the prayers with you. But they miss you, of course. And they can't possibly understand the charges against you. I'm still having trouble understanding it all."

"I can't discuss the charges. Thompson warned me not to. Did you know that he's going to Pakistan? He thinks the answer to getting me out of here is in Karachi."

Rebounding

"I know. He left yesterday. Did you know that your mother went with him?"

"She did? Why? What about her business? What's going on?"

"She said she wants to find the answers herself. She is determined to clear your name and bring you home. She has become a very good investigator. Her assistant, Charlene, will take care of the business while she's gone. I think there might be another reason, too, why she went. Did you know that Walt is divorced?"

"He mentioned it the other day. Mom and Walter Thompson? He said that they're good friends, but. . .no, I don't think so."

"I think it's possible. These last few weeks, she's been so worried about you, but I've never seen her look happier. What's wrong? You look shocked."

"I could never imagine Mom being involved with a man. Not even Sam, actually. I mean, I don't think there was any kind of immaculate conception, but, well, my life would be a whole lot easier if I didn't have a father."

"Seriously, Isa, didn't she ever see anyone while you were growing up?"

"Never. Whatever time she didn't spend at the office, she spent with us boys."

"Don't you think she could have been seeing someone and you just didn't know? Maybe she wasn't at work all that time after all."

"I don't know. I don't think so. Anyway, we never met anyone."

"Well, whether or not you want to admit it, I think she has someone now." She pauses.

"Do you remember when we were first married? You always told me how your mother was never there for you, but I have a hard time believing that now. She didn't date. She worked and took care of you boys. And now she's your greatest advocate."

"I guess the present colors our memories of the past. Back in those days, Mom and I weren't getting along, and all I could remember was the loneliness of my childhood, but now, when she's in my corner, I remember how hard she worked to raise us. And she had to do it alone. It probably helps, too, now that I'm a full-time father, or I was until they took me in."

"You're still their daddy. They know you didn't leave them on purpose. They look at your picture and talk about you all the time. Don't worry. They haven't forgotten you."

"I know. I just miss them so much. I wish I could come home with you."

"I wish I could smuggle you out of here. I miss you, Hon."

Our time is running out. We spend a few quiet minutes, again, before the guard takes me back to my cell. At least I'm better off than Troy. He doesn't have anyone to come visit him.

～

The next two weeks are the loneliest yet. Thompson doesn't come around because he's still in Pakistan. Yahya comes once, but he has to leave too soon. Troy is quiet. I guess he's thinking about his kids. I've met a few other guys, but I never feel comfortable because I never forget where I am.

The next time Aisha comes, she doesn't have a picture for me. "It's been so hectic lately. I thought about bringing Jamal, but I just don't know. It is a prison."

"The first time I met The Doc, he asked me if I had been involved in any terrorist activities. He said he didn't want to see my name up on the news. What do you think he would say now, seeing his daughter going to prison to visit her husband?"

"I think he would say you don't belong here."

"I hope that's what he would say. So how's Umar holding up?"

"He's having a hard time. He still feels bad about getting out while you're here, and he misses you. I never realized how close you two are."

"He's been my brother, too, all these years. I don't know what else to say."

"He contacted some of the old supporters for The Caring Center. He wants to see if he can get something going again, but

Rebounding

I don't think it's going to happen with the charges still standing. Hopefully Walt and Evie will bring some good news from Karachi."

"When are they coming back?"

"This Thursday. Evie called a couple of days ago. She sounded happy. Maybe they found the evidence they need to get you out of here and bring you home."

"Or maybe she's just having a good time over there with Thompson."

"That really bothers you, doesn't it? I guess it's hard to think of our parents as real people, even at our ages."

"Well how would you feel if Sharon started seeing someone?"

"Mom? She wouldn't. She was too devoted to Dad."

"It's possible, you know."

"I don't want to think about it. I could never imagine my mom with another man. It would be like she was cheating on Dad."

"But she's been widowed for eleven years now."

"Okay, Isa, that's enough. I get your point."

"And what about you? Your man is in prison. Are you sure you want to stick with me?"

She smiles and looks into my eyes. "Always."

Every time she comes, I have mixed emotions. Seeing her is so nice, but saying goodbye really hurts. Still, I'd rather have to say goodbye than never see her at all.

On my way back to the cell, I remember that our wedding anniversary was a few days ago. No flowers this year.

∞

Now I'm counting the days until Thompson gets back. I wonder what he found out. I wonder if he can get me out of here. I wonder what his relationship is with my mother.

Troy and I get along pretty well now. It's nothing like what I have with Umar or the guys, but at least it's something. He's settling down now, too. I think he's going to make it this time.

He's been asking me questions about Islam. He started out with the same questions I used to ask. Like, why are Muslims so strict about everything? Lately we've been talking about God. I guess he figures that since Islam helped me get out of my mess of a life, maybe it can help him too. I hope he keeps asking.

I've been wondering if he learned anything about Islam while he was in Iraq. I tried to ask him, once, about how it was over there. He wouldn't tell me. The only thing he would say was, "If you have to kill people, you have to learn how to hate them first."

※

I have a couple of other friends in this place—just guys I know I can talk to. And there are a few guys I know enough to stay away from. I give them a wide berth.

A new guy just came in. He has a real bad attitude. I don't know what his name is, but they call him Spider. He hangs with the other guys, the ones who mean trouble. I don't talk to him. I just try to stay out of his way.

On Wednesday at lunch time, I'm standing in line, waiting for my food, when somebody pushes me. I lose my balance and bump into Spider. He grabs my shirt.

"Hey man. Don't you mess with me." Then he looks at me. "You the Moslem terrorist I heard about?"

My heart beats fast. I don't want trouble. I have to stay calm. "I'm a Muslim."

"You know the guys who killed my brother?"

"No, I don't know anything about your brother."

"Sure you do. You know them. One of them terrorist snipers picked off my brother in Syria."

"I'm sorry. I've never been to Syria."

"It don't matter. All you Moslems, you're all the same. Turn your countries into shit and then pick off the soldiers who come to help you. You're just another goddamned terrorist."

"I'm an American."

"Don't give me that shit. If you're one of them, you're a terrorist."

"Look, I don't want any trouble. I just want to eat my lunch."

"That's all you Moslems are is trouble." He's screaming in my face now.

"Just let me go and I promise I'll leave you alone."

"I think I'd rather kick your goddamned terrorist ass."

Everyone else is quiet. Everyone is watching. Someone will stop him.

But no one stops him. He's Spider.

For a moment he just stands there, still holding me by my collar. The cafeteria is quiet. I look into his eyes. I don't like what I see.

He starts with my face. He's a little guy, but it hurts when he gets me in the jaw. He follows with a couple quick punches to the middle of my face. He's let go of me now. I want to fight back. I could probably beat him up, if I wanted to. I clench my fists, but I hold back. I don't want to get into trouble.

He keeps going after my face. I dodge his blows. That just makes him mad. He punches me harder, faster. It's really starting to hurt.

I have to get out of here, but I don't want to fight him. I keep blocking and dodging, but he lands a few good shots. My face bleeds.

I don't want to hit him, but it's too hard to hold back. I throw a few jabs to his jaw. He keeps on coming. He goes for my stomach. My weak spot. I push him away. He comes back harder. I throw a few more punches, just trying to keep him off of me.

Spider and I are still dancing around when this other guy comes over. I know his name is Joe, and I know he's trouble. And he's a whole lot bigger than Spider.

"Yo, Spider, let me have a piece of that terrorist. They blew up my daddy in Afghanistan."

I'm fast, but Joe is faster. He lands a couple sharp blows to my stomach, and I'm down on my knees.

It's time to fight back. I have to defend myself, but now I have two guys to take on. I can beat Spider, but Joe's another story.

I stand up and get off a few more good shots to Spider's face. Now he's bleeding too. That just makes him madder. He starts up rapid fire. And while I'm trying to fend him off, Joe gets a crushing blow to my side.

I'm shaky. I have to hold on to a table. In the few seconds it takes me to catch my breath, Spider lands another punch to my jaw. That one really hurt. To hell with getting in trouble. I lunge at him with everything I've got.

For a few minutes, it's just Spider and me. I haven't fought anyone for about fifteen years now but I remember what to do. He gets a few more punches in, but I come back and I have him on his knees. Then I see Joe in my face.

I go after Joe, too, but he's big. I manage to bust his lip, but that's about all. He gets me a couple of times to the head and I'm holding on to a table. A few more blows and I'm kneeling down on the floor.

"Go ahead and pray, terrorist. It ain't gonna do you no good." Spider laughs as he takes a few more shots to my head and face.

I need to fight back, but I can't get up. It hurts too much. Another couple of blows from Joe and I'm flat on the floor.

I'm down, flat on my stomach. Then they start kicking me. Joe, Spider, and a few other guys. I struggle until I manage to roll over onto my back. I try to get up, but they're on top of me now, pounding my face, kicking me in the side.

I kick them away, but there's too many of them, and it hurts too much. I want them to stop.

I hear Troy's voice.

"I was killing Iraqis while you bastards were knocking over liquor stores. You don't know what the hell you're talking about."

He curses them as he pulls them off of me. He gets a few shots in, too, but they keep at it until the guards run in and break it up.

They're off of me now, but I can't get up. Troy comes over and helps me. He has to hold me up. It hurts all over.

One of the guards takes charge. "What happened here?"

Rebounding

"It was Adams, the terrorist. He started it." Spider rubs the left side of his face. I did get off a few good shots—his face is swelling and his mouth is bleeding—but I think he got me worse.

Nobody else says anything. No one wants to answer to Spider.

"Let's go, Adams." Two guards come over and grab my arms. It hurts. I wince.

Troy gently pats my shoulder and whispers, "Be strong, man."

The guards start to lead me away. It hurts to stand. I lean on one of the guards. He shoves me against a table.

"Don't give me any trouble, terrorist." I suck it up and walk with them, pain in every step.

They take me to a different part of the prison. I've never been here before, and hoped I never would be.

"A couple of weeks in solitary should cool you off, terrorist."

They push me in and slam the door.

The cell is small and poorly-lit. No cell mate here. I hurt. I'm hungry. And I'm alone.

I can barely breathe, I can't move my jaw, and when I try to move my left arm pain shoots all down it. I'm bleeding all over. I try to wash myself up, but some of the cuts are too deep, and it's hard, using only one arm. I let the blood run down my face. In a few places, blood seeps through my prison uniform. Mostly on my thighs. They kicked me pretty hard. I leave those cuts alone.

When I go to pray, it hurts to stand. I kneel down on the floor and do the best I can.

After the prayer, I crawl over to the bed and lie in a daze. It hurts too much. It even hurts to breathe. I can barely move. I can't think at all. I lie here and stare, until I fall asleep.

A guard brings me my dinner on a tray. The noise wakes me up. I missed my late afternoon prayer. I wash up and sit down on the floor to pray. I can't stand too well. My head hurts. The room spins.

I stuff the food in my mouth. It isn't too good, but it isn't bread and water, and I'm too hungry to care. I try to chew, and wish I hadn't. I have to spit the food out and break it up into bits.

When I'm finished, I lie down again, praying that the pain will stop.

I toss and turn all night. Every time I move, it hurts, so I wake up a little and fall back to sleep again. A couple of times I vomit, and I can't make it to the toilet, so it lands on the floor. My head hurts so bad. I keep on feeling like I'm out of breath. I have to rest.

Every time I do sleep, I'm being kicked in my dreams, but there aren't just a few guys now, there are a hundred. One after another, they keep on coming. And they all look like Sam.

When I wake up, I try to wash up for my prayers. Everything hurts. I can barely move my left arm. My uniform sticks to those places where I was bleeding, but I can't do anything about it.

I have no idea about time now. I can't remember which prayer I'm supposed to be making, but I kneel down on the floor anyway and make my prayers sitting up—it hurts too much to bend my head down to the floor—and hope I'm right. I don't have a prayer rug here, or a copy of the Qur'an. I don't have anything. Just my faith.

Why is this happening to me? I thought I already paid for all my mistakes. And I've been good these last few years. I've been so good. Just taking care of my family, raising my kids, and trying to help people.

Except for that one time. When I cursed my father. But I think he's been cursing me since the day I was born. And I couldn't let him curse my family.

I need my family. I need Aisha. I need my kids. Why am I here? Why am I alone? What have I done wrong?

I have to hold on, but it hurts so bad, and I'm alone.

I keep drifting in and out of sleep. I vomit every time I manage to eat something. Half of the time, I don't make it to the toilet. The guard curses me when he brings my dinner and sees the vomit on the floor, but he leaves it there.

I pray when I think I should, but I'm never quite sure. I try to recite Qur'an, but there are voices in my brain. The demons are back. The demons keep telling me to give up. And this time I can't go to Umar. I'm alone.

Rebounding

Whenever I can, I sleep. I sleep to get away from the demons. Away from the pain.

When I'm awake, the demons taunt me. They whisper. I'll never see my family again. I'll never be with Aisha again. I'll never be any good. I'll never get out of here alive.

I sleep and I pray, trying to make them shut up, but they're loud. Louder than the Qur'an. Louder than my prayers. They are echoes, rebounding off the wall of the cell. And they make me hurt. My body hurts. My brain hurts.

I can't go on.

Finally I sleep, and they stop. It's a long sleep, a quiet sleep.

Part Six

Everything is quiet. Everything is black.

∽

I see a light. An unusual light. Bright and bold. I feel peace. I don't know anything, except peace.

∽

I dream. A woman's voice softly calling my name. A woman's hand gently touching my face. Aisha. I try to reach for her, but I can't move my arm.

"Good, you're awake. Stay still. You need to rest."

Who is she? That's not Aisha. She's wearing a white dress. I look around. My head hurts. I'm in a bed. There are machines in the room, a tube pushing air into my nose, and an IV in my right arm. My left arm feels stiff and heavy.

My throat is dry.

"I need water."

I can barely talk.

She brings me a cup with a straw. The cool water runs slowly down my throat.

I want to know how I got here—How long have I been here? Why do I still hurt?—but I'm too tired to talk. I drift back to sleep.

When I wake up again, my head is clearer. The tube is gone from my nose. I'm alone in the room. I see a single window on the far side of the room. It's light outside.

I have to pray. I don't know how long it's been since I prayed last. I try to get out of the bed, but I fall back down, tied down by the IV and my own weakness.

She comes back a while later. I don't think it was too long, but I have no sense of time.

"How are you this morning, Joshua? You're looking better."
"Where am I?"
"The prison hospital."
"How did I get here?"
"A guard found you passed out in your cell when he brought you your breakfast."
"How long ago?"
"Five days."
Five days? "What's wrong with me?"
"I don't know who you were fighting, but it looks like he won. You have two broken ribs, a punctured lung, a broken left arm, a broken jaw, a ruptured eardrum, a skull fracture, and a concussion. For a while there, we were worried about permanent brain damage. And there are cuts and bruises all over your body. A few of your cuts were so bad that they needed sutures. You're awfully lucky your lung didn't collapse completely, and that the fracture to your jaw isn't serious enough to warrant wiring your mouth shut for six weeks. You need to be careful who you mess with in a place like this."
"I know."
"You must be hungry."
"Yes, I am. Um, I need to pray. I have to go wash up."
"You're not going anywhere. Whatever you do, you're going to have to do it right there in that bed. I'll go tell someone to bring you breakfast."
I make tayammum in the bed, trying to make myself clean for the prayer. I raise my hands to Allah. I can't move much. My right arm is tied to the IV and my left arm is in a cast. Most of the motions I have to imagine. My body isn't going anywhere.

How long ago was the fight? More than five days. Was it a week? Two weeks? I don't know. Is Thompson back? Is Aisha coming to see me? Is anyone coming? Or am I forgotten?

They bring me some soft food to eat. Oatmeal and scrambled eggs. It's not bad, but I'd rather have something more solid. A pizza would taste real good right now. Extra cheese, thick crust. Maybe some black olives. And mushrooms. Definitely mushrooms.

I spend the day in a daze. Other nurses come in to check on me from time to time. They bring me tuna and cottage cheese for lunch. For dinner, they give me mashed potatoes with some kind of pureed mystery meat. It tastes like chicken. I get vanilla ice cream for dessert. No pizza. I pray the best I can. I recite verses of the Qur'an in my head. And this time I can hear them; the demons are gone.

In the morning, my favorite nurse returns. The one who gave me water. She smiles.

"You're looking good this morning. You have some color in your face. Someone wants to see you. Are you ready for a visitor?"

Yes. I want to see someone. Anyone. Except Sam. And Spider. And Joe.

"Yes, please."

She goes out, and when she comes back someone is following her. Mom.

She comes over and touches my face. I must be bruised. It hurts where she touches.

"They roughed you up, didn't they? We've been worried." She smiles a little. "What happened? You used to win all of your fights."

"This time I was outnumbered. And I tried not to fight back."

"Sometimes you just can't win for losing, can you?" She brushes her fingers through my hair. I close my eyes. I am six years old. I have the flu, and her touch makes me feel good again.

I open my eyes. "How was your trip?"

"Later. We'll talk about that later. Walt will come in and tell you about it. I did meet Abdul-Qadir. He said to tell you salaam. I know why you care for him. He is special."

"Yes."

"I won't stay long. You need to rest. They'll let Aisha come to see you today or tomorrow. And Walt will be in later. Rest, Joshua. I love you." She kisses me on the cheek, and then she's gone. Later I wonder if she was really here at all.

Rebounding

~

No more visitors today, but I eat well, and I feel stronger. I still hurt, but not like I did before. Back there in solitary. In the evening, a nurse removes the IV. I sit up and swing my legs over the side of the bed. I'm dizzy, but I manage to walk slowly to the bathroom by myself.

Thompson comes right after breakfast. I don't ask him if Mom came. It might have been real, or it might have been an illusion. Whatever it was, I want to hold on to it.

He sits next to the bed and puts his hand on my arm. "How are you, Joshua? We were worried."

"I'm better now. Much better."

"I've called for an investigation into the incident. This Spider person has a record a mile long. And Joe Nelson is in here for murder. He beat a man to death. If you hadn't passed out, they would have gotten away with what they did to you. Now they're the ones in solitary. I'm going after the whole prison administration. You should have received immediate medical treatment. It was insanity, the way they left you in that cell. You could have died." He briefly closes his eyes and grips my arm.

I've never seen Thompson get emotional. "Thank you for helping me."

"Are you ready for some news? Because my trip to Pakistan was very productive."

"Yes. Anything."

"First of all, Abdul-Qadir sent his salaams. And he gave your mother a package for you. She'll give it to you later.

"I talked with many people who knew Ahmed. It took some time, but eventually I was able to trace his movements for the past eight years. The same time frame the government gave for his alleged terrorist activities. It's all been fabricated. Ahmed never went to Kashmir. That was easy to prove. And he was never involved in any bombings. He was studying Qur'an on the night he was killed. There were no weapons in that apartment. I have sworn depositions accounting for all of his movements. I

143

have already filed a motion for a hearing before the judge. I am going to get this entire case thrown out."

"What about Al-Jahidia?"

"If they do exist, they are so far underground that I don't know how anyone could find them. Everyone I spoke with in Karachi said what you first told me, that the organization sounds bogus. At any rate, I have never seen the alleged documentation connecting you with them. My guess is that they fabricated those allegations and hoped your attorney would accept them on face value. It does sell newspapers, but it won't hold up in court."

"What are my chances?"

"I'd say they are very good. And this fight incident won't hurt. I know you took hell for not fighting back, but it was the right thing to do."

"I got a few punches in."

"I know. That Spider fellow was moaning and groaning about his injuries. And it worked, until you passed out and it looked like you were going to die on us. Now I have them on civil rights abuses. They are going to regret the day those agents walked into your office."

"How is my family?"

"They're good. Aisha will be coming to see you this evening."

I have to ask. "Did Mom come yesterday?"

"Yes. Don't you remember? Your injuries must be more severe than I thought."

I thought it was her.

"In a few days, they'll release you from the hospital and put you back into your old cell. Be patient. You should be having your new hearing soon. Then I'll get you out of here and back home where you belong."

"Thank you, Mr. Thompson, for everything you're doing for me."

"I've enjoyed working with you, Joshua. You have definitely expanded my horizons." He shakes my hand gently before he leaves. I know he was here because I see him walk out.

Aisha is coming. I don't want her to see me looking like this. I push the call button. My favorite nurse comes in.

"What do you need, Joshua?"

"My wife is coming. I'd like to get cleaned up."

"I'm sure you're ready for a shower. We gave you a sponge bath when they first brought you in, but that just doesn't do it. We can get you back into a prison uniform, if you like. I'll see if the barber can come over to give you a haircut and shave."

Sponge bath? I really was passed out. "Not a shave. Just a trim, please."

I have to remember how to take a shower with a cast on. I got hurt all the time when I was younger—pushing the limits—but it's been a while.

By the time Aisha walks in, I'm a whole lot cleaner. I can't wait to get back into my own clothes though.

"Assalaamu alaikum. You're looking good. You got a trim." She smiles.

"You're the one who looks good to me. Come here." She sits on the bed and I hold her close. It's been so long since I've touched her. "How have you been?" I stroke her cheek.

"We're okay. I was worried about you. They called our house and told me about the fight. They said that Evie and I should come. When they first brought you here, they weren't sure you were going to make it."

"You were here?"

"Yes. I called your name, but you wouldn't wake up. I was so afraid. Does your arm hurt? How is your head now? You have so many bruises."

That was her. "Don't worry. I'm okay. Nothing hurts now, now that you're here. How are the kids?"

"They're good kids, all of them. Every time it snows, Jeremy comes over to shovel our walk and driveway. We had another big storm just last week. Yesterday my car's battery died and Michael came over to put in a new battery and get me going again. Jennifer is my right hand. I couldn't keep things going without her. And our kids are great. Maryam is trying to roll over. The boys are praying for you. Even Luqman. You would be proud of them."

"That's what Sharon said about you and your brothers when The Doc was dying. It feels like I'm dead already. Do they remember me?"

"All the time, Isa. They talk about you all the time, but we do have to go on with our lives. You're right, in some ways it is like when Dad died, but I can still come here to see you and talk to you. And this time I'm able to touch you. To me you're always very much alive."

I miss her so much. I want to be at home with her, alone, but we're in the prison hospital, and far from alone. I have to be content just to be with her.

"How is everyone else?"

"They're all good. Marcus came into town a week ago, while you were unconscious. He wanted to visit, but they wouldn't let him see you. Umar is still struggling. He asked me to give you his salaam. I know he's been worried about you. He is spending more time with his kids, and he's waiting to see if John Williams will contact him and let him know about Derek. It's been almost three months now."

"Three months? Maryam is three months old?"

"Yes, almost. You would hardly recognize her."

"That's what I'm afraid of. I ignored my first daughter. Now I'm missing out on my second daughter, too."

"Don't worry. Walt will get you out soon. Insha Allah, you'll have the rest of your life to be with her. But I was so worried when they told me about the fight. You were so still." She stops, and the tears come. "I was so afraid, Isa. You wouldn't wake up. I thought I had lost you."

We hold and comfort each other. I wish she didn't have to leave.

Before she goes, she mentions Michael again. "He's looking forward to his graduation. I hope Walt can get you released by then. Michael needs you to be there."

I smile. "What is it?" she says.

"When I went to Pakistan, that first time, Mom told me to try to come back before Michael graduates from high school. She was being sarcastic, of course, but in some ways I am still coming back. When this is over, I'll be back."

"You will. I know you will."

A nurse comes in. "You'll need to leave now, Mrs. Adams."

Aisha stands. I hold her hand. I don't want her to go.

"Oh, I almost forgot," she says. "I have a picture for you."

She hands it to me. All of my kids standing in front of the house, smiling and waving. Michael has Luqman on his shoulders, and Jennifer holds Maryam. Jeremy stands behind Jamal and Muhammad, his arms around them. There's a lump in my throat.

"You can keep it. Maybe it will help."

I nod, still choked up. There is no way anyone is going to take this picture away from me.

The nurse speaks up. "I'm sorry, but your time is up."

I kiss Aisha goodbye, and I'm alone again.

I say my prayers. Then I go to sleep, staring at the picture of my kids.

∽

The next morning, my favorite nurse brings me my scrambled eggs. "You look much better," she says. "They'll let you out of here in a few days."

I wish she meant the prison and not just the hospital.

"Do you know why I'm in prison?"

"Yes. Why do you ask?"

"They say I'm a terrorist. Why are you so kind to me?"

"I'm not the judge or the jury. My job is to help you get well."

"You do your job well. Thank you."

I feel so grateful that I want to kiss her. I smile instead.

Part Seven

They take me back to my old cell after breakfast a few days later. Troy is gone. He might have been called up for trial and sent to another prison. Or he might still be in solitary for helping me in the fight. I hope I see him again. I pray for him. I pray that he gets away from the drugs and back to his kids.

I'm very careful when I go to lunch. I stand at the back of the line, away from everyone. While I wait, one of the guys I used to get along with comes up next to me.

"You'd better watch your back," he whispers. "They got Troy."

A chill runs through me, but I hope I'm wrong. "What do you mean?"

"They stabbed him two days back. He's not going to be seeing those kids of his again."

"Why did they do it?" I ask, but I know that answer too.

"Because he helped you, fool. Watch your back."

I don't eat much. I keep thinking about Troy. And I keep wondering which man is waiting for the right moment to stab me, too.

❦

When I get back to my cell, I wash up to pray, but I suddenly realize how defenseless I am during the prayers. Bowing down, my head to the floor, would be an open invitation to anyone who wants to take care of me. I wish Yahya was here. Forget football. I need to know how to pray.

I remember hearing something about the fear prayer. The Prophet used to perform it during times of war. It's in the Qur'an, too, I think. I wish I could look it up, but I haven't been able to touch a Qur'an since they took me away.

Rebounding

As well as I can remember, one group of men would pray while the others guarded. Then they would switch. They also shortened their prayers.

There's no one here to guard me. No one I can trust. No one I could ask to risk his neck. The guy who tipped me off was already taking a chance.

But I can shorten my prayers. I've done that before as a traveler, going back and forth to Pakistan. Then I'll only be in danger three times a day, instead of five.

I could just skip my prayers. I have to take care of myself and get back to my family. Does it make sense to put myself in danger? I'll recite more Qur'an and hope that Allah understands and accepts my intention.

But I've never been a coward. I never in my life ran away from a fight. I never took the easy way out. There are worse times to die than during the prayer. My life span has already been written. Whether I will die today or fifty years from today. When my time comes, I don't want to die a coward.

I stand as far away from the door of the cell as possible and squeeze myself into a corner. If they do get me while I'm praying, my kids will know that their father wasn't a coward.

I raise my hands and begin to recite. And the threat leaves my mind as I am carried away in my prayers. Sometimes my prayer is little more than physical exercise. Sometimes, like now, I feel connected. I really am communicating with Allah.

I finish the prayer and take a deep breath. I'm still alive. Now I just have to keep it up.

At dinner time I walk cautiously to the cafeteria, talking to no one, making eye contact with no one. I wait until everyone has been served before I get my food. I sit down at the nearest table and eat quickly, finishing up and hurrying back to my cell.

I make my prayers while most of the other prisoners are still in the cafeteria. I'm still alive.

I hadn't thought about what I would do at night time, but now, as the lights are turned down and I start to yawn, I realize that this will be the hardest part of it all. I suddenly have visions of being stabbed in my sleep. I'd better not sleep, even though my cell door is locked, and the other prisoners are supposed to be locked in their cells. I don't know who I can trust. A few of the guards scare me as much as the prisoners.

I sit on my bed, facing the door, my back against the wall, and recite Qur'an. When I get tired, I walk around the cell, always with my eyes on the door. I exercise a little, stretching my arms and legs, to keep myself alert. I can't move very much. It still hurts, but the pain helps me stay awake.

I used to stay up all night, playing video games or hanging out with my friends and my beer. Sometimes I'd pick up a girl. Then I'd go home around noon and crash. It wasn't hard, in those days. I had company. I had entertainment. I wish I had Islam then. I wasted my youth.

I'm older now, and it's hard. I didn't get much sleep on the night Maryam was born, but then I was running on adrenaline. And that was before the fight. I still don't feel as strong as I did before, but I can't give up. I have to stay awake.

The minutes, the hours pass slowly. Once or twice I start to drift off. Then visions come to me. Sam holding a knife. And I wake up and go back to my vigil.

Sometimes I look at the picture of my kids. The one Aisha gave me. I study it, then put it back in my pocket. I have to get through this and get back to my kids.

It's time for the morning prayer. I still don't have a watch, but I know.

The halls are quiet. I don't think there's anyone waiting for me in the shadows, but I still feel a fear as I raise my hands and pray to Allah. After the prayer I just sit here, in the corner, up against the wall, and beg Allah to let me go home to my kids.

Breakfast is another challenge. My assassin, whoever he is, is coming in fresh from a good night's sleep. My lack of sleep shows in my eyes, I'm sure. I put on a smile and walk briskly to the cafeteria. I eat quickly and head back to the refuge of my cell. I'm still alive.

I'm still alive in the late afternoon when the guard comes to get me. I've made it through another lunch and another prayer, but I can't get too confident.

Rebounding

I used to trust the guards, but I remember what happened after the fight. The guard shoving me into the table, pushing me into the cell. I walk down the hall with the guard, still on my guard. Watching him, and watching every man who approaches. Looking at every man's hands.

He takes me to the room where I meet with Thompson. Good. I'll tell Thompson about the danger I'm in. He'll get me out of here. Even the strictest judge will let me go when he knows that my life is in danger.

I've been here for just a few minutes, waiting for Thompson, when I hear shouting and other noises in the hall outside. I look through the small window.

I see a man down on the floor. He's bleeding. He's not a prisoner. He's wearing a gray three-piece suit. I recognize that suit. He was wearing that suit the first time I met him.

Two guards are holding someone. The guy who warned me. I thought I could trust him. They take him away. As he walks past he looks right at me, and smiles.

There's blood everywhere. Thompson is very still. I stare at him, lying there. After a few minutes, he's taken away on a stretcher. I can't tell if he's breathing. He doesn't move. And there's so much blood. All over the left side of his gray three-piece suit.

Why didn't that guy go after me? I trusted him. I wouldn't have seen it coming. If he was able to get Thompson just now, why didn't he get me? Is he alone, or are there others? Are they toying with me, watching me sweat?

I sit at the table, stunned. First Troy. Now Thompson. Will I be next?

∞

I don't know how much time has passed when the door opens. I jump. Two guards walk in.

"Adams, you're coming with us."

"Where?"

"Solitary. We have orders."

151

"I didn't do anything wrong."

The younger one starts in on me. "The hell you didn't, terrorist. And it's for your own protection."

I'm walking down the hall, with a guard on each side of me, when the younger one starts up again. "Don't try to give me a hard time, because I can shoot you and make it look like self-defense. I've got a kid fighting in Syria and I swear to God, if she doesn't come back alive, I'm going to shoot up all you goddamn terrorists."

I see the older one shake his head. And I see his mouth moving, but I can barely hear what he's saying. He's on my left side. I remember what the nurse said about my eardrum. I turn my head so I can hear him. "Take it easy, Nat. This guy's lawyer is going after the whole prison. He can have your job."

Nat laughs, and I turn my head back toward him. "Did you get a good look at that lawyer? Did you see the way he was bleeding? I don't think I have to worry about him anymore."

They take me to solitary and push me into a cell. Before he leaves, Nat says, "My kid had better come back alive. If she don't, then none of your Moslem kids is safe."

I heard that. And I shudder. Troy is dead. Thompson is dead. Now there might be someone out there gunning for my kids. The safest place to be right now is locked up. I wish I could lock them up with me.

※

I'm safe to make my prayers now, and safe to eat and sleep in the solitude of my cell, but I don't feel safe. They got Troy. They got Thompson. Were they really coming after me?

Or were they after the people who are close to me? Who would be next? Yahya? Aisha? I hope she stays far away. Please, Allah, keep her far away from here.

I think about Nat, too, and what he said. I can't blame him for being worried. Marcus served his two years, and he wasn't sent overseas. In a few years, Michael will get called up. I hope he doesn't get sent to Syria.

Rebounding

That's what it is. Spider's brother. Joe's father. Nat's daughter. The people close to them, who have died or are in danger because they're in Muslim countries. Because I'm a Muslim, they blame me for their deaths. Now they're going after the people who are close to me. I hope Aisha stays very, very far away from here.

A feeling of dread overpowers me. Aisha is in danger. And what if she brings Jamal? Would they go after my wife, and my son, to get revenge for the deaths of the people they love? Because they think I'm a terrorist. They think I killed them.

I throw myself on the floor, begging Allah to protect them. Please, Allah. Please, Allah. Please keep them safe. I pray until the tears are gone. And then I sleep. I sleep without dreams, this time.

I wake up when the guard brings me my dinner. I can barely eat. Thinking about Aisha and Jamal. Thinking about Thompson and Troy. Thinking about Ahmed.

When I try to sleep again, I am haunted. I close my eyes, and I see Thompson lying there, bleeding, on the floor.

I miss Thompson. He was a good man. And I think about Mom. Aisha was probably right. There probably was something between them. What will Mom do now?

Evie's Interlude: Fear and Prayer

Walt's secretary called me. I rushed to the hospital, my heart racing. I sat in traffic, willing the car in front of me to move. I cried. And I prayed.

He was still in the emergency room. They wouldn't let me see him. I argued with the nurse on duty, but she wouldn't budge. I sat nervously in the waiting room, and I waited. Until I saw his daughter Jean.

Jean barely saw me as she rushed to her father, but she came back fifteen minutes later.

"You can come see him now, Evie."

"How is he?"

"He'll live." She hugged me. Then we walked to his room together.

Karen sat at his side, holding his hand. When Jean and I walked in, he smiled.

"Evie. You're here."

Tiffany came a few minutes later. He looked at the four of us. "My girls," he said softly.

∞

He's been resting for the last three days. Visitors keep coming. Flowers, balloons, and fruit baskets fill his room. I stay with him as much as I can. I bring him magazines and keep him company. Charlene runs the business while I'm gone.

His ex-wife came yesterday. Meg walked in carrying a large fruit basket. I recognized her from the family pictures in the photo albums. She glanced in my direction, then turned to Walt. I am hardly the other woman—they've been divorced for almost twenty years—but I still felt uncomfortable. I left the room, and didn't go back in until she was gone.

When I did go back, Walt smiled and reached for me.

"You didn't have to leave, Evie."

"I know, but it didn't feel right."

"Meg is just an old friend now. The girls have told her all about you, and she has no problem with our relationship." He reached out with his good arm and pulled me closer. "Don't you know how much I love you?"

Sam used to say that, too, in the early days, but I know Walt means it.

The doctor says he can go home tomorrow. He needs to take it easy for the next month or two. That's all.

We haven't talked too much about the attack. I don't want to think about it. Walt reassures me that everything will be okay. He survived the attack. Joshua is safe. He has the depositions from Pakistan. He loves me.

～

As I drive home from the hospital, I think about God.

I used to pray when I was younger. I prayed that Sam would change, and he didn't. I prayed that my mother wouldn't die, and she did. After my mother died, I was afraid to pray, but I prayed again when I learned about the cancer. And I survived. I prayed when Joshua was attacked. And he's alive.

For the last three days, I have prayed that Walt would be okay. And he is.

Maybe there is a God. And maybe He really does listen.

Joshua

Part Eight

My days are long and silent. No visitors. No cell mate. No one left to die. This time, at least there are no demons.

I lose track of time again. I eat my meals and say my prayers. I sleep when I'm tired of living, and wake when I'm tired of dreaming.

I recite every verse of the Qur'an that I know. Over and over again. One verse I recite the most. "Surely, after difficulty comes ease." I have to believe that.

At least I'm still alive.

After a week maybe—I'm not really sure—I fall into a routine. I pray in the mornings, then sleep. When I wake up, I recite the Qur'an until the guard brings me my lunch. I eat, pray, and sleep again. All day long, a cycle of Qur'an, prayer, food, and sleep. Until nighttime. Then the nightmares come back.

It's almost always Sam. Chasing me. Torturing me. Hating me.

Sam is my father. He is also the monster of my dreams, lurking in the shadows, waiting to destroy me.

Every few nights I get a break. Everything is over and I'm back in Aisha's arms. I reach out to touch her. I'm playing with my kids. I hear their laughter. Dad is here with me in the cell, keeping me company and teaching me how to be strong. Thompson sits with me, his hand on my arm. Troy smiles as he talks about Courtney and their kids. Ahmed and I pray together, shoulder to shoulder. Umar and I eat lunch together in the office. And everything is good.

But then I wake up to the hard concrete around me and it starts all over again.

Before I go to sleep each night, I think about the center. The death of a dream.

I think about Aisha and the kids, caressing the images in the picture.

I think about Mom. Thompson is dead and she's alone again. I need to tell her about Islam. She doesn't want to hear it, but if I get out of here, I have to tell her. Before she dies like so many other people I have loved.

~

I can almost stand the loss of freedom. I can almost stand the hard concrete and metal bars. I can almost stand the slop they call food. But I can't stand the loneliness.

One hour a day, they let me out to take a shower and get some exercise. Two guards for one terrorist. I never see anyone else other than the guard who brings me my food each day. He doesn't talk. I thank him, and he nods. Then he's gone.

One day they take me to the infirmary. Two guards I don't recognize come to get me. They don't talk. I'm not sure I remember how to talk to anyone, anyway. The doctor comes in and, without a word, takes off my cast, quickly checks out my arm, and sends me back to my solitude.

There are the cockroaches and sometimes a rat. They come out at night to keep me company. I don't like them, but at least I'm not alone. Some nights I start naming them, but even the cockroaches don't talk to me.

I don't talk to anyone. I don't see anyone. I sit in my six by nine foot cell and wait. I don't know what I'm waiting for. I'm alive, but I'm not living.

The silence is deafening.

~

I don't know how long I've been here when they come to get me. I know it's been weeks. It could be four or five, or it could be nine or ten. Trying to keep track of time was driving me crazy, so I stopped trying.

There are two guards again—the older one who brought me to solitary and the one who brings me my food. I don't see Nat. I don't want to see Nat.

Rebounding

They take me to a small room. It looks like the room where they kept me right after the arrest. Just a table and two chairs. And the room is very small. When they arrested me, I felt like the walls were closing in on me. Now, after weeks in solitary confinement, it reminds me of home.

They leave me in here, and the door slams. I'm used to slamming doors now. At first it rattled me—it felt like someone was always angry—but I'm used to it now.

I wait. I'm used to waiting. I vaguely remember when I became impatient waiting the few seconds it took for my computer to boot up. I think I remember becoming annoyed when I had to sit at a red light. I guess that's how I used to be.

I don't know who I'm waiting for. I want it to be Aisha, but I hope it's not her. She shouldn't be here. It's not safe.

The door opens, and Thompson walks in. Is it him, or am I imagining that it's him? He looks real.

He smiles. "Joshua, how are you?"

I stare. I saw him. Bleeding on the floor. I open my mouth, but I think I have forgotten how to talk.

"Joshua. Joshua. Are you okay?"

I look at him. I clear my throat and I manage to say, "You're alive."

"Yes, I'm alive. Either my attacker had bad aim or he just wanted to scare us. I have a nasty scar on the left side of my chest, but he missed my heart by an inch or so." He stops and smiles again. "That's why you look like you've seen a ghost." He puts his hand on my arm. It's not a dream. "How have you been?"

How have I been? I've been scared. I've been lonely. I've been feeling guilty that you died because of me. If you're alive, what about Ahmed and Troy? Could they still be alive too?

But I can't talk. It's been so long since I've talked to someone. I blink my eyes, trying to reboot my mind. It takes more than a few seconds.

He grips my arm. "We have to get you out of here."

"Will you?" There are tears in my eyes.

For a long moment we just sit.

163

I'm glad to see Thompson—very glad that he's still alive—but I wish it could be Aisha. If it was Aisha, she would hold me, and I would find the strength I need in her arms. Thompson won't hold me, and I don't want him to. He just looks at me, his hand on my arm, and waits for me to adjust to the light. The light of human companionship.

I don't know how long it takes, but I'm starting to remember. How it is to talk to someone. How it is to not be alone.

"I, uh, I'm glad you're here. I thought you were dead."

"For a few minutes there, I thought I was, too. In all the confusion I didn't know, at first, how bad it was. Had you received threats?"

"Yes. That's what I wanted to tell you. And they killed my cell mate."

"I'm glad Aisha didn't come to visit you then. I had a feeling she shouldn't. I made sure they put you in solitary, as soon as I knew I would live. It's for your own protection, but I didn't know it would be like this. We have to get you out of here."

"Can you?"

"I've been working very hard on it. I've filed the motions and submitted the depositions we obtained during our time in Pakistan. I've been pressuring the judge to grant you another hearing in light of the new evidence. And I have good news. You will be going to court again next Wednesday."

"Wednesday? How many days is that?"

"Today is Thursday. You have six more days. Can you hold on for just six more days?"

"I must. Today is Thursday. What month is it?"

"It's the end of April."

"I have to get out. Michael is graduating in May. I have to be there."

"I know. I'm doing everything I can to help you be there."

"I have to come back from Pakistan."

He stares at me. "You're not in Pakistan, Joshua. You're in Chicago."

"No, I'm still in Pakistan. I have to get back for Michael's graduation. I have to be there for him."

Rebounding

I let go. I can't hold on anymore. I sob. Thompson puts his arm around me as I sob into the shoulder of his suit coat. He's not Aisha, but he's not a guard and he's not a cockroach. He's alive. And he's here.

The shoulder of Thompson's expensive suit is wet, but he doesn't seem to mind. I sit up straight. "I'm sorry."

"That's okay. I don't know how long I could take it, either. Remember, your next hearing is in six more days. Hold on to that. Six more days."

"And if the judge won't let me go?"

"You will come back here to await your trial, but I have the evidence. Be strong. Be positive. Hold on." He stops. "Why are you turning your head like that?"

"You're sitting on my left side. I can barely hear with that ear. Ever since the fight."

He looks down and shakes his head. Then he reaches out and touches my arm again. "I'm going to get you out of here," he says softly. "Just hold on."

"I will." I pause. "Um. . .you're alive. What about Ahmed and Troy, my cell mate? Could they be alive too?"

"No, Ahmed is dead. And I'm sure Troy is too. I'm sorry."

"At least you're alive."

"Yes." He smiles. "I was very happy when I learned that I would live. I have to go now, Joshua. I'm sorry I can't stay longer."

"How is Aisha?"

"Aisha and your children are doing well. You will see her at the hearing. I hope you will be able to go home with her."

"That's not possible."

"It is possible. Just hold on. Six more days."

Then he leaves, the door slamming behind him.

～

Now I have to keep track of time. I know it is afternoon because I had lunch before Thompson came. When I get back to the cell, I make my late afternoon prayers and I start the countdown. Six more days.

Three days later, the guards come for me again. This time they take me to the barber. Thompson wants me to look good in court. I catch a glimpse of myself in the mirror. My beard is long and tangled. My hair is down around my shoulders. My face is pale.

I'm a little nervous about being around a man with scissors, but the barber doesn't care why I'm here. He's just doing his job. He takes care of my beard and my hair. He can't do anything about my face.

Three more days.

I keep on counting, and I pray. Almost every second, surely every minute that I'm awake, I pray. I want to go home. Please, Allah, let me go home. Whatever it takes, I have to go home.

I don't dream these days. I'm too excited to dream about Sam, and I'm too afraid to dream about home. Afraid it won't happen.

One more day, and I keep hoping. This is the last time I will eat breakfast from a tray. This is the last time I will say my prayers on a hard concrete floor. This is the last time I will sleep with cockroaches. This is the last time I will wake up without seeing Aisha sleeping next to me.

∽

On the day of the hearing, I wash up as well as I can. I don't want to go in there looking like a man who has been in solitary for the last several weeks.

The guards come to get me and lead me out to the front where a car is waiting. One of the guards is Nat, but he's quiet this time. His daughter must still be alive. I glance at him, and I see hatred in his eyes, but he doesn't say anything.

I walk outside, and the glare of the sunlight attacks my vision. I stop, even while the guards move me forward. For a moment I can't see anything, until my eyes adjust. It's May. We're in the

Rebounding

middle of the city and I don't see the flowers or the birds, but I can tell by the strength of the sunlight. It's May.

I get into the car and look around, and all of my senses are assaulted. The noise of the tires on the pavement, the smell of a coffee shop, the feel of the soft vinyl seats. During the short drive to the courthouse I keep looking around, filling my senses.

Thompson greets me at the courthouse. He shakes my hand and smiles. "You're looking better. How do you feel?"

"Better, but I'm worried."

He nods. "I understand."

He walks with me into the courtroom and I look around. She's here. She smiles. And I can't take my eyes off of her. Mom is with her.

Thompson leads me to the table. I have to turn away from Aisha. I see Umar, sitting at the table. He nods, and rises to greet me. We shake hands. Then he looks down. That's strange, but I'm too overwhelmed to think about it.

The three people in my life who give me strength. Aisha, Umar, and Mom. No crowd of supporters this time, but they are all the support I need. I keep looking at them, back and forth. If I stop looking at them, they might disappear.

Thompson calls my name and I have to look away from Aisha. "Joshua, Tony is here because I'm going to try to get the charges dismissed for both of you today."

I nod, still overwhelmed. I can't even think about the charges right now. I just want to go home.

I quickly glance back. Aisha is still there.

The judge comes in, and we rise. I still don't like to stand up when the judge enters. It's against the teachings of Islam, but in prison I learned to do as I am told.

Thompson briefly presents the case and the judge says that he has received the new evidence. Then he delivers his verdict.

"I have read the depositions. I am rejecting the plea to have the case dismissed. I am not prepared to examine the evidence at this time, and the charges against the two defendants, Joshua Adams and Anthony Evans, will stand.

"However, I have come to a decision regarding the health and safety concerns raised by counsel on behalf of Joshua Adams. Mr. Adams, please rise."

I stand for his decision. I remember the stories I have heard about the Day of Judgment. This moment isn't anywhere near as important, but it's the most important moment I have ever experienced. I'm terrified now. How will I feel then?

"I have decided to allow you to be released on bail. You will remain free from incarceration until the date of your trial. However, you must be certain to follow the conditions of your release. Failure to do so will result in your return to the federal prison. Do you understand?"

"Yes, sir." I was probably supposed to say "your honor," but my heart is practically jumping out of my chest. I can't think about protocol right now.

He goes on, talking about the conditions of my release, but I'm in a daze. I can go home.

I pay attention when he concludes, "Joshua Michael Adams, you are hereby released, according to the conditions of your bail." He strikes the gavel, giving finality to his decision.

I stand here, stunned. I can go home. Mom and Aisha come up. They both hug me tightly. I hold on to them, afraid to let go in case they slip away from me again.

Aisha whispers, "I love you, Hon." I guess that's what she says. I can't really hear the words she speaks softly into my left ear, but I hear her with my heart.

First, we take care of all the paperwork. I am being placed under house arrest. I guess I should have listened to the judge's speech. I have to wear an electronic monitoring device. An ankle bracelet, they call it. I can't go to the mosque. I can't go anywhere without permission from my parole officer.

I'm not quite free, but at least I'm with Aisha again.

Mom pays my bail. She smiles as she signs the check. I remember my wild years. If I had been arrested then, she would not have been smiling.

Aisha and I walk toward the entrance, our arms around each other. Mom and Thompson walk together. Umar walks alone, his

Rebounding

head down. Something's wrong. I don't know what it is, but I know there is something wrong with him. I can't think about it now. I want to concentrate on his sister.

We get to the parking lot. Mom and Thompson came together, Umar came alone, and Aisha brought my car. The car where Maryam was born. The car I left in the parking lot while I ran in to my office to check on a few things.

I shake Thompson's hand again. "Thank you for everything."

"It's not over. There is still the trial, but I will keep working to have the charges dismissed."

"Thank you. And thanks, Mom, for standing by me."

"What else was I supposed to do?" She strokes my face. I close my eyes. I remember that time when I was four and I got lost in a store. I remember how I felt when she found me. Safe.

I open my eyes. Umar stands in front of me. I look at him, and smile. "I've missed you, Brother."

"Yes," he says. He looks down. Then he heads for his car and drives away.

Mom and Thompson come with us back to the federal prison. I have to get my things.

A guard brings me my clothes and lets me change. My pants are too large. I cinch the belt up to the last hole, and still they sag, but it feels so good to wear them again.

As we walk to the parking lot, I finger my car keys.

"Do you want to drive?" Aisha says.

"No, Aisha, you drive. I'm a little out of practice."

"We'll meet you at the house," Mom calls out.

We climb into the car. Going home.

Part Nine

I almost wish that Mom wasn't coming to the house. I'm tempted to tell Aisha to stay on the highway. We could drive up to Wisconsin for a second honeymoon. But I'm not allowed to travel. And I need to see my kids.

On the way home, I sit as close to her as possible. I don't want to let her go. I never want to let her out of my sight again.

As we drive down our street, my heart pounds. It's a different kind of restlessness. I can't wait to be home again.

I see our house. There's a huge banner in front. "Welcome Home, Dad." The kids are all lined up on the front porch, cheering.

"So, that's why you took the long way home. I thought you just wanted to be with me."

She smiles. I spent so many hours dreaming of that smile. "That too."

I step out of the car, and they crowd around me. Michael, Jeremy, Jennifer, Jamal, Muhammad, Luqman, and, in Sharon's arms, Maryam. I reach out and hold all the big ones in my arms. Little Luqman holds on to my leg. Maryam stares at all the crazy people. She probably wonders why they're making such a fuss over this strange man.

I want to tell my older children how proud I am of them, and I want to tell the younger ones how much I missed them, but for now it's enough just to hold them.

I don't want to let go of any of them, but I have to hold Maryam. We had just one day together. Her birth day. I'll always remember that day. I hug and kiss my other children one more time; then I take Maryam from Sharon's arms.

She fusses. She wants to go back to Sharon, but I hold her close and try to calm her. I softly recite the call to prayer in her ear, and she settles down. She snuggles against my chest. She remembers.

Rebounding

Yesterday, this morning, I was alone. Now I'm surrounded by the people I love. If I could, I would hold them all and never let go.

Suddenly I feel dizzy. I kiss the baby and give her back to Sharon. I try to take a step, but I feel like I'm going to fall.

Michael grabs my arm. "Are you okay, Dad?"

"Just overwhelmed, I guess."

"Let me help you."

I lean on Michael, and Aisha comes to my other side. We walk into the house together. In these five and a half months, Michael has turned into a man. He has strong arms, and whiskers on his chin. I lean on him as he helps me into the house.

"Sit down over here." He helps me to my favorite, soft, blue chair. I remember soft chairs.

Brad and Chris come over. I didn't see them outside. I try to get up.

"That's okay, man. Sit down. Take it easy." Brad leans over for a long hug. Then Chris.

"Man, I could have used a spiritual advisor in that federal prison."

Chris laughs. "I tried. They were stricter over there."

All of my friends come over next. Ismail, Mahmoud, Tariq, Fawad.

"You look so thin, Isa. Come into Karachi Kitchen and I'll fatten you up. On the house."

"I'll do that, Fawad. Thank you."

Dora cries as she greets me. "I've been so worried about you, Joshua. I shouldn't have let them come in. I should have called and warned you, but they said they were from the government, and I was afraid."

"It's not your fault, Dora. You did the best you could. And you called my mother. Thank you."

There are so many others. Marcus flew in from Boston. How did he know they would let me out?

"Assalaamu alaikum, Joshua. Or should I call you Isa now? It's good to see you again."

"It's great to see you, Marcus. Walaikum assalaam. And you can call me anything you like."

Aunt Arlene comes next. The stroke slowed her down, but she still smiles and gives me one of her hugs. Her hugs always remind me of the day I married Aisha.

"It's good to see you, Joshua. I know you've been terribly missed."

"Thank you, Aunt Arlene. I've been wondering. What would The Doc say if he knew I went to prison?"

"He would have done everything he could to get you out of there. We all know you didn't belong there."

Even Peter and Heather are here. Peter shakes my hand. "I'd like to hear about your experience sometime. When you feel up to it, that is."

"Sure, Peter. When I'm up to it."

Heather smiles. "I feel bad about what happened to you, Joshua. I know you didn't deserve that."

I'm stunned. No insults? "Thank you."

One after another, they greet me and welcome me back. Yesterday, I slept with cockroaches. Today, I am surrounded by my family and friends. I feel like a king.

Aisha stays by me through it all. I don't want her to leave me. Ever.

The last in the line are Umar's children. They're getting so big. One by one, they come to give their uncle a hug. Except for Raheema, who smiles shyly. "Welcome back, Uncle Isa. I'm glad that you're safe."

"Thank you, Raheema."

She nods, and turns back toward the party. Jeremy walks with her. It's nice that Umar's children and my children are so close.

Safa hands me a package with a wonderful aroma. One of her special breads. "Welcome home, Isa. I hope you enjoy this."

"I know I will."

Then Umar again. He walks up to me quietly, almost shyly, and he says, "I'm sorry, Isa. I shouldn't have left you there." We hug. And we cry. For the center, now dead, and for all the lunches we didn't eat together.

When he pulls away, I say, "Don't be sorry. You didn't have a choice." Then I remember. "How is Derek?"

"I don't know. No one has let me know yet." His voice is soft and low.

No wonder something seemed wrong. He is still carrying a lot of weight on his shoulders.

Mom comes up to me again. "You look so thin. You must be hungry."

"I sure am. What do you have?"

"How about spaghetti and apple pie?"

My last meal as a free man was Mom's spaghetti and apple pie. On the day Maryam was born. She knows what I need.

"That sounds great."

She brings me a plate, Chris brings me a root beer, and everyone starts to eat. I sit in my favorite chair, eating my favorite foods, surrounded by my favorite people. I am home.

I turn to Umar, who stands silently behind me. "Go get a plate, Brother. We can eat lunch together, just like in the old days."

"No, I'm not hungry."

Something is very wrong, but I can't think about it now.

～

It's been great, but after a couple of hours I start to get edgy. I spent ten weeks in near silence. Now, I can't take the noise. I whisper to Aisha that it's too noisy, and I'm getting tired.

"Of course. Why don't you go rest a little? Do you need help?"

"No, I'm fine." I try to stand up, but I get dizzy again and fall back into the chair.

Brad notices. "This would be a good time to challenge you to a soccer game. I could finally beat you." He helps me up and walks with me upstairs to the bedroom. Aisha follows.

"Have a good rest, Old Man. It's really good to have you back." He pats my shoulder and goes back to the party.

Aisha stays. I hold her hand and pull her close.

"Why don't you go lock the door?"

She smiles. "You need to get some rest and we have a house full of guests. Take a nap. I'll see you later."

"Okay, later. I love you. Would you stay with me a while, though? I don't want to be alone again."

"Of course. I love you, too. I've missed you, Isa." She takes me in her arms and holds me close. She strokes my head and gently rocks me. I fall asleep in her arms, listening to her heartbeat.

I'm floating. No more dreams of yearning. No more nightmares of Sam. I do see Dad. He doesn't say anything. He just smiles. Then he floats away.

∾

I sleep. When I wake up, everything is dark. Aisha lies sleeping in bed next to me. I gaze at her. I'm home. And she's here. It's not a dream. I want to touch her, but I don't want to wake her. For now, it's enough just to look at her.

It's a little after midnight. I get up and make my prayers. Then I walk around, remembering our house. After a while, I go to sit in my chair. I drink a tall glass of milk and eat Safa's homemade banana nut bread while I read the newspaper. Mario curls up in my lap, and Luigi goes to sleep on my shoulder.

"Did you miss me, guys?" I whisper. "I missed you too." I stay up, reading and enjoying the quiet of home until it's time for the morning prayer. I pray alone, then head for the stairs.

Sharon is walking down the stairs, ready to cook breakfast and start another day. We meet at the first step. She hugs me.

"I didn't have a chance to talk with you yesterday. You were very popular. It is so good to have you back." She hugs me again. Then she looks at me. "Arlene told me that you asked her about Jim. What he would say. He would be proud of you for coming through this and being so strong. That's what he would say."

"So he wouldn't wonder if I really was a terrorist?"

"You've been like another son to us, Joshua. We know who you are. He knew what a good man you are. And he would be very proud of you."

"I hope so."

"Are you still hungry for some of my beef stew?"

"I thought about it every day while I ate my lunch from a tray. I knew I had to be patient so I could get back to my wife, my kids, and my mother-in-law's beef stew."

"I'll get started on it right after breakfast then."

"Well, I need to go rest a little. Still getting used to being home."

She gives me one more hug before I go. "Welcome home, Joshua."

I think about Sharon's beef stew all the way up the stairs. The big chunks of beef. The potatoes. The carrots. Her own special seasoning. I can practically taste it.

I walk back into the bedroom and stare at Aisha. She looks so beautiful. I hate to disturb her, but she has to pray. I kiss her softly on the cheek. She opens her eyes.

"Assalaamu alaikum."

She smiles. She reaches up and puts her arms around my neck. "Walaikum assalaam. You're really here. It's not a dream."

I kiss her. I missed her kisses. I want to keep her here, warm and close, but then I remember. "You have to go pray, Hon. I already did. And you need to wake up the kids, too."

"Are you going back to bed?"

"Yes. I'm tired. Wake me up after you get the kids off to school."

"Okay. I'll see you soon." One more kiss, and she has to go.

I put my head on the pillow, and float.

I wake up again to an empty bedroom. I walk downstairs. All of the kids are in the rec room, watching television, and Aisha is in the kitchen, setting the table.

"There you are. Do you feel better?"

"Why are Jennifer, Jamal, and Muhammad still here? Don't they have school today?"

"They went to school. I picked up the boys more than two hours ago. Michael just dropped Jennifer off. She had a yearbook meeting after school."

"I guess I was pretty tired."

"You must have been. I sat with you for a while, and I whispered your name, but you wouldn't wake up."

"Did you whisper into my left ear?"

"I don't know. I guess so. Why?"

"I can't really hear in that ear. They damaged my eardrum in the fight. While they were kicking me, I guess."

"I didn't know." She touches my ear. "I'm sorry, Hon. I don't know what to say."

"It's okay. I'll get used to it, but next time, be sure to whisper into my right ear because I want to spend every minute I can with you."

She still looks worried. "You look tired. Go ahead and pray. Then you can eat and go back to bed if you want."

I grab her around the waist. "Do you want to come with me?"

"You're getting stronger, aren't you? You need to make up your prayers, though, and I need to feed the kids."

"I dreamed about you all the time," I say as I kiss her neck.

"I dreamed you were home," she says softly. "Almost every night. I woke up and reached for you, but you weren't there. Where were you last night?"

"I couldn't sleep. It was different in there. It's going to take some time."

Another long kiss, then she whispers into my right ear, "Go pray. Then let me feed you, and take care of you."

It is so good to be home.

∞

I wake up again a little after midnight. First, I peek into their rooms, looking at each of my kids. Then I wash up and pray. After the prayer, I settle in to read the paper, with Mario and

Luigi to keep me company. I'm absorbed in the quiet when I hear a knock at the front door.

I jump. I heard noises in the prison at night, and I never felt safe there, but I'm home now, and I'm safe. It was just a knock. I wonder who it is at this time of night.

I look out the window first. It's Umar. What is he doing here? I open the door.

"Assalaamu alaikum, Umar. Is everything okay?"

"I need to talk. Come outside."

I go out on the porch and sit on the porch swing. Umar stands.

"So what are you doing here this late?"

He talks fast. "I can't sleep. I don't sleep much anymore."

"I know. . . me neither. I'm still trying to get used to a normal life."

"There is no normal life, Isa. No work, no life. Just sitting and waiting."

He's not talking about prison. "It will get better."

"I have been waiting for five lousy months for it to get better," he snaps. "When the hell is it going to change? Can you tell me that? Because I am awfully damned tired of waiting." He paces across the porch.

"Take it easy, Brother. What's going on?"

"Nothing. I'm sorry. I don't know where to turn these days. And I get so damned tired of all this shit." His hands are clenched. "They close the center, they close our accounts, and they call us terrorists." He punches the air. "When will it end?"

"I don't know, but at least I'm not in prison."

He looks at my ankle and scowls. "Yes you are. What do you call that shit?" He shakes his head. "You shouldn't have stayed there. I shouldn't have left you there."

"It wasn't your fault. Nobody could do anything. Not even Thompson. And I'm the one who went to Pakistan and sent money to Ahmed. You shouldn't have been arrested in the first place."

"I should have stayed with you. I know they wouldn't have dared mess with you if I had been there."

"Maybe. Or they might have beaten you up too."

"They would have had to kill me. Which doesn't sound like such a bad idea sometimes."

I think of Troy. Umar doesn't know what he's talking about. He's just letting off steam. "Brother, if you had been there, you wouldn't talk like that."

"But I wasn't. I was enjoying my wife and children while you paid the price. It's not right." He sits down now and puts his face in his hands.

"No, Umar, that's not what I meant."

He cries, sobbing softly. I can count the number of times I've seen Umar cry, probably on one hand. It's the pressure from being arrested and losing the center. And he's worried about Derek.

"It's okay, Brother. I know how you feel." I put my arm around his shoulders, and we sit together in the quiet of the night.

When he's finished crying, he stands up. "I need to go home now. I'll see you later."

"Assalaamu alaikum," I call out as he walks away. He doesn't answer.

I sit out on the porch swing for a while and think about Umar. What's happening with him? The anger, the cursing. What is wrong?

I want to help him, but I'm tired. I go back into the house and crawl into bed next to Aisha. No more loneliness.

～

While I get stronger, I concentrate on getting to know my family again.

Jamal hasn't said ten words to me since I came home. On Saturday afternoon, after the prayer, he comes over and sits next to me.

I'm reading the Qur'an. In prison, I relied on my memory. It feels so good to hold the Qur'an in my hands again. I don't notice Jamal at first, until he puts his head on my arm. I finish reading, close the Qur'an, and put it aside.

"How are you doing?"

"I'm okay."

"I thought about you every day while I was gone."

"Yeah, I know. I'm glad you're back."

"Me too."

"Why did they take you away?"

"I don't know. They said they wanted to ask me some questions, and then they put me in handcuffs. I still don't know exactly what happened, but I'm home now."

"On Thursday, I told my teacher that you came home. Then, during recess, one of the other kids called you a terrorist. He made me mad. I wanted to hit him."

I'm surprised, because all of the kids at his school are Muslims, but I remember how I used to jump to conclusions when I heard someone had been accused of terrorism.

"Don't hit him, Jamal. Fighting never solved anything. He doesn't know any better, but you know who I am, don't you?" I hug his shoulders, pulling him close to me, and kiss the top of his head.

"Yeah, Dad, I know. And I'm glad you're back."

We sit together for a while and I hold him close. I haven't held him like this since he was a little boy, before he discovered video games and friends. I think I see a little tear run down his cheek, but he quickly wipes it away. It's too bad that boys have to reach the age when they think they're too big to cry. Abdul-Qadir taught me that it's okay for a man to cry once in a while.

Muhammad has so many questions about prison life. He throws them at me all weekend long—during dinner, while we're watching a movie, and while I'm trying to get him to go to sleep.

"What did they feed you?"

"Did they torture you?"

"Why do you have to wear that thing on your leg?"

"Did you remember me?"

"Were you afraid?"

I answer all of his questions as well as I can. Some, like whether the prison had rats and cockroaches, are easy. Some, like being afraid, are much harder. I can't tell him how afraid I was of never seeing him and his brothers and sisters again.

Luqman clings to me. I hold him and play some games with him. I try to fly him around the room like I did when he was little, but I still don't have the strength for it. And he's getting bigger, too.

Maryam knows me. I was so afraid she wouldn't. This morning she laughed out loud when I made a funny face. I loved it. She wants to sit up now. She grabs my fingers and lets me pull her up. Last night she fell asleep while I held her, curling up tight against my chest.

Jennifer lives here now, in the room she used to share with Raheema. I can't believe she's the same girl who screamed at me and sulked in the basement. She smiles. That's the biggest difference. And she's quick to help. The first time I saw her cooking dinner, I had to sit down. That must be how Mom felt when she saw me in the kitchen. But Jennifer is a lot younger than I was when I finally got myself turned around. I think I'll hold my breath for a few more years, watching for signs of a relapse.

I don't see my older boys much. They both have jobs, and they like to hang out with their friends. I remember hanging out with my friends when I was a teenager. Their friends don't brag about their conquests or smoke weed. Michael's friends are all high achievers who plan to go to good colleges, and Jeremy's friends are well-behaved Muslim kids. Heather and I had a rough start, but our kids have turned out awfully well. I know that she deserves a lot of the credit.

Michael comes over on Sunday night to eat dinner with us. I don't even try to talk with him during dinner. During those months in prison, I forgot how noisy and hectic it can be to eat with a family. The kids are talking and the bird is squawking. Michael helps, though. He fills everyone's plate, reminds Luqman not to drop his rice, and even feeds Maryam her cereal. He never took that much interest in the smaller ones before. It must have happened while I was away.

After dinner, I sit with him in the family room, and we talk. "So, you have two more weeks. You must be excited."

He grins. "I can't wait. I have my cap and gown now. Yearbooks came out last week. I'm actually going to miss a couple of my teachers, but I can't wait."

"Are you ready to head off for college yet?"

"Not yet. I want to take a couple of weeks off after graduation, just to relax. I will be going up there at the end of June to visit Marcus and find an apartment. He and I are going to room together."

"Is Boston that close to Worcester?"

"I guess so. From what Marcus says, lots of people commute into Boston. He says it's nice up there. I can't wait to see it."

"What's the name of the school you'll be going to again?"

"Worcester Polytechnic Institute. I haven't been able to get up there for a visit, but everyone says it's good. I want to be an engineer, like Uncle Brad."

"So you're all set to study engineering?"

"I've been thinking about it for a while now. My guidance counselor suggested it. And Uncle Brad let me spend some time with him at his office last summer. He showed me what he does. That's what I want to be doing."

"That's great. And you have a full scholarship. I am very proud of you, Michael."

"Thanks, Dad. I'm just glad you're here with us again. I didn't know if you'd be able to make it to my graduation." He stops, and looks into my eyes. He has my eyes. "You know, the day they took you in, I keep replaying that morning in my mind. You called Mom's place and wanted to tell us about Maryam, but I was in a hurry to get to school. I should have talked with you. I didn't know that it could have been the last time. I'm sorry."

"That's okay. Like you said, you didn't know. I sure didn't know, either, what I was going to be walking into."

"I know, but I've felt bad, all this time. Especially after I heard about the fight and I thought I might never see you again."

181

He stops, and looks down. "I guess I never told you that I love you."

"No, not since you were four, but I know how it is. I love you too, Michael. You were the first person I was ever able to love, since the minute I held you in my arms. I guess I never told you that, either."

We hug, and then he has to leave. I stand by the front door long after he's gone, thinking about Michael. I was there in the room when he was born, I watched him grow up, and, in a couple of weeks, I'll see him graduate. It has never been easy, but I've always been able to be there.

Jeremy took off one day of work and turned down invitations from his friends so he could be with me this weekend. We've talked, especially in the mornings after the prayer. He wants to know more about my experience. I've told him about most of it, especially the loneliness, but I haven't told him about Troy. I still have a hard time thinking about his death. I wish I could have seen him one more time.

Aisha has asked me, too. She knows about the fight, of course, but she wants to know why they had to put me in solitary for those last several weeks. I guess Mom didn't tell her about what happened to Thompson. I've told her that I can't talk about it yet. She accepts that answer, for now.

∼

Mom comes on Monday carrying bags of food. Sharon and Aisha feed the kids in the kitchen while Mom and I eat in the family room.

She's brought me a special treat. A large deep dish pizza from Giordano's, piled high with mushrooms and olives, and loaded with fresh Parmesan cheese. How does she know me so well?

We talk while we eat. "Dora called me that morning and told me what had happened. I couldn't believe it. Especially after all these years. I didn't know why they would come for you now. Charlene took over running the business for a week or so while I worked on getting you out of there. I could barely believe what was happening."

"Did you ever think that maybe the charges were right, that I was a terrorist?"

"Absolutely not. Thirteen years ago, I would have thought that, but not now. Let me show you something."

We go into the rec room and she puts in a DVD. We watch her interviews with the media. She shouts down every reporter who dares to imply that I might be guilty. She stands up in front of the cameras and defends me, over and over again. When the DVD is finished, I take her hand.

"Thanks, Mom, for believing in me."

"I know you, Joshua. You have been many things over the years, but you have never been a very good liar." She smiles. "It is so good to have you home. You can't imagine the terror I felt when they told me about the fight. I came there, before you woke up. Did you know that? You were so still."

"Aisha told me you two had come. I don't remember."

"I was so afraid that we would lose you. Then a few days later, that man stabbed Walt. Did you see the attack?"

"Yes. Well, right after the attack. And I heard it." I tell her about the threat, and my night of fear. "When I heard the noise, I looked outside and I saw Mr. Thompson on the floor. I thought he was dead."

"His office called me, and I rushed to the hospital. I thought we had lost him." She shakes her head. "Those were such frightening times. Thank God you both survived."

Thompson isn't dead and Mom isn't alone, but I still want to talk to her about Islam. "Do you mean that? Do you thank God?"

"It's just a figure of speech. You know that."

"I know, but do you thank God?"

"Let's not get into that again. I told you that what I believe is very personal. I thought you accepted that."

"I did, but I've had a lot of time to think. Ahmed is dead. I came close to dying in prison. None of us will live forever. Have you ever thought about what happens after we die?"

183

She looks down and says quietly, "I used to think about it. When my mother died. You don't remember her. You were too young. She was too young to die, and I wasn't ready to say goodbye to her. During the funeral, the reverend kept saying we should be happy, because her suffering was over and she was in heaven. I wanted to scream at him. I certainly was not happy that she was gone, and I didn't see any blessing in it. Since then, I've tried not to think about heaven and hell. I want to do everything I can to enjoy the life I have here and now."

"But there is more, Mom. There really is."

"Maybe there is, maybe there isn't, but all this talk about death is depressing me. We should be celebrating. Walt and you both survived, and you're home. Oh, by the way, we decided not to tell Aisha about the attack. We didn't want her to worry." She smiles again. "Walt had his arm in a sling for over a month. We told her it was a tennis injury."

I laugh. "And she believed you?"

"Of course. Walt and I have been playing tennis at least once a week for, oh, I suppose about ten years now. He's quite good."

"I didn't know that." I can't imagine my mother playing tennis. And I still can't imagine her having a man in her life. This would be a good time to ask, but I guess I don't really want to know.

Before she leaves, she hands me a simply-wrapped package. It's from Abdul-Qadir. Inside is a Qur'an, a prayer rug, and a note written in Urdu.

"Assalaamu alaikum, Isa. I am very sorry to hear about your imprisonment. May Allah give you the strength you need for this ordeal. This is Ahmed's Qur'an. He was reading it on the night he was killed. I am also sending his prayer rug. I know he would want you to have them. My heart is broken, but I know it is the will of Allah. Ahmed's mother and Ahmed's wife cannot stop crying, but I know we must be strong. Please pray for us, and for his children. I pray that you return safely to your family. With love in Islam, Abdul-Qadir."

Tears run down my cheeks. Mom reaches over and wipes them away. "What did he say?"

Rebounding

"These belonged to Ahmed. Abdul-Qadir wants me to have them." I close my eyes. I can see Ahmed. Laughing as he runs down the soccer field. Playing with his son. Praying next to me in the masjid. I still can't imagine him dead. "He was so young."

"Abdul-Qadir is very strong. I don't know where he gets his strength, to bury a son. You were right. Life is more real there."

Sometimes life is too real.

Part Ten

Some mornings when I wake up, before I open my eyes, I think I am still in prison. The feeling I get when I open my eyes and see home. I can't describe it.

I'm still trying to adjust. For one thing, I still have trouble with noise. I've been home for a week when Jamal and Muhammad come running into the family room, where I'm reading the paper, and start wrestling with one another. I feel like screaming at them to stop. I stop myself. I take a deep breath and head upstairs to the bedroom for some quiet. Aisha notices and sends the boys outside to play.

An hour later, Aisha tells me she needs to buy some groceries. I feel an intense fear.

"I want you to stay home. We have enough food in the house, don't we?"

"We're out of some basics . . . like milk, eggs, and flour. Jamal's class is having a bake sale tomorrow. I promised I would make cookies."

"You don't have to go."

"What's wrong? You never had trouble with me going out before."

"I'll miss you," I lie. Though I will miss her.

"I'll miss you too, Hon, but I'll be right back, insha Allah."

"Okay, but come right back. And be careful."

"You know I'm always a careful driver." She heads out, calling "Assalaamu alaikum" as she walks away.

"Walaikum assalaam," I say quietly as a knot forms in my stomach. I don't tell her that I'm really worried about nuts like Nat. Syrian fighters ambushed an Army convoy this morning, killing eighteen American soldiers. A grieving father seeing a woman in a scarf may decide to take his revenge. But I can't tell her that. I just say a short prayer and go to read the Qur'an until I hear her pull up in the driveway.

Rebounding

I have smaller problems, too. Sometimes in the middle of the night, if Aisha brushes against me, I open my eyes, expecting to find cockroaches. Brad could still beat me in a soccer game. Mom and Sharon both make sure I eat well; I rest when I'm tired, and work around the house when I feel rested. I'm getting there.

I still wake up every night. Sometimes Aisha gets up with me. We're awake at midnight when there's a light knock at the door.

I turn on the porch light and open the door. It's Umar again. He doesn't move. He doesn't say salaam. He just stands there.

"Assalaamu alaikum, Brother. Is everything okay?"

He stands there. Then he cries. Three times in one week. I don't think I've seen Umar cry three times in the last ten years.

I go outside and stand next to him. I touch his arm. "Let's sit down." But he doesn't move. Something is very wrong. The way he is right now, I don't know how he even managed to get to our house.

Aisha comes to the front door and looks out. "Isa, who is it? Is everything okay?"

"It's Umar. You can go on to bed. I think Umar and I need to talk."

"Okay, Hon." She comes out and kisses me. "Try not to be too late. Assalaamu alaikum, Umar."

He doesn't respond. Aisha looks at me. "Just go to bed, Hon."

"Okay." She goes back inside, leaving us on the porch.

"Let's go sit down." I take Umar's arm and guide him to the porch swing. He still hasn't said a word.

"It's been rough for you too, hasn't it?"

"I shouldn't have left you there. I went home with my wife and I left you there." He speaks slowly, in a monotone.

"It's okay, Brother. You couldn't do anything about it. I know you refused to testify against me. I know you wouldn't really leave me."

"I can't do it. I can't go on. It's too much."

"We have to go on. We don't have a choice."

"I can't work. I can't think. I sit at home. Waiting for it to be over. I'm a man, but I sit in front of the television. Day after day. I don't work. I don't pray. I don't know how to pray these days."

"It will get better. I'm out of prison now. Thompson will get the charges dismissed. We'll get back to work. Remember what you told me? Trust in Allah. Turn to Allah."

"Even Safa has had enough of me. She told me so tonight. She yelled at me. She said I can't just sit. But I don't know what to do. Everything is gone."

"Don't give up, Brother."

"No one needs me. No one wants me. I'm tired. It's no use."

"Everyone needs you, Umar. I need you. Just hold on." I hold on to his arm. Trying to keep him from slipping further away.

We stay out here on the porch until dawn; then I bring him into the house to wash up and pray. I have to walk with him to the bathroom. I have to bring him over to stand next to me in the prayer. He acts helpless, or lost. I have never seen Umar like this before.

Soon after the prayer, Sharon comes downstairs to start breakfast. When she glances into the family room and sees Umar here she stops. "What is going on?"

He looks at her. She takes one look at him, and she seems to understand. She kneels down next to him and puts her arms around his shoulders. He puts his head in her lap and sobs.

I leave them and go to make breakfast for the kids. When I come back into the family room, he's still sitting there, not moving or speaking. Sharon sits on the floor next to him, talking gently. He doesn't respond.

Safa comes soon, carrying Ahmad and dragging Tasneema behind her. She says she had to feed the kids first. She asks us to keep Tasneema and Ahmad while she takes Umar to the doctor. Aisha helps him out to the car while I stand on the porch and watch. Sharon goes with them to the doctor.

After they leave, I turn to Aisha. "What just happened?"

"Safa called last night, right after Umar came. She was crying. She said that his depression has been getting worse. He hasn't done anything for the last few weeks except sit on the couch. He's even neglected to make his prayers. Safa was upset that he wasn't praying, and she was getting tired of doing all the work while he just sat there. Last night they had a fight. She yelled at him. Then, she said, he started yelling and cursing. He punched a hole in the kitchen wall. He screamed that he wanted to die and stormed out of the house. She didn't know where he had gone. She was frantic. She was afraid he would hurt himself."

"I didn't know."

"But you did the right thing. You took care of him until Safa could come. That's what I told her, that we would take care of him and keep him safe until she could come."

"I never thought anyone would have to take care of Umar."

"I'm worried, Isa. Do you think he'll be okay?"

"I think so." *I hope so.* "Sharon will make sure he gets the help he needs."

Safa comes in the afternoon to get Tasneema and Ahmad. Her eyes are red. "They will keep Umar in the hospital for a few days. They say he needs medication, and he needs to be watched for now. I am so afraid."

Aisha holds her. I know she's worried about Umar, too, but she sounds confident as she comforts Safa. "It will be okay. My brother is strong. He'll get through this, insha Allah."

"It's my fault. I yelled at him. A wife should never yell at her husband. I didn't understand what was going on. I didn't know why he was sitting, and why he wouldn't pray. What if he had hurt himself? It would have been my fault." She cries while Aisha holds her.

Sharon walks down the stairs carrying a suitcase. I didn't see her come in. "I'm going to stay with Safa and help her with the children. I plan to be there for a while after Tony comes home. I think he needs me."

She pats Safa's arm. "Don't worry. They'll take good care of him. And don't blame yourself. You didn't know. I didn't realize, either, what was happening. I knew he was upset, what with the arrest and losing the center, but he has always been so strong, I was sure he would snap out of it. Let's go. I'll drive you home."

She bends down and scoops Ahmad up in her arms. "Grandma's going to go to your house and play with you. Okay?"

Ahmad and Tasneema both cheer. They're too young to understand.

Umar is released five days later. He's on medication, and he needs to return as an outpatient for therapy. Sharon is there to make sure he takes his medication and keeps up with his therapy schedule. I wish I could have been here for him, before it got this bad.

Aisha goes to see him when he comes home. I want to go too, but I'm still a prisoner.

As soon as she walks in the door, I ask, "How is he?"

"He still sits on the couch. He looks so very sad. Mom says he should come around soon, now that he's getting help."

"I need to see him."

"Why don't you call?"

"It's not the same."

"No, but it's better than nothing."

Sharon answers the phone. "Hold on, Joshua, he's right here."

"Assalaamu alaikum, Brother. How are you?"

"I'm sorry. I wasn't strong." He does sound sad. Not like Umar at all.

"Don't worry about that. Just remember everyone who loves you."

"I know."

"And hold on to your faith, Brother."

"That's why I came to you. Instead of jumping off a bridge."

I never imagined Umar could have those thoughts. He has always been so strong. Or he has always seemed so strong. "Remember, after hardship comes ease. Just hold on."

I need to be there. I could try to give him strength.

"I think I'll be okay," he says very quietly.

"You will, Umar. I know you will."

We talk a little before I hang up. I tell him about how Luqman ran through the house after his bath last night, buck naked, and nearly ran out the front door. I remind him about the

Rebounding

time Sakeena got stuck in that tree in their front yard and he had to climb up after her. I want to make him happy again, but all I can do is talk. I can't be there with him. We can't eat lunch together. We can't pray together.

~

While Umar struggles with depression, I keep struggling to get back to everyday life. I think I'm almost back to normal. Except for the noise.

And this damn ankle bracelet. I can't leave the house, except to go out on the front porch for fresh air. And to meet with my parole officer. I can't go near the computer, either. I guess an alarm will go off somewhere. I don't feel like testing it. I can't be around Muslims, except for my family and a few others, like Fawad, Ismail, and Mahmoud. Thompson said something about some kind of clearance. The imam hasn't come by. I remember some of the sermons he's given, talking about the injustice of U.S. military presence in Muslim countries. He must be on somebody's list.

When they released me, they returned my wallet. I was surprised to find some cash still in it. I want to take Jennifer out for lunch, but I can't leave. Instead, Jennifer and Aisha go to the burger place and order take-out. Aisha takes care of the other kids so I can have my time alone with my oldest daughter. It's the best we can do.

While we eat our burgers at the kitchen table, she catches me up on her life. She's on the yearbook staff at her school, and she has discovered that she likes to write. The school newspaper published one of her poems a few months ago. She shows it to me.

Gone
No more smile when he sees me
No more warm hug to soothe me
No more laughter, loud and strong
No more "looks" when I am wrong

I didn't know, that November day
That they would take him far away
Away from friends and family
Away from home
Away from me

Even when we fought, I knew he loved me
But now he's gone

I don't think I've ever cried in front of her. I hide the tears behind my napkin.
"Do you like it?"
It takes me a moment before I can answer. "It's beautiful."
She looks down. "I'm glad you like it," she says softly.
I get control of myself, and we talk about us. The anger, the fighting, and how much we missed each other. The sweetest words are the ones she says to me as we're finishing our banana splits. "You were right, Dad. Thanks for believing in me."
I go over and hug her. She starts to cry. "What's wrong, Jenny?"
"I was afraid that you wouldn't come back."
I soothe her, just like in the poem. *I know, Jenny. I was afraid, too.*
She's quiet as we finish up, but before we leave the kitchen she says, "I'm sorry, Dad. I was so mean to you. I even thought about running away and never coming back. But then they took you away. And I thought that I would never see you again. Are you mad at me?"
"No, Jennifer, I'm not mad at you. I love you." I hug her again.
She kisses me on the cheek. "And I love you too."
My little girl is back.

∼

I go out onto the front porch to pick up the mail. My daily dose of fresh air.

Rebounding

When I was in prison, I missed the simple things, like sitting in my chair to read the paper and going out to pick up the mail. It's all billing statements today. One is from a credit card company. They must have delivered it to the wrong house.

But it's addressed to Angela Evans. When did Aisha get a credit card? We've always tried to stay out of debt.

It hits me. I can't pay these. We had some money in our account when they took me in, but I can't get to it. Our accounts are still frozen.

Aisha is sitting on the couch, nursing Maryam. She reaches out, and I go over to kiss her. She notices the envelopes in my hand.

"Anything interesting in the mail today?"

"No, it's all bills."

"Oh, I'll just give those to Brad. He'll take care of it."

"That's how it's been, all these months. Hasn't it?"

"Yes. You knew that."

"Yes, I knew, but it seems different now. The thought that I have to rely on my brother to take care of my family. And why did you get a credit card?"

"I had to, Isa. That's what I've been using to buy gas for the car, and clothes for the kids, and even groceries. Don't worry. Brad takes care of that bill, too."

"This is all wrong. We've been so careful all these years. We always agreed that we would only pay cash. We don't go into debt, and we don't even come close to paying interest. I can't believe that everything has changed."

"I can't get to our account, and there's no money coming in. It's the only way the kids and I have been able to survive. I didn't know what else to do."

"There must be a better way. I'll call Thompson."

I call him, but he doesn't have anything encouraging to tell me. We won't be able to get to the account until the charges are dropped. He's working on getting the charges dropped, but it will take time.

"Couldn't I get a job?"

"Joshua, you are under house arrest."

"I thought they encouraged parolees to find jobs."

"Usually, but your case is special. You would still be in prison, if I hadn't petitioned the court concerning the physical danger due to the terrorist label and the mental stress you were experiencing in solitary. House arrest was the only alternative."

I didn't know how hard he had worked to get me out, but I can't leave it alone. "Maybe I could work from home."

"Don't go near that computer. These devices are very sensitive. One wrong move, and they'll be out there in thirty minutes or less to throw you back into solitary. And next time they won't let you out."

"But how do they expect me to take care of my family?"

"Your brothers are helping, aren't they? And I think Aisha gets some help from the government."

"Yes, but I need to take care of my family. Not my brothers, and definitely not the government. They're the ones who did this to me in the first place. This isn't right."

"No, it isn't, but there's nothing you can do until the charges have been dismissed."

I'm still upset, but there's no use arguing with Thompson about it. "Okay, thanks anyway."

"I'm doing everything I can, Joshua. Just be patient."

"I know you are. I'll try."

In the evening, Brad comes to visit. He brings Kyle.

"I haven't seen you in a long time, man. You're taller than your dad now."

Kyle grins. He's a good looking kid.

I tell them about my frustration. "I'm happy to be with my family, of course, but I feel like I'm still in prison."

Brad pats my shoulder. "Don't worry about it. Everything's taken care of. Think of this as an extended vacation. No rush hour, no deadlines. Hell, I wish someone would put me under house arrest."

Yeah, sure.

When Brad excuses himself to use the restroom, Kyle comes closer to me. "I can help you, Uncle Joshua," he whispers.

"You can? How?"

"I know how these things work. Last year in social studies, we had to do reports about technological advances in fighting terrorism. I wrote about the electronic monitoring device, like the one you're wearing. This thing is hooked up to a central computer. It sends constant signals, every three minutes, but I know how to get around it."

"Okay. What do you know?" I don't want to encourage juvenile delinquency, but it can't hurt to ask.

"Most people try to remove them, but these things register body heat, so that never works. But, like I said, it sends signals to a computer. I can hack into their computer. If there's anywhere you want to go, I can buy you a little time."

This is wrong. I could go back to prison, and Kyle could be put into juvenile detention. Brad would never forgive me. Neither would Aisha. But I need to go to the masjid. I need to see Umar. I need to breathe fresh air, meet people, do something. I have to get out of here.

By the time Brad comes back, Kyle and I have it all worked out.

On Tuesday morning, I leave to meet with my parole officer. I kiss Aisha on my way out.

"Do you want me to come with you?"

"No, that's okay. I guess I'd better learn how to drive again."

"Okay, but be careful. And come right home."

"I will, Hon. Don't worry."

Jackson, my parole officer, reviews the rules with me. "Every week, you'll need to report any upcoming changes in your schedule. Do you have anything to report?"

"My son will be graduating from high school on Thursday. I need to go to his graduation. And there will be a reception at my mother's house afterwards."

"That sounds safe. Give me the times and places, and I'll make sure the system conforms to the variations."

I try to finish up our meeting as quickly as possible. Then I get back into my car and head for the masjid. Kyle called last night. We spoke in code, because I'm sure my phones are tapped. He let me know I have an extra hour.

The brothers look surprised to see me. I tell them I have special permission. I know I can trust them, but that's all they need to know.

It feels so good to be back. I've missed the frayed green carpet and the smell of incense hanging in the air, but I can't stay long. We talk for a few minutes and I pray with them, shoulder to shoulder again.

When I leave the masjid, I still have forty minutes to spare.

Fawad smiles when I walk in. "Isa. Welcome back."

It's not the Karachi Kitchen I remember. The metal tables are gone, replaced by red vinyl booths. A mural covers the back wall. Even the old green tile has disappeared. The new linoleum is a swirl of colors. "You fixed up the place."

"Yes, my wife thought the booths would look better. My son Mustapha painted the mural. He calls it 'Everyday Life in Karachi.'"

"It looks familiar. He's good. He'll be graduating soon, won't he?"

"Yes, he's the same age as Jeremy. One more year, and then Zainab and I will have an empty house."

I ask Fawad about each of his children. Then I talk with Adel, Fawad's assistant manager, a little. And I catch up with Khalid, the cook. I glance at my watch. Twenty-five minutes.

I don't want to cut it too close. I start to leave, but Fawad stops me. "Don't you want to eat before you go?"

"Thanks, but I need to get back. Aisha will worry."

"Wait a minute." He goes into the kitchen. He doesn't know what a minute means to me right now.

Five minutes pass before he returns with a plastic bag holding four Styrofoam containers. "For you and your family."

"Thank you, Fawad. I don't know what to say."

"Then don't say anything. Just go back home and enjoy the food. I'll see you later, insha Allah."

Insha Allah. Because we never know what will happen tomorrow. Now I know what that means.

Tomorrow will I be in prison again, or will I pull it off?

I stop by Umar's house on my way home.

Sharon answers the door. "Joshua, what are you doing here? Shouldn't you be at home?"

"I have a few minutes. I need to see Tony."

"He's in the family room. But what's going on?"

I walk quickly into the family room. He's sitting there on the couch.

"Assalaamu alaikum, Brother."

He looks at my ankle. "You shouldn't have come."

"It's okay. I have a few minutes. I wanted to see you. How are you?"

"I'm feeling better. I think I'll make it."

I hug him. I've missed him so much—since the day they took me away—but I won't get emotional. That's the last thing he needs.

"You'd better go home," he says. "I don't want to see you back in prison."

"Okay. Be strong, Brother. I'll see you again soon."

He nods. "Don't take any chances."

"No, I won't. Don't worry about me. Assalaamu alaikum." I rush to the front door, not stopping to say goodbye to the rest of the family.

"Walaikum assalaam," he shouts after me. His voice is stronger. That's good.

I pull into the driveway with a minute to spare. I sprint to the front porch, as quickly as my tired legs will take me. I made it. I hope it worked.

Aisha is standing by the open front door, her arms crossed. "Where have you been? I was worried sick. You could have been in an accident, or they could have taken you away again. You can't imagine what has been going through my mind."

I kiss her on the cheek, and squeeze her waist. "I'm home now. Everything's okay." I did it. I haven't felt this good in six months.

The phone rings. Aisha answers. "Yes, Mom, he's here. No, I think everything is okay. Let me call you back."

She hangs up and turns back to me. "What did you do, Isa?"

Twelve years ago, I swore I would never lie to Aisha again, but I wish I could do it now. "I stopped to pray at the masjid on my way home. And I went to see Fawad. And Umar. Here, I brought you something." I offer her the bag of food from Karachi Kitchen.

"You did what? You know the masjid is off limits. And they're keeping track of you every second. I don't believe you did that. They're probably on their way here right now to come get you." She looks nervously out the window.

"No, they're not. I don't think so anyway. I know someone who was able to hack into their computers. He bought me an extra hour."

"Who?"

I don't want to tell her—I'm in enough trouble already—but she insists. "Who?"

"Kyle."

"Kyle?" she screams. "You're telling me that you put your life into the hands of a fourteen-year-old? Are you crazy? And do you know what happens when you get caught? They'll arrest Kyle too. They'll probably shut down the masjid. Maybe even Fawad's restaurant. And I don't know what they could do to Umar. What in the world were you thinking?"

I look down at the floor and raise my hands in futility. I guess she's right. I put a lot on the line. Just for a few minutes of freedom.

We spend the next hour looking out the window, listening for the sirens. They'll take me away again. I'll go back into solitary. I don't know when I'll see my family.

But they don't come. It worked. Kyle is one smart kid. I breathe deeply. I did it!

Aisha comes close to me and softly growls into my face. "Don't you ever try that again." Then she goes outside to her garden, slamming the door behind her.

Rebounding

~

I want to buy something for Michael. My first son is graduating, and I have barely a dollar to my name. Even if I did have the money, I couldn't go to the store to spend it.

Aisha offers to buy something with her credit card, but I can't do it. I hate to go empty-handed, but I don't have any other choice.

On the morning of the graduation, I open my closet, and I see it. The leather briefcase Umar gave me when I finished college. I look inside and find a grant application, an email from Mr. Richards, and the press release on the Jim Evans Memorial Youth Center, along with other bits and pieces of my life before the arrest.

I tear up the papers and clean up the briefcase. It's meant a lot to me over the years, but I can't use it now. It's still in good shape. And it's a gift from the heart.

All of us—Adams family and Evans family—show up to cheer for Michael, though Umar is still very quiet. Heather, Peter, and Brianna come too, of course. When I hear "Michael Nathaniel Adams," and watch him go up to get his diploma, I jump to my feet and shout. My son is a man now. He really is a man.

We go to Mom's house for the reception. I see Heather's parents for the first time since Jennifer was born. Her father and I shake hands.

"He's a fine boy, Joshua. Somehow, Heather and you did a good job."

"It was mostly Heather. By the way, I'm sorry for all the trouble I caused you. Now that I have a teenage daughter, I understand."

"Does Jennifer have any boyfriends who give you gray hairs?"

"Not anymore. There was one boy. Long hair, bad attitude. You know the type."

"That does sound familiar. Did you chase him off?"

"Something like that. Now I know why you told Heather to stay away from me."

"You gave me many sleepless nights, but it looks like it has all turned out in the end."

"Yes sir, it has." *Alhamdulillah.*

I give Michael the briefcase. "Thanks, Dad. This was yours, wasn't it?"

"Yes, it was." *In a past life.*

He hugs me. "I know what this means to you. I'll take good care of it."

I know Michael appreciates the briefcase, but my gift is no match for what his grandmother gives him. In the middle of the evening, she hands over the keys to a brand-new car.

"Wow! Thanks, Gramma. Thanks!"

Later I talk to her. "Thanks, Mom. That's a great present. By the way, why didn't I get a new car when I graduated?"

"Joshua, if I had given you a new car when you were eighteen you would have wrapped it around a tree."

She's probably right.

We have to leave soon. My time is almost up. Maybe I should ask Kyle to buy me a little more time. Or maybe not.

We're heading for the front door when Thompson grabs my arm and pulls me aside. "I know about your little stunt. That was probably the stupidest thing you have ever done."

I didn't know Thompson used words like stupid. I guess that pretty well describes it though. "Aisha told you."

"She's worried about you. You have to be careful. What were you thinking?"

"I just wanted a little freedom."

"I worked very hard to get you out of there, and you had better not screw it up." He doesn't raise his voice, but there's no mistaking his tone. I didn't know he could get this angry. "And if you don't care about yourself, think about your mother. She put up your bail. If you mess this up, she'll lose her business. Is that what you want? She loses her business, you lose your freedom. I don't see any winners here. Do you?"

He's right, but I'm not happy about it. "You don't understand. I can't stay in the house all day, every day. I have to get out."

Rebounding

"Be patient. I'm working to get the charges dismissed, but you will have to wait."

"To hell with being patient." My voice gets louder. "I'm tired of this. When do I get to have a normal life again?"

"Lower your voice. You don't want to make a scene here. Think about Michael."

I take a deep breath and shake my head. He releases my arm and we both walk away, but nothing's settled.

I'm seething. I'm so angry that I barely notice the car tailing me all the way home.

I don't say a word to Aisha in the car. I wait until all of the kids are in bed and we're in our room.

She comes closer to me, smiling. I push her away.

"Isa, what's wrong?"

"Why did you tell Thompson?"

"I thought he needed to know."

"It's bad enough with the feds keeping track of me. Now I've got Thompson chewing me out. I don't need that. But I know what I do need. And you need to leave it alone."

"I can't, Isa. I'm afraid. What if you get caught? You'll go back to prison."

"Do you think I don't know what I'm doing?"

"You can't go back. It was so hard, being without you."

"You're going to tell me about hard? Try getting beaten up while you're waiting to eat your lunch. Try spending weeks in solitary without the sound of a human voice. Try being called terrorist by everyone you see."

"I know you had a rough time in prison. That's why you can't go back there. You have to be patient."

"Patient. There's that word again. You and Thompson don't know shit about being patient."

"I don't know patient? Who do you think was taking care of these kids while you were locked up? Getting them off to school every day. Seeing that they got their homework done. Being there when they missed you. Who had to come home with a new baby only to find out that her husband wouldn't be there? And now I have to put up with you and all of your mood swings. Trying not to upset you. Knowing the right words to say. Loving you enough. All that, on top of what the kids need from me every day. Don't tell me about patient."

"I didn't know I was such a burden. You should be happy that I'm taking risks. Maybe I will end up in prison again and you won't have to put up with me."

She starts to cry. "I don't want to do this, Isa. I don't want to fight with you. I just don't want them to take you away again."

"Do you think I enjoyed it? It was a laugh a minute. Oh yeah. I can't wait to go back there. Maybe I can get beaten up again. Maybe I can get another man killed."

She looks at me. "What? Who got killed? What happened?"

"Forget I said anything. I don't want to talk about it."

"Tell me. I want to help you."

"I told you, forget it." I shout at her. I don't want to shout, but I can't help it.

She's still crying, but she rubs my back. "It might help if you tell me. I know that something's bothering you. I can see that."

I lower my voice and look down. "It's nothing. Just leave it."

"It's okay. You're home now. Just tell me."

"I can't."

"Who died, Isa? What is it?"

I sit down on the bed and close my eyes. I picture Troy. And I remember Thompson, lying on the floor and covered in blood. I remember the fight, and the fear, and the loneliness. I start to cry. I reach for her. She holds me and rocks me while I get it out of my system. It takes a long time.

When I'm calm, I stroke her cheek. "I shouldn't have yelled at you."

"That's okay. You've been through a lot. Maybe if you tell me, it will help."

"It's hard. I don't even want to think about it, but I can't get it out of my head."

"It's okay. I'm here. You're safe now. And you can tell me anything."

"Okay." The only way I can do it is to say it fast. "There was this guy named Troy. We shared a cell. At first he didn't like me very well—and I guess I didn't like him either—but after a while we got to be friends. He got to be the best friend I had in there. When they were beating me up, Troy was the only one who stood up for me. He came to pull them off of me, and he got a few punches in, too. I don't know, he probably even stopped them from killing me. After I got out of the hospital, a guy told me that they had stabbed Troy. Because of what he did for me. He had two kids. A son and a daughter. And they'll never even know him. He died because of me. It's like I killed him."

"You didn't kill him, Hon. Those men killed him, the ones who..."

I shake my head. Now that I've started, I have to tell her everything. "There's more. I couldn't sleep, and I could hardly eat or pray, because that guy said they were coming after me too. Then Thompson came to see me. Before he came into the room, while I was waiting to talk to him, he got stabbed."

"Walt? But I saw him. He wasn't hurt. Well, except for that tennis injury."

"He had his left arm in a sling. Mom made up the part about the tennis injury to keep you from worrying. The guy stabbed him in the shoulder. I guess his aim was off."

"How did you know it was his left arm? By the time you got out he wasn't wearing the sling."

"Because I saw him down on the floor, after the stabbing. I was waiting for him, and I saw it through the window. Except I thought the guy got him in the chest. All that time I was in solitary, I thought he was dead."

She stares at me, then she says softly, "That's why you had to go back into solitary. And that's why Walt told me I couldn't come to see you."

"Yes."

She cries again. "I didn't know I came that close to losing you. And imagine if I had come, if I had brought Jamal with me. I can't even think about it."

"It's okay now, Hon. We're all safe now." I try to comfort her.

"I can't go through that again, Isa. I need you too much. You can't leave me again. You can't put us all in that kind of danger."

"I won't leave you. I'll never leave you."

"Then don't take chances. You can't go back to that place. Next time you won't come out."

She's huddled over, hugging herself. I put my arms around her. "Okay, I promise"

"Are you sure?"

"Ask Sharon if she can watch the kids next Tuesday. You can come with me to make sure I stay out of trouble."

She's right. And Thompson too. It was a stupid thing to do. I need to call Kyle tomorrow and tell him the deal is off.

He sure is one smart kid, though.

After talking with Kyle, I call Thompson on his cell.

"Hi. It's Joshua. I hope you're not busy."

"What is it?" He still sounds angry.

"You were right. That wasn't the stupidest thing I've ever done, but it does rank right up there. I'm sorry."

"I only want what's best for you, Joshua." He pauses. "I'm glad you called."

After I hang up, I think about Thompson. He's more than my lawyer. He's my friend. I don't want to do anything to lose his friendship.

I think about Sam too. My father never loved me. He also never corrected me. I remember Jay, a guy I knew back in high school. He was always getting chewed out by his father. At least once a week. No wonder Jay got so nervous when his father yelled at him. Now I know how he felt.

On Friday, I sulk around the house. I should be going to the prayer. And I should be supporting my family.

Rebounding

In the afternoon, the principal of the Islamic school calls Aisha and offers her a job in the fall, teaching fourth grade. She quickly accepts. If Thompson doesn't move quickly, I'll face the added embarrassment of being supported by my wife.

※

I don't know what to do with my days. Aisha spends her mornings working in the garden. I watch her sometimes, through the kitchen window. I do remember, a long time ago, when I thought I would like to work on things in the garage, but our garage is detached from the house, and I can't go out there. I probably wouldn't know what to do anyway. I walk back into the rec room and watch a movie.

Umar and I are like two old men. We can't work. We putter around our houses. Sometimes, about once a week, he comes over for lunch, but it's not the same. At the office we had energy. We were always working on something, looking forward to something, but now we have nothing. Just waking up, eating, living, and waiting. He struggles with his depression. I struggle with my frustration.

He is improving. I don't know if it's the therapy or the medication, or maybe both. He says that the therapy is helping him understand some things.

"I've had these feelings all these years. And I kept them secret. I was afraid, if I tried to confront them, they would make me weak."

"What kind of feelings?"

"It started with the day Michelle walked away from me. I did love her, but I wasn't ready to marry her, and I didn't know what to do. Since that day, I have felt a sadness which never went away, even after I married Safa. And I have felt guilty for loving Michelle all these years. It's as if I was cheating on my wife. I'm learning now, through therapy, how to put all of that in the past. I haven't been able to do it on my own. And then, when they closed the center, I felt that I had lost everything. I was nothing without my work. I was almost happier in prison than I was at home, sitting around and not able to work. That made me feel guilty, too. Because I do love Safa and the children. Then I forgot how to pray. I sat. I felt empty.

"Then when she yelled at me—the first time she ever yelled at me—I couldn't handle it any more. What she said was too close to the truth, and I couldn't take it. It was bad, Isa. You don't know how bad it was. I'm sure she didn't tell you that I almost hit her."

"No, she didn't."

"She wouldn't. I raised my fist. I was ready to hit her. She cried and begged me to stop, to calm down. I saw what I was doing. That's when I ran out of the house. I almost hit her. I wanted to hurt her. And if I had, if I had hit her, I would have jumped off a bridge that night." He closes his eyes and bows his head, as if in prayer.

I remember what Umar told me, a long time ago, about his temper. And I remember when he said he could have killed me that one night, the night I almost threw my life away. I remember his cursing and pacing before the breakdown. But I didn't know he still had that much rage.

I reach over and pat his arm. "At least you did the right thing."

"Yes, but you don't know how close I came. I am very lucky that Safa has forgiven me. For everything. I don't deserve her." He stops for a moment longer before he looks up.

"Anyway, I am learning quite a bit about myself these days. I guess one of the most important things I've learned is that I don't always have to be strong."

"Isn't that what I've been telling you all these years?"

"Yes, but you don't have a Ph.D. behind your name." He doesn't smile, but I do see the spark again in his eyes.

He wants to stop taking the medication, but his doctor tells him that he's not ready yet. He talks with Sharon, and she says the same thing. She doesn't want to see him like he was.

He tells me he's been praying again, too. And praying more. He also reads the Qur'an every day. Gradually, he's coming back to being the Umar I've always known.

It's a Tuesday morning when he comes over to tell me his news. This time he is smiling. I haven't seen him smile since the day before the bone marrow extraction. A lifetime ago.

"Assalaamu alaikum, Isa. How are you doing?"

"Walaikum assalaam. I'm okay. You look happy."

"John Williams finally emailed me. The transplant was successful. He said Derek is stronger and healthier than he's been in a long time."

"Allahu akbar. That's great news. You gave him back his life."

"Allah did that. I just did what I could. That's not all. They've decided to tell Derek about me."

"They haven't told him yet?"

"No. They wanted to wait until his health had improved. And John Williams asked me if I'm ready for Derek to know me."

"Are you?"

"You know I am. Even Safa wants to meet him. She understands now that he is my son, and we are connected. I've already replied to his email. Now I have to wait to find out if Derek wants to see me."

I hope Derek wants to see him. I think that will help Umar more than any therapy or medication.

He gets his answer on Friday. He comes over in the evening to tell me.

"I received an email from Derek this morning. He said he knows about me, and he wants to meet me. He gave me their phone number, and asked that I contact them to arrange a meeting. I called there this afternoon. Michelle answered."

"What did you say?"

"I froze. I couldn't say anything. I think she was ready to hang up. Then I told her who I was, and she was quiet. Finally, she called her husband to the phone. I asked him to bring his family to my house for dinner on Sunday. I'd like Aisha and you to keep the kids again. Derek should meet them later, but not this time."

"That's great. Just two more days. How did you feel, talking to Michelle?"

"She sounds the same. I started to remember how it felt to hear her voice. But we have different lives now. I have to remember that."

"I know you'll be okay. And Safa will be there to remind you of what you have now."

"I know. I can't forget the way she's stood by me all this time." He smiles again. "You can't imagine how it feels to hear from Derek and know he wants to see me. In two days, I will finally meet my son."

Sharon moves back into our house the next morning. Umar is back.

⌘

Thompson calls later in the day, right after I finish cleaning up from lunch.

"How are you, Joshua? Are you staying out of trouble?"

"My wife keeps close tabs on me, but it hasn't been easy."

"No, I'm sure it hasn't. I have good news for you. The judge has finally agreed to hear my petition to have the charges against Tony and you dismissed. The hearing will be held in three weeks."

"Do you think it's really going to happen this time?"

"I wouldn't be taking it to court if I didn't. You have to learn how to trust me. You have a hard time with that, don't you?"

"I guess I do. I'm not sure why." It probably has something to do with Sam and his broken promises.

"At any rate, I think Tony and you have a very good chance. Their whole case hinges on your connection with Ahmed Ali. I have the depositions disproving their allegations of terrorist activity on his part. So, if you were sending money to Ahmed, and he was not involved in terrorism, then you cannot be charged with supporting terrorism. The evidence allegedly proving ties to a shadowy terrorist group called Al-Jahidia has never materialized. I don't see how they can continue to claim any basis for their charges."

"I hope you're right. I haven't been a very easy client, have I? I was rude to you at Michael's reception. I jeopardized my own freedom. And I can never forget that you were stabbed on my account."

"You've had a very difficult time. As far as the stabbing is concerned, let's just say it was a different kind of experience. When I realized I wasn't going to die, I felt so relieved that the rest of it didn't seem quite so bad. As I said, your case can be my last hurrah."

"So you are going to retire?"

"I'll let you know after the hearing."

"Well, thanks. I appreciate everything you're doing for me."

"Don't forget about what your mother has done. I think she missed her calling. She should have been a lawyer."

"Yes, I can see that. I'll see you in three weeks then."

~

Umar drops all five of his kids off on Sunday afternoon. They're expecting Derek and his family in two hours. Umar doesn't stay long. "I have to get back to help Safa."

"Just let her be in charge of the cooking."

"It's okay," he says. "We're barbecuing."

While I play with little Ahmad, and boil the macaroni, I think about Umar. Derek must be there now. I wonder how it's going.

He doesn't call until nearly midnight. The kids are all asleep, even Raheema. "It was a good evening. They've just left. Could you keep the kids at your house tonight? I'll come get them sometime tomorrow."

"Sure, no problem. I'm glad it went well."

"It went very well, alhamdulillah. I'll tell you about it tomorrow. And Isa, thank you for being there when I really needed you."

"You've done the same for me. That's what brothers are for."

He doesn't come until after lunch. I've just finished cleaning up Ahmad's mess in the kitchen when Umar knocks. When I greet him at the front door, he says, "Could we talk out on the porch?"

I go out and we sit on the porch swing. "Why out here?"

"The kids don't know about Derek yet."

"After all this time?"

"I didn't know how to tell them. And I didn't want to tell them at all until we knew he would be okay. We'll have to tell them now, of course. Hopefully, the younger ones will just accept him as their brother. Safa says she'll talk to Raheema and Sakeena and try to explain it to them."

"So it must have gone well last night."

"Yes. At first, when I opened the door and saw Michelle standing there, I felt awkward. She hasn't changed. The last time I saw her, I still loved her, and she hasn't changed. When Safa saw me, standing there at the door and staring, she came over, put her arm around my waist, and invited them to come in. She stayed close to me all night."

"That doesn't sound like Safa."

"No. She's usually very shy in public—it's the way she was raised—but last night she made sure everyone knew I belonged to her. It was good."

"So how is Derek?"

"Derek is great. He looks just like I did when I was in college, maybe an inch or so taller. He's very polite. John and Michelle have raised him well. At first he called me Mr. Evans. I asked him to call me Tony. I don't think I can ever ask him to call me Dad. John has earned that title."

"And they didn't leave until nearly midnight?"

"There was so much to talk about. At first, I suppose, we were all a little uncomfortable. We chatted about the weather and traffic, things like that. Then Derek started to ask me questions. Things he wanted to know about me. After that, I had my own list of questions. Things I wanted to know about him. That's when I found out how alike we are. And guess what. Now that he's healthy again, he'll be going back to his studies at Northeastern next fall, and his major is psychology."

Umar isn't just smiling, he's practically grinning. I don't think I've ever seen him this happy.

"We started to become more comfortable as the evening went on. John said they had thought about contacting me sooner, but they held back because of the terrorism charges. He did a little investigating on his own, until he was satisfied that the charges were false.

"At one point, I asked Michelle to tell me what happened after she walked away from me. I've always wanted to know. She was reluctant to talk about it, so John told most of the story.

"After she left me, she went to her dorm room to call her parents and tell them about her situation. They told her to come right home. She skipped her finals and went back to Springfield. She and John had been friends in high school, and he showed up at her house as soon as she came into town. He asked her to marry him several times before she finally agreed. He was in the room when Derek was born, and his name is on the birth certificate as Derek's father. They were married in January, when Derek was five weeks old. All these years, they've told Derek that they were married the January before he was born, not after. Oh, and she took the money I had given her for the abortion, and put it into an account for Derek's college." He stops a moment, and nods to himself. Michelle sounds like a very special woman.

"On the day after I received the email from John, they sat down with Derek together and told him the truth about his biological father. He took two days to decide whether or not he wanted to meet me. Finally, he decided that he had to know who I am.

"Before they left, I apologized to Michelle, and I tried to explain to her, and to all of them, why I behaved the way I did. I was afraid to say anything because I don't want Derek to hate me for the way I treated his mother, but I felt that I had to clear things with her. Derek is a little older than I was then, and he said he thought he could understand. And Michelle said she forgave me. You can't imagine how important that was to me. After all these years."

I think Umar has been harder on himself than Michelle ever was. She named their son Derek Anthony. "So I guess you have plans to see him again?"

"Yes. First, we're going to tell the kids about him. He'll come over tomorrow evening to meet them. Michelle and John said they'd bring their children, too. They have two boys and a girl. And John and I plan to take Derek and all of our kids to a Cubs game soon."

"That's great."

"I hope we can have some one-on-one time later—just Derek and me—but Michelle and John seem to be uncomfortable with that for now. I think I can understand how they feel. They don't need to worry, though. They've been raising him and teaching him all these years. I'm still an outsider. I probably always will be."

"Do you think the rest of us will get to meet him?"

"I told him about his grandmother, aunt, uncles, and cousins. I even told him a little about Dad. He wants to meet all of you, especially Mom. I've already invited them for our July barbecue. You can meet him then, insha Allah. And you're going to love him. He really is a great kid."

Umar is still smiling broadly. He walks into the house and calls out, "Where are Baba's girls? Where is Ahmad? You'd better watch out. I'm coming to get you." Raheema saunters out, too old for the game. The other kids hide, except for Tasneema. She runs into his arms. "Baba, you're here!"

Umar lifts her up into the air and laughs out loud. His biggest laugh ever.

∞

A few days later, we see the new moon and begin the fast of Ramadan. So much has happened since last Ramadan.

I've been looking forward to Ramadan this year. When I first became a Muslim, the fasting was difficult, and I approached each Ramadan with the fear that I wouldn't be able to do it. In the last few years, I have been feeling more comfortable. This year, I'm excited. Being in prison was an experience I wouldn't wish on my worst enemy, not even Sam, but while I was in prison my faith became stronger. In prison, my faith was all I had.

Jamal is worried about fasting this year. On the first morning of Ramadan, I wake Aisha, Muhammad, and Jamal so they can eat suhur, the early morning meal. Then we pray. After the prayer, Jamal comes and sits next to me.

I had planned to read some Qur'an, but I can tell he needs to talk. I put the Qur'an back in its place.

"What is it, Jamal?"

"Do I have to fast the whole Ramadan this year?"

"You're eleven now. Practically a man. I think you're ready."

"But what if I get hungry during the day?"

"You'll be okay. You've fasted whole days before. Last Ramadan you fasted at least fifteen whole days, didn't you?"

"Seventeen. But when I got hungry, I could break my fast and eat lunch. What if I get really hungry again, like I did last year?"

"Then you can read Qur'an, or go play outside. Do something to get your mind off of food."

"But everyone else will be eating. Muhammad will probably just fast half a day. And Luqman will be eating all day long. Maryam's just a baby, but what about Muhammad and Luqman?"

"I'll remind your brothers not to eat in front of you. Will that help?"

"I guess, but what if I just can't take it any more. What if I have to eat? Or what if I get really, really thirsty?"

"Then you come to me. We'll be fasting together. I'll help you get through it."

"Okay," he finally agrees. "That might work."

Jamal makes it through his first day with only one moment of temptation, in the late afternoon when Muhammad decides to break his fast. He comes and tells me he's having a hard time, so we sit and read Qur'an together. We're still reading when Aisha calls out, "Ten more minutes to break fast."

"Already?" says Jamal. "That wasn't so bad."

"I knew you could do it."

We sit together as a family, and Aisha, Jamal, and I break our fast with water and dates. Muhammad and Luqman sit with us, and Maryam crawls around. Sharon sits with us too. She's still not a Muslim—and she says she doesn't intend to become one—but she respects the fast. If she does eat during the day, I never would know it.

Jennifer is out with some friends. Girls she met while working on the yearbook. She said that she won't fast, and I did see her eating once today, but she does it quietly. She's especially sensitive to Jamal and Muhammad because they are young and she knows they're trying to fast.

Muhammad and Luqman start to argue over a cookie, but when the time comes to break the fast I don't pay attention to anything else. I sip the water, and I pray for Abdul-Qadir and for Ahmed's children and for all of the oppressed Muslims of the world.

A few minutes later, we go to pray. Then I read the Qur'an again.

I've been reading for about twenty minutes when there's a knock on the door. Umar and Safa are here with their gang. Safa brought dinner. She's always a wonderful cook, and she's made a special biriyani for the first day of Ramadan. Everything looks and smells so good. I don't eat much, though. After a full day of fasting, I'm not really that hungry.

After dinner, we break into our groups. Umar and I go into the family room. Sharon, Aisha, and Safa stay in the kitchen. The kids take over the rest of the house.

I don't know if Umar fasted today. He's only been out of the hospital for a few weeks, and he needs to take the medication. Both Sharon and his doctor worry about a relapse.

"So how was your first day?" he says.

"It was good. Everything is more meaningful now, this year. How about you? Did you fast?"

"I fasted. I took the medication right after breaking my fast. That has to be good enough. This year was so rough. I need Ramadan more than ever."

"What did the doctor say?"

Rebounding

"I didn't talk with him about it. I will be going back in a couple of days, but he can't understand how important this is to me. I think fasting will help me far more than the medication will."

"Probably, but you have to be careful. Maybe you don't realize how bad it was, before Safa took you to the hospital."

"I know, believe me. I lived it. But I also know how I'll feel if I don't fast. I don't want to feel like a child, not ready to fast yet. I have fasted every day of every Ramadan since I made Shahadah. I won't give that up."

"But you know, Brother, that Allah allows exceptions for those with special needs."

"Special needs. Is that what I am now? Did my breakdown turn me into some kind of invalid?"

"No, but you were very sick. You might not be ready yet. It hasn't been that long."

"I have to fast. And I will continue to take my medication. Just a reduced dosage."

"Talk to your doctor. Can you promise me that?"

"But he won't understand. He's not a Muslim. He has never experienced Ramadan. He can't possibly know what fasting means to me."

"If you don't talk to him, then I'll have to go to Sharon. I'm worried about you, Brother."

He shakes his head. "You're tough. I suppose that's what I should expect from an ex-con." He smiles. "All right, I'll talk to him. Don't say anything to Mom. I don't want her to worry."

"Then take care of yourself, so she won't have anything to worry about."

He brings his family to our house again a few days later. Sharon makes fried chicken and her special mashed potatoes. I make the salad. We enjoy our dinner, then separate into our groups.

Umar and I sit in the family room with our tea. "What did the doctor say?"

"He told me I shouldn't cut down on my dosage like that. It's too much of a risk. That's what I thought he would say."

"So what are you going to do?"

"I argued with him, but he told me that he has researched the relationship between spirituality and mental health. He said he understands, on a theoretical level, why I insist on fasting every day, and he conceded that the spiritual benefits may be so great as to reduce my need for the medication, but he also pointed out that my breakdown was very recent. He doesn't think I should take that kind of risk at this time."

"I agree."

"I started thinking about the risk. The fact is that I don't know. I feel that fasting would be of great benefit to me, but I know enough about psychology and brain chemistry to understand the benefits of the medication. I don't want to go through that again—the despair I felt in the weeks leading up to my breakdown, the anger and hopelessness gripping me that night. And I don't want to put Mom and Safa through that again. I'm not sure my marriage could survive another episode like that.

"The doctor also reminded me that the conditions leading to my breakdown are still present. The charges against us still stand, and I will face extra stress as the date for the hearing approaches. I still can't work. The center is still gone. And my relationship with Derek is new and uncertain.

"I asked about switching medications to something I could take only once a day, but he didn't agree. I'm responding well to what I'm on now, and he doesn't think I should start experimenting with drugs." He laughs, and shakes his head. It takes me a minute. Umar just told a joke. Amazing. "Anyway, I asked him to tell me more about the chemical part of the equation. We talked about dosages and brain chemistry, and eventually we reached an agreement. I'll fast for two days, with a lower dosage, then take my full dose on the third day. It's not ideal, but he said it was the most he could allow. Oh, by the way," he raises his shirt, "you're not the only one who is wired."

He has a device attached to his chest. "What's that?"

"They use it to measure a patient's emotional well-being. Heart rate, perspiration, that kind of thing. They say it can indicate depression, anxiety, all kinds of emotions. In the past, it was used only when a patient was hospitalized. Over the last couple of years, they've started using it for outpatients, too. I have to wear it to give the doctor more feedback. If I pass, he may let me fast more."

"Machines to monitor emotions. Sounds crazy, but I hope it works for you. I may be an ex-con, but I'm not that tough."

He laughs again and pats my shoulder. "So they couldn't take away your humanity, could they? I'm glad to hear it."

I don't know what helps him the most. The fasting, the medication, the therapy, or seeing Derek, but it's good to hear him laugh.

∽

I barely sleep the night before the hearing. Aisha and I stay up late, discussing the possibilities. If the charges aren't dropped, we'll have to go on the way we are now until the trial. That could be another year or two. It wouldn't be easy, but at least we'd be together. As long as I didn't do anything to make them revoke my bail.

On the morning of the hearing, I wake up for suhur, then pray and read Qur'an until it's time to go to the courthouse. We meet Umar and Safa there. Sharon came with us. Mom is here too. Jennifer is taking care of our kids and Raheema is watching her little sisters and Ahmad.

Mom smiles. "Don't worry, Joshua. I think Walt will get through to that judge this time."

I wish I had her optimism.

The hearing itself is simple. I had imagined Thompson standing there, in front of a panel of men in robes, pacing up and down in his best effort to convince the justices of the grave injustice of charging two innocent men, but there are no fancy speeches. There is no panel, just the same judge we saw earlier. Thompson presents his argument, listing the reasons why the charges should be dismissed. The key to his argument, of course, is the evidence he found in Pakistan.

The judge states that he has read the depositions from Pakistan and the motion to dismiss the charges. He recognizes the link between Ahmed's activities and the charges against us. He tells Umar and me to rise. And he states, quietly and simply, that the case is dismissed.

Before we are dismissed, though, he tells us that our freedom is conditional. Neither of us will be allowed to travel to another country for the next two years. In addition, he says, neither of us will be allowed to oversee the funding of a nonprofit agency for the next five years. We will have access to the money in our personal accounts after the paperwork clears, sometime in the next few weeks. The funds belonging to the center will remain frozen indefinitely. All of the items they seized in the raid on our office, from the computers to the pencil sharpeners, will also remain in government possession. He pounds the gavel. We are free men.

Each of us shakes hands with Thompson, and we hug. Our wives come to the table to share the moment with us. Aisha laughs and hugs me tightly. I glance over to see Umar and Safa kissing. That is so unlike them. This time, though, the moment is too big. I forget about them and kiss my own wife.

Mom comes up and slips her arm around Thompson's waist. Now I'm sure there's something going on between them. "I know that you are all fasting," she says. "But I've made reservations for dinner tonight. It's time to celebrate."

"But how did you know the charges would be dismissed?"

"I know that Walt is the best there is." The way she says it, I'm not sure if she's talking about his legal skills or something else.

Before we leave, they remove the ankle bracelet. I'm finally free. The center is still gone, and we still have to rebuild our lives, but I'm free.

When we get home, I say prayers of thanks. As I sit down to read the Qur'an, I feel lighter. The burden is gone. The nightmare is over.

We break fast and pray, then go to meet Mom and Walt at the restaurant. Brad, Beth, Chris, and Melinda are here already.

Mom is laughing. She was laughing at the courthouse too. I have never seen her act like this before.

During dinner we talk quietly, still stunned and relieved that it's finally over.

We're eating our salads when Thompson says, "You know, Joshua, it isn't quite over. There is still the lawsuit over the civil rights abuses and negligence in connection with the fight and the prison's failure to provide you with prompt medical treatment."

"I almost forgot about that. I was just waiting to see if I would have to go back to prison."

"There's no way to forget about it, Hon," says Aisha. "Maybe you don't notice the scars any more, but I do. Besides, you still have some weakness in your left arm, and the hearing loss."

"I didn't know about your arm," says Thompson. "And I had hoped the hearing loss wouldn't be permanent. Often a ruptured eardrum will heal on its own. I'll send you back to the doctor soon for a full examination. These conditions need to be treated. And proof of ongoing injury could help the case."

"I don't know. I've had enough of courtrooms and judges. I keep thinking I should just let it go."

"Your rights were violated. Are you going to tell me that there were no guards in that cafeteria when Spider first attacked you? They were there. They simply watched while you got the stuffings beaten out of you. And if the guard who brought you your breakfast that morning didn't have some sense of right and wrong, you would be dead now. They locked you up in that cell and left you with serious injuries requiring immediate medical treatment. Fortunately, when that guard saw you lying there unconscious, he decided to call for help. At any rate, you must consider what this case will mean to other men who have to follow in your footsteps. You weren't the first, Joshua, and you won't be the last to be falsely arrested on charges of terrorism, but by pursuing this abuse case, you will be making a statement which will help the next man who is taken away."

"I guess you're right. Somebody has to take a stand."

"By the way, Walt," says Aisha, "what was all that business about restricting Joshua and Tony's rights to travel overseas and work with a nonprofit agency? The charges were dismissed. How can they be punished when they weren't even put on trial?"

"That's something new to me. We certainly didn't cover that back when I was in law school. I can tell you that it's been done to other men as well. I remember some cases, a few years ago, where men were held in prison for years without being charged. One man, Yaser Hamdi, had allegedly fought with the Taliban, but he was a U.S. citizen by birth. He was detained without formal charges and eventually deported without a trial. Another man, Jose Padilla, was arrested here in Chicago and held for years without being charged."

I'm getting uncomfortable. I prefer to forget about my five and a half months of hell. "Hey, remember, this is a celebration. Let's not get too serious here."

The conversation continues on a lighter note. We're almost finished with the main course when Thompson stands up and clears his throat.

"Now that Joshua and Tony are free, I have a couple of important announcements to make. First of all, as I told you earlier, Joshua, I have been thinking about retiring. This was a very good case to go out on. I plan to quit my practice and do some traveling. Going to Pakistan made me curious about what else there is to see out there."

"That's great," I say. "You've worked so hard. You deserve to take a break now."

"I'm not finished yet. You do have a hard time being patient, don't you, son?"

The only man who ever called me 'son' was my father-in-law, The Doc. What is going on?

"When I first took your case, I told you that I had been good friends with your mother for many years. During these last several months, we've had the opportunity to get to know each other in a different way. I have already asked Evie to marry me. Or do I need to get permission from your brothers and you?"

My mother. Getting married. I still can't picture it, but I know he's right for her. "I don't know about Brad and Chris, but it sounds good to me."

Rebounding

"I think it's a great idea," says Brad.

"Mom deserves to have someone who cares about her," says Chris. "I'm glad she's found you."

"Thank you. I promise you boys that I will do my best to make your mother happy. And Joshua, you have to stop calling me Mr. Thompson. I think Walt will be fine."

I look at Mom. I've never seen her look this happy. "What about your business?"

"Charlene wants to buy it from me. It's been fun, but I think I'm ready for a different adventure now."

As we leave the restaurant, I ask Walt, "Do you plan to come out of retirement to argue the civil rights lawsuit?"

"No. I'm primarily a criminal lawyer. Your case fell within the parameters of my practice, but there were times in the last several months when I felt I was in over my head. I have defended clients charged with burglary, arson, or murder, and I have argued some civil lawsuits, but I have never defended anyone against Homeland Security or taken on a federal prison. I wouldn't have even accepted a case like yours, but I couldn't say no to your mother. And I have received an education. At any rate, that kind of case needs someone more energetic. There is a bright young man who has been assisting me. He's familiar with all of the details and he's ready to take over the suit. Your mother and I have made all the arrangements. His name is Jared White. He's just opened his own practice. And he's a Muslim, so I think he can identify with what you've been going through. You should be hearing from him soon." He smiles and touches my arm. "Besides, it might look suspicious for me to represent my stepson."

Stepson. Almost a son. And I realize that over these last several months Thompson—Walt—has become almost a father to me.

They look good together. And I like it. Mom finally has someone special. And we finally have a father who cares about us.

All the way home, of course, Aisha reminds me that she knew it all along.

On Friday, I go to the masjid with Umar. Finally.

The imam gives a sermon about being patient. I guess I'll keep getting pounded over the head with it until I learn how to do it.

After the prayer, the imam stands up and welcomes me back. The brothers come all around me. They pat me on the back and hug me. I remember that Friday when I made the Shahadah. This is how I felt that day. Coming home.

On the day before Eid, the imam comes to visit. We talk a little. Then he hands me an envelope.

"What's this?"

"It's money from the zakat fund, to help you and your family at this difficult time."

I try to hand it back to him. "I'm sure there are other families who need it more."

He pats my hand. "Keep it, Isa. Use it for your children. Make sure they enjoy their Eid."

I protest, but he won't listen. Aisha and I were talking last night about not having money for Eid presents this year because our account hasn't been freed up yet. I know the imam didn't hear us, but Allah did.

At the Eid prayer, Umar tells me he also received an envelope. "I've been so focused on myself," he says, "that I forgot about the mercy of Allah and the love of our Muslim brothers."

After the prayer, we head over to the mall and let each kid pick out a present. Jamal gets a video game, Muhammad wants roller blades, and Luqman picks out a toy garage with figures, cars, and trucks. Aisha plans to choose Maryam's gift, but as we're walking down the aisle of the toy store, Maryam reaches out to a soft brown doll. Not quite eight months old, and she already knows what she wants. In the afternoon, Umar and his family come over for an Eid barbeque. Jeremy and Jennifer join us. Michael is visiting Marcus in Boston. Sharon made most of the meal this morning while we were at the prayer. And Umar takes his place by the grill.

In the evening, I take Jamal out for ice cream. He fasted the entire month.

As soon as our account is freed up, we plan to take a family vacation up through Wisconsin and Minnesota. Nothing spectacular. Just our own small celebration of freedom.

~

When Jamal and I get home, I call Abdul-Qadir. I've wanted to talk with him ever since I heard about Ahmed. I've thought about calling him many times since my release, but I couldn't pay for the long distance call. And I wanted to wait until it was all over. It's finally over. For me. Not for Abdul-Qadir.

He answers the phone this time. His kids are grown now. "Assalaamu alaikum. It's Isa. Eid Mubarak."

"Isa. Assalaamu alaikum. Eid Kareem. It's good to hear from you. How are you now?"

The last time I talked to him was a week or so before I saw Sam—not that long ago, but he sounds old.

"Alhamdulillah. They dismissed the charges. I'm out of prison. I'm doing well. My lawyer told me how much you helped him."

"I'm happy you're out. I worried about you."

"How was your Ramadan?"

"Ramadan is always good, but it was hard this year, without Ahmed. Alhamdulillah, we're managing."

"Abdul-Qadir, I don't know what to say."

"You don't have to say anything. We had Ahmed for a short while, and then he had to return to Allah. Everything is by the will of Allah." He says these words slowly, as if he's still trying to convince himself.

"Yes, that's right. We must all return to Allah. How is Hamza?"

"He's a good boy. He and his mother and baby sister live with us now. It's good to have him with me. He has just started school, and I take him to the masjid. He wanted to fast, but I told him he's too young. He is very much like his father."

"What about your other children?"

"Alhamdulillah, I have two more grandchildren. My youngest daughter will be married next month. And Ibrahim married last spring. He's gone to live up north, in Islamabad. They are all good."

"What about Nuruddin? How is he?"

"I worry about Nuruddin. He should be attending university now, but I want him to leave Karachi. I might send him to live with Ibrahim, but their house is small. It can be dangerous here, especially for our young men. Every day I ask Allah to spare him. I have buried one son. I don't want to bury two."

I know what I have to do. "Why don't you send him to America? I can take care of him here for you."

"Would you do that for me? I didn't want to ask."

"You can ask me for anything, Abdul-Qadir. Yes, I would like to have Nuruddin with me. Tell him to go to the American consulate and find out what he needs to do to get a visa. I'll contact some colleges here and see what I can do. Don't worry. I want to do something for you."

"Thank you, Isa. That would be everything."

We talk a while longer, about my children and my plans for getting back to work. Before we hangs up he says, "I enjoyed meeting your mother and her husband. They are very nice. Please tell them hello for me."

My mother and her husband? So they pretended to be married while they were in Pakistan. I need to pay more attention to what's going on.

Rebounding

Mom and Walt do get married one week later. They decided to wait until after Ramadan. That was Walt's idea. They have a simple ceremony at Mom's house. A judge, a friend of Walt's, performs the ceremony. I meet Walt's children. He has three daughters—Jean, Karen and Tiffany. I think they are about the same ages as the three of us. I guess it wouldn't be polite to ask. Among them they have seven children, mostly teenagers. They tell me that they first met Mom several months ago, soon after my arrest. They like her. And they're happy for their father.

Mom and Walt hired a photographer. He lines up several different shots of the new couple and their families. For one shot, he asks the three of us to stand over by Walt while his three daughters stand next to Mom. Brad remarks, "I'm starting to feel like the Brady Bunch."

During the reception I sit down and talk with Mom alone for a few minutes. "Are you sure about all of this?"

"It's too late now, isn't it? And yes, Joshua, I am. Walt is the kind of man I should have been looking for when I found Sam. We're good for each other. And he's everything that Sam wasn't. Most of all, he cares about me."

"Like Chris said, you deserve to have someone special."

"Yes I do, and I've finally found him. By the way, at our ages it would be cheaper to just live together. We talked about it, but I knew Chris and you wouldn't approve. And you boys deserve to have a father. I know it's a little late. I wish I had grabbed Walt right after his divorce, but in those days I was still waiting for Sam."

"That's right. I called Abdul-Qadir the other day. He asked me to say hello to my mother and her husband. I guess you were living together in Pakistan?"

"We are adults. And even though you're religious now, I would expect you, of all people, to understand."

"I do, in a way, but Islam has changed the way I think about things. And I have teenagers now. I need to be much more careful in how I think and feel about everything."

225

"I wish you had been that way when *you* were a teenager. It would have saved me a lot of headaches."

"I know. I put you through a lot. Um, Mom, did you ever date while we were growing up? Aisha asked me about that once. I don't ever remember you seeing anyone."

"No. In those days, I wanted to concentrate on you boys. And I was still too hurt by Sam. I wasted many years waiting for him to come back to us. I didn't realize that I was waiting for the wrong man. But I've found the right man now."

"I'm happy for you. I really am."

Walt comes over. "I've been looking for you, Evie. It's almost time to go."

"That's right. I need to get my things."

Mom walks off, and Walt follows her. Then he turns around. "You're going to be okay now, son."

"Yes, I think I am."

My brothers and I help Mom load her suitcases into the limo, and they're gone. They plan to spend their honeymoon cruising the Mediterranean.

Part Eleven

Umar and I are still getting our lives back on track. He applied to some places as a counselor, but everyone knows about the arrest. He points out that the charges have been dismissed, but even an accusation of terrorism makes some people nervous. And some places ask about his mental health history. Those echoes keep rebounding.

I don't know what I should do. Aisha typed up my resume but it's very short. The only two places I've worked in the last thirteen years are Karachi Kitchen and The Caring Center. And everyone knows I spent time in the federal prison. I send the resume to a few nonprofit agencies and a couple of restaurants. I don't know what will turn up.

～

We've been free for three weeks when it's time for the annual barbecue. It will be at Umar's house this year. We both have reasons to celebrate. We have our freedom. And we have more children to love. I have Maryam and Umar has Derek.

We talked about that last week. I told him, "This barbecue will be a celebration, because of Derek."

He shook his head. "I'm not sure I have the right to celebrate. I still have very mixed emotions over this whole situation. I have felt guilty for the last twenty-one years, and I still feel guilty for the things I did wrong. I regret not being a father to Derek when he was young. I also feel incredibly relieved that he's alive. And I love him, more than I could ever have imagined. Sometimes I think that I don't have the right to feel good about this. I should have been married to his mother. I should have taken care of them. At the very least, I should have told Safa about my past before she married me. I was afraid she wouldn't marry me, though, so I stayed quiet. I am very grateful that even though I did everything wrong, it still has turned out right. I don't deserve it." He shook his head again. "No, I don't think I have the right to celebrate."

"Allah knows what you deserve, Brother."

"Believe me, I never forget that."

On the morning of the barbecue, I fix the potato salad and cole slaw, and haul them, along with the three boys, into my car. Aisha, Sharon, and Jennifer went earlier to help Safa get things ready. They took Maryam with them.

As we pull up, I see a tall man walking into the house. The same man I saw in the hospital. John Williams. The woman with him must be Michelle. My first thought is that she looks like Umar's type. But that was in a past life. Umar told me that she's a high school guidance counselor now.

Jamal and Muhammad help me carry the food into the kitchen. Luqman runs ahead of us, looking for his cousins. Jeremy is already here, in the kitchen. As I walk in, he and Raheema are heading out, carrying pies. It's nice that he is so helpful.

After we get inside and put the food where it belongs, Umar introduces me to John and Derek. "Derek, this is my brother, Isa. And Isa, this is Derek." We shake hands. He does look a lot like Umar.

"I'm glad to finally meet you, Derek."

"Somehow, I don't think you're really Tony's brother." He smiles. He smiles like Umar.

"No, I'm his brother-in-law and his brother in faith, but that's good enough."

"So you are a Muslim, like Tony?"

"Yes. Are you surprised that a white guy could be a Muslim?"

Derek grins, and raises his eyebrows. "I was surprised when Mom and Dad told me that Tony is my father. After that, everything else is just interesting."

Michael and Marcus walk in. Marcus always comes back to Chicago for the annual July barbecue. After we greet them, I introduce the boys.

"Hey Derek," says Michael. "Are you any good at soccer?"

"I sure am. I played center on my team in high school."

"Let's go then."

Umar, John, and I follow the boys out. As Derek heads over to the makeshift soccer field with the other boys, I notice that he even walks like Umar.

Umar takes his place by the grill. John and I stand on the patio, watching the boys play. "Derek is good."

"It's good to see him out there again. He was so sick. I know Tony feels bad about not being around to raise Derek, but thank God he was there when we needed him."

It's a good day. Everyone is here. Except Mom and Walt. They're still on their honeymoon.

After lunch, I get out on the field with the rest of the old guys. Umar, Mahmoud, Ismail, Tariq, Brad, Chris, Peter, and John. Even Fawad joins in. As I run down the field, pushing the ball past Brad's defenses, I know that I am finally back.

∾

I get a job at one of the restaurants. The owner calls a few days after the barbecue. He hires me on the spot.

Tandooris is an Indian Muslim restaurant. I've known the owner, Parvez Khan, for several years. I'm the assistant manager again. I went in earlier today for my orientation. I miss Fawad, but he's satisfied with Adel, and it will be good to learn something from a new place.

Aisha is getting ready for the new school year. She hasn't taught since she was pregnant with Muhammad, nearly eight years ago, but she's excited to be going back. The school has an on-site day care for the teachers' children, so she'll be close to Maryam. Luqman will be in the pre-kindergarten class. Muhammad will be in second grade this year and Jamal is going into sixth grade. In another year, I think Jamal will be taller than Aisha.

Now that our personal account has been freed up and I'll be bringing home a salary, I can start supporting my family again. I've been trying to think of a way I can show my appreciation to my brothers. I start by offering them free meals at Tandooris, but it's not enough. I'll probably never be able to repay them.

A few days after Parvez hires me, Umar gets a job working with the homeless. He will be helping people who have been down on their luck get back on their feet. He tells me, "I think I know a little more about that now."

We're finally getting back to normal. We will always carry the emotional scars, and I have a few physical scars from the fight—including some mild but permanent nerve damage to my left arm and some hearing loss—but we're making it. I'm even getting used to the noise again.

Sometimes I still wonder who the informant was. I can't think of anyone who would have done that to us, except Sam. I wonder if I'll ever know for sure.

I wonder if I'll ever see him again. Or if I'll ever want to see him.

Evie's Interlude: Explorations

Our honeymoon has been wonderful. Walt is the perfect husband. I can't believe it took me so many years to fall in love with him. I always knew he was a good man; when he stepped in and took over Joshua's case, I saw just how good he is. And he refused to let me pay him for his services. A week after Joshua's arrest, I knew Walt was the man I had always hoped to find. And he had been right under my nose all those years.

After the wedding, we flew to Paris. We toured the Louvre, marveled at the Eiffel Tower, and ate romantic meals at small sidewalk cafes before taking a train down to Barcelona. There we boarded a cruise ship that took us to such beautiful places as Rome, Athens, Istanbul, and Alexandria. We returned to Spain yesterday afternoon.

With each new city, I realize how small my world has been. For so many years, while the boys were young, I simply went to work, returned home, and relaxed in front of the television. Even after the cancer, when I cancelled my cable service and started spending time on my deck, I was still wrapped up in my own little world. When Walt and I went to Pakistan, I had little inclination to enjoy the sights because I was so worried about Joshua, but for these last three months I have finally taken the time to learn and explore, with the man I love at my side.

I have enjoyed the art galleries and the cathedrals, the architecture and the history, but I have also found pleasure in simple things. Watching the children, the mothers and the fathers, as they live out their daily lives. Seeing the mountains. Looking out over the sea.

The two cities I remember most are Rome and Istanbul. Both very powerful, and so very different. Neither of us is religious, but we both savored the experience of standing in the Sistine Chapel, gazing at the beauty of it. We even stood with the crowds in St. Peter's Square and saw the pope. In Istanbul, we went to the Blue Mosque and soaked up the culture of a city that lies on two continents. The bridge between east and west.

In Rome, I looked at the art and the crosses, and I thought of Chris. In Istanbul, I peered up at the minarets, and I thought of Joshua.

I don't follow any religion. My heart does not beat faster when I view a cathedral or a mosque. They are interesting, nothing more. Sometimes I wonder what I am missing.

Joshua

Part Twelve

Six months ago, I came home. And life is good again.

Good, but not perfect. Last month, a couple of men in black suits walked into Tandooris. My heart pounded as they walked toward me. I recognized the voice of the taller one. I can still picture him looking through the file cabinet in my office.

"Hello, Adams. How are things?"

I tried to stay calm. "Everything's fine. What do you want?"

"Your lawyer got you off, but we're watching you."

"I'll remember that."

"Good. Have a nice day." They walked out. I sat down and breathed deeply while customers waited.

I told Aisha about their visit as soon as I got home.

"They can't do that. You need to report them."

"Who am I supposed to report them to? The police? They're law enforcement. I'm sure the police can't touch them."

"It's not right. Something should be done."

"I'll tell Walt about it. And I'll be careful. That's all I can do."

Aisha shakes her head. "This used to be a free country."

~

Fawad concentrates mainly on the food, but Parvez cares almost as much about the atmosphere. Plush booths. Controlled lighting. Indian classical music playing in the background. I'm learning ways to make the customers more comfortable. Little things most people don't notice.

At first, I worked the morning shift. Now we alternate. I work three evenings a week so Parvez can be home with his family. I still work mornings on the other days. And, of course, Tandooris is closed on Mondays. I always cook dinner at home on Mondays to give Aisha an easier start to her work week.

She loves being back in the classroom. She spends a few hours every weekend making sure her lesson plans are in order, and sometimes she has to grade papers in the evenings. She gets tired, but she's happy. And she's still close to all of our kids.

Umar and Derek are getting to know one another. Derek stops by sometimes after his classes. Safa makes her special curries when he comes. And the kids do accept him as their big brother.

When I heard Umar laughing again it sounded strange, but it also sounded familiar. He sounds like The Doc.

I miss Michael. He calls every couple of weeks. A few days before he left town, I took him out for dinner. We had Chinese food. And we talked.

"So you're going to be on your own now. Are you ready?"

"Sure. I don't think it's going to be a big deal. I've been pretty much taking care of myself for the last couple of years now."

"You have been pretty much taking care of yourself your whole life. Your mom and I always depended on you to take care of things. We probably put too much pressure on you sometimes, but you seem to have turned out okay."

"Yeah, I think so."

"Anyway, even though you know how to take care of yourself, it will be different when you're on your own."

"I won't be completely on my own. I'll have Marcus with me."

"Yes, but that's not what I wanted to talk to you about."

"What is it, Dad?"

"Okay. What about girls? You didn't have any girlfriends in high school—none that I knew of—but you must be thinking about it."

"So that's what this is about." He laughed. "Are you going to tell me about the facts of life?"

"No, I think you're probably way ahead of me on that, but I want to talk to you about life. And how you have to be careful."

"So I won't make the same mistakes you made?"

"Me, or Umar, or any number of young men. It isn't always easy, Michael. And sometimes something will seem like a good idea but it isn't."

Rebounding

"Don't worry. By the way, I have had a couple of girlfriends, but nothing serious. I don't want anything, or anyone, to distract me."

"I'm glad you feel that way, but there are temptations, you know."

"I know. Believe me, I notice girls. And I think about things sometimes, you know, but when I get tempted I think about you."

"And how I would yell at you if you did something wrong?"

"No. How you made the wrong choices. I guess you didn't know any better, and you've done a good job of trying to fix things, but I know what you went through. And what Mom went through. I went through it too. I don't want to go through that again, and I would never put anyone else through it. The fighting. I still remember the yelling and screaming. I still remember the day you left us. I remember it all. The custody battle. Mom bringing her boyfriends to the apartment. Trying to get to know you again, after you married Aisha. Do you remember that first time Mom brought us to see you in that apartment you used to live in?"

"I remember. You didn't want to stay with me."

"I was afraid of you. Partly because I remembered the yelling, and partly because of the beard. I knew you were my dad, but at the same time I wasn't quite sure because you were so different than the dad I remembered. It took me a long time to stop being afraid of you."

"I didn't know that. What made you stop being afraid?"

"You came to my games. You were there, with those balloons. And then we'd go out to eat. I was mad at you when you stopped coming because I thought you stopped loving me again. But then you called and told me about Aisha's father. You came to my last game. We went out to eat again. And after that you never left me."

"I never stopped loving you, Michael, even when I was away. The first time I went to Pakistan, I met a little boy who reminded me of you. He's Abdul-Qadir's youngest son. Nuruddin. I'm trying to bring him to the U.S. for college. Anyway, even when I

239

was all the way over in Pakistan, I never stopped thinking about you. And I have always loved you."

"I know that now. The thing is, when I get married, I'm going to marry someone I love. My children will never have to wonder where I am or if I love them. So don't worry about me. I'll be careful. And I'm sure I won't be ready to get serious about anyone for a long time yet."

We finished our rice and shrimp, and opened our fortune cookies. I don't remember what the fortunes said. It didn't matter. I knew Michael would be okay. I'm just sorry he had to learn it all the hard way, when he was a confused and frightened little boy.

He likes it up in New England. He and Marcus have already traveled down to New York City and up to Maine. I call him on a Sunday afternoon. He tells me about his most recent adventures. I tell him to concentrate on his studies.

"Of course, Dad," he says.

When I hang up, I think of Sam. I had wanted him to be a phone call away. Or closer. When I was younger, I fantasized about asking my father to help me with my problems. He would tell me how to improve my grades, how to get along with people, how to be happy with myself.

At least I can be there for my kids.

∽

I'm working on bringing Nuruddin over, but it will be harder than I thought. Especially with the link between Ahmed and me. When I told Walt about the men who came to the restaurant, he advised me to find someone else to sponsor Nuruddin. Someone who hasn't been labeled a terrorist. Brad agreed to do it.

After my release, Jennifer decided to keep living here with us. She goes to see Heather at least once a week, but she says she likes being here with the kids. I know I love having her here. I haven't seen any more boys around, but she has won three awards for her writing.

I talked with her the other day about Islam, and I asked if she was interested in becoming a Muslim.

"Not now, Dad. I think it's nice, the way you all pray and fast together, but it's not for me."

"Are you worried about wearing a scarf?"

"Not just that, though I do like fixing up my hair. And I kind of like getting looked at when I walk down the hall at school."

"I hope all they're doing is looking."

She laughed. "That's all. Don't worry. I think Islam is kind of nice, but it's not for me. Not now, anyway."

"Okay, fair enough. You will let me know, though, won't you?"

"As long as you promise not to go all crazy on me. I mean, you'd probably start jumping up and down, stuff like that."

"No jumping?"

"No jumping."

"Okay, I promise."

She has two more years of high school, then she wants to go away to college. I think I would miss her too much. We'll see.

Jeremy still lives with Heather and Peter. He comes over once or twice a week. He came for dinner tonight, which was strange because he usually waits until the weekend.

We finish eating and go to the family room to pray together. After the prayer, Jamal and Muhammad go to do their homework, and Aisha gets Luqman and Maryam ready for bed. Jeremy turns to me and says, "Dad, we need to talk."

I don't like the sound of that. I take a deep breath and brace myself. "Okay, Jeremy. What is it?"

"You know that I'm in my senior year. Pretty soon I'll be on my own, like Michael. And I think I'm ready. I'm an adult now."

"Yes, Jeremy, I'm very proud of you. You're responsible and mature, just like Michael. Have you decided where you want to apply?"

"Yes, but that's not what I wanted to talk to you about. The thing is, I'm a man now. And I'm ready for the responsibilities of a man."

I don't think this is about college. "What's going on?"

"I might as well just go ahead and say it. I want to get married."

Married? Jeremy? "But you're so young."

"You got married when you were eighteen."

"And I got divorced when I was twenty-three. I wasn't ready for marriage yet. And I don't see how you could possibly be ready, either."

"But your life was different. You weren't a Muslim. You were into all that other stuff. And you didn't really love Mom, did you?"

"No, not the way I love Aisha. I was too young to know what love is."

"Look, Dad, I don't fool around with girls the way you did, but, like I said, I'm a man. And I'm ready. Do you know what I mean?"

I think I do know, but he's just a little boy. He can't be a man yet. It's too soon. I'm not ready. "What about your education? How will you support a family?"

"We already have it all figured out."

"We? So you have someone in mind then. Do her parents know?"

"Not yet. I wanted to talk to you first."

"Who is she? Someone you met in school? Is she a Muslim?"

"Not in school. It's Raheema."

Who? "Raheema, your cousin?"

"She's not my cousin. Umar's not really her father and Aisha's not really my mother. I guess you could say we're cousins by marriage, but we're not really even related."

I close my eyes and rub my forehead. I didn't expect this. "What about Raheema? Have you two actually talked about marriage?"

"We've been talking about it for the last year or so. Actually, I decided I wanted to marry her when I was fifteen."

"I never noticed anything going on between the two of you."

"That's because you always thought of us as cousins."

I guess he's right. I start to remember all the times I've seen them together. "You said you have it figured out. How are you going to manage it?"

"Okay, Raheema and I both graduate this year. I already have a job, and she can get a job too. Raheema could probably get a scholarship from any college, but she wants to stay in Chicago. She's going to apply to Northeastern and the University of Chicago. In case she doesn't get in, there's always community college. My grades are okay, but I'm not Michael. And my language scores are good, but my math scores suck. Community college is good enough for me. That's what Mom and you both did."

"But we didn't have any other choices. We were restricted because we had gotten married so young."

"But it's not going to be like that for Raheema and me. I've known her practically all my life. I haven't even kissed her yet, though I might have by now if we weren't afraid of Uncle Umar. And I have my life together. I'm ready, Dad."

I guess he probably is ready—a lot more ready than I was—but he's so young. And Raheema. I never imagined it.

They've already been talking about marriage. And they're young. So far he's tried hard to follow Islam, but he's a young man. I know how it is.

"Okay, let's talk with Umar. You'll have to go to him anyway."

"You'll come with me, right?"

I laugh. "You really are afraid of him, aren't you?"

"I was when I was younger. I used to hide from him. Now I'm only afraid of what he'll say when I tell him I want to marry his stepdaughter."

"Okay. Let's find out."

I go into the bedroom to get into some warmer clothes. Aisha sits on the bed, grading papers.

"Where are you going?"

"To see Umar."

"Oh, okay." Nothing unusual about that.

"Um, Aisha, have you ever noticed anything about the kids? Anything unusual?"

"No. Everything's okay, isn't it?"

"Sure, but. . ."

"What is it, Isa?"

"Okay, I was talking with Jeremy just now. And he told me he wants to get married. To Raheema."

She looks up from her papers and stares into space. "Now that I think of it, those two do seem to be together a lot, but it's always at family gatherings and I never thought much about it. I mean, they're practically like brother and sister."

"But they're not. They're not even cousins."

"No, I guess they're not. Jeremy is a good boy. I think he'd make a good husband for Raheema. Yes, now that I think about it, I can see it."

"But they're so young."

"They are. Very young."

"Anyway, Jeremy insists that he's ready. We're going to talk with Umar. What do you think your brother will say?"

"I know you remember what Dad put you through to marry me. I think Umar will be tougher than Dad was."

"Well, if Jeremy can get through that then I guess he'll prove he's ready to get married."

"I guess so. And tell Jeremy I said good luck. I think they'd make a nice couple."

"If you don't mind, I'll tell him later. I'm not sure I want to encourage him."

"Whatever you say."

On the way to Umar's house, we talk some more. Apparently he and Raheema have been planning this for some time. It sounds like he knows her well. It also sounds like he really cares for her.

Raheema answers the door.

"Assalaamu alaikum, Raheema. Is Umar home?"

"Walaikum assalaam. Yes he is, Uncle Isa. Come in, please." I see Jeremy and Raheema exchange glances. She smiles. I never noticed it before.

Rebounding

Safa and Umar are cuddled on the couch, reading to Ahmad and Tasneema.

"Assalaamu alaikum."

"Walaikum assalaam." Umar stands up and shakes my hand. "How are you, Brother?"

"Come in and sit down, please," says Safa. "Can I get you something, Isa? I just made some sweets."

"And I helped," says Raheema.

"No, thank you, not now. Go ahead, Jeremy."

"Uncle Umar, my dad and I would like to talk to you. Alone, please."

Umar puts the book down and looks at us. He can usually read my face. "Okay. Ahmad and Tasneema, Baba needs to talk with Jeremy and Uncle Isa. I think you two need to get ready for bed. Safa, could you help them please? Raheema, go make sure Sakeena and Sabeera get their homework done. Jeremy, Isa, sit down."

We sit. I haven't felt this awkward around Umar since Aisha and I got engaged. Umar stares at Jeremy. My son looks at me, pleading.

"Go ahead, Jeremy. You're a man now."

He looks down as he talks. "Uncle Umar, I've known you since I was little. And I have always looked up to you. I still look up to you. I admire a lot of things you've done in your life."

The kid knows how to flatter.

He looks at Umar. "One of the things I admire is how you've taken care of Raheema." He starts to sound more confident. "I remember when she first came into our family. We used to play together. When I got older, I understood how her real father died when she was little, and you treated her like your own daughter. I think that's really great."

He's really laying it on, but I know he's sincere.

"So, the thing is, I've known Raheema for a long time. And as we got older we started talking more, getting to know more about each other. And I think she's really great, too. She's smart and polite, and she's a good Muslimah. I've been noticing that for a long time now, how good she is."

245

I can't read Umar's face. He doesn't smile, but he doesn't frown either. He just sits quietly and listens, occasionally nodding.

"For the last year or two, Raheema and I have been talking more seriously. I told her I have some feelings for her. She said she has some feelings for me, too. And, Uncle Umar, we would like to get married. May I please marry Raheema? I promise that I'll love her and take care of her."

Umar doesn't say anything at first. He strokes his beard. Next he closes his eyes, just like Dad did. When he opens his eyes, he looks straight at Jeremy. Then he goes on the offensive. I knew he would.

"Are you ready to get married? You're still in high school. What about your college?"

"We don't have to get married until we graduate. It's just a few more months. And Raheema is trying to get a scholarship for college. If she doesn't, we'll both go to community college for now. I already have a job, and after I graduate I can ask for more hours. And maybe Raheema can get a job, too. We have it all planned out."

"Raheema and you have already talked about marriage?"

"Yes sir. Just when we see each other. . .at family gatherings, things like that. We've been talking about it for a while now. And I knew a long time ago that I wanted to marry her. She's so special."

"Yes, I know she is. Why didn't you come to me earlier?"

"I wanted to wait until I was closer to graduating. I know we can't get married until we finish high school, but I would like to marry her right after graduation."

"So you're going to work and go to school? Do you know how difficult that is?"

"I think so. I watched my dad do it. And my mom too. And they both made it."

Jeremy handles himself well. I'm impressed.

"There's something else that bothers me," says Umar. "You're only eighteen. How do you know you're ready to love Raheema? You're too young to know what love is."

"I know what you're thinking. My parents got married when my dad was eighteen, and it didn't work. And you were in love with Derek's mom when you were eighteen, and it didn't work. But this is different. For one thing, Raheema and I are Muslims. I think she's beautiful, but I haven't even held her hand yet. I want to, though. And I don't want to marry Raheema because of her looks, or her wealth, or her family background. I want to marry her for her spirit, and her heart, and her faith."

Umar sighs. For a moment he just sits there, stroking his beard. Jeremy sits confidently, waiting.

Finally Umar says, "I don't know. I will have to think about this. You are a smart boy. Smarter than either your father or I was at your age. I'll talk with Raheema, and of course I will have to talk with Safa. And I'll pray about it. I suggest that you pray about it, also."

"I already have, but I will pray some more, if it will help."

"Good. I'll let you know soon, and we will have to talk some more. I'm glad you came to your father and me—that shows maturity—but I can't make any promises yet."

"I understand, Uncle Umar." They shake hands. "Go ahead and think it over first."

Umar smiles. "Have some of Safa's sweets before you leave. She'll be disappointed if you don't."

"Sure. I can't disappoint my future mother-in-law."

Umar chuckles. Later, as we're leaving, he whispers, "Your kid sure has a lot more confidence than you did. He's smooth, too."

He sure is. All of my kids are better than I was, in every way. It's amazing.

On the way back to our house, I tell Jeremy what Aisha said. I guess I can encourage him. He sounds like he's more mature at eighteen than I was at twenty-three.

Before we go to sleep, Aisha says, "I can see it. I think they'll make a cute couple."

"I guess. I was just thinking about how old I'm getting. I have one son in college and another one who wants to get married. How did that happen?"

"You're not old, Hon. You're as young and handsome as you were the day I met you."

"I thought you believed in being honest."

☙

Safa calls Aisha at school the next day and invites the two of us over for dinner, along with Jeremy. Jennifer will have to take care of the kids again, but she never seems to mind. Jeremy comes to our house and drives over with us. He's good at handling the car in the snow. We got a few more inches late last night.

Raheema meets us at the door. The house smells great. Safa must have been cooking all day. Or was it all night? Is she upset, or did she make something special to celebrate? We'll find out.

"Assalaamu alaikum, Aunt Aisha, Uncle Isa. How are you this evening?"

"We're fine, Raheema. Thank you." Aisha beams at Raheema and hugs her. She loves this. She has always been a romantic.

I see it again—that little spark between Jeremy and Raheema. I can't believe I never noticed it before. It seems so obvious now.

Umar and Safa are waiting for us in the family room. I can't tell what they're thinking.

"Assalaamu alaikum. Thank you for inviting us," says Aisha.

"We do have something important to discuss, don't we?" says Safa.

"Let's sit down," says Umar.

We're going to talk before we eat. That's an encouraging sign. I find myself rooting for Jeremy.

"Jeremy, Umar tells me that you want to marry my daughter."

"Yes, Aunt Safa, I do. If it's okay with Uncle Umar and you, of course."

"I have already spoken with my daughter about this in private, but I'm going to ask her again. Raheema, do you want to marry Jeremy?"

Raheema looks down and says softly, "Yes, Mama, I do."

Safa turns back to Jeremy. "How long have you been a Muslim? I've forgotten."

"Since I was ten. I went to the masjid with my dad and Uncle Umar and made Shahadah one day after the Friday prayer."

"And do you practice Islam?"

"Yes. I pray regularly. And I've fasted every day of Ramadan since I was eleven. I'm taking Arabic classes at the masjid, too."

"Do you have a Muslim name?"

"No. I like Jeremy. My mother chose it because she liked the way it sounds, but a few years ago I learned that it means 'appointed by God.' My name reminds me that I always have a responsibility to live my life to please Allah."

Safa nods. "There's something else I've wondered about. Why don't you live with your father instead of your mother? Wouldn't it be easier for you to live in a Muslim home?"

Jeremy smiles. I know his answer. "I love both of my parents. Dad and I have a bond through Islam, but I want to stay connected with my mother, too. I try to teach Mom and Peter about Islam. And she needs me to be there. Michael is away at school and Jennifer lives with Dad. I don't want her to be alone."

I can tell Safa likes that answer, but she's not finished with him yet. "Why do you want to marry my daughter?"

"I love her," he blurts out. Raheema looks down and smiles. Umar and Safa both look a little stunned at his bluntness.

Jeremy continues, in a softer voice. "You know that we see each other at family gatherings. And we started talking to one another. She's very smart, and polite. I've never met another girl like her. When we talk, we understand one another. I've prayed about it, and everything seems to tell me that Raheema is the right person for me to marry."

"I see. And Raheema. Why do you want to marry Jeremy?"

"He's very smart. He always has new plans and new ideas. I know he will be a kind and loving husband. As Jeremy said, we understand one another. His faith is sincere. And I do care for him also."

"Umar, do you have more questions?"

"I am still very concerned about your age. You were right, Jeremy. When I was eighteen I was in love with someone, but then I got older and my ideas changed. And I found a more mature love. Will Raheema and you fall out of love? Do you even know what love is?"

"Uncle Umar, Aunt Safa, Aisha, Dad, I don't think you all realize how much you have taught me about love and life.

"I've seen Dad, the way he cares for Aisha. I've noticed the way he treats her. I saw Aisha and Aunt Safa when Dad and Uncle Umar were arrested. I watched them as they held on and patiently waited. I saw you, Aunt Safa, when Uncle Umar was struggling with depression. I saw how you accepted Derek into the family. I've seen Aisha and Dad have a few fights over the years. And I've seen them make up. Through it all, you have always stayed together. Raheema and I are not like my mom and dad were. We're more mature, and more ready to be together. The four of you, and Mom and Peter, have taught us how to love someone, through your example.

"Besides, Raheema and I will also be joined together in our faith. No matter how angry Dad and Aisha have been with one another, I have never seen them angry after the prayer. Raheema and I have love, and we have Islam. That's what will keep us together, insha Allah."

Right now, I am pretty proud of my kid.

Safa is smiling. She speaks softly. "I married Raheema's father soon after I graduated from high school. We were both very young, but we cared for one another. He was my cousin. I know that I would be married to him still, if Allah had not taken him away from me and given me someone else to love. I know that it's possible to love someone at eighteen. And as long as you promise to always care for my daughter, Jeremy, and treat her well, then I can accept your intention to marry her."

"Thank you, Aunt Safa. I promise I will always love her."

Umar strokes his beard. He doesn't smile. He looks at Jeremy straight in the eye again. He reminds me of Dad. "I am not Raheema's father, but I have taken care of her since she was a little girl. I love her as my daughter, and as her guardian I must

Rebounding

protect her and make sure that she is always safe and always treated well.

"I have known you also since you were a little boy. And I have been impressed with your strength of character. I was there when you made Shahadah, and I have never seen you deviate from your faith. Marriage can be difficult at times, but both of you know that. You are young, but you are old enough. So, Jeremy, you have my permission to marry Raheema." He stands up and offers his hand.

Jeremy shakes Umar's hand, and smiles. "Thank you, Uncle Umar. Thank you both." Then he hugs Umar. "I won't disappoint you. I promise."

"There is one more thing," says Umar. "Until Raheema and you are married, there will be no more private talks between you. Whatever you need to discuss with her, you can do it in our presence. Now that you have the intention to marry, the temptation will be even stronger. Do you understand what I'm saying?"

"Yes, I think I do."

"If you're not sure, you can ask your father. I did the same to him when he wanted to marry my sister. You have to be very certain that when you do marry, you start off on the right foot."

"Yes, I understand."

"Then," says Safa, "I think we should go eat."

It is a celebration.

As we walk into the dining room, Umar puts his arm around Jeremy's shoulders. "Remember, son, marriage is supposed to last for a lifetime."

"Yes, Uncle Umar, I'll remember that."

While we eat, Jeremy and Raheema smile shyly at one another across the table. They try not to be obvious, but I notice. Sakeena notices too. She giggles.

"What's so funny?" asks Tasneema.

"You're too young to understand," says Sakeena.

Safa brings out shandesh for dessert. The names means "good news," and it's served at special occasions. I guess they had already made up their minds, even before we came.

251

On the way home, Jeremy can't stop talking. I think I remember being that young and enthusiastic. He has so many plans for his future with Raheema.

When we pull up in front of the house, I ask him, "Have you talked with your mother about this yet?"

"No, not yet. I think she'll say that I'm too young. I wanted to get Uncle Umar's approval first. If I can convince him, I think I can convince anyone."

Somehow, Heather and I ended up with pretty smart kids.

"And don't worry. I'll talk to her tomorrow."

⁂

Heather calls the next evening. "Joshua, what are you thinking?" I remember that tone of voice. The last time I heard it, she slapped me in the face. "Jeremy just told me that he's getting married. And you approve. Are you out of your mind?"

"He's eighteen now. I've talked with him about it, and I think he's mature enough to make this commitment."

"I don't believe you. You are just going to stand by and let our son ruin his life?"

I have to stay calm so I can talk her down. "Heather, Jeremy knows what he's doing. He's a smart boy."

"You sure knew what you were doing when you were eighteen, didn't you?"

"Jeremy is not me. I was screwed up and strung out. Jeremy has his head together. He doesn't use drugs, he doesn't drink, and he's never even kissed a girl yet."

"Maybe he should. Let him drink a few beers and kiss a few girls first before he throws his life away. He needs to experience life."

"He's a Muslim. He knows better than to get drunk and fool around like I did."

"What are you teaching our son, anyway?"

"I'm teaching him Islam, and it's the most natural thing in the world. To wait until you find the one you really care for, get married and *then* be intimate. That's the way it's supposed to work. I wish I had known that when I was his age."

"You're not the only one." Her voice has lost its edge, but she'll never lose the sarcasm. "And how is he going to support her? He can't take care of a family on minimum wage. I know you couldn't do it, anyway."

"Jeremy is not me. He is much more mature than I was at that age. He'll keep working, she'll probably work, and I'll be there to help him if he needs it."

"But I don't know anything about this girl. I've seen her a few times, and she seems nice. A little mousy maybe. How do you know she's the right girl for him?"

She is right about that. She barely knows Raheema. "Listen, I think you should talk with her yourself. Why don't Peter and you come over for dinner on Saturday? I'll invite Raheema and her parents, and you can talk to them about it. Bring Brianna too. She can play with Umar's daughters."

"Okay, we'll be there. I need to be a part of this. Don't try to block me out of my son's life."

"No, I won't."

"And I think we'll just leave Brianna with a sitter. Those little boys of yours are too wild."

"Okay, Heather. Whatever. See you on Saturday."

∾

I cook Pakistani on Saturday. I know Peter likes it and, since she's married him, Heather has become a little more adventurous.

Mom and Walt are coming too. They're in town for now, in between trips to far off places. When I called Mom and told her about Jeremy, all she said was, "At least he didn't get her pregnant."

I laughed. Then, after I hung up, I thought about it. I really gave my mother a hard time.

Umar, Safa, and Raheema get here first, with all the kids. Jeremy came over earlier today to help me with the cooking—he's pretty good in the kitchen—but as soon as Raheema walks in he goes over to talk to her. Once in a while, as I'm finishing up the meal, I glance over at Umar. He sits between Jeremy and Raheema as they talk. This is all so familiar.

By the time Heather and Peter come, the food is ready. Heather says hello to Aisha, and I shake hands with Peter. Then she looks around. "So where's the girl?"

"They're in the family room."

She walks in, then stops short. "They want to get married, and you won't even let them sit next to each other? You Muslims are so weird."

Umar laughs. "Jeremy is not going to get close to my Raheema until he's married to her."

Heather looks at me. "Is that what you had to go through before you married Aisha? No wonder you were all over me in that car."

"Yeah, Heather, thanks for bringing that up."

Aisha rolls her eyes and shakes her head.

Peter raises his eyebrows. "What are you talking about?"

Heather whispers, "I'll tell you later."

Jeremy looks across Umar to Raheema and grins. "Welcome to my family."

Mom and Walt arrive just before we sit down to eat. Mom looks great. She's lost a little weight over these past few months, and she must be dyeing her hair because there are no more gray hairs among the brown. It seems like she even has fewer wrinkles. Maybe because she's always smiling.

Walt looks good too. It still feels strange seeing him in a polo shirt rather than a suit and tie. When they walk into the house, they're arm in arm. They act like newlyweds.

Mom hands Aisha a package. "I got this for you in Istanbul. I think you'll like it."

It's a blue scarf, hand embroidered. "Thank you, Evie. It's beautiful. That was so thoughtful."

"So where are you two headed next?" I ask.

"I plan to take your mother to London in about a month."

"You will be here for the wedding, won't you, Gramma? We're thinking about next May probably, or maybe June."

Rebounding

"Of course, Jeremy. I'll be there for you."

Heather sits next to Raheema during dinner. Peter talks to me most of the time, chatting about the weather and the economy and whatever else happens to pop into his head, so I can't listen in on their conversation. As they get ready to leave, Heather says, "She's a very nice girl. They are young, but I think it will work."

"I'm glad you agree. I never told you this, but I think you did a real good job raising them."

"Once you decided you wanted to be their dad, you weren't so bad yourself."

She leaves with Peter, and I put my arms around Aisha. Heather and I had some rough years together, but we both moved on to find real love, alhamdulillah.

All evening I watched Mom and Walt cuddling together, and Jeremy and Raheema making eyes at one another when they thought nobody was looking. I'm feeling kind of romantic, too. I hold Aisha close to me as we walk slowly up the stairs.

Part Thirteen

One full year, and I'm still tying up the loose ends of my life. Maryam is one year old today. One year ago tomorrow, I walked into my office and ended up in a different world.

I suddenly remember something I meant to do before they took me away. I mention it to Aisha during dinner.

"Do you remember the evening after Maryam was born? I sat with you in the hospital room, and we talked about her aqiqah. I planned to make the arrangements the next day."

"That's right, but you never had the chance. Let's do it now."

We had aqiqahs for all of our boys within the first twenty-one days after their births, but poor little Maryam missed out. Aisha talks to the school secretary the next morning and reserves the gym. A few days later, she goes out and buys Maryam a beautiful frilly pink dress and a pink headband.

I call Kareem, the butcher, to arrange for a lamb. Then I decide to make it two—one for Maryam and one for me—because I do have my life back. We send out invitations to our friends so they can celebrate with us.

On the night before the aqiqah, I shave Maryam's head.

"She has such beautiful hair. I hate to see it go," says Aisha.

"It will come back thicker, insha Allah."

On Saturday, Aisha and Sharon decorate the gym while Jeremy and I cook the lamb and rice. Jennifer made the salad this morning before going over to Heather's place.

When I look at the decorations, I think of Aunt Arlene. Her health isn't good, and we haven't gone to see her in almost two months. We should go soon.

Umar, Safa, and their kids arrive before everyone else. Safa made sweets for the occasion. Soon our other guests come with presents for our baby, now more than a year old. She enjoys all the attention she gets while her brothers run around the gym with their friends.

Rebounding

Mom and Walt stop by. They have tickets for a play later this evening. I bring them plates and sit with them for a few minutes. "This is delicious. I had never tried lamb until we went to Pakistan," says Walt. "At any rate, I was wondering about the significance of this ceremony. Is it anything like a baptism?"

"No, nothing like that. It's a celebration, a way of thanking God for giving us our beautiful little girl."

"She is beautiful," says Mom.

I remember the conversation I tried to have with her about God. I know she's still not open to talking about religion, but I need to keep on trying. "Maryam is a beautiful gift from God," I say.

"Yes," says Mom, "I suppose she is." She takes another bite of lamb. "You are a very good cook, Joshua. That still amazes me."

They don't stay long. We talk a little about their trip to London next month, but I don't pay too much attention to the conversation. I keep wondering. Does she believe in God?

After Mom and Walt leave, I sit with Ismail. He and Amal brought their two boys. Zaid is enough of a handful. Now they have Yusuf too. He's a few months younger than Maryam. I was in prison when they had his aqiqah.

"Hey, man, this lamb is good. Did you cook it, Isa?"

"It was a family project. Jeremy did a lot of the cooking. He's pretty good in the kitchen."

"I heard he's going to be Umar's son-in-law."

"That's right. He's going to marry Raheema next spring."

"Man, he's brave."

"He can handle it. He's a man now."

"Dude, you're getting too old for me. Before you know it, you're going to be a grandfather."

I hadn't thought about that before. I am getting old.

I head back to the kitchen to check on things. I'm thinking about my children. My oldest are going to college and getting married. My youngest has just started walking. I'm lost in thought, and not looking where I'm going. I literally run into another brother.

"Oh, sorry."

He turns around. It's Yahya, the imam from the prison. "Assalaamu alaikum, Isa. How are you? It's good to see you again."

"Walaikum assalaam. It's great to see you. I didn't know you were going to be here."

"Our wives are friends. My wife teaches kindergarten here at the school."

"It's really good to see you, Brother." We hug.

"I heard that the charges were dismissed. That's wonderful news."

"Alhamdulillah. We're very relieved. We had a few rough months there, but at least it's over. I appreciate your help during those days. As you can see, I'm still taking care of unfinished business. My daughter was born the day before they took me in and I wasn't able to arrange for her aqiqah."

"You're looking good. I know you had some hard times in there. I feel like I didn't do enough to help you. I am also under scrutiny. I need to be careful."

"You were there. That's what counted."

"There's something I need to tell you. I know you remember Troy, your cell mate."

"Yes. I'll never forget him. I keep thinking about how he was killed just because he helped me. It wasn't right. He was trying to get his act together so he could see his children again."

"Isa, on the Friday before Troy died, he asked to see me. He told me about his friendship with you. He said that you had taught him about Islam. He asked me what he would have to do to become a Muslim. And, he made Shahadah."

I close my eyes for a moment, remembering Troy. I feel a heaviness lift from my heart.

"That's been the worst of it. He had been asking me questions. I wanted to get out of the hospital, so I could answer all of his questions. I hoped he would accept Islam, but by the time I got out he was dead."

"They killed him two days later. At the time of his Shahadah, I gave him some books and pamphlets about Islam, and I talked to him about making his prayers. He said he knew how to pray because he had been watching and listening to you. I didn't have the chance to see him after that Friday, but I believe he was sincere."

"When I first met him, he hated Islam. If he made Shahadah, I know he was sincere."

"I thought you should know. Your arrest and imprisonment were great hardships for you and your family—I know that—but something good has come out of it."

"Is there any way I could contact his family?"

"I'll have to check on that. Why?"

"I want to let his children know how much he loved them. He talked about them all the time, how he was going to get out and clean up his act so he could be with them again. They need to know who he was when he died."

"You're right. I'll see what I can do."

Something smells good. I remember the cakes in the oven. "I have to go check on the cakes, but it's good talking to you. Call me sometime. I'm sure your wife has our number."

"I'll do that. We'll have to invite you and your family for dinner one day soon."

"Good. I'll talk to you later then. Assalaamu alaikum."

"Walaikum assalaam."

The cakes are done. I get them cooled and served. By the time I'm finished in the kitchen, Yahya and his family have left.

We're getting ready to go to sleep when I tell Aisha the news.

"Did you know that the kindergarten teacher's husband is a prison chaplain?"

"Yes. I've known her for a few years now. She taught Muhammad. While you were in prison, she came over here sometimes, just to talk. And she never came empty-handed. She told me that her husband was meeting with you. That comforted me, to know you had someone in there who would help you."

"His name is Yahya. He did help me. I talked with him tonight."

"That's nice. I'm sure you were happy to see him again."

"And he told me that Troy made Shahadah before he died. While I was in the hospital."

"That's wonderful, Isa." She hugs me.

"Yeah, it's really great. It's what I was hoping for. The funny thing is, though, now I miss Troy more than ever."

⁓

The next time I see Umar, I tell him about Troy. About his rants, and his death, and his Shahadah.

"He just wanted to see his kids again."

"Why didn't you say anything before, when I was spouting all that foolishness about the fight? My comments must have hurt. I didn't know."

"That's right. You didn't know. And I had a hard time talking about it—it still hurts to think about Troy—but at least he was trying to get things right before he was killed."

Umar looks at me. "You've changed, Isa. I guess five months in prison can change a man."

I guess being close to death can change a man.

⁓

I've met with Jared White a few times. The first time we met, I didn't think he was really qualified to handle my case. I was used to Walt, with his gray hair and three-piece suits—that's how a lawyer is supposed to look—but Jared can't be much past thirty, and he likes to wear jeans. I had real misgivings about him for the first five minutes. Then I started listening to him. He knows what he's talking about.

He's enthusiastic, and very confident about the case. I got nervous when he started talking dollar figures. He wants to go for a settlement in the nine-figure range. I don't expect to get rich off of this. I just want them to answer for their mistakes.

We have another meeting today. When I walk into his office, he's eating pizza and listening to rap while reading some papers at his desk. When he sees me, he turns down the rap but keeps on eating. He does offer me a slice.

"Assalaamu alaikum, Joshua. I've been looking over these records of your injuries. I'll be calling medical experts in to testify about the severity of your injuries and the potential for long-term damage because of the prison's failure to provide you with prompt medical treatment. You haven't been having any unusual headaches or short-term memory loss, have you?"

"No, I'm fine, alhamdulillah."

"Good. I want to make sure there are no lasting effects from your head injuries. I have the records here on the nerve damage to your arm. The doctor who diagnosed the damage has already agreed to testify. I also have the report on your hearing loss, and I'm working on getting that doctor to testify. I want to be certain that all long-term effects have been well-documented. I think we'll need to schedule you for another physical soon, just to make sure everything checks out."

"Do you think that's really necessary?"

"I get the impression that you aren't very enthusiastic about this suit. Why is that?"

"It's over. I survived. Sometimes I just want to forget about the whole thing and concentrate on getting on with my life."

"Did you know that there were five guards standing around in the cafeteria watching the fight? They were there from the very beginning, and they let those prisoners beat the shit out of you. Then they tried to punish you by putting you into solitary, without medical attention, even though they knew full well that Spider attacked you. Doesn't that make you angry?"

"It would have. . .a couple of years ago. It does disturb me, but while I was in prison I guess I got used to the abuse. When the only people who talk to you call you a terrorist, I guess you start to believe it. I don't want to give them any reason to come after me again."

"You sound like my father. He always told me not to make waves. Learn how to work the system. Throw in a few yes sirs. Make them feel important so they'll like you. I'm going to tell you right now that I don't buy that shit. I didn't think you would either."

"I wouldn't have, a year or two ago, before they put me in prison." I like Jared. I like his nerve. Maybe he can help me regain my balance.

"They stole your thunder, didn't they? Well, Joshua, I'm going to help you get that back. And they are going to pay."

Jared sounds like he's ready to try the case tomorrow, but the wheels of justice move slowly. He tells me that the case won't come up until next year. At the earliest.

༄

We put everything on hold for a few days when we get the news about Aunt Arlene. She died last Wednesday, after another stroke.

Aisha, Umar, and I take Friday off and drive to Moline for the funeral. Sharon left on Wednesday. Safa and Jennifer stay behind to take care of the kids. Except for Maryam. We bring her with us.

After the funeral, the relatives ask about my time in prison and what I plan to do now. Then Aisha and I take some time to sit down with Aunt Helen. She can't stop crying. Aisha holds her hand.

"They're all gone now. I'm the last one."

"You'll be okay, Aunt Helen. You still have us."

"I've buried two brothers and my mother. Now my sister. I've never been far away from my big sister. She practically raised me after our daddy left. When we got older, we would wear each other's clothes. When I had my first baby, she came over and showed me what to do. And when our big brother died, your daddy, we cried together. We cried for days, until our tears were gone, but now who's going to cry with me?"

"I will, Aunt Helen." Aisha puts her arms around her, and they do cry together. I cry a little, too, but not just for Aunt Arlene. I cry for the changes that time brings. For that

Rebounding

Thanksgiving Day, when The Doc invited me into his family, and everybody was healthy and strong. And I cry for Dad.

We spend the night at the house. I haven't been here for at least two years, probably longer. I still feel Dad's presence in this house.

We leave on Saturday afternoon. Sharon stays.

"I need to be with Helen. And your grandmother. And my brother and sisters. I might not come back to Chicago. You children don't need me so much anymore."

"We always need you," says Aisha.

"Yes, but I think they need me more now. I expect to see you children here, too. Your grandmother is nearly ninety-one years old. She won't be with us forever. Make sure you come to see her while you still can."

"We will, Mom."

We say goodbye to Sharon in the driveway. I remember those days after Dad died. But she's strong now. I'll miss her, but I think she is ready to move back to Moline.

Before leaving town, we go to visit Grandma. Her hip healed well and she still insists on living by herself. She looks good, just smaller and grayer.

First we have a round of hugs. Then she looks at me and grins. "Angela, are you still married to that white boy?"

"Yes, Grandma, I think I'm stuck with him."

Grandma holds my hand. She's strong. "I know you're taking good care of my granddaughter, aren't you, Joshua?"

"Yes, Grandma, I always will."

"Let me look at that baby. She is the sweetest thing. Aren't you, Maryam? Do you want to come to your great-grandma?"

Aisha puts Maryam on Grandma's lap. Maryam snuggles close to her. Grandma smiles and puts her arms around her youngest great-grandchild.

We talk for a while before we leave. She says she's looking forward to coming to Chicago for Raheema and Jeremy's wedding. "If the Lord wills."

263

Those are the last words Dad said to me, on the day he said he loved me. I close my eyes and remember him. And I think about time.

~

The wedding plans are going smoothly now, with just a couple of glitches along the way. Setting the date was the biggest problem.

Jeremy said they wanted to get married right after graduation, but one evening while we were eating dinner together, soon after the engagement, Safa said, "You can't get married that soon. Ramadan will be coming at the end of May this year, insha Allah. You don't want to get married during Ramadan."

"That's okay. We can manage."

"No Jeremy," said Umar. "Ramadan should be a time for prayer and reflection. You'll have an easier start to your marriage if you wait."

Jeremy reluctantly agreed. We consulted the calendar and finally set the date for the last Sunday in June. There's a possibility that will also be the Eid day. "Then," said Aisha, "We'll have two reasons to celebrate."

Four months before the wedding, Jeremy and Raheema say they want to go looking for an apartment. We've just finished eating Safa's biriyani.

"Back home in Bangladesh," says Safa, "the new wife stays with her mother-in-law until the first child is born."

Raheema smiles. "Jeremy's mother is very nice, but I don't think there's room for us in the condo."

She's being diplomatic. Raheema and Heather seem to get along well, but I can't see them living in the same apartment.

"And we want to have a place of our own," says Jeremy.

"The first thing," says Umar, "is to determine what you can afford."

"How do we do that?" Jeremy asks.

Umar and I sit with Jeremy and Raheema for two hours, explaining how to follow a budget and helping them come up with a practical plan. At the end of the two hours, my son and future daughter-in-law are way ahead of where Heather and I were when we got married. We did it the hard way. I didn't have a father to teach me.

Umar writes down a figure and circles it. "This is what you have to work with."

"I didn't know it would be this complicated," says Jeremy.

"Do you see why we thought you might be too young to get married?"

"I guess, but don't worry. We can handle it, insha Allah."

The two of them spend the next week looking for a place. When we meet again, Jeremy looks upset. "I couldn't find anything we can afford."

"I found these eight places online," says Raheema.

Umar and I go through the list with them. They are all in rough neighborhoods.

"I'm sorry, Jeremy, but I'm not going to jeopardize Raheema's safety just because the two of you want some independence. I'm sure you don't want that either. Have you tried student housing at the university, Raheema?"

"I called. There's a long waiting list."

"So what should we do?" says Jeremy.

"You could move in with us," I say. "Sharon has moved back to Moline, and the house seems empty without her."

"But, Dad, I'm a man. If I'm old enough to get married, then I should be old enough to take care of my wife. And we'll want some privacy."

"It's okay to get help from your family. You were too young to know what your mom and I were fighting about, but most of the time it was money. We never had enough of it. And it took us years to pay off all the credit card debt we ran up. You don't want to start your marriage that way."

"No, I don't want to fight with Raheema about anything."

"You probably will fight once in a while. It happens. If Raheema is like her mother, I'm coming to your house to eat when she's mad at you."

Raheema laughs. "You'll be welcome any time, Uncle Isa. And Jeremy, it's okay with me if we have to stay with your dad and Aunt Aisha for a few months. If it was good for my mother and father, it will be good for us, insha Allah."

"If you say so, Raheema. Just for a few months, though."

A few days later, Jeremy mentions the arrangement to his grandmother, who has just come back from London.

"That's nonsense. Raheema and you will need to have your own home. Let me get a nice apartment for you. I'll pay your rent for a year. That should give you enough time to get yourselves established. It'll be my wedding present for you."

Later, I ask Mom why she didn't do that for Heather and me.

"We all lived different lives then. I was disgusted with you for getting Heather pregnant, I was fed up with your craziness, and, in those days, I still blamed you for Sam leaving us. Don't keep thinking about the past. Besides, I put up your bail and got you a good lawyer. Doesn't that count?"

"Of course, Mom, though you got a good deal on my lawyer."

"Yes, I did." She smiles. "I wasn't always the best mother—I know that—but I decided long ago that I would do everything I could for my grandchildren."

~

Umar and I have talked about starting up the center again. What we were doing worked very well before—before we were shut down. I wouldn't be allowed to manage the finances, but we could hire someone to do that. I could work with Umar on program development. I decide to test the waters.

On one of my days off, I call Mr. Richards. I was supposed to have met with him all those months ago. I want to see if he's still interested.

He congratulates me on having the charges dismissed. "So what can I do for you?"

"Tony Evans and I are thinking about rebuilding the center. I wondered if you would be willing to support our efforts, assuming we had a well-written business plan for you to examine."

He's silent for a moment. "I would like to be able to help you—Tony and you are very bright and committed, and I'm certain that you have the talent to rebuild your center—but people don't easily forget. For a couple of weeks there, the publicity was so great that some people here in Chicago still associate you with terrorism. I can't afford that association. You probably are not aware that after your arrest I also came under scrutiny. I was questioned by Homeland Security, and my own business records were examined. Guilt by association, you know. I'm sorry. I hope you can find the support you need. I'm sure you understand my position."

"Yes, Mr. Richards, of course. Thank you."

I take out the Rolodex I kept at home—one of the few things related to the center which was not confiscated—and try a few more of my old contacts. Only one can give me some assurance of support. Most of the others are like Jason Richards—kind, but not willing to commit. Three were also questioned by Homeland Security. One of my old contacts gets angry with me. He calls me a terrorist and shouts that I should still be in prison. This will be harder than I thought.

In the evening, I go to see Umar and tell him about my calls. "They're not willing to forget, even though we were never guilty."

"Just the hint of wrongdoing is enough for some people. It will probably take years and there will always be some who think of us as terrorists." He smiles. "Do you understand more about prejudice now?"

"I don't know. I guess I do."

"What about when they called you a terrorist there in the prison? Did you fight back, or did you say 'yes sir'?"

"I kept my head down and tried to stay out of trouble."

"But I thought you said we have to stand up for ourselves."

"I couldn't think about that then. I was just trying to survive."

He nods. "You understand."

I guess I do.

"So we're terrorists. If we don't fight, what do we do?"

"Forming another organization like The Caring Center is out of the question. It won't work. It was good, and I think we did some good, but the time is past. We could continue in our current jobs, but I know you're not really satisfied with what you're doing, and I miss the challenge of actually creating programs. Where I work now, I only follow the procedures that others have written. It's not enough."

"So nonprofit won't work. What if we open our own business, for profit?"

"But doing what?"

"I don't know. It would have to be something that serves the needs of others."

"That's nonprofit. We're back where we started."

"Why don't we sleep on it? We can ask our wives. Maybe they'll have some ideas."

"I'll do that, but I don't think Safa will be able to help us much. All she and Raheema think about these days is the wedding. Yesterday, I had to remind Raheema not to forget about her studies. Heather has been coming over too. She wants to be involved in every detail."

"I can't imagine Heather and Safa planning something together. They're so different."

"They are, but they're both mothers." He laughs. "And in a few months they'll be related."

"Now that's funny."

"What about Jeremy? Hasn't he said anything about getting ready for the wedding?"

"Don't you remember? All he has to do is show up."

"A couple of weeks ago he came over and asked Raheema what she wanted for her dowry."

"What did she say?"

"She wants him to take her for the hajj."

"She is a smart girl."

When I get home, I talk with Aisha about our business dilemma. She thinks about it for two days. On the third day, when I come home from work, she tells me she has a solution.

"Umar and you have so much experience. That's what you can sell. Your experience."

"How?"

"You can write books, give workshops and seminars. You two know how to build a good center. And if you can teach others how to do it, you will be able to help even more people."

"That might work, but how should we get started?"

"Sit down together and write a business plan. Divide up the tasks—just as you did before—but this time you will have to concentrate on publicity. Getting the word out. You do have a lot to offer. You just have to convince other people that you can help them build successful programs."

I pass Aisha's idea on to Umar. He likes it. We sit down for an hour or two to break it down. Then I go home to start on my share of the business plan. I think it just might work.

We meet again a month later to see what we have.

"I don't think writing a book is a good idea," I say. "What if I produce an interactive CD instead, and a short manual to go with it? We can use the material to help us in the seminars and workshops, and make it part of the fee."

"Good. You can work on that. I've been looking into how to promote our work. I think we can do this."

I hope so. I'm bored to death working at the restaurant. Parvez is nice, but I don't have the same relationship with him that I have with Fawad. Even more, I miss the kind of work I did at the center.

"By the way," says Umar, "I just sent in my application for graduate school. Do you remember when we first became friends? I told you I had been thinking about going back for my Masters. Now I want it in psychology, not social work."

"That was so long ago. Haven't we always been friends?"

"I'm going to do it now, Isa. It's not just what Mom and Dad expected of me. It's what I expected of myself. I just got sidetracked."

"So you're going to be one of those psychologists with a Ph.D. behind your name?"

"Could be, insha Allah."

Part Fourteen

Ramadan is here again.

A few days ago Jamal told me, "I can't wait until Ramadan comes, because now I know I can do it."

Umar got off the medication about four months ago, and he's looking forward to fasting a full Ramadan again.

Yesterday, we were talking about our families. "Last year I found my son. This year Jeremy will become my son-in-law. I wonder how much longer it will be before we're welcoming our grandchildren."

I'm still not ready to think about that yet.

❦

On the second day of Ramadan, I see them again. The men in the black suits. For the third time since the charges were dismissed. At least they come to the restaurant. I don't want them at our house, around my family.

"How is everything, Adams?"

"Everything is just fine."

"How is that lawsuit coming?"

"I don't know. You would have to ask my lawyer."

"You don't really think you're going to get away with it, do you?"

"Why not? I like to think that this is still a free country."

"We're watching you."

"Oh, I'm sure of that." I walk away, and they leave.

The first two times they came, my heart beat faster, I started sweating and I felt like running away. Now, I try to treat them the same way I treat Heather when she comes up with those little barbs. They're just another annoyance. But I am very careful. I return my library books on time. I don't use my cell phone while I'm driving. I don't jaywalk. And my heart still beats faster.

Rebounding

I'm still tense when I get home. I sit down and read the Qur'an until it's time to break fast.

I've just finished eating my third date when the doorbell rings. Muhammad runs to get it. He walks back into the family room a minute later, smiling and holding Mom's hand. "It's Gramma and Grandpa Walt!"

"Hi Mom. Hi Walt. We just broke our fast. Can you wait a minute? We need to pray."

"Go ahead," says Walt. "I'm sorry we disturbed you." Mom doesn't say anything.

"It's no problem. You know I'm always happy to see you. Just hold on a minute."

I pray, but I can't concentrate. Mom looks worried. I wonder what's wrong.

After the prayer, we invite them to eat dinner with us in the kitchen. They sit at the table, but they don't eat. Mom's lips are pressed tightly together.

Walt smiles. "You're looking good, Joshua. You've gained back all that weight, I see. Aisha must be a good cook."

I don't tell him that Jennifer and I do most of the cooking. Mom still hasn't said anything. "What's wrong, Mom?"

"Go ahead and finish eating first. Then we'll talk."

I don't have much of an appetite, anyway, after fasting all day. It's harder to eat now, worrying about whatever it is that's worrying Mom. I finish quickly. "Let's go sit in the family room. We can talk there." Aisha comes with us.

We go in and sit down. I study Mom's face. I haven't seen her look this tense in a long time, certainly not since she's been with Walt. "What is it, Mom? Is the cancer back?"

"No, Joshua, I'm fine, but we need to talk."

"What's going on?"

"Celia called. Sam's daughter."

Just the name is enough to make me tense again. "Tell me this isn't about Sam."

"He's dying. Prostate cancer."

271

My face is getting red. "I won't go to see him."

"Joshua, the way you left things with him. . . No matter how bad he is, he is still your father."

"Are you going?"

"Yes. Walt has said he'll come with me. I was cursing at him too, and I never curse. I have to go, to clear my own conscience."

"Then you can go ahead. That man tried to ruin my life."

"That man helped give you life."

My hands are clenched. Walt must have noticed. "Stay calm, Joshua. I know you've been hurt, but you know how it is to be a father. Think about it."

"I know, but I love my children. I'm a father to my children, and my children know who I am. My children know that I love them. I would never hurt or insult one of my children. I would never take my son's life away from him and have him locked up. I know how it is to be a father. Sam doesn't."

Mom raises her eyebrows. "What are you talking about, Joshua?"

"Mom, you know it was Sam who sent them after me. You know that too, Walt. Don't you?"

Walt leans over and reaches out to touch my arm, just as he did so many times while I was in prison. "If I tell you who the informant was, will it make a difference?"

"I already know who it was."

"Yes, you do know. I'm sorry, Joshua."

Mom looks hurt. She turns to Walt. "So it was him. You wouldn't tell me either, all those months. Why wouldn't you tell me?"

"I didn't see the point in it, Evie. The damage had already been done."

"I'm so sorry," says Aisha. "I can only imagine how much that hurts."

I shout at her. "No, you can't imagine. You don't know how it is to have a father who hates you. Do you know that they came to the restaurant again today? They practically threatened me, because of the lawsuit. They said I wouldn't get away with it. I'm going to have to spend the rest of my life looking over my shoulder. That's what my father did to me. And you'll never be able to understand."

"Don't do that to me, Isa. I'm not the one you should be angry with, and you know it. I know that your father has hurt you. I don't know what kind of man would do that to his child."

"He's not a man. He's a monster."

"He is your father. And he's dying. If you don't go to see him, you will only be hurting yourself."

I don't want to be angry with her, but she doesn't understand. Her father was The Doc. "You don't get it."

"Settle down, Joshua." Walt pats my arm. "I know you've been hurt, but we're not the ones who hurt you."

"Are you still going to see him, Mom?"

She's been quiet. Walt puts his arm around her shoulders and holds her close to him. "Remember what you said, Evie. You have to go to clear your own conscience. I promise I will be there, right beside you."

"You're right—I just get so angry with myself for ever bringing that man into my life—but you are right. I'll go. What about you, Joshua?"

"I can't. He's hurt me too much. Even the thought of him. I can't." The anger flashes again. I have to control it. I feel like screaming and cursing. I want to throw something, but Walt and Aisha are right. It's not their fault. It's time to change the subject. I take a deep breath and try to smile. "So, where are you two heading on your next trip?"

"We haven't decided yet. I wouldn't mind going back to Pakistan, but your mother says she's always wanted to go to Egypt."

Thank you, Walt, for understanding.

"Um, excuse me," I say, "I'll be right back."

I go to make some tea, kicking the wall a few times on my way into the kitchen. When the tea is ready, we sit and talk about their travels, Jeremy's wedding, our new business venture, Aisha's teaching, Jared White, and Aunt Arlene. We don't talk about Sam.

As they walk out, Mom hands me a piece of paper. "This is where your father is, in case you change your mind."

I crumple the paper and put it in my shirt pocket.

After they leave, I call the boys to pray with Aisha and me. Then I sit and read the Qur'an again, trying to block thoughts of Sam, but it doesn't work. I put the Qur'an aside and put my head in my hands.

Aisha sits next to me on the floor and rubs my back. "Why don't you go see Umar?"

I hug her, grab the car keys, and slip on my shoes.

She kisses me at the door. "I love you. Try not to be too late."

⌘

Jeremy's car is parked outside Umar's house. He comes here almost every night now. Umar and Safa are very patient. They know it will be only a few more weeks. Then Raheema will be gone.

Sabeera answers the door. "Assalaamu alaikum, Uncle Isa."

I still have a lump in my throat, but it's not Sabeera's fault either. I force a smile. "Sabeera! Walaikum assalaam. You get prettier every time I see you."

She giggles. "My Baba is in here." She takes my hand and leads me to the family room, skipping along the way.

Umar stands to greet me. "Assalaamu alaikum, Isa. What's wrong?"

I glance at Jeremy and Raheema. "I know you're busy, but can we talk? It's important."

"Of course. I'll ask Safa to come in." He heads for the kitchen.

"So how are the wedding plans coming along?"

"Gramma's going to take us this weekend to pick out some furniture. I think everything for the wedding itself is all set. Raheema has been working on it, along with Aunt Safa and Mom. I didn't really have much to do with it."

"That's usually the way it is."

Rebounding

Umar and Safa come in from the kitchen. Safa takes her place with my son and her daughter. "Let's go into my office, Isa," says Umar. "We can talk there."

Tasneema is in the office, playing on the computer. "Sorry, baby, but Baba needs the office. I think you need to go get ready for bed now, Sweetheart."

She leaves and he closes the door. "What is it, Isa? Don't tell me the government is giving you problems again."

"They did come by the restaurant today to remind me that I'm being watched, but it's more than that. Sam's daughter called Mom. Sam is dying. Mom thinks I should go see him before he dies."

"What do you think?"

"I can't. He's hurt me too many times."

"He is your father."

"He was also the informant. Walt finally told me. I always thought it was him. He's the one who took away our center and put us in prison. I don't owe him shit."

Umar flinches. "I'm sorry to hear that. I know it hurts. That would explain why they went after you so much harder than they went after me. I never imagined that a father could do that to his son."

"That's what I'm saying. What kind of father is he?"

Umar pauses a moment. Then he says softly, "He's the kind of father who gave you life."

"Yeah. Thanks a lot, Sam. He gave me life, and then he tried to take it all away from me."

"I understand how you feel."

"You don't understand. How could you? You had Dad."

"That's right. And I would give anything if I could see him just one more time."

"Because he was Dad. He was good. Sam is evil."

"If you hate him so much, why did you come to ask me whether or not you should go to see him?"

I have a hard time answering that, but Umar knows me too well. "Because I feel like I should go. Even knowing it was him.

I'm afraid if I don't see him again, then, somehow, it might come back to haunt me."

"Why? Because you have some feelings for Sam?"

"I don't love him," I answer quickly. "How could I? He never loved me. I've spent most of my life hating him. But. . .I don't know. . ."

"But he is your father. You look like him. Even though he never gave you anything else, he gave you life, and he gave you his last name. And that's something."

"But he left me. He took away the center. He took away five and a half months of my life. I'll never be as strong as I was. And I still have to keep looking over my shoulder, waiting for the men in black suits to show up."

"Listen to me, Isa. I tried to get rid of Derek. If it had been up to me, he would have never even been born. Not just five and half months of his life. His life itself. How do you think he should feel toward me now?"

"That's different."

"How is it different?"

It's different. It has to be different.

"I don't know. For one thing, you gave him some of your bone marrow. And you're trying to be a father to him. You two have a relationship now. I have never had a relationship with Sam." I look down. "And you love Derek."

"And that's what really bothers you, isn't it? You have always wanted his love."

"I don't know. I guess."

"You have tried to replace him with Abdul-Qadir and Dad and now Walt, but you have always wanted Sam to be a real father to you. After he dies you will never have another chance."

I don't want to cry—I stopped crying over Sam when I was ten—but I do anyway. Umar knows me too well.

He puts his arm around my shoulders. "Go see him. Not because he needs it. Because you do."

I nod. "I guess you're right. I'll go tomorrow, insha Allah."

"Good." He gives me a quick hug. "I just remembered. Safa said she has some bread in the oven, so we'd better go chaperone our kids."

"Can I have some tea to go with my bread?"

"Of course."

When I get into my car, I pull out the paper Mom gave me. She wrote down the name of the hospice and his room number. I'll go.

I guess I really do want to see him. I didn't toss the paper in the trash.

~

At first, I had planned to go right after work, but I decide that I really want to take Aisha with me. Maybe if he meets her, he'll know how special she is. Maybe then he'll stop being someone I hate. Maybe she can help me stop hating him.

We go before it's time to break fast. If we wait, visiting hours will be over. It's probably better, too, that I'm fasting when I go to confront him. I hope my fasting will help me get through this.

Jennifer is there to heat up dinner and take care of the kids. I worry sometimes about relying on her too much, but I give her a regular allowance now, and she has free time some evenings and on the weekends—as long as I know where she is and who she's with. I think she enjoys being with the kids. I know our boys think she's the greatest thing ever. Maryam is her shadow.

Aisha and I talk as I drive through the city streets. "I hope I know what I'm doing."

She reaches over and rubs my arm. "You're doing the right thing."

"I don't know. I keep thinking I should just stay away from Sam and his evil."

"He's not evil. There is some good in every person."

"Every person?"

"Yes. That's what I think—people do evil things sometimes, for a variety of reasons, but no person is completely evil."

"That's one of the things I love about you—your compassion. I guess that's why you wanted to marry me. You felt sorry for me."

She squeezes my arm. "I don't know if it was compassion, or just plain passion."

"We're fasting, remember?"

She laughs. "I remember. Just remember, too, that he is your father."

"He's not The Doc, though. Far from it."

"No, but he is your father."

What does it mean, I wonder, to be a father who hates his son?

We get to the hospice and I pull into the parking garage. We take the elevator up to the second floor. We don't talk. I hold her hand. I'm still not sure I should be here, but I know I wouldn't feel right if he died before I saw him one more time.

I squeeze Aisha's hand as we walk into the room. He doesn't have any other visitors. I can barely see him behind the rails of the hospital bed, surrounded by the bedclothes. There's an IV in his left arm. He looks frail. There's nothing frightening about him. He's just a sick, old man.

He's been watching television. When we walk in, he turns down the sound and looks toward the door. "Hello, Sam."

"Hello, Joshua. The last time I saw you, you told me to go to hell. It looks like I'm on my way there now. Are you happy?"

I almost answer that, but I decide to hold it. "Sam, this is Aisha. This is my wife."

"Hello, Sam," she says. "I'm glad to finally meet you."

He frowns and turns away.

I stand there with Aisha, waiting for him to turn back to us. He doesn't. After a few minutes I say, "I guess we'd better be going."

He looks at me, "So, you came to see the old man before he dies."

"I came to see my father, but I guess I'm wasting my time." I turn around and head for the door. Aisha walks with me, reluctantly.

"Come back here, boy. Don't you turn your back on your father."

I turn around so fast, still holding Aisha's hand, that she nearly loses her balance. "Like you turned your back on me all those years?" I shout. "You can't tell me what to do."

"The hell I can't. I am still your father."

"I shouldn't have come here." I turn to Aisha. "Do you see what I mean? There's no talking to him."

Aisha unlocks her hand from mine and walks over to Sam. She stands by his bed and touches his hand. He jerks away from her touch.

"See, I told you. Let's go home."

"No, Isa," she says gently. "You need to stay here and work this out with him."

"Are you crazy? He hates you as much as he hates me. Let's go."

"I don't hate you, Joshua," Sam says quietly.

"You don't? Well you sure put on a good act all these years. Do you remember when I was ten and you promised you would come?"

"No, I don't remember."

"I waited for you. You said you would take me to see the Cubs. And you never came."

He looks down. "I lie here in this bed, day after day, waiting to die. And I can't change what I've done. I probably am going to hell, you know."

"I hope you're not looking to me for sympathy, because you're not going to get any."

"I've done a lot more than you know. I am going to hell," he mutters softly.

There is no talking to him. Even fasting can't keep me from being angry. "Let's go, Hon. This is a waste of time."

"No, Isa. For fourteen years you've told me how much your father hurt you. Tell him."

"Go ahead," he smirks. "Tell me."

"Okay," I shout, "you left me. You almost never came to see me. You cursed my mother. You broke your promises. You cursed my wife and children. And if that wasn't enough, you had me arrested. They should name you father of the year!"

He shakes his head. "You're right. I was a terrible father, but I'm dying. Can't you think of anything good to say before you send me on my way?"

"No. Nothing."

"I've spent the last two weeks lying in this bed and thinking about my life. I wish I had it to do over again. There are many things I would have done differently."

"Would you be a father to me?"

"If, by some miracle, I was given the chance to live the past forty years over again then, yes, I would, but it's too late now."

"No, Sam. It's only too late when we're dead."

"What do you want me to do? I don't think I can make it to your ball games."

"No." I hesitate. I have to say it. "You can't make it my games, but you can love me."

He's quiet for a long time. Then he sighs and says, "I didn't want another child. You cried all the damn time. I tried to hold you, once or twice, but you always screamed in my arms. Then Cynthia came along and, well, I was a young man then. Every time I went to see you boys, I wound up fighting with your mother. That time in your mother's house, I did want to make things right, but it got screwed up pretty badly, didn't it? I never thought that one of my kids would go and marry a ni—" He stops, fumbling for a better word. "A black person. It never seemed right to me, but I guess dying changes things." He looks at Aisha. "You love my son, don't you?"

"Yes, I do."

"You seem decent. I guess he could have done worse."

Was that a compliment? I don't know what he's trying to say, but I decide to let it pass because there's something I need to know.

"Did you ever love me?"

He shakes his head. "Not the way a father should love his son. I didn't know how. Maybe because my old man didn't ever love me. He beat me and I never did know how to love a son."

"What about Brad and Chris? What about the son you had with Cynthia?"

"No, I never knew how to love a son."

"I have five sons, and they all know how much I love them."

"Congratulations," he says with a twist of sarcasm. "So how do you do it?"

"I treat them the way I wish my father had treated me," I say, with a twist of my own.

He looks at me and starts to say something, then stops and shakes his head. "I wish my old man had stopped beating me. And I wish that, just once, he had touched me in love instead of in anger, but he never did."

I suddenly realize how much I want to know him. I never knew who he was. I still don't know. I stare at him and a strange feeling comes over me. I see him for the sad man he is. I go close and take his hand. "Like this, Sam?" I bring his hand up to my lips, and kiss it.

He reaches up and touches my face. "Yes, Joshua, like that."

I have never kissed my father before and, as far as I know, my father has never kissed me. I'm hit by a wave of emotion. Love?

We look at each other for a long time. Then he pulls me close to him, puts his one free arm around me, and we both cry for wasted lives.

When I pull back, he says, "If I tell you that I love you, can you do something for me?"

That's the Sam I know. Always looking to see what he can get out of a deal. I ask him anyway. "What is it?"

"Could you call me Dad? I never acted like it, but I am your dad."

"But you're not my dad. You were never there for me. I barely even know you. And I already have a dad."

"Your father-in-law—I know—but why him? He doesn't look like you. He's not your kind. And he's not your father. I am."

"You sure didn't act like it. He loved me. You never did. And you had better not start with that racist shit again."

"You were about to build a center in his name, weren't you? 'The Jim Evans Memorial Youth Center.' What kind of memorial will you build for your real father?"

"My real father? I never had a real father."

"Don't you talk to me that way, boy. You take a good look in the mirror. Look at your eyes, your hair. Your skin. Don't you try to tell me that Jim Evans is your dad. You sure don't look like no ni—" He stops. He knows that I'm one second from walking away from him and never coming back. "What I mean is," he says quietly, "you're my son."

"Your son? You never treated me like your son."

"Doesn't matter how I treated you. You're still my son."

"Jim Evans treated me like a son. You treated me like dirt."

"I know I could have done better, but I'm still your father. How could you love him and not your own father?"

"How could you not love me?"

"If I tell you I love you, can you call me Dad?"

"Why now? Because you're dying?"

"Yes. Because I'm dying. And I know I'm going to hell. Just do this for me before I go."

He doesn't know what he's asking. In all my life, I've had only one Dad, the one who helped me get past not having a father in my life. And he's the only one I could ever think of as Dad.

But Sam, the man in front of me now, is my father. And he's dying. I don't know. Maybe it's not too much to ask. Somehow, I think The Doc would want me to do it.

I take a deep breath and look into his eyes. The same eyes I see every morning when I look into the mirror. The eyes he gave me. "Okay, Dad." I remember the ten-year old boy, waiting for him. I remember how much I wanted to see him then. And I whisper, "I have always loved you."

He traces my face with his fingers. "I love you too, Joshua."

And something changes in the world. Somehow, those words change everything.

But I can't let it go.

He said he loved me. I should let it go. But I can't.

"Then why did you do it? Why did you tell them to come after me?"

"I was angry. I wanted to hurt you, the way you hurt me that time in your mother's house. I'm an old man, and I just wanted the chance to know my sons before I die, but you turned against me, and you turned your brothers against me too." He looks down and shakes his head. "They weren't supposed to take it that far. I only wanted them to scare you a little. Shake you up. Teach you a lesson about having respect for your father. They were supposed to take you in for questioning, maybe hold you overnight. That's all. But once they got started, they wouldn't let up. It turned out all wrong."

"Did you know that I got beaten up? Did you know I almost died in there?"

"I heard. It wasn't supposed to happen like that."

"Did you know that they're still after me? I can't make a move now without them breathing down my neck."

"I didn't think it would go that far."

"And what about the raid that killed Ahmed and four other people, including a woman and a child? That was part of the setup, wasn't it? And Troy? Do you know he was killed because of me?"

"Part of their setup, yes. I had nothing to do with it. I said it got out of hand. It wasn't supposed to become an international incident. I only wanted to teach you a lesson."

"You can't play with people's lives, Sam. All your father did was beat you. You got people killed, Sam." I turn away from him and stare at the traffic outside his window.

The old man reaches out to me. "I'm sorry. I didn't know it would turn out that way. Do you think you could forgive me?"

I look at him and I still feel the anger. "Why should I forgive you? Did you ever forgive your old man for beating you?"

"Forgive him? Hell, I didn't even talk to him for the last ten years of his life. But don't be like me, Joshua. I'm just a bitter old man."

"You don't know what you did. Two of my friends were killed because of you. Both of them left fatherless children. And for five and a half months, you took me away from my children, too. Away from my newborn baby girl. You didn't want to be our father, but why did you have to take other men away from their children? You don't know how many people you hurt."

He tries to raise himself up. "That's enough, boy. I don't want to hear any more of your whining. You listen to me. Listen good. I'm a salesman. I go into people's homes and offices, and talk them into buying things I know they'll never need. Even so, people like me. I'm smooth, and I talk a good game, but I don't take crap from anyone. Not from my old man. Not from your mother. Not even from Cynthia. Why do you think she was plastered half the time? There were a few men, now and then, who tried to stand up to me and I always mowed them down. Then, my own boy, my flesh and blood, tells me to go to hell. I knew you needed to be cut down to size. All that other stuff that happened, I'm sorry for that. It wasn't supposed to be that way, but you cursed your father, boy, and you needed to be put in your place." The speech exhausts him. He lies back into the bed.

"But you cursed my wife and children. What if your old man had cursed your family? I know you would have told him to go to hell."

"Hell, boy, I would have slugged him."

The way he says it is comical. And sad. "I won't hit you, and I won't curse you again, but I need you to apologize. Like I said, this is my wife. She's the best thing that ever happened to me. If you can't accept her, then I have nothing else to say to you."

He looks at Aisha. "My old man used to spit on your kind. One time, a colored family tried to move next to our house over in Cicero. By the time he was finished with them, they couldn't pack up fast enough. And one day, some of those colored boys thought they were going to use our community swimming pool. My old man was real proud of me after I chased them off. He's the one who taught me to hate. The thing is. . ." He chuckles weakly. "I always hated my old man.

"Like *I* said, I never thought one of my boys would go and marry a colored girl. If my old man were alive to see this. . ." He shakes his head, and smiles. "Well, I guess you showed him,

Rebounding

didn't you, Joshua." He turns to Aisha. "So what do you think of Joshua's old man? I guess you hate me just as much as those boys did after I ran them off."

She looks straight at him, with that look of hers that could cut through glass, and says calmly, "No, Sam, I don't hate you. You were wrong, but I guess you already know that."

He shakes his head again, and smirks. "I never thought I'd be saying this about a. . . a black person, but it looks like you have more class than my son and me put together. You're a nice girl."

"I'm happy to finally meet you." She offers her hand.

He hesitates for a moment. Then he reaches out to her. She takes his hand. Then she bends down and kisses him on the forehead.

"Yes," he says, "you married a nice girl."

"That's the first thing you've said that makes any sense."

"So what's it going to be, boy? Are you going to walk out of here cursing the old man, or are you ready to forgive me? Or maybe you need to be taught another lesson?"

I raise my hands in frustration. I can't answer. I don't know whether to scream at him, or just walk away.

"You said you loved me. Did you mean it?"

I look at him. "Yes, I meant it. That's why it hurts so much. Why did you hurt me, Dad?"

"Because I'm a mean and bitter old man. Don't you know that you're the first man I have ever apologized to? It's not my style, but somehow, seeing you today, I feel like I need you to forgive me. I guess it's because I'm dying. And I meant it when I said I love you."

"Would you love me if you weren't dying?"

"I don't know. I never thought much about love. I can tell you that I never loved my old man. I didn't really love your mother. I didn't even love Cynthia half the time, but, Lord, she was a good looking woman.

"You're different, Joshua. I respect you. You're a lot like me. You know who you are and you won't take crap from anyone, but you have a good heart. That's what's different between us. I'm willing to love you, but you have to do your part, boy."

I look at him, lying there so small in his bed, and something happens to the anger. I can't keep it going. He'll never be the warm and loving man I'd like him to be. He's rough and crude and self-centered, but he's not a monster. Just a sad and bitter old man. He is my father. And I do love him.

"May God be with you, Dad." I gently hug him one more time and kiss him on the forehead. He pulls me close to him again and kisses me on the cheek. We stare at each other for a moment longer. I touch his face before I turn to walk out the door. And I whisper, "I forgive you." He has real tears in his eyes.

I walk away and stand in the doorway, watching as Aisha hugs him too. He holds on to her hand. "You are a fine woman. Joshua is a smart boy to have married you."

"God bless you, Dad," says Aisha. "And thank you for finally loving him."

She and I don't talk on the way to the parking garage. We're silent all the way home, but she sits close to me in the car and holds my hand. After I pull into the driveway and turn off the ignition, I pull her closer. "Thank you" is all I can manage to say.

∻

I think about him as the days go by. I wonder how he is and I think about going to see him again. I could tell him about Islam. I could find out who he is.

But we both said everything that really needed to be said. I decide it's better just to leave it.

One day, while I'm reading a book about Islam, I come across a hadith. I have to read it twice. Prophet Muhammad said, "Do not turn away from your fathers, for he who turns away from his father will be guilty of committing an act of disbelief."

He is my father and I did the right thing. I saw him. I forgave him. I told him I love him. And I meant it.

I don't go to see him again, but I do pray for him. Every day. Especially when I'm breaking my fast.

Rebounding

∽

Celia calls Mom three weeks later to tell her that Sam—Dad—has died. I don't mean to go to the funeral parlor, but, somehow, I feel restless and Aisha and I go out for a drive and we're in the neighborhood so we stop by.

Soon after we walk in, a woman comes up to greet me. She has curly black hair, like mine. "You must be Joshua."

"Yes. How did you know?"

"Because you look just like our father. I'm Celia." She offers her hand.

I'm about to tell her that, as a Muslim, I don't shake hands with women when Aisha whispers, "Go ahead. She's your sister."

That's right. I have a sister. I shake her hand.

"Your brothers came earlier. I'm glad to finally meet all of you."

"Don't you have a brother too?" I look around.

"Yes, but he's not here. He lives in Atlanta. The last time he saw Dad was about six months ago. They fought, and my brother left. Dad was diagnosed two weeks later, but Sean refused to come. They never got along. I guess because Dad hit Sean a lot when he was young. My brother has never been able to forgive him."

I know how that feels.

"Dad told me you came to see him. It meant more to him than you can ever imagine. A few days before he died, he asked me to tell you that he's sorry for everything. And he wanted me to thank you for calling him Dad. Do you know what he meant?"

"Yes, I do. Thank you for the message."

Aisha asks the question I wouldn't ask. "Joshua has always wondered how he was, as a father. I'm sorry, this might not be the right time to ask, but he's always wanted to know."

"My mom always told me I was lucky because I'm a girl. He was sweet to me, but not to my brother. I guess he didn't know what to do with a son, but he did try, in his own way. That one time—when he met with your brothers and you—he really did

287

want to know you, but he didn't know how to do it. He told me what happened."

"I'd rather just forget about it. We made our peace. I have the feeling that he was never very happy."

"No, not often. It's sad, really, that he spent all those years being bitter. He didn't get along with his father, either. If you want to know more about him, you can ask his sister. That's Aunt Janet over there. His brothers didn't come. They were never very close.

"There are just a few relatives here. The rest are people he knew through his business dealings. Other businessmen, and a few politicians too. He always bragged about all the friends he had downtown in city hall. He even used to talk about some connections he had in DC. He was a very successful salesman, and he had many friends."

He knew how to make friends. Just not how to treat the people who wanted to love him.

While she's talking, I look around and I see another face. Familiar, but not friendly. The man standing next to Aunt Janet. He's one of the agents who tried to interrogate me. The one who seemed to take pleasure in telling me that Ahmed was dead. I grab Aisha's hand and squeeze it tightly. A flash of anger bursts in my chest. Then it's gone.

Sam is lying in an open casket in the front of the room. "Excuse me." I leave Aisha and Celia, and walk up to take a look at him. Through the magic of mortuary science, he looks better than he did that time at Mom's house. I can see the resemblance between us. I reach over and touch his cold hand. "I still don't really understand why you did it, but it's done. I meant it when I said I always loved you. Goodbye. Dad."

I linger for a moment, lost in thought. We made our peace. I just wish we could have done it before he was dying. He was my father, my dad. It's too bad we wasted so many years before we could find some love between us. Now it is too late.

I come out of my daze and remember the man in the black suit. I walk back quickly and grab Aisha's arm. "We need to go."

"I wish you would stay," says Celia. "I've been wanting to get to know you."

"Call us later. I need to leave." Aisha quickly gives her our number.

I take Aisha's hand and we walk back to our car.

"What happened in there?" she asks as we pull away from the funeral parlor.

I can't answer. I prefer to concentrate on the traffic. I wait until the car is in the driveway before I turn to her.

"One of the agents who questioned me was there. One of Sam's friends. I couldn't bear to be in the same room with him. Every time I see one of them, I get a tight feeling in my chest. I'm afraid they're going to take me away again."

"I didn't know. I'm sorry, Hon."

"That's okay. That's who he was. I don't want to think about it. I want to remember my father, the one who finally said he loved me."

I sit and cry in the car, here in the driveway. Aisha holds me and rubs my back. He said he was sorry. We made our peace. That's what's important. By the time I get out of the car, I'm able to leave behind the thirty-nine years of pain. For the first time in my life, I am really free.

∾

On Sunday morning, I go to see Mom. We have to talk.

Walt lets me in. Mom is in the kitchen, making breakfast. They are both still in their bath robes.

"Oh, Joshua. I didn't expect to see you at this time of the morning. I'm not dressed or anything."

"That's okay. I just need to talk to you about something."

"Can I get you something? Have you had breakfast yet?"

"I'm fasting."

"That's right. I forgot. Okay, just give me a minute."

Walt takes the spatula from her hand. "I can finish cooking breakfast, Evie. You go talk with your son."

She pours herself a cup of coffee and walks with me into the patio room. When we sit down, she takes a sip, then stops. "I'm sorry. I guess I shouldn't drink in front of you."

"That's okay, Mom. Don't worry about it. I went to the funeral parlor yesterday. I met Celia."

"Yes, I know. Walt and I came later. Aisha and you had just left. Celia said you seemed to be in a hurry."

"One of the agents was there. The thing is, Mom, I looked at Sam lying there in the casket. You know that we're all going to end up that way someday."

"I've told you, I try not to think about it."

"But it's going to happen, whether you think about it or not. Sam, Ahmed, Aunt Arlene, Cynthia. They're all dead now. And I know I came close because I saw the white light people always talk about." *Allah only knows how close I came.*

"Can you just answer one question for me, Mom? Do you believe in God?"

She doesn't say no, but she's too quiet. She stares out the window for several minutes before she turns to me again. "I suppose I do. I don't know, really."

"What's holding you back?"

"I don't know. I don't like to think about it."

"About God?"

"God, death, everything. Can't we just enjoy our lives and hope for the best?"

"But there's more than that, Mom. More than this life."

"Joshua, I haven't even had my breakfast yet. Can't this wait?"

"I guess, but I worry about you."

"You do? I thought Chris was the only one who worried about my soul. And as long as we're baring our souls, you never did tell me if you went to see your father before he died."

"Yes, I went."

"And?"

"We made our peace."

"I'm glad you did that."

Rebounding

I leave so she and Walt can eat their breakfast without feeling awkward. As I drive home I keep wondering.

∽

I rest a little, then go to see Brad. Matt lets me in. Brad is in his home office, working at his computer. He almost never goes to church on Sundays, but he's almost always working.

I walk into his office. "Hey Brad, you have a few minutes?"

He saves his work, then turns around. "Sure. What's up?"

We talk about our families. Then we start talking about Sam. I ask him, "Did our father ever beat you?"

He looks down. "Yes, starting when I was four. I felt guilty when he left because in a way I was happy. The beatings stopped, and I was happy he was gone."

"Why didn't you ever say anything?"

"I thought it was my fault. He hit me because I was bad. He left me because I was bad."

"I never knew you had that kind of baggage. With all of that going on in your head, why didn't you get as messed up as I was?"

"When I was in high school and college, you were just a kid. I smoked some grass. And I messed around a little. Didn't you ever wonder how I knew the address of that abortion clinic I told you about when Heather ended up pregnant? There's a lot you don't know about me, but I never let any of that get me off track because, most of all, I wanted to succeed. I had to prove to Dad that I was good and I didn't deserve to be hit."

Brad's confession catches me off guard. He's right. I was just a kid. I never thought there were any flaws in my oldest brother. He was the first man who filled the role of father for me. I take a moment to process it all, then reach over and put my hand on his shoulder. "I never knew."

"You weren't supposed to know. I have always had an image to maintain." He tries to smile, but doesn't quite manage. It wasn't really a joke.

"Did Mom know about the beatings?"

"No. I'm sure she didn't. She couldn't have. She would have stopped him." He's quiet for a moment. I guess he's remembering. "He must have waited until she wasn't around. That part was really scary. He was so cool about it. He took his belt. Sometimes he used a piece of wood he kept around. He kept that wood just to beat me. He made me pull my pants down. And he let loose. While he was hitting me, he was angry, but not before, and not after. When he was done, he told me to pull up my pants. Then he smiled and, this is the strangest part, he kissed me on the cheek and told me I was a good boy."

"That's eerie. So Mom never saw the bruises?"

"No. There's no way she could have. He only hit me where they wouldn't show." He stops again and winces, as if he still feels the pain. "But that's not the worst of it. Two times, before he left, he hit me when I did something good, not because I was bad.

"When I won the first grade spelling bee, I came home with my certificate and my ribbon, and showed them to him. He took them away from me and beat me. Later I found them in the trash. I took them and cleaned them up after he went to sleep. And right before he left, I brought home my first straight A report card. That was the worst beating of all. Later I found my report card in the trash can, too, but it was torn up. He was supposed to sign it so I could take it back to my teacher. He was supposed to be proud of me. The next day, I told my teacher I had lost it. I couldn't tell her what my father did."

I'm not sure if I've ever seen Brad cry. I've seen him angry and upset, but I don't know if I've ever seen his tears. After everything he has done in his life, his degrees and his promotions, he still cries over the memory of his second grade report card and the hurt he suffered at the hands of our father. I'm not sure what I should do. He's my big brother. I glance at the books on the shelf. I don't look at him while he cries.

He quickly calms himself, and I turn toward him again. "It's not your fault. He was sick."

Rebounding

"Yes, he was. It helped when I became old enough to understand that, but it still hurts."

"Didn't you get angry?"

"Of course, but I felt guilty for being angry with my father. And I couldn't show my anger. The first couple of times he beat me, I tried to fight back. Then he beat me harder. I learned to take it. I was also afraid, and the fear lasted for many years. I was afraid of him, and I was afraid that I would grow up to be like him. That's why Beth and I waited so long before we had a child. I worried that I would beat my son. Beth is the one who helped me work through it."

"Did he beat Chris, too?"

"No, but I guess maybe he would have. Chris turned four about six months before he left. I suppose if he stayed he would have beaten Chris. And you. I think you would have ended up killing him."

"I probably would have. Can you imagine how badly that would have screwed up my life?" I almost laugh. It's so sad that it's funny. "But there's something I don't understand. After all that, all the times he abused you, it was still hard for you to walk away from him that time at Mom's house, wasn't it?"

"Yes. Because when I saw him, I was a little boy again. And I wanted him to love me. But I had to walk away. Not just because of what he said to you. I could still hear the anger in his voice when he talked to me. If he were younger, and I were smaller, I think he would have beaten me again."

"Did you go to see him before he died?"

"Yes. Beth came with me. It was like my wife had to protect me from him. Even though he was old and dying, I didn't know what he would do.

"He was civil. We talked for a while, about my career mostly. When I told him about my latest promotion, he smiled. Can you imagine? He didn't scream at me. I think he was proud of me. Right before we left, he said he was sorry, and he told me that he loved me. I think he meant it."

"I'm sure he did. Did you know that his father used to beat him?"

"No, but that doesn't surprise me. I remember his father, our grandfather. He seemed to be just a harmless old man. Not very friendly, but not dangerous. Whenever he was around, Dad used to cower. He became smaller. Then, when we were alone again, he would beat me."

I remember what Sam told me—that he would have hit his father—but he was really a coward. That's why he always had to act so tough. It was all an act.

"At least," I say, "you were able to make peace with him before he died."

"In a way." Brad shakes his head. "But it's too bad that it was forty years too late."

~

When I leave Brad's house I feel emotionally drained. All these years I have felt sorry for myself. I never imagined what Brad was going through.

This whole experience with Sam's death has been a roller coaster ride. I'm glad it happened during Ramadan.

By the time I get home, I know what I need to do. I talk with Aisha after we break our fast.

"I need some time to sort everything out. This whole Sam thing. I want to spend the last few days of Ramadan at the masjid. What do you think?"

"I'll miss you, but I think it's a good idea. Go ahead and get your things together. The kids and I can manage for a little while. Just don't talk to any men in black suits. I expect you to be back home for Eid."

I pack up my things—clothes, toiletries, bedding, Qur'an. I call Parvez and arrange to take a few days off. Business has been slow, anyway, during Ramadan.

Before I head out, I hand Aisha an envelope to mail. We can pay the annual zakah again. This year, it will go to Ahmed's widow and children.

I prepare another envelope which I'll hand to the imam. Our Zakatul Fitr can help another family enjoy Eid.

Rebounding

Everything's taken care of, but I feel I'm forgetting something.

During the prayer, I realize what it is. When I'm finished praying, I call Jeremy on his cell.

"Assalaamu alaikum, Dad."

I hear giggling in the background. It sounds like Sabeera. "Are you at Umar's house again?"

"Yes. What's wrong with that?"

"You'll be married to her in less than a week, Jeremy. I have a better way for you to spend your last few days as a bachelor. Come with me to the masjid. We'll make ittikhaf together. And I can tell you everything you need to know before you make the most important commitment of your life."

He's not easily convinced, but I have him put Umar on the phone, and together we get him to tear himself away from Raheema so he can spend a few days with his old man.

Before I leave for the masjid, I call Michael too. Just to hear his voice. And to tell him that I love him.

Evie's Interlude: Facing Death

Sam is dead.

God knows how many times I have wanted him dead. When he was beating me. When he was hitting Brad. When he left me for Cynthia. When Joshua was arrested, and I just knew Sam had to be behind it. There have been many times over the years when I would have gladly twisted his neck and watched while he took his last breath.

But he was my husband. And the father of my sons. As much as I hate him for everything he has done, part of me still feels something. I suppose it is pity. My love for him started to die the minute he first raised his hand to me.

I stood there yesterday at the funeral parlor and looked down at his lifeless body. He can never hurt me again. It's all gone now. The cruelty. The lies. And the boyish grin.

Joshua came to see me this morning. He wanted to talk with me about death. I told him I don't like to think about it. The truth is, I do think about it, but I certainly do not want to discuss it.

My mother suffered for four years before she died. During that last year or so, we knew the end was coming, but we never talked about death.

We didn't even talk about it during her last month, when we knew death was imminent. I clearly remember my last conversation with her. It was two days before she died. Right before she lapsed into a coma. She was so weak. I hated to see her like that. I knew she couldn't last long, but we kept pretending she would get well. She asked me about the boys, and I told her about Brad's latest report card, Chris's latest merit award, and Joshua's latest stunt. She asked me to kiss them for her. She told me she loved me, and I said I loved her too. She asked me to take care of Dad. I kissed her on the cheek, and she reached up to touch my face. Then I told her I had to leave to pick Brad and Chris up from baseball practice and get Joshua from the sitter. I said I would be back tomorrow.

A few hours later, Dad called and told me she was slipping away. I left Brad in charge of his brothers and rushed back to the hospital. She was still alive, but I would never hear her sweet voice again.

We never talked about dying.

※

In the evening, while Walt and I relax together, I say, "Do you think maybe we should update our wills?"

He looks up from his book. "I think that is an excellent idea."

A few days later, we meet with one of his friends who is still practicing law. Walt leaves a good part of his extensive book collection to my sons. I have decided to leave part of my art collection to his daughters.

"There is one more thing, Walt. You know how I feel about my grandchildren. I have been very generous to both Michael and Jeremy. Do you think it would be appropriate for me to establish a trust of some kind to ensure that all of my grandchildren receive something special when they are eighteen? Just in case I'm not around when Martha and Maryam reach that age?"

"I think that would be very appropriate."

I ask Walt's friend to make the necessary provisions.

On our way home, I ask Walt, "Are you sure this was the proper thing for us to do?"

"People update their wills all the time, Evie. There's nothing unusual about that."

"Then why does it make me feel so strange?"

He just reaches over and holds my hand.

※

Before I go to sleep, while Walt reads one of his books, I think about death. Sam is dead. I will die too one day, I suppose. My will is ready, but I'm not.

Joshua

Part Fifteen

These last few days with Jeremy were the best I've ever spent with any of my children. We prayed together, read Qur'an together, and we talked.

Today is the last day. Tomorrow is Eid. His wedding day. After the morning prayer, I decide that it's time to give him my speech.

I figure that, as the father of the groom, I have two main duties, aside from the financial. I fulfilled the first when I took Jeremy to talk to Umar. I put aside the Qur'an and turn to Jeremy so I can fulfill my second duty.

I clear my throat. "You're getting married tomorrow. And there are some things you need to know."

We talk for the next two hours, covering everything from Islamic teachings about intimacy to helping his wife with the housework. The most important thing I want to tell him is to treat his wife well, even when it's raining and the boss just yelled at him and the car needs major repairs.

"Remember, you are making the most important commitment of your life. I've said that already, I know. I'm not that old yet, but I can't say it enough. Nothing else you do—your work, your education—will be as important as the promise you will be making to Raheema."

"I know. Don't laugh, but it's a little scary to think about it."

"Sure it's scary. The marriage contract you sign tomorrow will affect everything you do for the rest of your life, but if you always respect her, and treat her the way you would like to be treated, then everything else will fall into place."

"I think I can do that."

"I don't need to know every time you have a fight with her—there are things that the two of you will have to work out on your own—but if you ever need me to remind you about the things we've talked about today, I'll always be there for you."

"Thanks, Dad. That's good to know."

We each take a nap, then pray together and read some more Qur'an. The day passes too quickly. Before I know it, we're breaking our fast. Then we pray and eat together one more time.

Jeremy is going back to spend his last night as a single man in his mother's home. "I'd better get moving. Mom said she has something special planned."

"I guess I'll see you tomorrow then."

"Yeah, Dad. I'll see you then."

I watch as he drives away. I miss him already. I stand outside the masjid for a minute, remembering my little boy, before getting into my car to head home.

When I walk in, I find Umar sitting in our family room, reading to the kids. "Assalaamu alaikum. What brings you here?"

"They've kicked me out of the house. They're having a henna party for the bride. Women everywhere, I imagine. It may run late. I hope you don't mind if I hang around."

"Never, Brother. And tomorrow we're going to become in-laws again. Where is my wife, anyway?"

"At the henna party, of course. She took Jennifer and Maryam with her."

"I know Jennifer will love that, especially since she and Raheema used to be so close. So it's just us guys. What do you think we should do?"

"It's Eid now, Dad," says Muhammad. "We have to celebrate. Let's go get some ice cream."

He takes after Aisha. "Sounds good to me. Let's go."

∽

I don't know what time it was when Aisha, Jennifer, and Maryam finally got home. I crashed right after we came back from getting our ice cream. Umar stayed up with the boys.

I wake everyone up for the prayer in the morning and cook a light breakfast. We eat, put on our new clothes, and get into Aisha's van to head for the Eid prayer. Jennifer isn't sure if she wants to be a Muslim, but she does want to celebrate with us. Aisha took her shopping a couple of days ago and bought her a

Rebounding

long dress to wear for Eid. She also agreed to wear a scarf, just for the Eid prayer. She looks beautiful, but I wonder what Heather would say if she saw our daughter right now.

Aisha hands me the van keys. "You drive. I'm too tired."

"When did you come home?"

"I don't know. One, maybe. Or two."

"More like two," says Jennifer. "It was great. I never laughed so hard."

"What do you women do at those parties?"

"That's something you'll never know," says Aisha. She smiles, then yawns again.

After the prayer, I greet my friends. It takes me a while to find Umar. He looks tired, too.

"What time did you leave last night?"

"I don't know. Sometime around two or three, I think. I slept on the couch until Aisha came and woke me up."

"Were they all gone?"

"The last ones were leaving just as I pulled up. Safa and Raheema didn't come to the prayer this morning. They're both tired. And nervous."

Jeremy walks up and gives me a hug. "Eid Mubarak."

"Eid Kareem, Son. So, are you ready?"

"Sure. It's what I've been waiting for. I saw Jennifer. She looks great. Is she ready to become a Muslim now?"

"Not yet, but she wanted to come with us. Don't tell your mom."

He laughs. "No, I don't think I want to do that. Anyway, she has other things to think about today."

"What are your plans for the rest of the day?"

"I'm going out to eat with a few of the guys. We thought about catching a movie too, but Mom wants me to come home and get ready."

"Aren't you nervous?"

"A little, but didn't you tell me that after I get married I won't have much time to hang out with my friends? Don't worry. I'll make sure I get there on time. Mom will probably be calling me every ten minutes to remind me to come home and get dressed."

305

"I'll see you tonight then." Another hug, and he's off with the guys.

Umar yawns. "What are Aisha and you going to do for Eid?"

"I think we'll just go home and let the kids play with their presents. Aisha and Jennifer barely slept last night, so I'm sure they'll both want to take naps. And we'll wait for tonight."

"It will be the same at our house, I'm sure. Eid is very different this year."

~

We get to the hotel in the late afternoon. The ceremony is scheduled for six.

Jennifer wears the same dress she wore to the prayer, but without the scarf. "You look very pretty today," I tell her as we leave the house.

"Thanks. I love this dress."

"How did you feel, wearing a scarf this morning?"

"It was different."

I decide to leave it at that.

At the hotel, I play a dual role, checking on the catering and helping to supervise while greeting the guests as they arrive. Everything is in place.

Jeremy arrives with Heather, Peter, and Brianna. He's dressed in special wedding clothes from Bangladesh. His white wedding suit is similar to the one I wore when I married Aisha, with a longer jacket. He also wears a white turban. He looks so grown up. My son, the handsome groom. My little Jeremy.

The rest of the family is in the spirit, too. Brianna just wears a pretty little dress, but Peter is wearing a Pakistani outfit, similar to mine. Heather is decked out in a bright orange sari, revealing quite a bit of skin. I take Jeremy aside.

"Didn't you tell your mother how to dress for an Islamic ceremony?"

"What was I supposed to say? She bought the sari a few months ago, and she likes to wear it that way. She was so excited about trying something different. And Peter likes it. It's okay, Dad. It's a special day for her, too."

That's Heather. She still looks good, too, for a woman who is old enough to be the mother of the groom. I put my arm around Aisha's waist.

I walk around the room, talking with friends and relatives. I know Safa's brother, Imran, and a few of her other relatives, but I meet many others I have never seen before. Another one of Raheema's uncles is here, too. Her father's oldest brother, Abdul-Malik, flew in from Miami. He introduces himself, and we shake hands.

"I wish Abdul-Aziz could be here to see her. He loved his little daughter very much. His wish was to see her grow up."

"I'm sure he would be proud of her."

"Yes, he would. Safa and Umar have raised her well. Abdul-Aziz would be very proud of the young woman she is now."

Many of Jeremy's and Raheema's friends are here. Jeremy's friends come in a variety of dress, everything from jeans to suits to robes. Raheema has several close girlfriends. A few of them are not Muslims, but they all dressed modestly.

Sharon has just arrived from Moline, with many of the relatives, including Grandma. She looks strong. She comes over and takes my hand.

"Now it's your turn, Joshua, to see your children marry and have children."

I look at her gray hair and wrinkled skin. She's seen her children and grandchildren marry. And two or three of her great-grandchildren. How much longer will it be before I am old, too?

Aunt Helen said she would try to come, but she doesn't get out much anymore. Sharon tells us that she's having a very hard time since Aunt Arlene died. Like she said, she's alone now.

Jeremy fidgets and talks nervously with his friends. I remember that feeling when I married Aisha. I hope their marriage is as good as ours.

The imam comes over and talks with Jeremy. Some final words of advice.

When Mom arrives, she gives Jeremy a big hug and a kiss on the cheek. He blushes. "Hi, Gramma. Where's Walt?"

"He went to pick up Michael and Marcus from the airport."

"They made it? Michael told me he wasn't sure he could get away."

"He wanted to surprise you. They should be here soon."

The guests keep arriving. This wedding is much bigger than ours was, or Umar and Safa's. These are our children and we want to do everything for them.

Michael and Marcus walk in, grinning. Michael and Jeremy hug. "My little brother is getting married. I can't believe it. Oh, assalaamu alaikum."

"Walaikum— Wait, are you a Muslim?"

"For over a month now. Assalaamu alaikum, Dad." The words I've waited to hear from him. He hugs me.

"What finally convinced you?"

"I don't know. I guess I just got away from the family and started thinking more about it. Marcus and I studied Islam together. It all started to make sense."

"And you fasted too?"

"I made it. It wasn't easy, but we helped each other out."

"Assalaamu alaikum, Marcus. It's good to see you. I'm glad you could make it."

"Walaikum assalaam. I always knew you'd be the first to take the plunge. All that shyness, that was just an act, wasn't it?"

Jeremy grins. "What about you? You're not getting any younger."

"We'll see, insha Allah."

"I've been trying to convince him," says Michael. "But we need Uncle Ismail to come up and help him find someone."

A few minutes later, my brothers walk in. Brad brought his whole family. Chris and Melinda left their children at home. They don't say why, but I know it's because Chris wants to limit their exposure to Islam. He won't be happy when he hears that Michael is a Muslim now, but Michael is my kid.

Brad pulls me aside. "I have some good news. Nuruddin has his visa. He'll be coming at the end of August."

"Great. Just two more months. Thanks for sponsoring him."

"No problem."

I'm looking at the door, waiting for Umar and his family, when John, Michelle, and their children arrive. Derek strolls in with a young woman on his arm. They all come over to greet Aisha and me.

"Hi Joshua. Are you ready for the big day?"

"I guess I am, John. I'm getting a little worried, though. Tony and his family aren't here yet."

"I'm sure they're on their way. I'd like you to meet Derek's fiancée. This is Keisha."

Keisha offers her hand, which Aisha accepts. "It's nice to meet you. Congratulations on your engagement. Does my brother know yet?"

"No," says Derek. "I finally convinced her to marry me just last night." He smiles and puts his arm around her waist.

"Well, I'm sure he'll be happy to hear the news. Welcome to the family, Keisha."

One way or another, I guess Umar will have a chance to start welcoming grandchildren.

We've been here for a while now. It's a few minutes after six. The younger ones are restless. I stop Luqman from chasing Muhammad around the hall.

I feel like I've shaken hundreds of hands tonight. The guests are waiting. The imam is waiting. The groom is waiting, but we're still missing the bride.

The imam comes over to me. "Is the young woman here yet?"

"No. I don't know what's keeping them."

Jeremy bounces from one foot to the other. He keeps looking at the door. I go out into the hallway to call Umar.

There's no answer at home, and I get the message on his cell. Where could they be?

I walk back in. Jeremy looks at me. I shake my head. He's rubbing his hands together. He can't stand still. He's nervous enough, without this delay.

309

I'm really starting to get worried, but a minute later Umar walks in with Sakeena and all his little ones. The bride stays out in the hallway with her mother, waiting to make her appearance.

"Assalaamu alaikum. Are we ready?"

"Just waiting for Raheema. What happened?"

"First we all took naps, and we overslept. Then she was so nervous that it took her hours to get ready."

Marcus comes up from behind him. "Assalaamu alaikum."

Umar rarely looks that surprised. He smiles and hugs Marcus tightly. "Walaikum assalaam. I'm glad you could make it."

"How could I miss this? I've known Jeremy and Raheema since they were little kids, running up and down the stairs and getting into my things. It's hard to believe that they're all grown up."

"When will it be your turn?"

"I'm still not as old as you were when you married Safa. I think I've got a couple of years yet, but I need to start collecting a dollar from everyone who asks me that tonight. I could probably get enough for a new computer."

The imam comes up to us. "We're ready now. You can take your places in front."

We had many discussions in the months leading up to the wedding about how the ceremony should be conducted. Safa told us about the customs in her country, where the bride and groom are separated during the ceremony, but Jeremy and Raheema are both American kids. We all talked about it and finally agreed on a ceremony similar to what Aisha and I had, but Umar will not be walking Raheema in.

We quietly take our places in front. Heather and I sit next to Jeremy. Umar and Safa will sit with Raheema. Abdul-Malik will sit next to Umar to represent his brother, Raheema's father. Imran and Michael sit with the party as witnesses. The imam sits in the middle.

Even though she doesn't make a grand entrance, everyone looks when Raheema walks into the room. Her dress is similar to the pictures I've seen of the Bangladeshi weddings of Safa's

Rebounding

relatives, but her hair is fully covered. Her sari is red, but she wears it modestly. She looks sweet. Jeremy stares at her, smiling.

The ceremony is like other Islamic weddings I have attended, but this time it is my son who is getting married.

They sign the contract, and the imam concludes the ceremony. They're married. I greet my new daughter-in-law with a hug.

"Welcome to the family, Raheema."

"Thank you, Uncle Isa."

"You can call me Dad now."

Jeremy greets his mother-in-law. The newlyweds look shyly at one another.

There is eating and talking and blessings for the newlyweds. Aisha and I talk with some of Raheema's family, the aunts and uncles I haven't seen since Umar and Safa got married, and a few I've never met before. Safa's mother couldn't make it to the wedding because of her health, but most of her family is here.

Heather and Peter try to learn new words and comment on the delicious food, while Brianna plays with Sabeera and Tasneema. Some of Raheema's relatives look surprised when they meet Heather, with her bright orange sari and flowing blonde hair. They knew that Jeremy and I are American Muslims. They didn't know how far we've come from that little apartment on the south side.

It's all over way too soon. Then Jeremy is the one who gets ready to leave with his wife. Tomorrow they'll fly to Charleston for a short honeymoon—a wedding present from Aisha and me. Tonight they'll go to their new apartment.

There are handshakes, hugs, and kisses. I'd like to give my son some more fatherly advice, but I can't think of anything and, besides, there is no time for a private moment with him. I already did that. And I'm glad I did. I just give him a hug, and then he's gone. With his wife.

The mothers cry. Heather and Safa, and Aisha too. And Mom. They're probably all remembering the shy little round-faced boy and the little girl who ran around with her braids bobbing in the air. I don't feel like crying. When I look at this young Muslim couple, I feel a great sense of pride in the adults they have become.

Jeremy has so much more going for him than I did at that age. I wonder if having a father made a difference. I hope it did.

Safa invites the family members back to her house after the other guests are gone. Just Aisha and me, Heather and Peter, Mom and Walt, Brad and Beth, Chris and Melinda, Imran and his wife, Abdul-Malik and his wife, Sharon and Marcus, John and Michelle, and Michael and all the rest of our children. She asks Grandma, Uncle Paul, Aunt Vivien and Aunt Debra to come too, but Grandma is tired, so they all decide to go back to the hotel. Safa invites them for brunch tomorrow.

She has tea and sweets for us when we walk in, even though we get there just a few minutes after they do. John and his family walk in right behind us.

I turn to Derek. "So, you're ready to get married?"

"Yes, of course. I'll finish my studies in December, and we plan to get married sometime next spring."

Umar walks in from the kitchen. I put my hand on his shoulder. "You know, Tony here is looking forward to having grandchildren."

Umar shakes his head. I've managed to embarrass him, which isn't easy. Keisha laughs. "We'll have to see about that."

Safa brings out the tea and sweets. We sit and talk about our married children while our other children either sit with us or run off to play. The two youngest, Maryam and Ahmad, are asleep.

"It was a very different kind of ceremony," says Peter. "Is that usual for Muslims?"

"In this country it is," says Safa. "Back home it is much different. The bride and groom do not even see each other during the ceremony. There are many rituals we perform during the marriage period, starting with the engagement. And the party sometimes lasts for days. But we're in America now, and even my daughter is an American."

"I like the part about the dowry. And the part where she had to give her consent. I thought that Muslim women were the properties of their husbands."

Rebounding

That's a strange comment, especially coming from Heather. I have treated Aisha, whom I married as a Muslim, much better than I ever treated Heather, but I don't want to go there.

"Not at all. Not even with Raheema's father. Though he was my cousin, and though our families arranged the marriage, I still had to give my consent. And he did have to give me the dowry."

"But," says Imran's wife, "there *are* families who force their daughters to marry someone they don't wish to marry. That is culture, though, not Islam."

"And," says Imran, "did you wish to marry me?"

She smiles. "We have five children. You figure it out."

Everyone laughs. And I realize that we have bridged the gap. My Islamic life and my non-Islamic life are together in this room. Friendship and understanding are here also.

In an odd moment, while everyone else is talking, I think of Sam. Even if he were still alive, he wouldn't be here tonight. When he walked away from us, he lost his place in our family. None of us—Brad, Chris, or I—really knew him, and his grandchildren never saw him.

I went away from my family too. Twice. While everyone talks, I silently thank Allah for bringing me back to them.

I am a father to my children. They know I will always be there for them. And they know who I am.

Evie: A Journey

"Take advantage of five before five: your youth before old age, your health before your sickness, your wealth before your poverty, your free time before you become occupied, and your life before your death."
— Prophet Muhammad

Part One

It was a lovely wedding. Raheema looked beautiful, as a bride should. And my grandson... I could barely recognize him, sitting there wearing the traditional Bangladeshi wedding clothes, but he looked very handsome.

The ceremony was quite different. Later, at Safa's house, Joshua said that it was similar to the ceremony they had when he married Aisha. I still regret not going to their wedding. Everything was different then. Anyway, it was so short and simple. In some ways it seemed more like a business arrangement, with the signing of the contract. Joshua told me that the greatest emphasis is not on the ceremony, but the marriage.

They are so young, but I do believe they are ready for marriage. Jeremy is much more mature than his father was at that age. Perhaps that is because he has seen what his parents did wrong. Heather and Joshua had such a rough time of it when the children were small. They must have done something right, though, because all of their children are such fine young people. Even Jennifer.

I'm sitting in the car, looking out the window and thinking about the night, while Walt drives us home through the nearly empty streets. It is far past midnight, and I usually go to sleep much earlier than this, but I don't feel tired yet. It was a lovely wedding.

"I forgot to ask Safa. I wonder why Raheema was wearing red." It's not so much a question as a spoken thought.

"In South Asia, red symbolizes life and joy," says Walt.

"You never stop learning, do you?"

"Not if I can help it. I had some interesting conversations with Safa's relatives. Maybe we could go to Bangladesh someday."

I don't think Walt has ever met a person he couldn't talk with.

317

He reaches over and pulls me closer to him. We're quiet the rest of the way home. He must be tired. I think I'm starting to become tired, too.

He pulls into the garage, we get out of the car, and he puts his arm around my shoulders. I am very tired now. I lean on him as we walk into the house.

We change our clothes and crawl into bed. I lay my head on my pillow. I'm just about to drift off when he says, "Evie, I have been thinking. I don't know what you believe."

I'm so tired I can barely talk, but his statement jars me. "What? Where did that come from?"

"We have been married for nearly a year now, and I don't know what you believe."

"Can't we talk about this in the morning?" I struggle to keep my eyes open.

"Of course." He kisses me. "Go to sleep. I love you."

He turns off the light and holds me as I drift away.

Sometime during the night, I dream that I'm sitting in church with Sam. He looks handsome in his suit and tie. I hold a baby on my lap. It must be Brad. He can't be more than a year old. The organ plays and I open the hymnal to page 114. Sam's deep voice belts out the hymn with vigor while I quietly sing along. Suddenly I look around me and wonder what I'm doing here. I want to go home. I grab the baby and walk up the aisle. I try to leave, but the exits are blocked. I start to cry. People look at me and shake their heads. Sam puts his arms around me and tries to lead me back to our pew. "Settle down, Evie," he says. "People are looking." I fight him, but I can't get away. He holds me tighter. "Settle down, Evie. It's okay."

I open my eyes. Walt is holding me. "It's okay, Evie." He soothes me as I drift back to sleep.

∾

In the morning, we eat a leisurely breakfast and talk about our plans for the day. Our first stop will be the travel agency. We want to look at their materials and make plans for our next trip.

Rebounding

When Brad or Walt's daughters travel, they arrange everything over the internet. That is much faster, but we're retired now, and we have time. I enjoy walking into the office and fantasizing about the wonderful places we could go.

On our way to the travel agency, Walt asks, "What happened last night? Why were you afraid?"

That's an odd question. "Afraid of what?"

"I don't know. Whatever it was you saw in your nightmare."

"I slept very well last night. I don't remember any nightmare."

He drops it. I don't know what he's talking about. I do vaguely remember a question he asked me, right before I went to sleep. Something philosophical. I suppose it was prompted by the wedding. There was no alcohol at the reception. Perhaps it was the Indian food.

∾

We walk into the travel agency and find our favorite agent. Amanda arranged our other trips for us, and she has a wonderful talent for locating the most culturally authentic hotels and restaurants with the best prices and all the amenities of home. Third world travel with first world comfort, she likes to say. As we sit down in front of her, it suddenly occurs to me how terribly ethnocentric that statement is.

"Good morning, Walt and Evie. It's nice to see you again."

"It's been a few months, I know. We've been busy. My grandson was just married."

"Oh, how nice. So where would you like to go this time?"

Ever since we started talking about the wedding, I have been curious about Bangladesh. Until I met Safa, I had not even known where Bangladesh was located. I would like to go there and experience, first hand, the culture of this small nation. I'll have to be sure to speak with Safa before we go, so she can give me some tips on the dos and don'ts of her culture.

Before I can open my mouth, Walt says, "We would like to go somewhere to learn more about the religious experience. What area of the world would you recommend?"

He never mentioned this before. I thought we were in agreement about going to Bangladesh. I shoot him a look. He doesn't seem to notice.

"That depends," says Amanda. "If you are interested in exploring Christianity, I would recommend Italy, of course. For Hinduism you could go to India, and for Buddhism you could go to China or perhaps Thailand. What exactly do you have in mind?"

"I would like to visit an area where I can find the full range of religious experience. Including Islam. Is that possible?"

"I think you might find Southeast Asia intriguing then. In Malaysia alone you can find Christianity and Islam, as well as Buddhism and some Hinduism. I could even help you find villages where animism is still practiced. Is that what you're looking for?"

"Yes, I believe it is. Could you book travel for us to Malaysia then?"

"Excuse me, Amanda," I say as politely as possible. "I think perhaps Walt and I should take more time to discuss this trip. We will be back later. I hope we haven't troubled you."

"No, no trouble at all. Please come back when you have decided."

Walt swallows hard. I can tell he's irritated, but so am I. "Let's go, Walt."

He gets up slowly. "Thank you, Amanda." It's the same voice he used when, in a moment of whimsy, I made a face at a guard at Buckingham Palace.

He waits until we're in the car. "What was that about, Evie?"

"What do you mean? Religious exploration? Southeast Asia? You didn't discuss this with me. I thought we had agreed to go to Bangladesh."

"No, we had not agreed. You had mentioned it. Along with half a dozen other places. I have never said that was where I wanted to go."

Rebounding

"Just last night you said you would like to go there. And when I brought it up two weeks ago, you nodded."

"I nod all the time. It doesn't mean that I agree with whatever you happened to have said in the last five minutes. As I said last night, I would like to go to Bangladesh, eventually, but I feel that I need to do this first."

"Why? You never talked about going to Southeast Asia before. I hear it's beautiful, but why now?" I vaguely remember his strange question last night, right before I fell asleep. "Does this have to do with that question you asked me? 'I don't know what you believe' or some kind of nonsense."

The engine has been running, cold air streaming from the vents. He opens the windows and turns off the ignition. "It is not nonsense, Evie. This is important to me. I hoped it would be important to you, also."

"Don't tell me I married some kind of closet religious fanatic."

"You are much too intelligent for that kind of remark. I can tell that you don't understand. I'll put it very simply. I have never believed in any type of higher power. I never even considered it. I was raised to be religious, but in a superficial way. We went to church every Sunday, and my father looked forward to conducting business after the service. My mother chatted and gossiped with her friends. By the time I entered college, I was tired of all the pretending, so I stopped going to church. Meg and I were married in the church, and she took the girls to Sunday School when they were small, but I treated church as a way to make business alliances and advertise my practice. I have not set foot in a church since the divorce, except when my daughters were married and my grandchildren were baptized. And I never thought about what I believed.

"Not until I met your sons and I saw how their faiths guide their lives. Not Brad—he is like me—but Chris and Joshua are both very serious about their respective faiths. Most remarkably, their faiths do seem to give them strength. Chris has a kind of calm about him which is very hard to find in most people these days. And, throughout his entire ordeal of arrest, imprisonment, and readjustment, Joshua withstood hardships which could have broken another man. I have been watching these two young men for some time and wondering from where they draw their strength."

"You must have been talking with Chris. Or did Joshua put you up to this?"

He smiles. "What about you? You never did answer me."

I don't really want to discuss this right now—it's hot, and we need to talk about our trip—but I have been thinking about it, since the day he was stabbed.

"My background is similar to yours. My sons have a hard time believing that I was the religious one. When the children were small, before Sam left, I made certain that our family was in church every Sunday. My boys were all baptized, even Joshua, and my older two were sent to Sunday School, where they were instructed to be good Christian children. When Sam left, my universe was disrupted to the point that I abandoned everything, including the church. We went to services for Christmas and Easter, of course, and a few other special occasions now and then. I continued to believe that the church teachings were correct, but they seemed to have no relevance to my life.

"When Chris found Jesus, I actually went further away from the church. I was happy for him, happy that he had found some stability, but I could not stand the way he talked about religion every chance he found. And he was far too judgmental. Then, when Joshua became a Muslim, I went through a full range of emotions. For a short while, I did worry about Joshua's soul, though I would never admit that to Chris. Then, after we reconciled, I could see how his faith helped him. So I decided, in order to be fair to both of my religious sons, that it would be better for me to believe in nothing. Both of them tried to convert me after my surgery, but I told them that my faith was a private matter. The truth is, I had no faith, except in a very general sense. I prayed before my surgery, though I haven't prayed very much since then. I do believe there is a God, somewhere out there, but it has been many years since I was able to subscribe to any particular set of religious beliefs. I decided long ago that religion was simply not necessary. Not for me."

"So we are just two faithless people, bouncing around without a spiritual anchor."

"You make it sound so bleak. We have our families. My sons have been my foundation. Until I married you, of course. And we both believe in certain values—love, compassion, commitment."

"Don't forget justice. Believing in values is very good, but from where do the values originate? Do they exist on their own, or do they emanate from another source?"

"Let's not get too philosophical," I say, wiping a drop of sweat from my forehead. "Why are you bringing this up? Why now?"

"I'll tell you 'why now.' It's because of four separate events. Four events which have changed the way I think about my beliefs.

"It started the day I met Joshua. He had just been arrested, on false charges, and he was worried about his wife and newborn daughter. Before I opened the door, I heard him saying something. Later, I learned that he had been reciting the Qur'an. All during that first interview, he was calm. If I myself had been in his shoes, I would have been anything but calm. I remembered what you told me about Joshua when we met. At that time, I believe, he had just married his first wife in front of a shotgun, so to speak. During those next few years, you were nearly sick with worry over him. When I thought of the boy you had worried over, then looked at the man sitting there in that room, I knew that something very significant had happened to cause him to change so drastically. Even though he didn't always keep his composure, throughout his long months of imprisonment he continued to hold strong to his faith.

"Then I talked with Abdul-Qadir. His oldest son had been killed, murdered. He should have been angry and bitter, but he was calm. Almost serene. He didn't dwell on his loss. Instead, he wanted to know what he could do to help Joshua. I was astonished by his selflessness and self-control. I know you were as impressed with him as I was. What if Joshua had died after the fight? Would you have accepted his death? I know I wouldn't have. I looked into Abdul-Qadir's eyes. I could see the pain as he spoke of his first-born son, but I saw something else, too, when he talked about the will of Allah. He loved his child, as much as any parent would, but his faith gave him the strength to bury his son. I know I couldn't be as strong.

"And then I was stabbed. I felt a tremendous pain in my left side. There was blood all over my clothes. I thought I was dying. My life did flash before my eyes, in the moment before I realized I had not been mortally wounded. And I did not like what I saw. I have my daughters, of course, and my law degree. Over the years, I built a successful practice. I drove a nice car and lived in a nice home. That was all. It occurred to me, as I was being rushed to the hospital, that, except for the stabbing, my life would make for a very dull movie.

"While I was in the hospital, I often thought about that moment. I came face to face with my own mortality. And what then? What would come next? That's when I began to wonder what it is I believe, and I realized that I have no belief at all. I believe in justice, of course. And I believe that nearly all people, men and women, are basically good. But I never turn to a higher power. My wound was not fatal, but it forced me to admit that I will die someday. And I began to wonder, for the first time, about life after death. Do we simply cease to exist, or is there a state of being beyond this present life? I must know."

"But how can we know until we actually experience death ourselves?"

"I don't know if we can, but it certainly is worth the effort. I have carefully planned out every aspect of my life, from my career to my children. Do you think it would be wise to leave my eternity simply to chance?"

"I have never thought about it that way. Do you think it's possible to plan for something such as that? I have always looked at death, and the possibility of life after death, as the last great surprise."

"Maybe, but you know I don't like surprises. I need to make the effort to know, at least."

Rebounding

"It sounds to me as if you're simply chasing phantoms."

"Perhaps, but I believe there are some people who do have the answers. It shows in the way they conduct themselves, the way they live their lives.

"The fourth event was the wedding last night. Did you take a good look at the newlyweds? I studied their faces. Here were two young people, both healthy and attractive. I noticed how shy they were with one another. How many eighteen-year-olds do you think there are in this country, or in this world, who possess the innocence, the purity, I saw in the faces of Jeremy and Raheema? It was rare even in our day, and it is nearly impossible to find now. These people—Chris, Joshua, Abdul-Qadir, Jeremy, Raheema—know something I don't know. They draw on something I cannot even imagine. I would like to know what it is. I don't know if Christianity is the most correct, or Islam, or perhaps they are the same. Maybe it doesn't even matter what you call it. I do know that some people, who are very important to me as well as to you, follow these faiths, and I see a peace in them. I would like to be able to experience that peace in my life. Even if I cannot ensure peace after my death, I would like to have that peace before I die."

I am very hot and uncomfortable, but I cannot bring myself to complain about the heat. There is something in what he said. I've noticed it too—the peace, the strength, and the innocence—but I have never yet wanted it for myself. Not the way Walt does. Even when I thought I might die of breast cancer, as my mother had, I simply did my very best to hold on to what I had.

Walt wants it, though. I can hear it in his voice. This man, who has presented so many arguments over the course of his career, has just argued his most important case to me. The search for his own spirituality.

"Evie, I want our trips to be about more than just seeing the sights. I've loved all of our trips, but the best one was when you went with me to Pakistan to help clear Joshua. We were working together for a cause. Then the cause was Joshua's freedom. Now the cause is my own spiritual discovery. Please work with me on this."

He's serious. And it means so much to him. "A spiritual odyssey. What an interesting idea. Do you really think that Malaysia is the best place to start?"

"It's not conventionally known as a place of pilgrimage, is it? But it does intrigue me because of the coexistence of different cultures. And we don't always have to be conventional, do we?"

"A tropical vacation does sound nice. We can get a house on the beach. And try to discover the meaning of life on moonlit nights."

"I'm not sure that's the concept I'm going for, but it does sound nice."

We go back inside and ask Amanda to arrange for our trip to Malaysia. She books our flight for the middle of September.

I bought some tour books about Malaysia yesterday, and started reading about the beaches, the sights, and the people. I'm starting to get excited about our trip. This will be a different type of adventure.

We invite the newlyweds over for dinner, about three weeks before we leave. Two days before they come, we go to visit Umar and Safa. I ask Safa to teach me how to cook basmati rice so that it turns out perfectly. She also shows me how to make chicken makhani, one of Raheema's favorites. I enjoy expanding my repertoire. While Safa and I talk about spices, Walt sits with Umar and discusses his spiritual quest.

On the way home, I ask him about their conversation. "Do you have any new insights?"

"He told me about his journey to Islam, and what being a Muslim means to him. He didn't try to convert me—not exactly—but he did give me some things to think about."

Rebounding

"Such as?"

"Such as creation and eternal life. Whether there is a God, and what His role is in this world. And monotheism. Did you know that Muslims have a very strict monotheism?"

"I know they believe in one God, of course. What do you mean by strict?"

"Umar said that the worship or association of others with God is the worst sin, the worst crime essentially, a person can commit." He laughs. "I told Umar that I've had many clients acquitted of serious crimes such as murder or robbery, and I wondered how it would be to face The Big Judge and try to get a client acquitted of polytheism. Umar didn't see the humor in that. He looked at me straight in the eye, and he said that when it's finally time to be judged, there will be no more lawyers. It will be every man for himself." Walt stares ahead through the windshield. I know he's deep in thought. At times like this, it's best to leave him to his meditations.

～

Jeremy and Raheema arrive promptly at seven. They make a lovely couple. Jeremy has Joshua's hair, with Heather's soft features and light complexion. Raheema is dark and exotic-looking with her black eyes and full face. They will have beautiful children.

We sit in the family room and talk for a few minutes before we eat. They look so sweet together. He holds her hand, and he smiles at her when she talks.

Walt tells them about his spiritual hunger. "I have been looking for something. I'm not certain what it is, or if it even has a name, but the two of you have it. I can see it in your faces."

"I would like to help you, but I'm not sure how," says Jeremy. "We do have Islam, and our faith is very important to us, but what you're describing isn't just a set of beliefs, or a set of teachings about right and wrong. What you're talking about comes from the heart, the soul."

"Yes, that's it. All of my life I have been very good at reading books and learning from them, but I don't think that what I am seeking this time can be found just in a book. I feel that I need to travel, and speak with many different people, before I can discover it and have it for myself."

"No, it's not only not in a book," says Raheema. "But it is also not in traveling. When your heart is ready, you will find it. Your travels may help your heart become ready, insha Allah."

Walt smiles. I can tell he likes that answer better than anything anyone else has told him. Especially me. He tells me I am far too practical to truly understand.

We sit at the table and I bring out the basmati rice and chicken makhani. Raheema smiles. "You have gone to a great deal of trouble. Thank you, Gramma."

"Taste it. I want to see if I made it correctly."

She tries it. "Yes, this is wonderful. Maybe you should open another catering business."

"No," says Walt, "I need my travel buddy."

During dinner, they tell us about their studies. Raheema has a scholarship to Northeastern Illinois University, the same school from which Aisha and Umar graduated. She is majoring in environmental studies. "I hope to learn ways to help people work in closer harmony with our natural environment." Jeremy is taking classes at Wilbur Wright College, where Joshua started his studies. He plans to pursue a degree in criminal justice. "I became interested in that because of Dad's experience in prison. I would like to be able to work for real prison reform."

Before they leave, Raheema says, "Oh, Gramma, I almost forgot. I wanted to thank you again for the apartment. It's beautiful."

"You're welcome, Raheema. I want you to enjoy it."

"Why don't the two of you come over for dinner sometime before you leave?"

Walt smiles. "If you cook like your mother does, Raheema, we'll be there every night before we leave."

"Raheema is an excellent cook," says Jeremy. "Haven't you noticed? We've only been married for eight weeks and already I'm gaining weight."

We had a wonderful evening. They are young, but they are so much more mature than Joshua and Heather. Or Sam and me.

Two days later, we eat dinner at their apartment. Raheema is an excellent cook, like her mother.

∞

Before we leave for Malaysia, we go to visit each of his daughters and my sons.

When we go to Brad and Beth's house, they serve seafood. "I imagine you'll be eating quite a bit of seafood in Malaysia. When you do, we want you to think of us," says Beth.

"Could you bring me back some shells?" says Matt.

"Of course we will, Matt," I tell him. "Beth, where is Kyle tonight?"

"He's at football practice. He should be home soon. I know he wants to see you."

"He's not driving yet, is he?"

"No, not yet," says Brad. "He'll be catching a ride from one of the guys on the team. But it won't be long before he does start driving. And I'm worried."

"I can imagine. It would be like Kyle to take off speeding as soon as he gets behind the wheel."

"I know, but, unfortunately, we can't keep them children forever. I'll send him to a driver's education class soon, and I have been thinking about putting one of those monitors in the car. It will record his speed and let me know if he's driving recklessly."

"I don't know if that will help. Mostly, at his age, they just need a great deal of reminding. And, though I'm still not big on this, maybe some prayer would help."

"That's right," says Brad. "I heard about the reason for your next trip. A spiritual odyssey. Very interesting, Walt. What made you think of that?"

"Don't you ever feel that there's something missing in your life? You have a very nice wife, two bright, healthy sons and a successful career, but don't you ever wonder if there's anything more?"

"I don't have time to wonder. I always have ten different projects to juggle at the office, the boys are always going in different directions, and Beth and I have our own interests we like to pursue in whatever spare time we can manage. Not to mention the business trips and dinner parties. I barely have enough time to sleep."

"But you made time for Evie and me tonight."

"That's different. I always have time for Mom and you."

"That's good. I'm glad to hear it. I have found, Brad, in my long years of life that we always have time for what's important to us."

"I guess that's true. Spirituality simply isn't high on my to-do list. Right now, I have more important things to think about."

"You sound just like me thirty or forty years ago. But, as they used to say when I was a young man, don't forget to take time to 'stop and smell the roses.' At the time, I thought it was just a bunch of silly talk from all those hippie types. I was a young lawyer who was going places in life, not one of those dreamy flower children. Now I can see that there is some truth in what they said."

"Tell you what, Walt. You come back from Malaysia and let me know where you are in your journey. Maybe then you'll be able to convince me."

"That sounds fair enough."

I'm still more with Brad in this whole business. I remember those starry-eyed visionaries who were trying to find themselves. I knew who I was. I just wanted to see how far I could go. I can't change my way of thinking as easily as Walt has changed his, but I do keep thinking about my beliefs. I still haven't talked to Walt about it. I need to work through this on my own.

Rebounding

We go to Chris and Melinda's house a few days later. They serve fried chicken, mashed potatoes, and okra. Chris instructs Isaiah to lead us in grace before we eat.

"This is a good dinner, Melinda. I like to try all kinds of food, but my favorite is still the down home kind. It reminds me of those leisurely Sunday dinners at my grandmother's house, back in the days when everything was closed on Sundays."

"Yes, Walt, my mother has told me about those days. It sounds so nice. She said they would even take Sunday drives out in the country, for no particular reason. Don't get Chris started on what they've done with Sundays now. You'll be here all night."

"Okay, I promise I won't start my sermon about Sundays. Not tonight, anyway. So I've heard that this trip is some kind of spiritual journey. Is that right?"

"Yes, Chris. As a matter of fact, you are one of the people who inspired me. You, and Joshua. How old were you when you made your decision of faith?"

"I discovered Christianity when I was fourteen. That sounds strange, because we went to church off and on when I was growing up, but, when I was fourteen, I found out what Christianity is all about, and the true meaning of faith."

"Why is that? What happened to you when you were fourteen? Was there a special event which brought about your spiritual awakening?"

"No, no special event. I had just started high school and I felt lost. There were too many kids in the school and too much stuff going on in the hallways. I felt awkward, as if I didn't belong there. But I didn't belong anywhere else either. A girl in my algebra class invited me to go with her to a Bible study one night."

"A girl? I never knew that your conversion was because of a girl."

"It wasn't like that, Mom. She was nice, and I think she may have been interested in me, but I was only fourteen and I didn't care much about girls yet. I did meet some other people at the

Bible study, though, and they helped me find what I had been searching for."

"What was it, Chris? What had you been searching for?"

"At first, it was a sense of belonging. The people at the Bible study called me brother, and they cared about me. It soon became something much deeper. I learned that I didn't just belong to that group of people. I belonged to God. I knew I wasn't alone. My faith has given strength and structure to my life."

"I suppose that is what I am looking for, but how do I find it?"

"The best way, I believe, is to keep searching and studying. If you are sincere, it will find you."

"I thought, when we came over here, that you were going to try to convert Walt and make him join your church."

"Not exactly. Though I do encourage you both to read the Scriptures, and listen with your heart. Once you come to the realization, as I did, that Christ was sent to save us, your life will never be the same."

I look around the table at Ruthie, Isaiah, Jacob, Benjamin, and Martha. Ruthie is a nice young woman. I need to remember that she likes to be called Ruth now.

She will be graduating next May. I know she has never dated. Chris and Melinda would not admit to following the same principles of dating and marriage which Joshua and Aisha follow, but, in practice, I think Ruthie's—Ruth's—experience will be very similar to that of Joshua's children.

They are all good children. They have given Chris and Melinda very little trouble. They are children, of course, and they have the usual problems that children have, but I have never heard them talk back to their parents or seriously fight with one another.

I wonder if there is something to all of this, after all.

❧

Two days later, we sit at the table in Joshua's kitchen.

Rebounding

Abdul-Qadir's son, Nuruddin, is here now. I know Joshua has been trying for several months to bring him to this country. He's a very nice young man. A little quiet, but he has just arrived.

Joshua made Pakistani food, which he knows we both like.

I praise Joshua for his cooking skills. He continues to amaze me.

"I like to cook too," says Jennifer. "I like to try new things."

"Yes, Jennifer made the salad and dessert for tonight."

"This salad is good," says Walt. "And I can't wait to dig into that chocolate cake. Speaking of trying new things, Joshua, what do you think about our little pilgrimage?"

"I was surprised when Mom first told me. I never thought of either of you as being religious."

"Neither did I, but that first time I met you, you impressed me with your calm. Your life had just been stolen away from you, but you read the Qur'an and controlled your emotions. I've told Evie that I don't think I could have done the same."

"You knew Mom when I was younger, didn't you?"

"Yes, we knew each other casually for many years."

"In those days, I would have been ready to beat up anyone who came within five feet of me. I had a lot of rage then. It still surfaces, once in a while, but I can keep it under control. When I do feel distressed, I pray and ask Allah for help. That's how I find my peace." He stops, and grins. "And these days, frankly, I'm too tired to get so upset about things."

"Your journey inspires me. I want to know what it is that you've found."

"I've found peace, that's all. The main thing that brings me peace is knowing that I'm not alone. Even when I was in solitary, I knew that Allah would give me the strength I needed to get through it. Except for those hours when I was injured, before I passed out. Those were the times when I really had to fight to hold on."

"But you did hold on. I want to experience that kind of strength. I've listened to Chris and you talk about your faiths, and I can understand, on an intellectual level, what you're telling me, but I don't feel it in my heart. That's what I am hoping for."

"I'm glad you're looking. God, Allah, is always there, whether you know it or not. He is as close to you as your jugular vein."

"That's poetic," I say. "Did you make that up?"

"No, Mom, I didn't. It's in the Qur'an."

"How did Muhammad know about the jugular vein?"

"Prophet Muhammad didn't write the Qur'an. Allah did."

I nod politely and ask Aisha about her fourth-graders. I don't like discussing religion, but I must admit that I am still astonished at the changes in Joshua. Could a man change that much simply because of a religious experience? Could faith be that powerful?

Before we leave, Joshua tells us that his business plans are coming along well. "I'm still experimenting with the CD, but it's almost there. The manual is ready. Umar is making the contacts. We have two presentations lined up for next month, and a few more leads. Of course, for now we're going to keep our day jobs."

"I like what you're doing," says Walt. "Even with all of the obstacles, you are able to use your expertise to help others do what you love."

"Umar and I still hope to reopen the center one day. We have at least two or three solid supporters from the old days. We're hoping that this consulting venture will eventually lead us back to where we started."

"Just be very careful. Stay in touch with Jared, and let him know the next time those men show up. I don't want to receive a call when I'm somewhere halfway around the world, telling me you've been arrested again. I am enjoying retirement far too much."

"Don't worry, Walt," says Aisha. "I've made it my business to make sure he never ends up like that again. We need him with us here at home."

∞

Two days before we're due to leave, my sons and their wives take us out for dinner. Each of my boys makes a short speech and presents us with a gift. Joshua gives us a copy of the Qur'an,

Rebounding

all in English. Chris gives us a copy of the Bible. Brad grins. "Sorry, but I've always been the practical one. This is a set of CDs to help you learn Malay. And this is a book about the customs of Southeast Asia."

"We will use all of these to help us in our journey," says Walt. "The spiritual, and the practical. Thank you, boys. Getting to know the three of you has been one of the best experiences of my life. I have truly enjoyed being your stepfather."

"That sounded like a farewell speech. We expect to see you in a few months."

"But we never know, Joshua, what lies ahead."

Part Two

We climb into bed and Walt picks up a book to read, as usual. This time he's reading the Qur'an.

"Why are you reading that? Don't you at least want to read the Bible first?"

"I have never actually read the Bible, but I know the stories. Most of them, anyway. I know nothing, really, about the Qur'an. At any rate, Umar told me that Muslims believe the Qur'an has no mistakes because it was divinely revealed. At least I can look for the mistakes and inconsistencies."

After forty years of breaking down the prosecution, he should be good at that. "All right, then."

He puts the book down and looks at me. "Joshua converted fifteen years ago, but you are still very uncomfortable with Islam. Aren't you?"

"Yes. Islam still seems very strange to me. Headscarves, and praying and fasting all the time. It's so rigid."

"Then I'm going to ask you a hypothetical question. What would you do if I decided to become a Muslim?"

"Why do you always like to ask me difficult questions at bedtime?"

He laughs. "Go to sleep then, but I want you to think about it. Hypothetically speaking, of course." We kiss. "Goodnight. I love you."

I don't know what time it was when he finally turned out the light and snuggled next to me. I fell asleep right after "I love you."

֍

On the night before we leave, I lie awake in the dark long after Walt has gone to sleep. Usually I sleep first while he stays up and reads, but tonight I cannot stop thinking.

Rebounding

What do I believe? When I was younger, I believed in the teachings of the church. When Sam left me, I stopped believing. When I had breast cancer, I prayed to God. And when the doctor pronounced me cured, I stopped praying.

And why am I against Islam? It has certainly been good for Joshua and his family. And even though he practices his faith diligently, Joshua is not rigid. He still knows how to smile and joke and have fun with his children. I suppose it's all those images I've seen over the years. Hijackers, suicide bombers, kidnappers. Terrorists.

Joshua is not a terrorist—and neither was Abdul-Qadir's son—but what about the others?

It's not important. I need to go to sleep. We have a busy day tomorrow. I still have a little packing to do. And we need to get to the airport early enough to get through all the security.

I close my eyes and try to relax. I'm very tired, but my mind keeps racing. What do I believe?

∽

I wake up still tired, but excited. I finish my packing. Walt's middle daughter, Karen, drives us to the airport. We go through security, board the plane, and wait to take off on our newest adventure.

It's a beautiful, sunny Thursday afternoon. As we take off, I look out the window and say goodbye to Chicago. There's a little turbulence as we gain altitude. I close my eyes and think about the beaches of Malaysia.

We change planes in Los Angeles. I have time to call my brother Rob and tell him I'm in town. We talk about our families. I tell him about our upcoming trip. He tells me about a new idea he has for a novel. We talk and talk, just like we used to when we were young.

I'm still talking when Walt whispers, "Evie, we have to board now."

"I need to go, Rob. Is there anything you want me to bring back for you from Malaysia?"

337

He laughs. "I already have it all. The palm trees, the sun, and the ocean. Have a good trip, Evie. Drop me an email and let me know how it's going."

"I'll talk to you later, then." He's the first one who called me Evie, because he couldn't say Evelyn when he was small. Coming from him, it feels like a very special name.

For so many years, we barely spoke. Then, I received an email from him, out of the blue, about four years ago. We've spent the last four years catching up. After this trip, I think Walt and I need to spend time with him in Los Angeles. I'll talk to Walt about it later.

᠅

We board, and wait for take-off. I look through one of the books I bought about Southeast Asia. Walt is still reading the Qur'an. He's always reading something. The stewardess tells us to fasten our seat belts, and we head out over the Pacific on our spiritual adventure.

We've been flying for an hour or so when he closes his book and asks me, "So what would you do if I decided to become a Muslim?"

"Hypothetically speaking, I don't know. I wouldn't divorce you, but I wouldn't wear a scarf. And I certainly would not allow you to take another wife."

"I haven't found any mistakes yet. I have found verses referring to contracts and witnesses. And many verses speak of justice. Both in this life and the next." He looks down and continues his reading.

᠅

After several hours, we land in Honolulu. It is as beautiful as they say. We plan to spend two days here before continuing to Malaysia.

We take a taxi to our hotel, then head for the beach. We swim and play in the ocean for a few hours, until dinner. I fantasize

Rebounding

about living close to the ocean and coming to the beach every day. No wonder my brother won't leave California.

In the morning, we take off on a helicopter tour of the islands. The vibrant colors, the volcanoes, the ocean. "Maybe we should look into real estate while we're here," I tease Walt. The buildings and pavement of Chicago are no match, but I know neither of us wants to move. We both want to stay close to our children. We spend the rest of the day on the beach. I wonder if we could get our children to move here.

We take a walk along the beach in the moonlight before returning to our hotel room. I'm so exhausted that I crawl into bed much earlier than usual. Walt is still awake, still reading.

I wake up and reach for him, but he's not there. His pillow looks untouched. I find him on the balcony, looking out over the ocean.

I walk out and kiss him on the cheek. "You're certainly up early this morning."

"I didn't sleep last night."

"Why not?"

"I was thinking, that's all." He puts his arm around my shoulders, and keeps looking out at the ocean.

I want to ask him what he's been thinking about all night, but he has that far away look in his eyes. After a few more minutes, he says, "I think I'm ready for breakfast."

We eat a wonderful breakfast. Pineapple never tasted this good before. Then we have time for another walk along the beach. Our flight to Malaysia doesn't leave until after noon.

On our way to the airport Walt tells me, "I finished reading the Qur'an last night. I couldn't find any mistakes."

I don't respond. I don't know what to say. I don't want to have to think beyond the hypothetical.

∾

I don't like to fly, but I love to travel to new places. Especially when I'm with Walt.

We spend hours over the ocean, with no land in sight. I find this both calming and unsettling. Before take-off, the stewardess reviewed the procedures in case we need to make an emergency landing on the water. I still don't know, though, how I would be able to pry the cushion off my seat and use it as a flotation device.

I gaze out over the endless miles of water. They say that Earth is two-thirds water, but I never imagined there was so much of it.

"This reminds me of something I read the other day." Walt opens the Qur'an and searches for a few minutes. He has a very good memory, even at his age. "Here it is. 'And if all the trees on earth were pens and the ocean were ink, with seven oceans behind it to add to its supply, yet would not the Word of Allah be exhausted: for Allah is Exalted in power, full of wisdom.' If all this water were ink. Can you imagine?"

I suppose he wants me to discuss the wonders of that verse with him, but all I can think is, "He's quoting the Qur'an. Do I need to start worrying?"

∾

We have a smooth landing in Kuala Lumpur and take a taxi to our hotel. On the way there, I look out the window and start planning our days, but for now I'm too tired to do any sightseeing. We left Honolulu on Sunday. Now it is Tuesday. We lost an entire day, crossing over the International Date Line. I'm glad Walt is as tired as I am. We check in and spend the rest of the day adjusting to a new time zone.

For the next two days, we tour the city, mostly by taxi. I love the architecture. A mixture of Chinese, Indian, Islamic, and modern. And the food. From the ayam goreng—their own special fried chicken—to the steamed crabsticks. On Thursday, we find a vendor who sells hamburgers that are simply heavenly--piled with toppings and covered in a very special sauce. Tangy, but not hot. At dinner, I try the Chinese sausage. I offer some to Walt, but he declines.

Rebounding

For two days, Walt has patiently followed me as I explored department stores and outdoor markets. On Friday, during breakfast, he tells me he wants to go the mosque.

"That is why we came," I reply. "Are you sure you want to start with the mosques, or should we go to a temple first? I saw a beautiful temple while we were out yesterday."

"I was talking with Harun. He works at the front desk. He said he could take us to the National Mosque in the afternoon."

"In that case, I suppose we'll go to the mosque with Harun. Did he say anything about how I should dress? I don't want to offend anyone."

"Dress modestly. He said you will be given a robe and scarf to wear at the mosque."

"That should be interesting. Be sure to bring the camera. I'm sure Joshua would love to see that."

"Evie," he says. Then he pauses. He takes my hand and looks into my eyes. I recognize that look. I saw it in Joshua's eyes on the day he told me he was going to Pakistan. Don't say it, Walt. Please don't.

"Evie, I have been thinking. I've read the Qur'an, and I like what I read. What would you think if I became a Muslim?"

I try to stay calm. "Hypothetically speaking?"

"No."

"I don't know what to say," I whisper.

"It won't have to change our relationship," he says softly. "The words I read in the Qur'an touched my heart. I understand, now, about believing in God. I'm ready to do this."

"But how can you be certain?"

"In the same way I was certain my clients weren't guilty. I examined the evidence, and I went with my heart. From what the feds told me, by the way, Joshua looked guilty as hell, but I went with my heart."

"And I always thought you were so rational."

"This is what I want, Evie. Please don't be upset."

"I don't know what to say." I try to think of something practical that will help me stay calm. "How are you going to do it? Do you have to go through some kind of formal ceremony?"

341

"I only need to recite the Shahadah. The confession of faith. I plan to do that at the mosque today."

"Do you have to do this today? We just arrived. You haven't taken time to explore other religions. Isn't that why we came?"

"It is, but Raheema was right. She said I wouldn't find it in traveling. I would find it, she said, when my heart was ready. And my heart is ready now."

I don't know what to say. Walt hugs me tightly. "Don't worry, my love. It won't change anything between us."

We spend the morning near the hotel. I try to get Walt to go with me to a temple. He refuses. He's very quiet.

We eat lunch at an Indian restaurant. Their tandoori chicken is delectable, but I don't have much of an appetite.

Harun meets us in the hotel lobby. I offer my hand, but he withholds his own hand and shakes his head. I remember. Joshua doesn't shake hands with women either.

He does smile. "It's very nice to meet you, Mrs. Thompson."

That's all he says to me. Then he turns to Walt, and the two of them begin an animated conversation. I almost laugh at the contrast when he and Walt walk together. One is tall and very white. The other is shorter and darker. They've known each other for only two days, or maybe three, but the way they talk with one another, they could be brothers.

All the way to the mosque, it is Walt and Harun. I sit in the back seat of Harun's car, silent and invisible.

He does talk to me when we get to the mosque. "You will have to wear a scarf and a robe when you go inside, Mrs. Thompson."

I nod. "Yes, I know. That's fine."

I put on the apparel, we remove our shoes, and we follow Harun through the main entrance. I look around me. This building is tremendous, both in size and design. The columns. The high domed ceiling. The whiteness. I have never seen anything like it.

Harun leads us to an older man who sits near the wall, reading. "Assalaamu alaikum, Dato Adam. This is Mr. Walter

Thompson, from America. He would like to make the Shahadah."

Dato Adam stands and shakes hands with Walt and Harun. "Walaikum assalaam. It is very nice to meet you." He glances at me. "And this is Mrs. Thompson?"

"Yes. It's nice to meet you." I don't know what else to say. I can't believe I'm standing here, dressed like this.

He turns to Walt. "Are you certain you are ready for the Shahadah?"

"Yes. I've been thinking about my faith for some time now. That's why my wife and I decided to come to Malaysia. I wanted to explore. I've read the Qur'an, I've spoken with Harun, and I am convinced."

"Do you know the meaning of the Shahadah?"

"I testify that there is no god but Allah, and Muhammad is His messenger."

"Very good. Now would you please repeat after me?"

Dato Adam says some words in Arabic, and Walt echoes them. I have heard those words before, while we were in Pakistan. I listen to Walt's recitation, not knowing what to say or think.

The men hug. Walt looks at me, and smiles.

Before we go back to the hotel, Harun takes a picture of Walt and me outside of the mosque. I wear the robe and scarf for the picture.

When we get back to our room he holds me close. "This is the right thing, Evie. I'm sure of it."

"You look the same. Are you planning to grow a beard now?"

He smiles. "I don't know. What do you think?"

∞

Walt became a Muslim a month ago. In some ways, nothing has changed. He talks the same, walks the same. Loves me the same.

But he prays regularly throughout the day, and we have to arrange our schedule around his prayer times. He won't eat pork.

He won't have a drink with me. Fortunately, I never cared much for drinking anyway. He thought about it for two weeks before he decided to stop shaving. Right now sharp stubble covers his face. When I complain, he assures me that soon he'll have a nice soft beard.

He bought CDs of the Qur'an on the day after his conversion, and he listens to them every night. Harun gave him some books, and now he reads more than ever. He always wants to learn.

We decided not to tell our children yet. His daughters will be shocked. Joshua will be happy, of course, but Chris will be upset. I don't know what Brad will say. He'll probably just crack a joke.

~

We've been in Southeast Asia for almost three months, and we've traveled all over the region. We spent quiet days and nights on the beach. We had a hectic week navigating around Singapore, which is the cleanest city I've ever seen. We stayed in Thailand for two weeks, exploring the natural beauty of the south and sitting in traffic in Bangkok. We even flew down to Jakarta for a few days, another city with both natural beauty and the blight of urbanization. We rode on elephants and watched monkeys carouse in the trees above the road. We battled mosquitoes and listened to the nightly clicking of the geckos. And we visited so many mosques that I lost count.

At every mosque we went to, the women greeted me warmly. The men looked at Walt, with his white skin and western build, and marveled when he recited a little Qur'an and prayed next to them.

Every day, Walt tells me a little about Islam. I never liked it when Joshua discussed his faith, but I have an easier time listening to Walt. Maybe because he is my husband. Maybe because I have always had so much respect for him. Maybe because I know he has never had an irrational thought in his life.

I am especially interested when he tells me about the life of Muhammad. I had dismissed him as a fanatic with impossible

Rebounding

visions, but Walt tells me about the Muhammad I didn't know. The one who was orphaned at a young age. The one who was always considered trustworthy. The one who loved children and helped with the housework. Walt portrays Muhammad as a gentle man, as gentle as Abdul-Qadir, who always cared about those around him. It is so much different than the image I've had of the man all these years.

If anyone else tried to tell me these things, I don't think I would listen, but I have always trusted Walt. Completely.

His beard has grown out now. It's softer, and I'm starting to like it. It looks good on him.

We've taken hundreds of pictures, and sent some of them home. Even the one Harun took in front of the National Mosque. And some showing me next to my bearded husband. I wonder what our children will say.

∽

Ten days before we're due to leave, Walt asks me again, "What about you, Evie? What do you believe?"

"Honestly?"

"Of course. You have to stop worrying about what other people think."

"I believe in God. I have a new appreciation for Muhammad. There are many things I like about Islam. I can see now how the discipline helped Joshua, but I don't know if it's for me."

"Why not?"

"For one thing, I do not want to wear a scarf."

I've never heard him laugh so hard.

"What's so funny?"

It takes him a moment to control himself. "I read a verse in the Qur'an. Apparently, when a woman becomes elderly she doesn't have to cover."

I toss my pillow at him. "I am not elderly!"

"I know you're not, love. You're beautiful." He reaches for my hand. "At any rate, you can decide whether or not to wear a scarf. What else?"

"I don't know. All the praying and fasting. I certainly will not pray in public. Religion should be private."

"You don't have to pray in public. Most Muslim women choose to pray at home. Anything else?"

"Walt, you are talking about a life-altering experience."

"I know. I've done it. And these past ten weeks have been the happiest of my life."

He is more relaxed. I can see the peace in him, but I'm not ready to make that kind of decision.

"I don't know. Let me think about it."

We go to sleep. Sometime during the night, I dream. Sam and I sit in church. My little Brad sits on my lap. We turn to the hymn on page 99 and start to sing. Suddenly I feel trapped. I stand up, carrying Brad, and hurry toward the exit. Sam tries to stop me. He grabs my arm and won't let go. When I resist, he slaps me. I struggle. Finally I get away from him and run through the door. On the other side of the door, I find Walt. He takes me into his arms. And I know I am safe.

I sit up straight and open my eyes. I replay the dream. Now I remember my earlier dream. This time I escaped. What was I trying to get away from? Sam? Or something more?

I reach for Walt, but he's gone. I hear his noises in the bathroom. Time for the morning prayer.

I watch him as he prays, bowing down to the floor and standing up again. Suddenly I feel like joining him.

After his prayer, he comes over and sits next to me on the bed. I touch his cheek. "When I was a little girl, the minister taught us that anyone who wasn't a Christian would go to hell. I don't want to go to hell."

"I thought you didn't believe in heaven and hell."

"I was bluffing."

"Do you still believe what your minister taught you?"

"When we decided to come to Malaysia, you said you wanted peace in this life, even if you couldn't ensure it after you die. I want that too. I have never had it. Not the way you do."

He holds my hand and listens quietly as I say the words. I know them by heart now. I've heard them so many times, called

Rebounding

from the mosques of Pakistan, Turkey, Egypt, Indonesia, Thailand, and Malaysia. He hugs me. Then he shows me how to make ablutions, and how to pray.

There is no god but The One God, Allah, and Muhammad is His Prophet. That is what I believe.

But what will people say?

~

Later in the day, while we're walking through an outdoor market, we see a woman selling scarves. Walt looks at me. "What do you think?"

"I told you. I will not wear a scarf."

He picks up a dark blue one. "This is nice. It would look good on you."

"Haven't you been listening?"

The vendor smiles. "It would look very pretty on you," she says.

By the end of the day, I have two scarves, two long dresses, and two tunics with matching skirts. Walt insisted on buying them for me. I didn't promise I would wear them, but I do wear one of the scarves when I pray with Walt in our hotel room.

~

The next morning, Walt walks out of the bathroom and says, "I need to show you how to take a bath."

"Excuse me?"

"You need to take a special bath. I should have shown you earlier."

"I won't have to do this in public, will I?"

"No, of course not—you know Muslim don't baptize—but I do want you to go with me to the mosque today for the Friday prayer. You can wear one of your new outfits."

While I shower, I wonder what I am doing. I must be insane. Wearing a scarf. Going to the mosque. Changing religions.

But I remember the special feeling I have when I pray.

Harun drives us to the mosque. He smiles broadly when Walt tells him about my conversion. "That's wonderful. Congratulations, Mrs. Thompson." I don't know how many times I have asked him to call me Evie, but it's always Mrs. Thompson.

We get to the mosque, and I start to follow Walt into the prayer area. He stops. "Oh, I forgot to tell you. The women pray upstairs." He points to a balcony and shows me to the stairs.

The balcony is already crowded. Some women talk quietly with one another while others read the Qur'an or work their prayer beads. I find a corner and sit down, hoping no one will notice me. I feel so strange.

The sermon is in Malay, and I wonder why I came. Then the women stand and begin lining up. I watch, not sure what I should do, until they begin to pray. I secure a place at the end of the back line and pray with them.

When it's over, I work my way slowly through the crowd and wait for Walt outside. Harun and Dato Adam are with him. "Evie, I told Dato about your conversion. He wants to give you the Shahadah formally in the mosque."

Dato Adam nods at me. "Assalaamu alaikum, Mrs. Thompson."

I know I'm supposed to reply, but suddenly I can't remember how to say it. I smile and nod.

After the crowd thins a little, I go back into the mosque and say the words. I suppose there's no turning back now.

Before we leave the mosque, Harun takes our picture. Walt in his long robe and beard. Me in my long dress and scarf. What will the Meyers say?

~

We've spent the last few days buying gifts to take back. When we were at the beach a few weeks ago, I made sure to collect some shells for Matt. Tomorrow we will fly out of Kuala Lumpur. Going back home. I don't know if I'm ready to leave.

Rebounding

On our last night here, we take Harun and his wife, Huda, out for dinner. I wear the scarf again. At least I don't have to worry about fixing my hair.

Huda is very nice. We chat about our families. She and Harun have a son and a daughter, and four grandchildren.

Before we part, we exchange email addresses and phone numbers. "I hope you can come to visit us sometime in Chicago," I say.

"That would be very nice. I'm so glad to know you, Evie." We hug.

Three months ago, I never imagined I could feel so close to someone who lived on the other side of the world. There are many things I couldn't have imagined three months ago.

※

In the morning, before we leave for the airport, Walt goes on the computer.

"Hurry up, Walt. We're going to be late."

"I have a couple of emails to send. It won't take long."

"Who are you writing to?"

"Karen. I want to remind her when to pick us up. And Joshua."

"Why Joshua?"

"I'm sending him the picture of you at the mosque last Friday."

"But I thought we weren't going to tell the children yet."

"I didn't tell him."

※

Our plane takes off into clear blue skies. I relax into my seat and take a nap.

When I wake up, the plane is shaking. I check my watch. We still have many hours before we land in Honolulu. I squeeze Walt's hand.

"It's okay, Evie. There must be a storm."

The turbulence increases. The plane is tossed. The pilot turns on the seat belt sign.

Suddenly the plane drops. My heart catches in my throat. We level off again, and I breathe. "We hit an air pocket," says Walt. "It happens sometimes. We're okay now."

But the plane keeps tossing and shaking. And the storm is getting worse. The sky is dark, even though it's still daytime. Lightning flashes.

I'm holding on to Walt, terrified. Suddenly there's a flash right outside the window, followed by a sharp noise. We drop again, and keep on dropping. The oxygen masks come down. Walt helps me with mine before he puts his on.

I want to stand up and try to pry the seat loose—my flotation device—but the seat belt light is on. Should I sit, and get ready for the impact, or stand up and try to get this seat loose? I hold on to Walt and cry softly into his chest. "I love you."

He caresses me. "I love you, too," he says

We keep falling. The plane shakes violently, heading down toward the ocean. And I know we are on the threshold of the unknown.

Suddenly I feel very calm. It's going to happen, and there's nothing I can do about it. I hope I'm ready.

I suppose it doesn't matter now what my sons will think. It doesn't matter what the Meyers will say. Now it is between God and me.

Epilogue

When Brad Adams was forty-seven years old, he became an orphan.

First there were the initial reports that the plane was missing. Then the wreckage was found, and crews were sent out to search for survivors. After that came the grisly task of collecting and identifying remains. When it was all over, Walter and Evelyn Thompson remained among the missing.

Their six children came together and decided to hold a memorial service. After much discussion, they finally decided that, in honor of the couple's spiritual quest, the service would include elements of both Christianity and Islam, along with general expressions of spirituality.

They rented a hall and invited all of Walt and Evie's friends. Evie's brother, Rob, flew in from California for the service.

Walt's oldest daughter, Jean, recited a poem she had written about her father. His youngest daughter, Tiffany, a gifted pianist, played Gershwin's Rhapsody in Blue, Walt's favorite piece. His granddaughter, Megan, read an essay about her grandfather. Chris and Joshua each gave a short eulogy. Ruth sang a song about heaven. Jeremy made a short speech about finding peace through faith.

Michael flew in from Boston for the service, but he couldn't find the right words to express his love for his Gramma.

Brad stood in the back of the hall and cried. He thought about his mother, and all the words that had never been said. And he wondered how people could talk about God at a time like this.

Jamilah Kolocotronis is an American Muslim, married, and the mother of six sons. She has a doctorate in Social Science Education and has worked as a teacher in several Islamic schools throughout the US. Her published books include *Islamic Jihad*, a nonfiction work about the principles and practices of military jihad; *Innocent People*, a novel exploring the lives of American Muslims after 9/11; and *Echoes*, the first novel in her Echoes Series. Visit Jamilah's website at http://jamilahkolocotronis.writerswebpages.com